An excerpt from *Just a Few Fake Kisses...* by Jayci Lee

"What do you *want*, Anthony?"

Chloe sounded tired...and hopeful.

He swallowed after several tries. "Something I can't want."

"Then what *can* you want?" she whispered.

"Can I want to kiss you? To really kiss you. Not because someone is watching."

"No faking? No kittens?"

"No. No faking. As for kittens—" he chuckled "—I don't see why we can't have kittens. I like thinking of you as one."

"M-me?"

"Yes, kitten," he purred against her ear. She stiffened against him and pulled back to stare at him. *Damn it.* Had he pushed his luck?

"I've never had a nickname before." Her mouth curved into a naughty smile. "So do you want to kiss me, Anthony?"

"I—" He sucked in a sharp breath. "I shouldn't."

"You *shouldn't*? Well, then. How can you resist?"

"I can't." He lowered his head slowly, then stopped a whisper away from her lips.

An excerpt from *The True Love Experiment* by Anne Marsh

"I'd like a second chance."

Wren met Nash's eyes.

"At kissing you," Nash clarified.

"Why on earth would that be a good idea?"

"Because I can do better." He pulled her toward him.

Standing this close, she could feel his heat. His mouth closed that last small distance between them and he kissed her.

"Wren—" He groaned her name.

She was dizzy, body on fire, head spinning. She looked up.

Concern was painted across his face. He didn't seem swept away anymore. "I can't be your one and only. You deserve that." And then he said the last thing that she expected. "Good night."

He turned and walked down the hallway and out of sight.

Fake date, fake kiss, totally fake expectations.

It sucked.

JAYCI LEE

&

NEW YORK TIMES BESTSELLING AUTHOR
ANNE MARSH

JUST A FEW FAKE KISSES...
&
THE TRUE LOVE EXPERIMENT

HARLEQUIN
DESIRE

Recycling programs for this product may not exist in your area.

ISBN-13: 978-1-335-45777-6

Just a Few Fake Kisses… & The True Love Experiment

Copyright © 2023 by Harlequin Enterprises ULC

Just a Few Fake Kisses…
Copyright © 2023 by Judith J. Yi

The True Love Experiment
Copyright © 2023 by Anne Marsh

For questions and comments about the quality of this book, please contact us at CustomerService@Harlequin.com.

Harlequin Enterprises ULC
22 Adelaide St. West, 41st Floor
Toronto, Ontario M5H 4E3, Canada
www.Harlequin.com

Printed in U.S.A.

CONTENTS

Jayci Lee writes poignant, sexy and laugh-out-loud romance every free second she can scavenge. She lives in sunny California with her tall, dark and handsome husband, two amazing boys with boundless energy, and a fluffy rescue whose cuteness is a major distraction. At times, she cannot accommodate reality because her brain is full of drool-worthy heroes and badass heroines clamoring to come to life.

Because of all the books demanding to be written, Jayci writes full-time now and is semiretired from her fifteen-year career as a defense litigator. She loves food, wine and traveling, and incidentally, so do her characters. Books have always helped her grow, dream and heal, and she hopes her books will do the same for you.

Books by Jayci Lee

Harlequin Desire

Hana Trio

A Song of Secrets
One Night Only
Just a Few Fake Kisses...

The Heirs of Hansol

Temporary Wife Temptation
Secret Crush Seduction
Off Limits Attraction

Visit the Author Profile page
at Harlequin.com for more titles.

You can also find Jayci Lee on Facebook,
along with other Harlequin Desire authors,
at Facebook.com/HarlequinDesireAuthors!

Dear Reader,

I feel like I wrote this book on a dare. Like someone said, "I bet you can't add any more tropes." And I said, "Well, I bet you I can!"

Let's make a list of all the tropes in *Just a Few Fake Kisses...*, shall we? Fake dating, former crush and age gap with a hint of enemies to lovers and secret identity... I'd say I won the imaginary bet. Wouldn't you?

Needless to say, this book was a lot of fun to write. Chloe and Anthony are so sexy and adorable together that I admit to squealing once or twice as I wrote their story. I hope you have as much fun reading *Just a Few Fake Kisses...* as I had writing it.

Thank you again for choosing to read my book when you have so many books to choose from and every spare minute of your time is precious.

With love,

Jayci Lee

JUST A FEW FAKE KISSES...

Jayci Lee

To Gloria, my dear friend and sister of my heart

One

Chloe Han saw the folly of secrets, especially the ones you kept from your family…

Her eldest sister, Angie, and her now husband, Joshua Shin, had kept his alter ego as a composer—plus their love affair—a secret until it bit them both in the ass. Her second older sister, Megan, had kept the identity of her one-night stand turned baby daddy, Daniel Pak—plus *their* love affair—a secret until shit inevitably hit the fan.

Although everyone had gotten their heart's desire in the end, her sisters' road to happiness was a big old mess of secrets refusing to stay hidden. Thankfully, Chloe was an open book. She was the constant in her family and that was exactly how she wanted it. She would never do anything to rock the boat. Besides, she had nothing juicy enough in her life worth keeping a secret. A forlorn sigh slipped past her lips.

"What's wrong?" Angie peered at her, a slight frown marring her forehead.

"Nothing." Chloe brushed some imaginary dust off her jeans. "Why do you ask?"

"I *ask* because you just sighed like you were doing your best impersonation of Eeyore."

"It wasn't a sigh. It was a long exhale," Chloe said. "Where is Megan anyway? And why is she keeping the substitute violinist's identity a secret?"

She sighed again. Megan had yet another secret. *Oh, joy.* Chloe realized she was in a crummy mood due in large part to lack of sleep. And the fact that she'd gotten her ass handed to her on *League of Legends* last night by her archnemesis, SerialFiddler. It was infuriating. She refrained from kicking the music stand in front of her.

"She said it was a *surprise*. Not a secret," Angie reminded her. "And whoever they may be, they're only a candidate. You and I will have the final say in who temporarily joins our trio while Megan's on her maternity leave. We're the ones who need to play with them."

Some of Chloe's ire left her as she thought about the impending arrival of her new nephew. In less than two months, she was going to be an auntie and she planned on spoiling that baby rotten. Angie would no doubt do the same.

"Are you ready to get your socks blown off?" Chloe and Angie started when Megan and her huge stomach burst into the rehearsal room they rented from the community college.

Megan's near maniacal grin faltered when a deep

voice—so the candidate was a man—murmured through the crack in the door.

"Embarrassing?" Megan frowned. "How is this even remotely embarrassing? I just want to set things up for your grand entrance."

The murmuring grew a bit more urgent. Chloe's ears and curiosity perked up. She kind of liked the smooth tenor of the mystery man's voice.

"Nonsense," her sister retorted. "Of course you want to make a grand entrance. Just stay put for a second."

"Megan, sweetie," Angie intervened. "Stop embarrassing the poor man and let him come inside. We promise to be properly impressed."

"Yeah, Unni," Chloe said a tad impatiently. "Honestly, I don't know why you're making such a fuss. Who could it possibly be—"

Her words died a quiet death on her tongue when the door opened wide and *Anthony Larsen* walked into the room. She shot to her feet from her chair, her eyes frantically searching the room…for what? An exit. She was searching for an exit. Why? Because one of the most talented and best-looking violinists of their time—who also happened to be her teenage crush—had just walked through the door. It. Was. Too. Much.

"Wow. You're Anthony Larsen." Angie rose from her seat at a normal speed like a normal person and continued speaking in the most annoyingly normal voice. "I can see why Megan wanted to preen over your introduction. I'm Angie. It's an absolute pleasure to meet you."

Anthony smiled and Chloe might have squeaked. His quizzical gaze shot briefly to her before he turned back to Angie. "The pleasure is entirely mine."

When Chloe stood like a statue—a blotchy red statue—Megan came to her side and wrapped her arm around her shoulders with a sly grin. "Chloe, aren't you going to say hello to *Anthony*?"

God help her, she was going to kill her very pregnant sister. With her bare hands. As soon as she could move. Or breathe.

Anthony's head cocked to the side but his tone was friendly when he said, "It's nice to meet you, Chloe. Megan has told me so much about you."

Her mouth decided to form words at that moment. "I'm Chloe."

Megan snorted beside her, and her fury finally broke the shock paralyzing her. She gave her sister a look that would've shriveled a lesser woman and met Anthony Larsen's eyes—the most beautiful hazel eyes she'd ever seen. Oh, how she used to dream of staring into them... like she was now. *Snap out of it, Chloe.* She gave herself a firm mental shake.

"I mean... It's nice to meet you as well, Anthony." Chloe was proud of how steady and casual her voice sounded. "My sister wasn't kidding when she said she had a surprise for us."

It was Anthony's turn to blush and he looked almost boyish—which was kind of a weird thought since he was at least ten years older than her. But still, he looked endearingly bashful as he said, "I wish she hadn't done that. I'm not some celebrity. If anything, I was probably more excited about meeting the rest of the Hana Trio."

"Isn't he the sweetest?" Megan said unrepentantly and grinned as Anthony cleared his throat.

"Megan, stop making him uncomfortable," Angie chastised.

"Oh, all right. Ruin my fun, why don't you." Megan was still all smiles as she waddled to the side of the room and maneuvered herself onto a chair. "Okay, Anthony. Ready for your audition?"

"Not as much as I'd like to be," he said, rubbing the back of his neck. "Megan said Mozart's Divertimento in E-flat Major is in your repertoire for this season. Should we play a movement from that piece?"

"Good choice." Chloe took her seat and pulled out her viola. Having her instrument in her hands centered her and made her feel less starstruck. "Why don't we try the second movement?"

"The Adagio?" Angie arched her eyebrow and settled her cello between her jean-clad legs. "I guess we're not taking it easy on Anthony."

"Of course not," Megan said with a sly glance at the world-renowned violinist. "We wouldn't want to insult him."

"Goodness no." Chloe shot him a cheeky smile as anticipation coursed through her. "Let's see what you're made of, Larsen."

His eyes seemed to darken as they lingered on her lips, and she felt her hard-earned calm trip and stumble under his gaze. Before she could wonder what the hell was happening, he sat down beside her and grinned. "Bring it on."

He brought his violin under his chin and took a deep breath. After meeting both Angie's and Chloe's eyes, he nodded as he played the first note. To anyone listening, it would've sounded like the three of them came in at the exact same time, but Chloe and her sisters knew that the start was slightly off. There was something tentative about the first few notes. By the grim set of Anthony's lips, he probably sensed it, too.

They rallied until the music swelled and ebbed in melancholy waves around them. There were a couple of instances where Chloe sought to catch Anthony's attention to anticipate the next phrase but his head was bowed, reading the music. Even so, she was impressed by how attuned he was to her and Angie. He didn't play as though he was the solo performer while they provided the accompaniment. He faded back when necessary to highlight the cello and the viola, and remembered their harmonious interplay even during the violin-forward parts. They played the last notes in sync and lowered their instruments.

"That was a valiant first effort," Angie said, smiling.

"Very promising," Chloe added.

She couldn't help being awed by how beautifully he played. He imbued such power and passion into his music that she felt a little out of breath. While they wouldn't be able to play with the same unity and grace that the Hana Trio was known for, their temporary trio would bring an added edge and excitement to the pieces.

"Can we go again?" Anthony asked, running a hand through his hair. "I can do better."

"That's what practice is for." Megan laughed as she got up from her seat. "Okay, Mr. Larsen. Please step outside so we can talk about you. My sisters might even decide to have a full practice session with you today, so tell your inner perfectionist to chill for a minute."

"God, I can't remember the last time I was this nervous." Anthony chuckled, shaking his head. "Be gentle with me, ladies."

"We will," Chloe reassured him. She wanted to blurt out that he got the job to ease his anxiety, but her sisters had a say in this as well. "We won't be long."

He tilted his head and stared at her for two heartbeats before he nodded and walked out of the room. She had to be imagining these drawn-out looks. Not that she was unaccustomed to men looking at her. She wasn't as beautiful as Angie and Megan, but she had her own appeal that garnered plenty of interest. She just couldn't fathom *the* Anthony Larsen finding her attractive or whatever.

"Blah blah. Blah blah blah," Megan said. When Angie frowned at her like she'd lost her marbles, Megan just shrugged. "We have to at least *pretend* to discuss his audition, don't we? But let's be realistic. What's there to discuss? He's in."

"You're not the one who has to play with him." Angie rolled her eyes. "What do you think, Chloe?"

"Shouldn't someone ultra-famous like him be a little more egotistical?" Chloe huffed, crossing her arms in front of her chest. She still couldn't believe how down-to-earth Anthony seemed. "I half expected him to hijack the piece and turn it into his solo performance, but he didn't do that. Not once."

"You almost sound like you're disappointed." Megan glanced sideways at her.

"Of course I'm not disappointed," Chloe said.

Honestly, it would've been more convenient if he was a bit of an asshole. She didn't want to relapse into her infatuation with him, which went on a lot longer than even her sisters suspected. Of course, she wouldn't let that happen, especially if they were going to work together. But it would've helped if he was less appealing.

"His talent is unquestionable, but I'm really impressed with his willingness to work as a team," Angie said. "We have over a month until Megan leaves on her maternity leave. That should give Anthony plenty of time to get acclimated to our style and for all of us to become attuned to one another."

"See? He's in." Megan's attempt to gloat lost some of its impact as she struggled to her feet with a groan. "Chloe, go get him so we can share the good news."

"Why me?" Chloe asked.

"Because you're the youngest and you have to do everything we tell you to," Megan said. "Plus, I need to catch my breath. I don't have the strength to get out of a chair *and* walk across the room."

Ignoring the butterfly swarm in her stomach, Chloe strode to the door and flung it open before she lost her nerve. She took one step into the hallway and nearly slammed into Anthony. She stopped just in time to avoid the collision but couldn't stop her squeal of alarm.

"Shit. Sorry," Anthony said. "I didn't mean to startle you."

"That's okay." She glanced up to meet his eyes and almost yelped again. He was very tall and very close. "I, um, rushed out without looking."

"Still. I'm sorry." He made no move to step back as his gaze roamed her face—his expression warred between confusion and fascination. She sucked in a quick breath and his nostrils flared ever so slightly. Tension built and charged the air around them.

"I… I was rushing because we have good news," she said a tad too loudly. "Please come in."

Chloe forgot to move aside as Anthony took a measured step forward, closing the bit of space that remained between them. Her body hummed like a plucked string at his proximity. She swayed toward him before she caught herself and cast a panicked glance up at his face. The dark heat in his eyes singed her. She took a stumbling step away from him and practically ran toward her sisters, counting on them to ground her before she climbed the man like a tree.

Two

Anthony blinked and Chloe was out of his reach. When she rejoined her sisters, she spun to face him with a flustered expression. He wasn't the only one who felt whatever it was that passed between them. But he needed to get it together. There were three pairs of eyes on him and he was expected to join them inside the room.

Closing the door behind him, he strolled toward them as casually as he could. He stopped at a respectable distance and shoved his hands inside his pockets, doing his utmost not to stare at Chloe.

"Welcome to the Hana Trio," Angie said with a warm smile.

"Really?" He laughed with relief. "I'll do my best to deserve the honor."

"I can't even roll my eyes because I know he actually means that." Megan let out an exaggerated sigh.

"So can I have another go at the Adagio?" he asked, chancing only a brief glance at Chloe. He was acting like it was the first time he met a beautiful woman. "I would like to redeem myself."

"Redeem yourself from an exceptional audition?" A teasing smile danced around Chloe's lips, and his heart thudded against his rib cage.

"Why don't you listen to the three of us run through it first?" Angie suggested. "Then you can get a better feel for our interpretation of the piece."

"That's a good idea." Chloe tapped her chin in contemplation. "We should try that system with the rest of the pieces as well. First with Megan, then Anthony. That way Megan won't get rusty—while Anthony gets acclimated to our sound."

"You'll find that our little sister *loves* systems," Megan said with an affectionate smile.

"That I do." Chloe's voice took on a dreamy lilt. "Systems are the best."

"Are they?" Anthony wasn't entirely sure what they were talking about, but he was all for it, if it made Chloe sound soft and husky like that.

"Yes." She nodded enthusiastically, dispelling her faraway look. "Systems are the superior approach to everything in life. They provide maximum efficiency and effectiveness."

He couldn't stop his lips from quirking into a grin. "That all sounds so…productive."

"It's not as boring as you make it out to be." Chloe narrowed her eyes at him. "Whatever. You'll thank me later."

"All right." Angie clasped her hands together. "Let's play some music, shall we?"

Goose bumps prickled across his arms as their music swept him away. It was truly remarkable how attuned the Han sisters were to one another. They played together their whole lives, but he still couldn't fathom how they seemed to be able to read each other's minds—how their three instruments came together so seamlessly to create one sound. His applause rang through the room when they finished the piece.

"That's a hard act to follow," he said.

"Just try your best, Mr. Greatest Violinist of Our Time." Megan rolled her eyes but her face softened as she said, "My sisters will have your back."

Angie nodded her agreement. "It's just a matter of learning to trust each other."

"We got you, Larsen." Chloe's tone was light, but the kind encouragement in her gaze made his heart drum deep and heavy in his chest. He gave her a single firm nod.

Hard work. That was what would get him through this. Most people thought some magic genius gene made him a successful violinist, but talent only got you so far. It was hard work—hours after hours of practicing and practicing again—that made him the musician he was today. And while playing as a part of the Hana Trio was different from performing on his own, he would work hard to not let the Han sisters down.

Anthony took the seat that Megan vacated and raised his violin, tucking it under his chin. The simple act was so familiar and *right* that it almost felt like a position of repose. It grounded him like nothing else. With a deep breath, he brought his bow down. This time the three of them struck the first note as one. And Angie and Chloe indeed had his back, steadying him when he stumbled and nudging him along when he hesitated.

Not only did Chloe play exquisitely but the sound of her viola felt like a warm hand wrapped around his own, guiding him through the entire piece. Even while he was absorbed in the music, his eyes strayed toward her again and again. His first taste of playing as part of a trio was exhilarating. It held an allure that was entirely different from performing as a soloist. The closing notes still hung in the air when they brought their instruments down.

"I'll be damned," Megan murmured. "Do I need to be worried about Anthony taking my place permanently?"

He chuckled. "It was an improvement but nowhere near where it needs to be. I still have a long way to go."

"But we'll get there," Angie said confidently.

"Okay. Let's move on to the next piece. It's your turn, Megan." Chloe clapped her hands. "Come on, people."

"Right." Anthony rose to his feet and grinned at Chloe. "The system."

"That's right, Larsen," she said with a playful wink that made his breath hitch. "You're learning."

Anthony felt a pang of disappointment when the three-hour rehearsal drew to a close. He couldn't remember the last time he'd enjoyed himself so much.

"Can I take you ladies to lunch?" He glanced at the three sisters as he packed up his violin.

"Sure," Chloe chirped. "I'm starving."

"I'm always starving these days," Megan muttered.

"But I can't today. I'm meeting Daniel for a prenatal appointment."

"And I'm having lunch with Joshua and his grandfather," Angie said with genuine regret. "Can I take a rain check?"

"Absolutely." He turned to Chloe, who stood beside him with her bottom lip snagged between her teeth. It took some effort to keep his gaze focused on her eyes. "I guess it'll be just the two of us."

"Um, we could do it another time when all of us are available…" Chloe began.

"I was hoping to discuss the pieces I need to familiarize myself with," he said in a rush, which was utter bullshit. Megan could easily text him the works he would be performing with the trio. "That way I can hit the ground running during our rehearsals."

"He's right." Angie glanced at her youngest sister as she hoisted her cello case onto her shoulder. "You should bring him up to speed."

"I guess so." Chloe shrugged.

It wasn't the most enthusiastic acquiescence he'd gotten from a woman, but he would take it. Besides, she wasn't a woman *per se*—she was his colleague and Daniel's sister-in-law. His friend would have his hide if Anthony so much as held Chloe's hand. He would keep this lunch—and his every interaction with her from this point forward—strictly professional.

"Do you like sushi?" he asked. There was a sushi bar he made sure to visit every time he was in Los Angeles.

"That depends. Are you buying?" Chloe grinned, a dimple winking in her right cheek.

He almost choked on his own saliva at the bewitching sight. *Strictly professional,* he reminded himself. He managed to wheeze, "I sure am."

"Then I *love* sushi," she said.

After saying their goodbyes to Angie and Megan at the parking lot, they drove to the restaurant separately. He bought a car when he came to LA since he would be there until the Chamber Music Society's season ended. If the car worked out for him, he might take it back to New York. He never got around to buying one after he moved to Manhattan—he traveled too often and public transportation was more than adequate—but it might help him feel more settled if he had his own car.

He parked at a corner lot by the sushi bar. As he neared the restaurant, he bit out a curse because there was a line a block long. He'd forgotten how busy it got during lunch. He scanned the crowd of people and spotted Chloe near the end of the queue.

"I'm sorry about the wait," he said, making sure not to stand too close to her.

"Don't be silly." She crinkled her nose at him. "There's always a long line at this restaurant. That's how you know it's good."

He chuckled. "I can't argue with that logic."

"So how will this work for you?" She cocked her head to the side. "Will you be able to attend all our rehearsals and performances? You always seem to have a jam-packed schedule with concerts all over the world. I don't know how you'll be able to manage."

"How do you know about my jam-packed schedule?" His eyebrows rose into his forehead.

"I… You have great marketing." Chloe fiddled with

the hem of her shirt. "It's hard to miss all the hoopla about your performances."

"Hoopla. Right." He nodded as if he understood. In truth, he relied on his manager and good friend, Tanner Moates, to handle the business aspect of his career. "Well, my schedule has been cleared for the next couple months. The Hana Trio will have my undivided attention."

A crease formed between her eyebrows as she studied him for a moment. She opened her mouth, then closed it and shook her head as though to say never mind.

Curiosity got the best of him. "What is it?"

"I was wondering if this has anything to do with... Let's just say there's a lot of hoopla about your personal life as well, and they're not all flattering." A blush crept cross her cheeks. "Words like *reckless* and *out of control* have been thrown about."

"I hope you don't believe *everything* you read," he muttered, raking his fingers through his hair. He typically didn't give a damn about his less-than-stellar reputation—especially since he contributed to much of it—but Chloe's opinion mattered to him.

"Of course not," she quickly averred.

He was too mortified to confess that Tanner had strongly recommended that Anthony stay low for a while. His latest hookup turned out to be the girlfriend of the golden boy conductor Javier Morales. Anthony wouldn't have gone near Scarlett Harding if she'd so much as implied that she was in a relationship with someone, much less someone he actually respected.

Their one-night stand was a mistake he didn't intend to repeat.

Thanks to being voted *People Magazine*'s Sexiest Man Alive two years ago, his every move—mostly regarding his love life—was reported and judged by the world. The last thing he needed was to get entangled in Javier and Scarlett's highly publicized, tumultuous relationship—something he would've known about if he didn't assiduously avoid social media. If he was involved in yet another scandal, his role as the luxury watchmaker Soleil's spokesperson would be on the line. He couldn't risk that.

"I cleared my calendar for a much-needed break from all the traveling." It was the truth—just not the whole truth. "I didn't want to push myself into a burnout."

"That's smart," Chloe said with eyes full of concern and understanding. Anthony couldn't look away even if he'd wanted to. "It's important to take care of yourself. We can burn out even when we're doing something we love and are passionate about."

"You're very wise for someone so young." Her compassion made something twist in his chest.

Her chin lifted a notch. "Twenty-five isn't that young."

Rachel was twenty-five when she died. She had been much too young for her life to be senselessly cut short. He chased the painful memory away and forced himself to smile. "It is when you're approaching middle age like myself."

"Thirty-five isn't that old," Chloe retorted with an indignant huff.

"You're too kind," he said wryly. But she really was

kind—kind, endearing and sweet—not to mention beautiful. He backed away from the not-at-all professional thoughts. Her talent. He would focus on her substantial talent as a musician. "You're exquisite."

Her jaw dropped. "What?"

Anthony closed his eyes for two seconds. Fucking Freudian slip.

"Your *playing* is exquisite." He enunciated carefully, making sure his brain and his mouth were on the same wavelength.

"Oh." She blinked rapidly. "Th…thank you. That means a lot coming from you."

"You're welcome." *Keep talking shop, Larsen.* "I'm very excited about being a temporary member of the Hana Trio."

"We're excited to have you, too," she said with a warm smile. "I'd be happy to answer any questions. You must have quite a few."

"Mmm-hmm. So many." But he couldn't remember a single one of them because the thoroughly distracting dimple had made its appearance again. Before he made a complete ass of himself, the restaurant server called Chloe's name and they were shown to their seats.

"I hope you don't mind sitting at the bar," she said, hanging her purse on the back of her chair.

"Not at all." But the seating at the bar was rather tight and they'd already bumped their knees twice. The second time might not have been an accident. And it was more of a brush than a bump. She smelled so damn good that he felt slightly off-kilter.

"I like chatting with the sushi chef and watching them do their thing," Chloe continued, oblivious to his wayward thoughts. "Did you know that the perfect ni-giri is supposed to have two hundred forty seven grains of rice?"

"That specific?" He turned toward her, then quickly faced the bar again. It was hard to ignore how close she was.

"They do it by feel." She made *feel* sound like *magic*. "I watched a show where they had this sushi chef make a nigiri, then they actually counted the grains. It was exactly two hundred forty seven."

Anthony added *interesting* to the list of Chloe Han's beguiling qualities. Wait, why was he making a fucking list about her? He promptly scattered the list, leaving only *talented* behind. She was his very talented—very young—colleague, who happened to be his dear friend's sister-in-law. He would keep things strictly professional between them even if it killed him.

"It must take years of dedication to achieve that kind of precision," he droned, instead of suggesting that they count the rice in their first nigiri. "It's not unlike what we strive for as classical musicians…"

Three

Anthony Larsen was polite, professional and...astonishingly boring. *Everything* he brought up had something to do with classical music. Yeah, it was their profession. But did the man have no other interests?

Chloe sighed as she unlocked the door to her apartment, a tiny one-bedroom in the graduate housing building. She wasn't being fair. It wasn't his fault that she knew every minute detail about his career. Otherwise, it would have been fascinating to learn about the life of a child prodigy turned brilliant virtuoso.

She dropped her purse, viola and keys on the well-worn couch in the cramped living room and padded into the kitchen. After clicking on her electric kettle, she plopped down next to her discarded belongings and grabbed her laptop off the coffee table. She hesitated for a moment before launching *League of Legends*. She usually didn't play until the evening—she was a disciplined, high-functioning gamer—but it had been a wild day and she felt like she earned a game.

The hot water for her tea forgotten, Chloe idly skimmed to see if any of her *LoL* friends were playing. *SerialFiddler*. She narrowed her eyes and growled at the screen. Of course *he* was online. He obviously didn't have the kind of discipline she had. She wouldn't be surprised if he played eighteen hours a day, crouched in his mom's dank basement. That would explain how he bested her at nearly every game they've had the misfortune of playing against one another.

She didn't know why they'd friended each other but they had. It probably had something to do with the "Keep your friends close; keep your enemies closer" philosophy. Before she could form additional unflattering thoughts about her nemesis, a message arrived from SerialFiddler.

Fancy seeing you here at this hour, NightMusic. Did you finally lose your day job?

"Asshole," she hissed. She considered ignoring him for all of three seconds before pounding out:

I know having a real job is a foreign concept to you, so I won't confuse you with an actual answer.

She grinned with petty satisfaction. Snark came so naturally with her archnemesis. But her smile disappeared when SerialFiddler's next message popped up.

Who says professional gaming isn't a real job? I always knew you lacked imagination, but I can't help feeling disappointed in you.

Her nostrils flared with annoyance as she typed:

Considering your amateur skill set, I bet my most prized possession that professional gaming is a sad, little pipedream for you.

There was a pause and she wondered if he went to lick his wounds in the corner. When his next message arrived, Chloe frowned in confusion.

What is your most prized possession?

That sounded like an actual question—a serious, personal question. They didn't do that. They bickered and took cheap shots at each other. It was their unwritten code. Chloe snapped her laptop closed in a sudden panic. *League of Legends* was her escape. Somewhere she didn't have to be upbeat and cheerful all the time. Somewhere she could rock the boat and screw up however much she wanted. The real her had no place in *LoL*.

Chloe made herself a cup of tea and sat down at her desk. She might as well get some work done. She opened her laptop with every intent of working on her term paper but found herself stalking Anthony Larsen on the internet instead. She didn't question what he said about wanting to avoid a burnout but she had a feeling there was more to his decision to join the Hana Trio and buckle down in LA for the next couple of months.

The articles she pulled up were old news she'd read

about months ago. His brief relationship with the prima ballerina of the famous French Ballet. And an even briefer relationship with the lead actress of *Virtuoso*, a film about a violinist's tumultuous life during World War II—Anthony was the artistic consultant and body double for the lead actor. Then there was always this model and that socialite in between anything that lasted long enough to be called a relationship. That had been his MO ever since his wife died.

Anthony Larsen was and would always be way the hell out of her league. It was a good thing he was so dull. She would never truly fall for someone who bored her to tears. Of course, it hadn't been boring to catch him looking at her with searing heat in his eyes several times during lunch. *Searing heat? Nah.* It must've been the lighting at the sushi bar.

Chloe shook her head and returned to her recon mission, which had nothing to do with his seemingly smoldering looks or her old infatuation with him. It was only mild curiosity about a musician she admired—a musician who would be a part of the Hana Trio for the next couple of months.

The gossip columns had been unusually quiet about Anthony lately, but one article snagged her attention. It included a statement from Soleil, the Bentley of watchmakers, about their decision to choose Anthony as their newest spokesperson. In response to an inquiry about any concerns they might have regarding the violinist's eventful love life, the luxury watchmaker responded:

Anthony Larsen is a brilliant musician. His passion for his work and pursuit of perfection embody the spirit of Soleil watches. His personal life is just that. Personal. It shouldn't in any way be a reflection on who he is as a violinist and a spokesperson for our brand.

She read what they didn't say between the lines. *We want nothing to do with his playboy bullshit.* She worried her bottom lip. His latest breakup with the actress *was* rather messy. It happened a few weeks ago—after the actress threw champagne in the prima ballerina's face at a gala in New York. Could that be why he disappeared from the gossip columns? Was he lying low to appease Soleil and rehabilitate his playboy image?

Chloe closed the browser with a determined click. She had a term paper to finish and a concert in two days. *No more procrastinating.* If she made significant headway on her paper, she would reward herself with a game of *LoL*. She didn't pay any attention to the flicker of anticipation that ran through her at the thought of going head-to-head with her archnemesis.

Anthony came to the Chamber Music Society's concert to familiarize himself with the Hana Trio's performance style. His presence in the audience had nothing to do with seeing Chloe again. He was there for purely professional reasons. Never mind that time seemed to drag on endlessly since he saw her two days ago.

He couldn't remember half the stuff he blabbered on about over lunch—he nearly put himself to sleep with boredom—but Chloe gave him her full attention throughout and didn't display one iota of annoyance. Even so, he had no doubt he'd firmly established himself as a dull older man in her mind. And he was completely fine with that. In fact, it was exactly what he wanted. Maintaining a strictly professional relationship with her should be a breeze now.

He held on to that delusion until the Hana Trio took stage, the three sisters wearing red formal dresses in various styles. Chloe took his breath away in a strapless gown that hugged her luscious curves and left her creamy shoulders bare for his eyes to devour. She exuded a graceful sensuality that he yearned to explore. He shifted in his seat, his slacks suddenly too tight. But the only exploring he intended to do was studying her musicianship.

The Hana Trio's performance was powerful and moving. He felt truly honored to have the opportunity to work with such phenomenal musicians. And to ensure that he did nothing to taint his working relationship with the Hana Trio, Anthony left as soon as the concert ended. He didn't trust himself to be within six feet of Chloe in that damn red dress.

He had one foot out the entrance when a hand gripped his arm and pulled him to the side of the building. Once he ascertained the owner of the hand, he shook his arm out of her grip.

"Anthony," Scarlett Harding purred. "How lovely to see you in LA."

"What an unexpected…pleasure," he said in a tone that made it clear that it was anything but. "Is Morales with you?"

"Not at the moment." Her smile was positively feline. "He's busy chatting with the Chamber Orchestra's conductor. It's always work, work, work with him."

"His dedication is reflected in his craft. He's one hell

of a conductor." Anthony hoped to work with Javier Morales one day. All the more reason to cut this encounter short. "Enjoy the rest of your evening."

But when he made to step away, the blonde bombshell put a possessive hand on his arm. Anthony noticed that a new diamond ring graced her ring finger.

"I was disappointed when you didn't call," she said with a practiced pout.

"I'm sure you recovered with admirable speed," he drawled, not bothering to hide his derision. She was still pulling this shit when she was engaged? "That night would never have happened if I'd known you were with Morales."

"Didn't you know a night with me is habit forming?" she said coyly, making his stomach heave with distaste. "Javier is always so busy, and I'm lonely."

"Then find someone else to keep you company because I'm not interested." He once again moved to walked around her, but she stepped closer to him, blocking his way. He had no choice but to stop. No matter how irritating she was, he couldn't bowl her over.

"I find that hard to believe." The beginnings of an ugly snarl twisted her pretty face. "You couldn't keep your hands off me that night."

"Sure." He shrugged callously. "I must've gotten my fill, then, because I have no desire to lay a finger on you ever again."

"You—" she hissed and planted her palm on his chest "—are going to regret this."

"Sheath your claws, sweetheart." He didn't bother keeping his voice civil. "You're drawing a crowd."

She glanced over her shoulder and turned back to

him with a vicious grin. "You're right. I even see a couple of our paparazzi friends lurking down the stairs."

His eyes darted to where two men climbed the steps with cameras hanging from their necks. *Shit.* "We're done here, Scarlett."

"No, I don't think we are." She leaned in to kiss him and his fury momentarily paralyzed him.

"Keep your overinjected lips to yourself." Two fingers pressed into Scarlett's forehead, pushing her away from him. He recognized that clear, ringing voice and slowly turned his head to confirm the identity of its owner. *Chloe.* His rescuer moved close to his side, her arm brushing his reassuringly. "And do not *ever* touch him without his consent again."

It took the other woman a few seconds to find her voice, which came out shrill and whiny. "Who the hell are you?"

"I am—" Chloe's gaze darted to the paparazzi now snapping away at them "—Anthony's girlfriend."

Something primal awoke at her words. She was *his*. He didn't care that she was just trying to save his ass. He *wanted* her to be his. To grab hold of her and never let go. Before he could formulate any rational thought—because this need churning through him was the farthest thing from rational—Anthony spun Chloe to face him and crushed his lips against hers.

Four

Chloe's lips parted on a gasp and the breath got caught in her chest when Anthony swept his tongue into her mouth. He was kissing her. Anthony Fucking Larsen was kissing her as though she tasted like heaven. She couldn't stifle the little moan that escaped her. With an answering growl, he hauled her soft, pliant body against the hard planes of his own.

And she was lost. She wrapped her arms around his neck and buried her hand in his hair. Her fist clenched when he bit her bottom lip, then lightly licked the sting away. She entwined her tongue with his, reminding him to play nice—not at all sure she wanted *nice*. His hands splayed across her back and tugged her even closer.

She rose on her tiptoes because she needed more of this. More of him. The feel of his muscular body against hers made warmth pool between her legs. The taut, hard arms encircling her felt like bands of iron and her breasts might as well have been pressed against a brick wall. She gripped the lapels of his suit jacket with half a mind to rip it off him. She wanted to feel his bare skin beneath her hands. She wanted to touch him everywhere—and *be* touched.

The muted chuckling and the flash of cameras brought her back to her senses. This was pretend. Anthony was only kissing her to maintain her outrageous claim that she was his girlfriend. She must've been out of her mind. But in that moment, all she'd been able to think was that he couldn't afford another scandal…and that she wanted to get that blonde viper's hands off him.

The lightest push against his chest had Anthony stepping back immediately. She barely registered that the blonde was nowhere in sight. Unable to meet his eyes, she linked her fingers through his and waved breezily at the paparazzi with her other hand. "Good night, boys."

Anthony followed where she led without a word. She pulled him down a hallway that housed the offices at the concert hall. It was late enough in the evening that they lay empty. She stopped at a dim alcove and released his hand. It felt as though he held on a second longer than necessary… She blew out a breath, preparing to apologize for sticking her nose in where it didn't belong.

"Thank you." The quiet sincerity in Anthony's voice had her eyes flying up to meet his. "She was a mistake I didn't want to repeat. And with the paparazzi there… The whole thing would've been a disaster without your help."

"It wasn't my place…" she demurred.

"You were thinking quickly on your feet." His lips

quirked into a half grin, which disappeared much too quickly. "If you didn't intervene and claim to be my girlfriend, the media would have gleefully painted me as a cad having an affair with an engaged woman."

"That woman. The paparazzi. The media. They're all awful." A blush crept across her cheeks. "And I guess that kiss convinced them that you're happily in a relationship."

"Yes," he said in a low voice as his gaze dipped to her lips.

"Well, I'm glad I was able to help out," she said with forced cheer as the alcove grew ten degrees warmer.

"Here's where things get a bit awkward." Anthony rubbed a weary hand over his face.

"Awkward? No, no, no." *Jeez.* She couldn't be more awkward if she tried. "I know the kiss was pretend. It was just for show. We're both adults. It's not a big deal *at all*. It was nothing. Really."

"Nothing?" A small groove formed between his eyebrows. "Okay. Sure. But that wasn't what I was getting at."

"Then what were you getting at?" It was her turn to frown.

"I need you to keep pretending that you're my girlfriend."

Her mouth dropped open. "Come again?"

"At least until the end of the season," he said, his expression solemn. "With your declaration that you're my girlfriend followed by that very convincing kiss, we've basically confirmed to the paparazzi that we're dating. If we turn around and say that we were just pretending, it'll garner unwanted talk and speculation. And

God knows what Scarlett will say or do if she thinks we duped her."

"Scarlett?" Her eyebrows knitted together, then all the social media posts she'd seen flooded back to her. "That was Scarlett Harding? Javier Morales's fiancée?"

"Yes." Anthony pinched the bridge of his nose.

"She's all over social media, glomming for attention," Chloe whispered, dread twisting in her gut. What had she gotten herself into? "She has enough followers to do some real damage if she puts her mind to it."

"More reason for us to present a unified front. If we show the world that we're in a solid, committed relationship, even her drama can't touch us." His gaze held hers without wavering. "I know I'm asking for a lot."

"Is it because you don't want to be dropped as Soleil's spokesperson?" she blurted.

His eyes widened. "How did you know about that?"

"I kind of put two and two together." She would die if he knew how closely she followed his career. She took a deep breath. "But faking a relationship? Isn't that a bit extreme?"

"Yes, it is." He dragged his fingers through his hair and paced a few steps. "My wife—my late wife—was a special education teacher."

Chloe nodded because words were beyond her as a torrent of emotions slammed into her.

"When she—" his Adam's apple bobbed as he swallowed "—passed away, I vowed to do everything in my power to honor her memory. Every last penny I earn from Soleil is meant to go to Life Village, a foundation for children with developmental disabilities."

"You… You must have loved her very much," she whispered.

"I did." A muscle in his jaw ticked. "I do. I always will."

She was only twelve or thirteen when Anthony married his college sweetheart but Chloe had been heartbroken. But she was even more shattered when she heard the news of his wife's death a few years later. The details were kept private but Rachel Larsen died as a result of a bungled robbery.

Even now, she couldn't begin to fathom what Anthony went through. To lose someone you love so suddenly and violently… And he must still be hurting, holding on to that love all these years. *Oh, Anthony.* She blinked away the hot tears that threatened to spill over.

"With that donation, Life Village will finally have enough money to build a housing community to help the children transition into adulthood and live independently," he continued in a rush as though he was desperate to convince her to help him—as though she needed any more convincing. "If Soleil fires me and I don't come through with those funds, it might indefinitely delay the construction. I can't do that to the foundation…to the children."

"Oh, Anthony." She wanted to take his face in her hands and smooth away the lines of worry, but she held herself back. He didn't need her sympathy. He just needed her to be his fake girlfriend.

"I know it's selfish of me to ask so much of you—"

"Selfish?" Incredulous laughter huffed out of her. "Oh, yes. You're *so* selfish for wanting to help those kids."

"Does… Does that mean you'll help me?" The uncertainty in his voice made something tighten in her chest.

"I'll help you," Chloe said, even though she had a sinking feeling that she wasn't going to walk away from this unscathed. "But on one condition."

"Of course." Anthony took a step closer to her, hope glowing in his eyes. "I'll do anything you want."

"I…" She shivered at his words—his closeness—and lost track of her thoughts for a moment. "We can dupe the whole world into believing that we're dating, but I'm telling my family the truth."

"Of course." He nodded solemnly. "Will you allow me to tell Daniel myself?"

"Okay."

Chloe blew out a long breath. She couldn't believe she just agreed to be Anthony Larsen's fake girlfriend. What was going to happen to her calm, steady life? She ducked her chin as a secret smile blossomed on her face.

"I think it goes without saying that I will kick your sorry ass all the way to New York if you hurt Chloe," Daniel said with steely calm.

"Whoa." Anthony held up his hands. They were sitting on opposite ends of the sofa in his hotel suite, so Daniel could technically kick his ass without even getting out of his seat. "Why would I hurt Chloe? All we need to do is go out on a few fake dates and smile prettily for the cameras."

"You. Kissed. Her." His friend shoved his phone so close to Anthony's face that he had to back up to be able to see the screen.

The paparazzi had gotten a good shot of their kiss.

Chloe's arms were wrapped around his neck, one hand buried in his hair, and her body was arched against his. Just remembering how sweet she tasted made his blood hum with desire, and a stupid smile tugged at his lips.

"Anthony." Daniel's voice rumbled with warning.

"I panicked." Or temporarily lost his mind. How else could he explain that surge of primal need?

"You panicked by shoving your tongue down my sister-in-law's throat?" His usually levelheaded friend was as close to losing his temper as Anthony had ever seen him.

"When Chloe said she was my girlfriend, it looked as though Scarlett couldn't decide whether to laugh in her face or scratch her eyes out," Anthony said, hoping to convince himself as much as his friend. He was the cause of this whole fiasco, but he wanted to believe he had nobler reasons than lust motivating him. "Either option would've been a disaster, especially with the paparazzi circling us like piranhas. What she said couldn't be unsaid, so I made the best of the situation by convincing both Scarlett and the paparazzi that Chloe is truly my girlfriend."

"You were very convincing," Daniel grumbled.

"I'm sorry I got her involved in this." But no matter how bad he felt about involving Chloe in his mess, Anthony couldn't stop his heart from speeding up at the thought of spending more time with her. "But being in a healthy, committed relationship will go a long way in rehabilitating my image with Soleil. You know I can't let Life Village down."

"I know. I don't like it, but I know." His friend sighed.

"So how long do you need to keep this ridiculous farce going?"

"Until the end of the Chamber Music Society's season." He and Chloe had decided this would be the best option. "Once I'm done playing with the Hana Trio, I'll go home to New York. After a couple of weeks, we'll say that a long-distance relationship isn't for us and amicably part ways."

"That sounds positively boring. Even the most creative gossip columnist wouldn't be able to spin that into a scandal."

"Exactly." Anthony raised his glass of scotch in mock salute.

"Megan is going to kill me for telling you this." Daniel knocked back his drink. "Chloe would probably die if she ever found out."

"Tell me what?"

"Chloe used to have a diehard crush on you when she was a teenager. For years."

"Really?" Anthony kept his expression neutral with some effort. He was a bastard but he couldn't suppress the brief surge of male pride—couldn't ignore the kernel of hope that the grown-up Chloe might still feel something for him. "I'm sure it was nothing."

"Maybe. But I wanted you to know."

"Why?"

"You know I don't take our friendship for granted. Far from it." Daniel walked to the wet bar and refilled his drink. He turned around and raised his eyebrows in question. When Anthony lifted his empty glass in answer, his friend brought the bottle back to the sofa. "But Chloe is family."

"Daniel—"

"You still love Rachel and can't bear to move on," Daniel interrupted. Anthony didn't bother denying it. "That's why you flit from one woman to the next. I feel for you, man. But that doesn't mean I'll stand by and watch you treat Chloe like your latest flavor of the week."

Anthony had a reputation with women. He knew Daniel only wanted to protect his sister-in-law. But his fists clenched on his thighs as he said, "She is a grown woman who can take care of herself."

"No doubt, but she has a soft spot for you. If you seduce her, you'll not only be using her body," his friend said bluntly, "but risking her heart, *knowing* you can't give yours in return."

"Fuck you," Anthony growled and tipped his drink back. The burn of alcohol did nothing to ease the chill in his chest. As his burst of anger seeped out of him, he rested his head on the back of the couch and stared unseeingly at the ceiling. "I will *never* risk breaking her heart."

"Do I have your word?" Daniel asked.

"You have my word." Anthony glanced at his friend and drawled, "Do you want a blood oath?"

"Sure. Why not? Write 'I will keep my hands and dick to myself' in blood." Daniel smirked. "If you break your oath, said dick will shrivel up and fall off."

"Asshole." Anthony chuckled even though the conversation weighed heavily on him.

"And on that lovely note, I'll bid you good night." His friend rose to his feet.

"Is Megan waiting up for you?"

"Probably. She usually can't fall asleep when I'm not there—it's funny how quickly you get used to someone sleeping next to you. But I'm actually rushing home because I get nervous if I'm more than two feet away from her lately. I feel like she's going to go into labor the minute I leave her side." Daniel laughed sheepishly. "I think she's getting sick of me following her around like a Velcro dog."

"Doesn't she have a few more weeks to go?" Anthony walked his friend to the door.

"Eight." Daniel heaved a sigh. "I don't know if I'll make it."

Anthony chuckled. "I never thought I'd see the day you became a Velcro husband."

"You and me both." Daniel walked out to the hall-way and waved over his shoulder.

After closing the door behind him, Anthony retrieved his scotch from the coffee table and headed toward the bedroom. He sat on the bed and leaned back against the headrest with a weary sigh. Nursing his drink, he mulled over his conversation with Daniel.

Anthony meant what he'd said—he would never risk breaking Chloe's heart. Just the thought of her hurting made his chest clench painfully. But being around her without touching her... That was going to be torture.

Having her in his arms, her soft, generous curves molded against his body, had felt almost too good to be true. And she tasted as sweet as a summer nectarine. He could easily become addicted to kissing her.

"Hell," he muttered as his blood rushed south.

He shifted on the bed and shunned any thought of

giving himself the release his body craved. The more
he fantasized about their kiss, the harder it would be to
keep his hands off Chloe. For the sake of his sanity, he
could never kiss her again.

Five

"Anthony kissed you?" Angie asked, straightening in her seat.

Chloe and her sisters reconvened at Megan's place as soon as she and Anthony parted ways at the concert hall. She needed to tell them her secret before the news of Anthony and her "relationship" became public.

"No," Chloe said, then quickly amended, "Yes. But it wasn't a real kiss. We were just pretending."

"Sure as hell looks like a real kiss," Megan muttered, glancing down at her phone.

"What?" Chloe reached for Megan's phone but Angie snagged it first. "There's already a picture online?"

"This definitely looks like a real kiss," her eldest sister pronounced.

"Oh, jeez." Chloe scooted to Angie's side and peered at the picture. She gulped. It did look real. It had felt real, too—at least for her. She cleared her throat. "Well, we had to be convincing. Otherwise, what's the point?"

"Well, the point is… Why do you have to do this in the first place?" Angie threw her hands up in exasperation.

"I had to do something because—" Chloe dug deep for her patience as she repeated her reasons for the third time "—that handsy blonde was about to ruin Anthony's reputation. Telling her that I'm his girlfriend, then kissing the hell out of him in front of the paparazzi might have been a bit rash, but what's done is done. Now that the media believes we're dating, we can't come clean without risking a backlash."

"And any more bad publicity would mean that Soleil will drop Anthony and those innocent children will ultimately pay the price." Genuine concern clouded Angie's face, banking some of Chloe's frustration. "I understand all that, but why *you*?"

"Because I have impeccable timing." Chloe smirked with feigned bravado. "If I didn't show up right that second, Anthony would be neck-deep in a scandal right now."

She hadn't realized how big of a scandal until he explained that the bombshell blonde was Scarlett Harding. Javier Morales was the hottest thing in the classical music scene at the moment. If people thought Anthony was having an affair with his fiancée, Soleil wouldn't be the only thing he would lose.

"Helping those kids is important to Anthony because it was what Rachel would have wanted," Megan said in an unusually subdued voice. "He would do anything to keep his wife's memory alive. I don't think he ever stopped loving her. You can't forget that, Chloe."

"I… I know." She swallowed past the sudden constriction in her throat.

"You're a grown woman and I can't tell you how to live your life." Megan held her gaze. "But I hope you don't let this become anything more than one friend helping out another."

"You guys are taking this much too seriously." Chloe forced a light laugh. "Celebrities have fake relationships all the time as publicity maneuvers. This isn't much different from that. Anthony and I'll be seen in public on a few strategic dates, then he'll be off to New York once the season is over."

Her sisters exchanged a speaking glance. Chloe understood why they were worried, but she was over her childish crush on Anthony. She wasn't an impressionable teenager anymore. She knew better than to fall for someone who was still hung up on his late wife.

"When are you going to tell Dad?" Angie sounded resigned.

"It's too late to talk to him tonight," Chloe said after glancing at the wall clock. "I'll tell him tomorrow. The last thing he needs is one of us keeping yet another secret from him."

"No," Megan groaned. "I think the poor man has had enough secrets exploding in his face to last a lifetime."

"Do you need backup?" Angie reached out and squeezed Chloe's hand. "I doubt he'll take kindly to this fake-dating scheme."

"No, having you two there will probably remind him of all the heartache *you* caused him." Chloe smiled at her sisters to take the sting out of her words. "Besides, if I don't make a big deal out of it, maybe he won't either."

"Good luck with that," Megan said past a yawn.

"The pregnant woman needs her sleep." Angie got to her feet and gathered her purse. "But report back after you speak with Dad. Okay, Chloe?"

"Yeah, yeah." Chloe gave Megan a hug and patted her stomach in fond farewell to her nephew. "I'll keep you guys posted on everything but this really isn't a big deal."

"Of course. Faking dating the greatest violinist of our time is *so* pedestrian." Megan rolled her eyes as she walked them to the door.

Angie chortled and Chloe glared at her sisters. "Mark my words. I'm going to keep this fake-dating thing so practical and sensible that it'll bore you to death."

"Oh, no." Megan clapped her hands on her cheeks in mock horror. "Anything but death by boredom."

"Go to sleep, you silly woman," Angie said fondly as she stepped outside.

Chloe waved goodbye to Megan and joined her eldest sister on the sidewalk. She smothered a yawn behind her hand as exhaustion came crashing down on her.

"Good night, Unni," she said when they reached her car.

"Chloe." Angie placed a hand on her arm. "Your heart has a mind of its own. Logic and determination have no sway over it. Just… Don't let yourself get too close to Anthony."

Annoyance flashed through Chloe. "He's a good man."

"I know." Her sister sighed. "That's what I'm afraid of."

Inexplicable tears filled Chloe's eyes but she blinked them away. "I need to get home."

"Okay. Drive safe."

Chloe sat in her car, gripping the steering wheel. Her sisters were overreacting. Even if she *was* smitten with Anthony—and she wasn't—nothing was going to happen because *he* wasn't interested in her in that way. He made it clear that he admired her as a musician but that was all. They couldn't even think of a common topic to discuss over lunch. Besides, he was out of her league by a mile. This was going to be the most uneventful fake-dating scheme in the history of fake-dating schemes.

Now all she had to do was stop replaying their kiss—the best kiss of her life—over and over in her head.

For their first fake date, Chloe suggested dinner at an upscale French restaurant in Santa Monica. She said it was a good place to be seen without looking like they wanted to be seen. By the third course of their thirteen-course meal, Anthony couldn't care less about *why* they were there. The food was exquisite and the company was…captivating.

His eyes followed the finger Chloe languidly trailed around the rim of her wineglass. He wondered how she would react if he ran his tongue along her finger with the same lazy strokes she was bestowing on the glass.

"Anthony?"

"Yes?" The rasp of his voice was barely audible. He cleared his throat and tried again, "Excuse me. Yes?"

"What do you think about this dish?" she said, taking a delicate bite of the succulent beef tartar. Her eyelashes fluttered and a dreamy smile stole across her face. If Anthony gripped his fork any tighter, he was certain the silverware would bend in half.

"The ratatouille pearls on top take the tartar to another level." He somehow managed to string words together.

He forced himself to look away from Chloe and stared down at his dish. The gastro pearls engineered by the chef looked like salmon roe at first glance, but it was filled with the bright, refreshing flavors of summer vegetables. He would be enjoying the surprising texture and unique presentation more if he wasn't busy drooling over his date.

"Right?" Chloe grinned. "I love how they pop in my mouth like caviar. It's so much fun."

Anthony couldn't help smiling back because *she* was so much fun. She exuded the warmth of sunshine in the spring. He wanted to soak her up until the ice around his shattered heart melted, so he could *feel* again—and one day heal.

The only time he truly felt alive was when he was playing his violin—when he allowed the vise of his guilt to recede into the background. With Chloe by his side, he might finally be able to *live* every moment of his life. He caught himself short and took a sip of his wine to regain his equilibrium.

"Speaking of fun," she said, taking a sip of her wine, "we never talked about our…expectations from this *dating* arrangement."

"Expectations?" His eyebrows drew together. "Other than what we already discussed, what more could I expect from you?"

Chloe was a colleague who was doing him a huge

favor. That was all. She was already giving him more than he deserved. He couldn't ask for anything more from her no matter how much he wanted her.

She leaned in close and lowered her voice. "There will obviously be no sex."

Unfortunately, he was in the process of drinking some water to wash away the bitter taste in his mouth. Most of it and possibly an ice cube went down the wrong pipe. Chloe pounded his back with some force as he coughed until his eyes watered.

"I'm going to take that as a yes to the no-sex rule," she murmured. "I also don't want you to fall in love with me. I don't want breaking your heart etched into my conscience."

He stared at her, wheezing slightly—at a loss for words. When her dimple winked by her mouth, he realized she was messing with him. He let out an awkward laugh. "No sex. No love. Got it."

"We have a deal." She held out her hand across the table. "Shake on it?"

He accepted the handshake—eager for the fleeting touch—and regretted it almost instantly as heat shot up his arm. Her hand was small, warm and so damn soft. His jaw clenched from the strain of stopping himself from brushing his thumb across her knuckles and kissing the sensitive skin at her wrist.

He forced himself to drop her hand before he gave himself a full-blown hard-on. From fucking shaking her hand. *Get a grip, Larsen.*

"Beethoven's Serenade in D major sounded solid this morning," he said, falling back on the safe topic of their mutual profession.

"Oh... You want to talk about work...again." The barest hint of a cringe swept across Chloe's face. "Well, yes. It sounded wonderful. We were definitely in sync."

"It helped me a great deal to listen to Megan play with you and Angie first," he continued, relieved his heart rate was slowing down. Perhaps having a professional and cordial relationship with Chloe wasn't as hopeless as it seemed. "Your system really works."

"Of course it does." She perked up at the mention of her system. "I told you systems unfailingly provide maximum efficiency and effectiveness."

He chuckled at her unabashed enthusiasm. His laugh turned into a dopey smile as he stared at Chloe. *For fuck's sake.* He gave himself a mental shake. "I hope it works just as well when we practice Schubert's String Trio in B-Major."

"Mmm-hmm," she said, sounding a bit distracted. "Everything will click during the practice. You'll see."

"Good. Of course. Yes." He sounded like a stuffy bore even to his own ears. Their scintillating conversation lulled as their plates were taken away.

Chloe drew lines across the condensation on her water glass to entertain herself. He swallowed all the questions he wanted to ask about her life—about her. The more he knew about her, the harder it would be to keep his distance. Before the silence between them could become too uncomfortable, their server presented them with the next course.

"Oh, my God," Chloe whispered with reverence. "I *love* duck."

It was served in three ways—a bite each of rich, melt-in-your-mouth confit, medium-rare roast with black truffle and crispy skin atop a mini bao. He fought to ignore the low moans of appreciation coming from across the table after each morsel. He was dying to watch Chloe eat—wondering what kind of expressions accompanied the sinful noises she was making—but he didn't dare. He doggedly focused on the food in front of him and actually managed to register that everything was delicious.

"I've been thinking about something." He couldn't quite look Chloe in the eye, so he resumed the shop talk to distract himself from her allure. "For the summer concert at the Hollywood Bowl, I thought it might be fun to play 'Por Una Cabeza' as part of our program. I could write an arrangement for a string trio."

"Oooh." She looked almost as excited about the idea as she did about the duck. That was definitely *not* what he was going for. "'Por Una Cabeza' is one of the sexiest pieces of music ever written. It would be amazing to perform ensconced in the night with stars spilling from the sky. Mixing that piece with the romance of the outdoor venue and the heat of summer is sure to get the audiences hot and bothered."

Anthony loved taking passionate pieces of classical music—such as arias from grand, iconic operas—and reinterpreting them for the violin. They were such a thrill to perform. But playing the sultry tango with Chloe would give him more than a thrill. *Forget the audience.* He would be the first one to get hot and bothered…and hard. He obviously hadn't thought this through before he opened his big mouth about "Por Una Cabeza."

"How did your talk with your father go?" He asked the

question he really cared about. It suddenly seemed safer than talking about music. "If my conversation with Daniel is anything to go by, your father must've been livid."

"Um…yeah." Chloe blinked at his abrupt change of topic. "Let's just say he wasn't overjoyed at the news."

"I'm sorry." He wouldn't be causing her so much trouble if he didn't have such a sordid reputation. For the first time, he regretted the reckless choices he had made in the last decade—for throwing his body around like it was worthless…like *he* was worthless.

"Don't worry about it." She waved aside his apology. "We have good reasons for doing this."

"Yes, but it isn't fair to you—"

"What has *fair* got to do with anything? Nothing about life is fair," she said with a hint of sadness. He remembered that she lost her mother to cancer several years ago. And he thought about Rachel's life being cut short so senselessly. No, life wasn't fair. "Let's not overthink this."

"Okay." He should stop trying to convince her that this sucks for her. She was letting him off easy. "Thank you, Chloe."

"You're welcome." A soft blush stole across her cheeks.

She was so lovely. He let himself stare at her for a moment because it was impossible not to. Then he needlessly adjusted the napkin on his lap to give himself some time to recover.

"So after dinner," she said, "I was thinking we could stroll down Third Street Promenade. It's a very date-y thing to do in LA with plenty of camera happy tourists around."

"Did you take walks there with your real boy-friends?" The question flew out of his mouth before he could stop it, his back teeth clenching at the thought of her with other men.

"Real boyfriends?" She giggled with an embarrassed wince. "Yeah…um… I haven't had one of those in a while."

"Oh?" He hoped his tone conveyed casual interest rather than heartfelt relief. Something was seriously wrong with him. "I find that hard to believe."

"Being a member of the Hana Trio while getting myself through graduate school is more than enough to juggle." She shook her head. "The last thing I need is a man thrown into the mix."

Anthony arched an eyebrow.

"No, no. I don't mean you," she quickly amended. "I mean a man that I would be romantically interested in. You know, the kind of man that I'd lose sleep over—the kind I wouldn't be able to get out of my mind."

"Yes, of course," he muttered, more than a touch peeved. It sounded as though she was speaking from experience. "I'm certainly not that kind of man."

"No, you're not. At least for me. We work together. It would be unprofessional." A small frown marred her forehead. "And I don't plan on letting our fake relation-ship interfere with my real life in any way."

"I see." His index finger tapped restlessly on the table. "That's very reassuring."

"I'm glad," she said with a resolute nod. "I want you to stop worrying and apologizing, Anthony. This is no big deal."

"Okay." His lips felt stiff as he forced them into a smile.

Daniel needn't have worried. *Nothing* remained of Chloe's teenage infatuation with Anthony. She wasn't the least bit interested in him. It was for the best. The stifling weight of his disappointment was of no consequence.

Six

No boy had ever interested Chloe's teenage self because they all paled in comparison with Anthony Larsen. Then her mom had gotten sick and nothing else seemed to matter. She did everything she could to make her mom smile during those long, hard years. After she died, Chloe focused on holding her dad together so he wouldn't fall apart, especially after Angie left home. When the cloud of grief finally lifted for all of them, she threw herself into the Hana Trio and her master's program. There had been no time for a man in her life.

The only man she had lost sleep over—the only one she hadn't been able to get out of her mind—was Anthony. But she would die before she told that to him. Besides, her teenage crush on him was ancient history. Now they were colleagues and temporary co-conspirators in a preposterous fake-dating scheme.

Chloe couldn't stop herself from sneaking a glance at her "boyfriend" as they walked down Third Street Promenade. A small smile played around his full lips as he took in the brightly lit shops on the wide pedestrian street and the lively throng of people walking alongside them. She found herself smiling, too. It'd been a while since she went out for fun, doing something as simple as taking a stroll. The tall, handsome man by her side might have contributed to her lighthearted mood.

They passed by street performers doing harrowing juggling tricks and impressive dance moves but the soulful crooning of a singer on his acoustic guitar caught Chloe's attention. She scanned the street until she spotted the source.

"Come on." She grabbed Anthony's hand and made a beeline for the talented singer.

The crowd gathered around him wasn't as big as the other flashy performances but everyone seemed enthralled by the husky, plaintive sound of his voice and the soft thrumming of his guitar. It wasn't until the song ended that Chloe realized she was still holding Anthony's hand. Heat rushing to her cheeks, she tugged her hand free and clapped enthusiastically.

She felt Anthony's eyes on her as the singer continued on to the next song but she was suddenly too shy to meet his gaze. That didn't seem like the actions of a woman whose crush was *ancient history* so she forced herself to look at him and raised an eyebrow in cool inquiry.

"You know—" the warmth of his breath teased her ear and his fingers lightly brushed against the back of her hand "—the handholding probably helps."

"Helps with what?" she asked, unintentionally leaning closer to him.

"With our lovers act." The low rumble of his voice felt like a caress down the side of her neck. A tremor quaked through her and the song filling the night faded into a faint hum. She held his gaze and laced her fingers through his, praying that her knees wouldn't give out.

"Anything for the kids," she said to hide her reaction to him.

It wasn't until the next song that Chloe was able to focus on the performance again. *Focus* might be an overstatement. She could barely discern the lyrics but her world was no longer narrowed down to the heat spreading from her hand to every last cell in her body.

"Is that Anthony Larsen?" a woman said from somewhere beside them.

The whisper scraped against Chloe's ears like sandpaper. She stopped herself at the last second from turning to identify the speaker. Anthony squeezed her hand to let her know that he heard, too. A quick peek at his profile showed that he was completely relaxed. He must be used to this kind of attention.

"Oh, my God. It is him," another woman replied in a louder voice. "Who is that girl standing with him? Are they holding hands?"

Chloe didn't miss the slight emphasis on *girl* as though she wasn't mature or sophisticated enough to be deemed a woman—at least a woman worthy of Anthony Larsen's attention.

"He can't possibly be with her." The woman snorted. "I mean, I guess she's pretty enough. But she is so not his type."

Chloe's nostrils flared. Who made her the fucking expert on his *type*? She surreptitiously blew out a long breath. *Relax, Chloe.* To be fair, the women who'd been photographed with Anthony had all been stunning and glamorous. The deep breathing wasn't working. She was smart, funny and accomplished. She was a goddamn catch.

She jumped when Anthony's mouth brushed against her ear. "What do you say we convince those busybodies otherwise?"

Before she could think of a response, he cupped her cheek and tilted her face toward him. She only had time to grab a fistful of his shirt to steady herself when he brushed his lips against hers—soft and questioning. He seemed to be asking, *Yes?*

"Yes," she whispered without breaking the kiss. It was the only answer her mind could formulate—the one her body craved.

His other hand reached up to cradle her face and he ran his thumbs cross her cheekbones as he kissed her. His lips were gentle but curious as he explored her mouth. The patience and thoroughness of his kiss made her toes curl in her shoes. She gripped his shirt tighter but didn't touch him anywhere else.

She couldn't hold back a small whimper when he sucked her bottom lip into the warmth of his mouth. His breathing seemed to quicken as he caressed the sides of her neck with trembling hands. With a low growl rumbling in his chest, he buried his fingers in her hair that hung in loose waves down her back and deepened the kiss at last.

No matter how much she reminded herself that this

wasn't real—that it was all for show—she couldn't stop herself from closing the distance between them. She placed her hands, fingers spread wide, on the hard wall of his chest. She reveled in the frantic pounding of his heart, which echoed the beat of her own. Driven by instinct, she ran her tongue inside his bottom lip, drawing a strangled groan from him.

His hands fisted in her hair as he angled her head and delved his tongue into her mouth as though the last tether of his control had snapped. A secret smile stole across her face but soon she grabbed the lapels of his jacket and rose on her tiptoes as their kiss grew wild.

"Did I mention my songs are potent aphrodisiacs?" the singer said with wicked amusement. "If you want that kind of action, you might want to download a copy of my album for your next date."

Chloe heard the performer's good-natured joke somewhere in the recesses of her mind and understood that was the reason Anthony was slowing down their kiss. The laughter bubbling up around them finally jolted her back to the present—back to the busy street.

"I guess she *is* his type after all." The woman from earlier guffawed with her friend, snapping pictures of them with their phones.

"Oh, God." She'd practically climbed Anthony in front of a bunch of strangers. And she'd forgotten all about it being pretend.

In a blind panic, she spun away from Anthony with a vague notion of running far, *far* away from there. Before she could take more than a stumbling step, his hands clamped down on top of her shoulders and pulled her flush against him, her back pressing into his chest and his—she swallowed the gasp that rose to her lips—his unmistakable hardness digging into the small of her back.

"I need a minute," he growled into her ear.

"I, um, sure. Mmm-hmm. Yeah," she prattled. "We could listen to one more song."

The singer obliged and launched into a catchy, upbeat song. Anthony swept his hands up and down her arms in soothing strokes—at least what he probably meant to be soothing. Unfortunately for Chloe, they were distracting as hell and did nothing to slow down her pulse.

Pretend or not, there was no denying that the kiss had been sexy as sin. But what did it even mean? Was her teenage crush resurfacing as this white-hot attraction? Was she doing the exact opposite of what she assured her sisters of? Falling for someone whose heart belonged to another? And what about his reaction to her? He *definitely* was not faking that hard-on.

She needed to take her own advice and not overthink this. Their bodies were responding naturally to their fake kiss. Even professional actors sometimes got aroused while filming steamy scenes. Maybe she should develop a system of distracting her mind while they put on public displays of affection.

As the song came to an end with the soft thrum of the guitar, Anthony took hold of her hand and led them down the street. They didn't speak until they reached the end of the promenade and crossed over to the other side of the street to make their way back.

"Chloe," he said, tugging her to a stop.

Something in his expression made her think that he

was about to apologize again. And for some reason, she absolutely did not want him to apologize for the kiss.

"We sure laid it on thick for those ladies." Her voice was half an octave higher than usual and carried far enough to turn a couple of heads.

"I—"

"I've come up with the perfect system for our future *fake*—" she made exaggerated air quotes "—kisses."

"A system?" His eyebrows climbed into his hairline.

"We're two healthy adults and things could get inadvertently heavy at times." She paused briefly to suck in some air. "So we should think about kittens when we kiss."

"Kittens?" Anthony enunciated carefully as though doubting his hearing.

"Yes. Soft, cuddly kittens." Chloe bobbed her head up and down fast enough to blur her vision. "There is nothing sexy about cute, little kittens, so we can kiss all we want without…you know…getting turned on."

Myriad emotions flickered across his face—amusement, tenderness, panic and fear? Before she could parse out what any of it meant, Anthony blinked his eyes and wiped away the emotions. He took a measured step toward her with a smile that held a cruel edge. She was tempted to retreat a step but she held her position and lifted her chin.

"Did our kiss turn you on, Chloe?" The seductive croon of his voice sent a shiver down her back.

"Yes," she squeaked.

He chuckled darkly and she squeezed her thighs together. *Oh, God.* If Anthony Larsen ever decided to seduce her, she didn't stand a chance of resisting him. Even if she put on an iron chastity belt and threw away the key, she would claw the thing off with her bare hands to offer herself to him.

"I noticed that you were—" she waved her hand toward his nether region before she caught herself "—*on* as well."

"And did my arousal turn you on even more?" The arrogant arch of his eyebrow told her he already knew the answer to his question.

It simultaneously made her want to kick him in the shin and to kiss him again. In the end, anger triumphed over lust. She was suddenly livid. Here she was terrified that she might fall for him when his heart belonged to someone else, and he was *flirting* with her. Maybe he really was a callous playboy out to score an easy hookup. Did he enjoy toying with her? How *dare* he?

"Perhaps," she said with icy composure, "but not enough to want to fuck you."

She didn't stay to enjoy the shock washing over his handsome face. Instead, she spun on her heels and marched away from him.

Lust he could handle. Even the kind of lust that came over him when he was near Chloe—something that felt like a riptide sucking him underwater, relentlessly tossing him around. But the rush of tenderness that overtook him when she mentioned a system of kittens scared the shit out of him. So he had gone and ruined it all by being a complete asshole.

The dull weight of remorse replaced his fear as he

watched Chloe walk away from him. Before she disappeared into the crowd, he followed her with heavy steps, keeping a wide berth between them. She didn't look back once as though she was done with him. As far as she was concerned, she'd left him staring after her like a fool at the end of the promenade.

But was she really done with him? Had he ruined it all—robbed those children of the future they deserved—out of pure cowardice? They deserved better. Chloe deserved better. He ran his hand down his face as shame washed over him in hot, oily waves.

She paused when she reached the opposite end of the promenade and glanced around as though she couldn't recall how she got there. Not giving himself a chance to chicken out, he caught up with her and turned her toward him with a light grasp on her arm. Her eyes widened and she snatched her arm out of his reach like his touch repulsed her.

"Let me drive you home," he said quietly. He wouldn't apologize because he didn't deserve her forgiveness for the way he'd behaved.

She narrowed her eyes at him and opened her mouth—the *no* plain on her face—but she glanced at the people strolling past them and slowly pressed her lips together. She jerked her chin at him, commanding him to lead the way. After a brief hesitation, he headed toward the parking structure where they'd parked earlier. She fell into step beside him, close enough that their shoulders occasionally brushed against each other's. A flicker of hope lit up inside him, which he hastily stomped out.

He shouldn't have kissed her again. No matter how furious he had been at the nosy women talking about Chloe as though they had the right to judge her...as though *she* wasn't worthy of *him*. They had no idea how amazing and *good* she was—how she was worth ten of him, a glorified fuckboy with enough emotional baggage to sink a barge. He couldn't resist the impulse to put them in their place. He wanted to show them how exquisite and irresistible Chloe was to him. But he'd underestimated *how* irresistible she was.

Once his lips met hers, all the hunger he'd been holding back combusted inside him, and he'd kissed her as though she was the air he needed to survive. There was no pretense on his side. It didn't even occur to him that they were performing for an audience. He even forgot that they were standing in the middle of a crowded street. There was only Chloe and the heady pleasure of kissing her. He wanted to soak up the feel of her. From the soft, whimpering noises she made against his lips to the sweet, heady scent of her. He wanted to spend eternity kissing her.

Suffocating silence accompanied them on their walk to his car. As soon as they turned off onto a side street and the crowds thinned to a trickle, Chloe put enough distance between them so there was no more accidental touching. It was ridiculous how keenly he felt the loss.

He opened the door for her when they reached his car and she slid in past him without breaking the silence. Once he settled into the driver's seat, he turned toward her, ready to face the music.

"I understand if you want to back out of our arrangement." Regret thickened his voice.

"Is Soleil still poised to fire you if you're involved in another scandal?" She stared out the windshield as she spoke.

"Yes," he said curtly. "But—"

"Does Life Village still need your donation to break ground on the housing community for the children?"

"Yes, but I—" He raked his fingers through his hair. Panic coiled through him. He didn't recognize this cool, distant person sitting beside him.

"Then our arrangement will remain as it is." She took a shuddering breath. "I… I thought for a moment that you were toying with me because you really are a man-slut like the media makes you out to be."

"Man…slut?" Not the most flattering thing he'd been called but he deserved it.

"But I realized that it was your way of telling me to keep my distance," she continued as though he hadn't spoken. "I don't know what I did to make you feel… threatened, but you don't need to worry. I won't delude myself into thinking there is anything more than a business arrangement between us."

"Chloe, please." He didn't understand what he was pleading for—what it was he wanted from her.

"I've always respected you as a musician, and I also respect what you're doing for those children." She finally glanced at him but nothing remained of her warmth and openness, like a dark cloud had hidden the sun from sight. "I have no issue with us continuing to perform together and maintaining this fake-dating farce. Especially since both arrangements are temporary."

"I…" He swallowed. "Thank you."

What else could he say? Wasn't this exactly what he wanted? He fucked up tonight but maybe it was for the best. He couldn't stop wanting her but he could at least respect the line that she had drawn.

Seven

Chloe and her sisters took the stage to the enthusiastic applause of the audience packing the concert hall. She had been dreading another fake date with Anthony after the Third Street Promenade fiasco. But now that a week had passed without any such invitation, she couldn't help but feel slighted.

She took her seat and smoothed out her dress across her thighs. As she promised, she'd been perfectly professional to him during their rehearsals and he had been professional right back at her. They were so polite and proper to each other that she felt like she should serve tea and drink it with her pinkie held high. *Ugh.*

The more she thought back to that night, the more convinced she became that she'd done nothing wrong. Well, *wrong* wasn't the right word. Of course, she hadn't done anything *wrong*, but she'd been worried that she might have been…overly familiar? She thought she must have done something—crossed some invisible line—to make Anthony shift into his man-slut mode. But she was certain she hadn't. All she'd done was be herself. If that made him feel threatened, then tough. It was his problem. Not hers.

Megan raised her violin and Chloe followed suit. The three of them caught each other's eyes and at Megan's subtle nod, they swooped into the piece as effortlessly as taking their next breath. As always, Chloe fell in love with her viola and the music like it was for the first time.

The initial intoxicating flush of love naturally waned into something milder and more steadfast because it was necessary. If the frantic, all-consuming fire of first love lasted too long, no one would survive it. But there was no other way to create music—at least while they performed—but to be consumed by the fire.

For Chloe, performing for the audience meant that she had to become a phoenix. To burst into fire and burn herself into cinders until she was born again for the next concert. She had to give it her all every time. As their music filled her—burned through her—she knew that her sisters felt the same way. That was what made them the Hana Trio.

As the echo of their last notes dissipated into the air, applause roared through the auditorium. She and her sisters rose and bowed, and retook their seats. A low murmur grew into a cacophony of sound as the audience wondered what was happening. An awed silence descended as Anthony Larsen walked onto the stage. He bowed formally to Megan and helped her stand from her chair. She strode to the front of the stage as he lowered himself into the vacated seat.

"I have to say goodbye for a short while to welcome a new life into this beautiful world," Megan said with a tender touch to her stomach. "But I'm leaving you and my sisters in the best hands. Please welcome Anthony Larsen as the Hana Trio's violinist for the remainder of this season."

Anthony rose to his feet as the audience clapped their hands raw. Then Chloe and Angie stood to applaud their sister as she walked off the stage. Once they sat back down to perform together for the first time as the Hana Trio, Chloe glanced at Anthony to find the telltale signs of his unease in the tense line of his shoulders and the grim set of his mouth. She was beyond surprised that the veteran musician was nervous but it also touched her that he cared so much about their trio.

"Trust in the system, Anthony." She leaned close with a gentle hand on his back. To hell with stiff professionalism. He needed her support. Besides, she was done playing that game. "We sounded amazing during the rehearsals. You got this."

A soft smile spread across his lips as his eyes roamed her face. It seemed he was done playing that game, too. She blushed as her heart fluttered at the tender affection in his gaze. After giving him a small answering smile, she drew back her hand and took a steadying breath. They could resume their silent conversation after the concert.

Their performance was flawless—different but no less beautiful. After bowing to the ecstatic audience, the three of them filed off the stage. Without the music to hold her attention, Chloe was much too aware of the gorgeous man standing behind her.

"Thank you for the pep talk," he said in a low voice only she could hear. "I haven't had stage fright in a long time."

"Of course." Chloe glanced over her shoulder and quickly looked forward again. He was so close that their faces were mere inches apart. "It's so different from what you're used to. I bet you couldn't decide whether you were excited or nervous."

"Nerves were edging out excitement until you talked to me," he murmured.

Again, he didn't bother to hide the affection in his voice. She gulped.

Before Chloe could respond, Megan rushed toward them with Daniel by her side. "You guys were fan-freaking-tastic."

Their whole family had gathered backstage to greet them. Joshua pulled Angie into his arms and kissed her soundly on the lips. Her dad harrumphed at the PDA but couldn't quite hide his fond smile.

"It's good to see you again, Mr. Han," Anthony said to her dad. They'd met briefly at Megan and Daniel's wedding.

"Larsen," her dad said curtly. "I can't wait to see the back of you."

"Appa!" Chloe and her sisters said in unison.

"What?" He had the grace to look abashed. "The man's proving to be a pain in my ass."

Joshua and Daniel guffawed until their wives glared at them.

"Appa, please." Chloe employed her most powerful puppy-dog eyes. "Don't make a fuss. It really isn't a big deal."

"Mr. Han, I sincerely apologize for the trouble I'm causing you and Chloe." Anthony bowed his head. "If there's any way I can make it up to you—"

"Never mind all that." Her dad clicked his tongue. "I'll book your ticket to New York myself once the season's over."

Before Chloe could die from mortification, a familiar voice called out, "Chloe."

"Johnny." She'd never been happier to see her childhood friend as he enfolded her in a bear hug. He'd come in the nick of time to end her father's tirade. "I didn't know you were coming tonight."

"I had to see Megan Noona's farewell concert, didn't I?" Johnny grinned, stepping back from Chloe to bow to her dad and her brothers-in-law. Then he tipped his chin at her sisters in a much more casual greeting.

"Nice try, you suck-up." Megan rolled her eyes in the most affectionate way possible. Johnny Park was a long-time favorite among the Han family. He and Chloe had been friends since kindergarten. "We all know you're here to see Anthony Larsen."

"Well, you have me there," her friend said with easy charm. He extended his hand to Anthony, who had come to stand stiffly beside her. She snuck a peek at his tense profile with a small frown tugging at her eyebrows. "It's a pleasure to meet you, Mr. Larsen. I'm a big fan."

"Pleased to meet you." Anthony shook Johnny's hand, while his other arm wrapped possessively around Chloe's waist.

Her friend's smile faltered for a second as his attention snagged on Anthony's hand. Unfortunately for Chloe, Johnny wasn't the only one who noticed. Her dad's mouth turned down into a disapproving frown as he shot poison daggers at Anthony with his eyes.

What was Anthony thinking? There were no nosy tourists or paparazzi to convince back here. Was he putting on a show for Johnny's benefit? He was practically family. It wasn't worth incurring her father's wrath. The fact that her dad didn't roar his fury at Anthony was a testament to his consideration for the children whom the fake dating was meant to benefit.

What really baffled her, however, was that it didn't even occur to her to move away from Anthony. She just stood there, her toes curling in her shoes, as though she belonged tucked in tight against his side.

She and Anthony were both perfectionists. They were merely giving their arrangement the attention they would normally give to any endeavor they undertook. In order to do that, they had to keep up appearances at all times wherever they were. It was like method acting. They had to be immersed in their fake-lovers roles so they wouldn't slip up. They couldn't risk letting down the children.

Chloe glanced up at Anthony and met his eyes. A faint whirring sound began humming in her ears as she fell into his hazel gaze. The grim line of his lips softened into a gentle smile and she couldn't help returning it. He tucked a wayward strand of her hair behind her ear and she leaned into his touch.

"It's a rare occasion to have the whole gang together." Daniel's booming voice seemed to reach her from far-away. She remembered in the back of her mind that they were standing backstage surrounded by her family. But Anthony's eyes still held hers and she had no desire to look away. "Why don't we head out to grab a bite to eat? I'm going to go out on a limb and say that Megan is probably starving. Right, honey?"

"Mmm-hmm. I could definitely eat a burger or two," Megan said, coming to link her arm through Chloe's and pulling her away from Anthony. Angie took her other arm and steered her toward the dressing room.

"Just give us a minute to change out of our dresses. We'll meet you guys at the front lobby," Angie said breezily over her shoulder.

Chloe looked between her sisters with her mouth hanging open. They were running interference between her and Anthony. Like she was a child.

"Our baby sister is in so much trouble, Angie," Megan murmured just as Chloe was about to give them a piece of her mind.

"I know, Megan." Her eldest sister sighed. "But that's what we're here for."

"To shake some sense into her?" Megan offered.

A gurgling sound escaped Chloe's throat as her outrage grew. They were talking about her like she wasn't there, wedged tightly between them.

"No," Angie said. "For her to lean on when she needs us."

"I won't need to lean on you guys," Chloe snapped without much heat. Her sister's sweet words had doused her anger. "At least not where Anthony Larsen is concerned."

Anthony found himself sandwiched between Daniel and Joshua at the diner while Chloe sat between her sisters at the opposite end of the table. *Johnny* sat right across from him and he found it difficult not to glare at the guy. He just rubbed Anthony the wrong way.

Perhaps it was the affectionate way Minsung Han nudged Johnny's shoulder and guffawed at every quip he made. Or how the Han sisters joked around with him as though he were a part of the family. Maybe it was because he looked like one of those ridiculously attractive K-pop stars. Or it might be how the man stared at one particular Han sister when he didn't think anyone was looking. That *definitely* rubbed Anthony the wrong way. The fact that it was none of his business pissed him off even more.

"How does it feel to be a part of the Hana Trio?" Joshua Shin, the renowned composer, asked him, munching on some fries. It was always refreshing to meet someone he admired to find that they were delightfully normal.

"It's something of a thrill," Anthony said, shaking off his foul mood. "Performing on my own or as a soloist with an orchestra feels more straightforward in some ways. My focus in on my interpretation of the music. For the trio, I have to develop a hive mind with two other musicians in order to create one harmonious sound. It's a bit of a juggling act but it feels exhilarating when everything lines up—like hitting the sweet spot."

"You mean the *suite* spot. Get it?" Joshua grinned and Daniel groaned.

All it took was a brief lull in their conversation for Anthony's eyes to find their way to Chloe again. She burst out laughing at something Megan whispered in her ear, clapping her hand over her mouth to prevent spewing milkshake all over the table. He stared in awe as her infectious joy seemed to brighten up the whole restaurant.

"Close your mouth," Daniel muttered beside him. "You look absurd."

"The Han sisters have a knack for turning men into idiots." Joshua chuckled.

"You know you're being much more lenient toward Anthony than you were with me when we first met." Daniel huffed.

"Unless someone failed to inform me that Anthony knocked up Chloe, I think the two instances are completely different." Joshua leaned back in his chair with a smirk.

Anthony choked on his root beer and Daniel pounded on his back with more force than necessary. "That's not going to happen unless our friend here wishes to part with his balls."

"What are you?" Anthony rasped. "The fucking mafia?"

"Nah." Joshua met his eyes with steely intensity. "Just a close-knit family. Besides, it's not Daniel and me you need to worry about. Angie and Megan are the ones you need to fear. They would do *anything* for their baby sister."

"What the hell do you guys even think I'm going to do to Chloe?" Anthony sputtered.

"From the way you stare at her, you probably have a *lot* of things you want to do to her." Daniel glowered at him.

Anthony dragged a weary hand down his face. He had nothing to say to that. He wasn't foolish enough to think he could deny his attraction to Chloe with any plausibility.

"It's not the way he stares at her that I'm worried about." Joshua took a bite out of his club sandwich. "It's the way she stares at him."

"What way?" Anthony stole a glance at Chloe, who was sticking her tongue out at Johnny. Was that really necessary? She looked much too adorable. "Besides, she does *not* stare at me."

"That's right. She doesn't stare at you." Daniel shot his brother-in-law a warning glance. "Let's not plant any ideas in the man's head. Chloe would never be interested in this boring old white dude."

"Thanks." Anthony snorted. "You're a true friend."

"Just keeping it real," his *friend* said with a shit-eating grin.

Anthony knew he should not want Chloe staring at him but a small, greedy part of him wanted just that. It didn't seem fair that he should feel tortured by being near her and not have her feel anything in return. He'd always thought he was a pretty decent guy but he might actually be something of an asshole. He took a sip of water to wash away the bitter taste in his mouth.

He wasn't a man who wandered aimlessly through life. He knew what he wanted. Before Rachel died, his life centered on perfecting his craft and establishing himself as the best violinist in the world. After she died, his focus shifted to keeping her memory alive, which required him to continue succeeding in his career. He knew himself, flaws and all—he was a workaholic and a womanizer with enough baggage to drown a man. But when it came to Chloe Han, he was...lost.

Contradictory thoughts filled his mind and refused to line up in a neat row.

Anthony shouldn't want her but he did…desperately. He shouldn't—wouldn't—act on his desires, but he wanted them reciprocated even though that would make resisting her nearly impossible. He longed to bask in her light and let her chase away the darkness inside him. He wished he could absorb her joy and let himself heal even though he didn't deserve her. Chloe deserved someone whole—someone *good* like her. But he wanted her more than he wanted anything in his life. And that—*that*—was why he could never have her.

Rachel died alone because of his selfishness. Maybe she died *because* of him—because he wasn't there that night. He didn't get to move on from that and lead a happy, fulfilling life. He might be a selfish bastard but he would never go as far as to forgive himself.

Yet, he couldn't stop his gaze from seeking out Chloe again and again. And when their eyes collided, her lips parted as though she felt his desire like a physical touch. His heart lurched in his chest. His glance dipped to her mouth and the tip of her tongue flicked out to wet her bottom lip.

"Excuse me for a minute." She shot to her feet with enough force to make her chair slide back with a loud screech. "I need to run to the restroom."

Without thinking, Anthony pushed back his chair as well. Daniel's hand clamped down on his shoulder.

"Anthony." His friend's voice held no warning—only concern.

Even so, he shook off Daniel's hand and followed Chloe to the back of the restaurant. He had no capacity to care about the eyes he must be drawing from their table—the concern he must be causing his friends. He only knew he had to get to Chloe.

She was leaning back next to an old-fashioned pay phone mounted on the wall in a long hallway that led to the restrooms. Her expression was wary when he approached her. That was enough to halt him in his steps.

"Chloe—"

"What do you *want*, Anthony?" She sounded tired... and hopeful.

He swallowed after several tries. "Something I can't want."

"Then what *can* you want?" she whispered.

"Can I want to kiss you?" He stepped closer to her and planted his hands by the sides of her head. "To really kiss you. Not because someone is watching."

"No faking?" Chloe blinked rapidly. "No kittens?"

"No. No faking. As for kittens—" he chuckled, brushing the tip of his nose against hers "—I don't see why we can't have kittens. I like thinking of you as one."

"M...me?"

"Yes, kitten," he purred against her ear. She stiffened against him and pulled back to stare at him. *Damn it.* Had he pushed his luck?

"I've never had a nickname before." Her mouth curved into a naughty smile. "So do you want to kiss me, Anthony?"

"I—" He sucked in a sharp breath. "I shouldn't."

"You *shouldn't*?" Chloe arched an eyebrow. "Well, then. How can you resist?"

"I can't." He lowered his head slowly, never breaking eye contact, then stopped a whisper away from her lips.

"Excuse me. Pregnant woman coming through," Megan announced loudly. "This kid is jumping on my bladder like it's a trampoline."

Chloe started and pushed against his chest but it took Anthony a tremendous amount of willpower to step away from her—like he was fighting against quicksand. He took one step back, then another. Then he spun on his heels and walked off without a word. It was either that or throw her over his shoulder and run off like a caveman.

He wished he was a caveman.

Eight

It was Chloe Han up against the whole freaking world. Or at least her whole freaking family.

She had half expected Daniel and Joshua to come in with their heavy-handed tactics to warn Anthony away from her. After all, they could always blame their over-abundance of testosterone for their idiocy. But her sisters were blatantly meddling, too—even after she told them she could take care of herself where Anthony was concerned.

Then Megan pulled that stunt at the diner. She didn't even bother with subtlety. And no, her sister couldn't blame pregnancy hormones for what she did. Women were stronger than that. Even with so-called pregnancy brain, Megan was as smart as a whip. She knew exactly what she was doing.

Bottom line? Her sisters didn't trust her. It was as

simple as that. They couldn't accept that she was a grown woman capable of making her own choices and living with the consequences. No, they thought they were better judges of how Chloe should live her life.

Not to mention the man himself. Anthony was so afraid of intimacy that he pushed her away at the first sign of a real connection. And he apparently convinced himself that it was *wrong* for him to want her.

Fuck it all to hell.

She scrubbed off her makeup with extra vigor in the dim light of her cramped bathroom. One of the light bulbs died two weeks ago. She really should change that. She shrugged and squeezed the last bit of toothpaste—hand shaking with the effort—onto her toothbrush. Yeah, she should pick up some more toothpaste as well. She stuck her tongue out at her reflection. Rehearsals, concerts and finishing her master's degree held precedence over everyday adulting.

With her nighttime ritual complete, Chloe plunked down on her sofa and pulled her laptop onto her thighs. She felt some of the tension from the day leaving her shoulders as she logged in to *League of Legends*. She couldn't help the grin that tugged at her lips when she found SerialFiddler in the lobby. It didn't mean she was happy to find him there. It was more of a menacing, bloodthirsty smile. She tapped the keys with a light, jaunty touch.

I see you couldn't find a game to join. No one wants to play with you, SerialFiddler?

His response popped up almost immediately.

I'm actually trying to decide which invitation to accept. I have to handle this delicately so no one feels spurned. Dominating in every game comes with great responsibility...but you wouldn't know what that's like.

Chloe burst out laughing. He was funny. She had to give him that.

Does being an asshole come with any responsibility? If so, you must be overwhelmed.

Language, NightMusic. I might have to report your use of "a**hole" to the LoL authorities.

You're a narc now?

Just a respectful member of the community.

She crossed her legs and tried to get more comfortable on her couch. The seat cushions had seen better days and her butt sank too deeply, making her laptop wobble on its perch.

I must not be keeping up with the times. Does "respectful" have a new definition nowadays?

A longish pause ensued.

NightMusic, you want to play a game with me?

Her mouth dropped open and she pushed her face into the screen to see if she was reading his message right.

Play a game…with you? Like on the same side?

I know. Wild, right? But I'm feeling a little wild tonight.

Chloe gulped as her heart tripped in her chest. She was being ridiculous. He was probably a pimply teenage boy. Why was she getting breathless over this? Even so, she was suddenly curious why his name was SerialFiddler. Did he play the violin? She shook her head. It was none of her business. It didn't matter who he was in real life. They left all that IRL stuff out of the game. They could be whoever they wanted to be without worrying about rocking the boat. *League of Legends* was pretend.

How ironic that her personal life now involved pretense as well. But which part was she really pretending? Was she faking the passion that ignited between Anthony and her when they kissed? Or was she pretending that the passion wasn't real? Did she want it to be real? She felt a headache gathering at her temples. There were no easy answers.

She shook out her arms. Enough with the soul-searching. What she needed now was some escape—escape from responsibilities, hard answers and complicated situations.

Why not? she typed. One little game with her enemy wouldn't hurt anyone. Just don't shoot me in the back.

You wound me, NightMusic. I may be ruthless but I'm honorable.

Sure, SerialFiddler. Whatever you say, buddy.

Buddy? Does that mean we're friends now?

Whoa. I'm agreeing to play on the same side with you for ONE game. Let's not get ahead of ourselves.

Chloe found herself smiling again—much less menacing and bloodthirsty this time. They bickered back and forth for a few more minutes after they were queued in for the next game. And once their game started, she and SerialFiddler became the freaking dynamic duo.

"Yeah!" she yelled into her empty apartment. They had to carry half of the players on their team but they defeated their opponents with ease. "That's what I'm talking about."

This was exactly what she needed. She could finally take a full breath without her chest clenching up. *League* was her happy place. And maybe SerialFiddler was her new best friend. She cackled at the thought. Not going to happen.

Good game. She nibbled on her bottom lip, debating how she wanted to leave things with him. I wouldn't make a habit out of it, but there is a small chance that I might play on the same side as you again.

I'll try not to hold my breath, he typed.

Yes, I wouldn't want to be responsible for your asphyxiation.

See you around, NightMusic.

See you, SerialFiddler.

With a contented sigh, Chloe plugged her laptop into a charger and headed for bed. She crawled under the covers and yawned sleepily into her hand. By the time she drifted off to sleep, she'd almost forgotten about the real kiss she didn't get.

"Sometimes I can't remember whether I'm your babysitter or your manager, Larsen," Tanner muttered from the other end of the call.

"Fuck you kindly, Moates." Anthony returned home from his late dinner with the Han family in a foul mood. It might've had something to do with the kiss he didn't get—the kiss he shouldn't want. "Don't you ever sleep? It's almost two in the morning over there."

"Anything for my number one client." Sarcasm dripped from his friend's tired voice. "Especially when he doesn't call me back for three hours when I specifically said it was urgent."

"I told you I was otherwise occupied." Anthony nudged his laptop aside on the coffee table to make more room for his feet and leaned back on the sofa. He'd needed to let off some steam before he called his manager back.

"With that sweet Chloe Han?" Tanner teased. "From the pictures plastered on the internet, it seems like you occupy all your free time kissing her."

"Watch it," he warned.

"Erica from Soleil has been in touch." Tanner switched to his manager mode. "It seems the powers that be over there are very happy about your involvement with Chloe Han. They think a steady relationship with someone with her stellar reputation would be the perfect way to rehabilitate your image. They even mentioned the possibility of signing Ms. Han for a limited campaign to promote their couple's watches with the two of you."

"I don't want to extend this fake-dating scheme longer than strictly necessary." Anthony pinched the bridge of his nose.

"Fake dating?" Tanner sounded more inquisitive than shocked.

"I ran into Scarlett Harding and Chloe rescued me from a potential nightmare."

"Shit."

"Chloe has agreed to play my devoted girlfriend until I return to New York, at which time we'll quietly end our supposed long-distance relationship."

Anthony pushed off the couch to pour himself a drink. He didn't like any of it—involving Chloe in his messy life, the distance that would soon yawn between them and the end of their fake relationship.

Tanner whistled softly. "I had a feeling it might be something like that, but I was hoping you finally found someone good for you."

"Even though I'm bad for her?" He scoffed. "Isn't that a bit selfish?"

His friend was quiet for a moment on the other end. "You could be good for her, Anthony. You're a good man."

He let the whiskey burn its way down his throat and settle like molten lava in his stomach. Perhaps he could be a good man for Chloe…but how could he when he'd been a bad man to Rachel? That wasn't a choice he could make.

"My only concern right now is keeping Soleil happy so Life Village gets the donation I promised them."

Tanner sighed. "Then I suggest you go the extra mile and make your fake romance even more public."

"What do you mean?" Anthony tilted his head back and squeezed the back of his neck.

"Make Soleil happy," his manager advised. "Go on more dates. In public. Be seen. Be talked about. Hell, go on a romantic weekend getaway. People are going to eat that shit up. Make the most out of the lovely Ms. Chloe Han's cooperation while you can."

"You do know that we have to work occasionally, don't you?" Anthony said dryly. "Chloe and I are musicians first and foremost. I thought you were my manager. Do I really need to remind you of this?"

"Oh, please. You're at the top of your game as a violinist, and the Hana Trio is the classical world's sweethearts. You two are already doing the best thing for your careers with your collaboration." Tanner paused to take a breath. "The only *managing* you need from me right now is to salvage your tattered reputation and save your contract with Soleil."

"I appreciate that." And he meant it. He was lucky to have him as his manager and his friend. "But I'll handle my fake relationship with Chloe. Don't worry about it."

"All right, then." That was one of the great things about Tanner. He knew when to back off. "I'll be here if you need me."

"Thank you," Anthony said. "Sorry for keeping you up."

"Don't worry about it," Tanner said around a yawn. "We'll talk soon."

Without Tanner's practical voice to fill his ear, Anthony's mind shot straight to the hallway at the diner. *Well, then. How can you resist?* Chloe's words danced around his head—at once a taunt and a sultry invitation. How indeed?

Suddenly, he was desperate to hear her voice. Was she still awake? Even if she was, what excuse could he make up to call her? There was always the romantic weekend they needed to plan. He laughed at himself. There was no way they were going on a weekend trip. A trip with just the two of them… With no Daniel breathing down his neck. With no interfering sisters jumping in to rescue her. *God.* It sounded like heaven.

Anthony gave his head a sharp shake. Not heaven. It would be hell to have Chloe to himself and not be able to touch her. He downed his drink and marched toward the bathroom. He was going to take a shower. A cold shower. And forget all about a weekend getaway with Chloe.

Nine

"A weekend getaway?" Chloe asked, her fork clatter-
ing to her plate. She quickly picked it up and stuffed
a bite of walnut pear salad in her mouth. She couldn't
let Anthony see how flustered she felt at the thought of
spending a weekend alone with him.

"My manager thought it would be good for publicity." Anthony shrugged with one shoulder. He was the
picture of nonchalance as though they were discussing some mundane business. Maybe that was all it was
to him.

It was as though the almost real kiss had never happened. He came to rehearsal in the morning and greeted
her in a perfectly pleasant way. He practiced the pieces
they were performing next with his usual dedication
and professionalism. Megan pretended she didn't practically throw herself between them to stop them from

kissing in the diner hallway. All in all, it was a fantastic practice.

It pissed Chloe off to no end.

"So not only do I need to go out with you multiple times a week, now you're asking me to spend my weekend pretending to be your girlfriend, too?"

"Is spending time with me such a chore?" His full lips quirked into a lopsided grin.

She hated how her heart stuttered at the sight. "Honestly, we don't have very much in common."

Chloe was being inexcusably rude but it wasn't fair that she was the only one who couldn't forget about their almost kiss. Besides, it was true that they didn't have much in common.

His eyebrows rose in surprise. "But we're both classical musicians."

"Yes, but there's only so much we can talk about classical music," she muttered.

"The complexities of music range far and wide..."

How could someone that could make her catch fire with a mere glance bore her to death? Her body was humming with electricity just sitting next to him, their knees grazing each other with every shift of their body. But her mind had all but checked out.

"Okay. Fine. Why not?" she blurted. Anything to stop talking about *the complexities of music*.

"Why not what?" He cocked his head. She loved the way his head tilted just a little to the side in question. It was ridiculously endearing.

She scowled and stuffed a giant bite of salad into her mouth and chewed like she had a vendetta against lettuce. "I'll go on a weekend getaway with you."

"You will?" The genuine surprise on his face eased some of Chloe's annoyance at his nonchalance.

"Yes," she said. "So what were you thinking? Somewhere nauseatingly romantic like Napa Valley?"

"If we were in New York, I would suggest Paris but it'll take us a good twelve hours to get there from LA." He cupped his chin and tapped his finger on his cheek. "I am kind of curious about the Pacific Northwest. I've performed in Portland and Seattle but there was rarely time for sightseeing."

"Huh." She wrinkled her nose. "PNW?"

That was rather unexpected. She hadn't pegged Anthony for someone who was outdoorsy. She herself was definitely most comfortable snuggled in her couch with her notebook on her lap. But since they were aiming for publicity, they should probably venture outside.

"Have you been?" he asked and bit into his croissant sandwich.

She looked longingly at the brie-and-fig-filled sandwich. He somehow managed to eat it without getting croissant flakes all over his mouth like she would've, which was why she had opted for the salad.

"Other than to perform? No." She quickly shifted her gaze to her plate when she realized that she was staring longingly at his mouth. She knew it wasn't entirely because of the sandwich. "But I heard that Bend is beautiful."

"Then it's settled. We'll go to Bend." His eyes crinkled at the corners as his face lit up with a giant grin. He must really be excited to visit the PNW.

"We can't go this weekend. We have back-to-back concerts." Chloe scrolled through her calendar. "But we might be able to finagle next weekend. We just have one performance on Saturday evening, so we could fly out on Sunday morning and spend a couple of nights…"

Spend a couple of nights. With Anthony. Her mouth dried out. Not that she would actually *spend* any nights with him. They couldn't get separate rooms because of the optics but they could easily get a suite and have one of them sleep on the sofa or something. She took a long sip of her iced tea.

"I'll arrange for our flight and hotel." A blush spread across the bridge of his nose. "Of course, I'll—"

"A suite is fine," she cut in. "There's no reason to be awkward about it. It's not a big deal. We're both adults…"

She stopped blabbering when she realized she was totally being awkward about it. They ate in silence for a few minutes. She glanced out into the street and watched the pedestrians pass them by loaded with shopping bags hanging off the crooks of their elbows.

She'd suggested this café on Rodeo Drive as the perfect spot for their lunch date. It was a good place to be seen and there were bound to be paparazzi behind every shrub, so Soleil would see fresh pictures of them on the internet within the hour. *Oh, there's one right there.*

Chloe let out a bright, twinkling laugh and reached across the table for Anthony's hand. His eyebrows shot up into his forehead but he flipped his hand and linked his fingers through hers as though on instinct.

She brought her glass to her lips and said, "Paparazzi at two o'clock."

His smile turned lazy and his thumb drew slow circles on the back of her hand. Her heart halted for a split second before taking off in a sprint. *It's all pretend, Chloe.* Her body didn't give a hoot as it tensed and melted at the same time.

"Are you blushing, kitten?" Something hot and teasing sparked in his eyes.

How the hell did he go from bland and boring to *that* in a second flat?

"Don't call me that," she croaked. His thumb had moved onto the sensitive skin of her inner wrist and a shiver made its way down her spine.

"Why not?" His eyes dipped to her lips and his voice grew husky. "It suits you."

She snatched her hand out of his and sat on it for good measure. Their paparazzo had stopped taking pictures of them and was scrolling through his phone. "I think he got enough."

"I'm not sure I did." The raw hunger on his face took her breath away. It was nothing like the irreverent playboy move he'd pulled in Santa Monica. This was...real.

"I'd be more careful about flirting with me if I were you." She smiled with something that felt like triumph.

"And why is that?" he said in a low growl.

"Because I might decide to flirt back." She bit her bottom lip and glanced up at him from beneath her lashes. "Then you really might do something you *shouldn't.*"

His body lurched forward as though he wanted to grab her. But he took a deep breath and clenched his hands into white-knuckled fists on the table. He smoothed the feral yearning on his face into an insipid smile.

"Speaking of something we shouldn't do," he said.

"I don't think we should take the Allegro movement in Joshua's string trio quite so fast…"

God save her from mental whiplashes. Boring Anthony was back with a vengeance. This version of him was infinitely safer than the churning intensity of his sexier side, but Chloe was growing tired of safe.

Anthony thought back to a childhood cartoon that had aliens taking over human bodies. Too bad he couldn't use that as an excuse for why he convinced Chloe into letting him whisk her away for a romantic weekend. *Fake* romantic weekend but one where he would nonetheless have her all to himself.

He stole a glance at her, sitting next to him on their flight to Bend. She wore a T-shirt that said *Classical music rocks* with a long, flowing skirt. Other than some glistening pink lip gloss, she was fresh faced and makeup free. She was so lovely that something simultaneously burst free and tightened in his chest.

Chloe was poring over a book on baroque music for a paper she had to write for her early music class. He sometimes forgot how young she was. She was still a student for God's sake. Sure, she was a graduate student, but he was nevertheless years past that period in his life.

She glanced up and smiled distractedly at him, and he returned her smile with his heart pounding like a fool. When she returned to her book, he forced himself to look away and released a long breath.

Aliens didn't take him over but something definitely did. He could flippantly blame lust—yeah, he was thinking with his dick…hardy har har—and be done with it. But he couldn't bury his head in the sand anymore. It was more than lust. It was greed.

He was greedy for Chloe's company. He was addicted to how alive she made him feel when he was with her. Sure, he forced himself to stick to shop talk to keep her at arm's length but he couldn't stop himself from teasing her more often than wise until that fiery spark lit in her eyes. Or from making wry observations to draw that twinkling laugh from her.

The distant, superficial relationships that he had so easily cultivated since Rachel's death—the only kind of relationships he felt *able* to endure—felt almost impossible to maintain with Chloe. He wanted more of her. And because he *shouldn't* want more, she was becoming fucking irresistible.

He gripped the armrest between them and forced himself to remember. Rachel died alone because he cared more about his career than getting home to her. He saw the broken glass and overturned furniture, his heart dropping like a boulder to his stomach. He remembered holding her cold, lifeless body in his arms, blood soaking her chest like a scarlet dahlia. He couldn't forget. He wasn't about to erase Rachel's memory—forget his selfishness—by falling for another woman. He had to resist being drawn to Chloe no matter how impossible it seemed.

"You're not afraid of flying, are you?" she suddenly asked from beside him.

"What?" His question sounded like a whoosh of air. He didn't realize he'd been holding his breath.

Chloe looked pointedly at the hand he had wrapped around the armrest, his white knuckles straining against his skin. She gently covered it with her own. "I used to be afraid of flying."

"I'm not…" He trailed off, realizing he couldn't explain what he really feared.

"Whenever I locked up with terror, my mom would whisper in my ear, 'You're a monarch butterfly. Strong and graceful.'" Chloe squeezed his hand. "And I would imagine flaring my wings, welcoming the air that would carry me away. After a while, I wasn't scared anymore."

"Your mother sounds like she was an amazing woman." He flipped his hand to link their fingers together. The gesture was so intuitive that he didn't remember deciding to do it.

"She was." Chloe leaned closer and drew something on the back of his hand with an index finger. "I wish I'd known her longer."

"How old were you when she passed away?" He peered down at their hands, trying to see and feel what she was drawing.

"Eighteen." She finally leaned back in her chair. "There."

"What were you drawing?" he asked softly.

"A butterfly." She smiled sweetly at him. "Now you don't have to be afraid anymore."

He swallowed a lump that formed in his throat. He didn't remember how to live without fear. He was afraid of forgetting. Of letting go. Of forgiving himself. He lifted her hand and placed a feather-light kiss on her knuckles, letting his lips linger against her soft skin.

If he let her, maybe she could teach him how not to be afraid anymore. And *that* scared him more than anything.

Ten

"So we just…float for two hours?" Anthony cocked his head to the side as though doing nothing but chilling for couple of hours was a foreign concept to him.

"Trust me," Chloe said with utmost confidence even though she'd never done this before. But she read that tubing down the Deschutes River was *the* thing to do when in Bend during summer. It wasn't quite summer, yet, but it was close enough, and she was dying to try.

She loved the bustling energy of Los Angeles but the quiet calm of Bend was working its way through her—slowing her down, making her take in her surroundings. It was so green and there was a gorgeous river running through the middle of town. How could she not fall in love with it?

"Let's go line up." Chloe grabbed Anthony by his wrist and tugged. "Hurry. They close in ten minutes."

Once they were in line to rent their bright orange tubes, she practically threw his arm back at him because her knees were turning wobbly from the innocuous touch. It might've had something to do with the fact that Anthony was bare-chested with only a pair of board shorts slung low on his slim hips. All in all, he looked unfairly fantastic without his shirt. He had a golden tan like he spent his days on the beach rather than in rehearsal rooms and concert halls. And the gym. He must spend a lot of time in the gym. The man was chiseled like a marble statue.

She, on the other hand, looked fairly okay in her favorite red bikini. Her curves were fuller than her willowy older sisters but she never minded. There was nothing wrong with being cuddly. But she was waiting until the last minute to take off her jean shorts because she felt ridiculously shy about being half-naked around Anthony.

Not picking up on her mildly aroused state, he lifted her hand and kissed it as he'd done on the plane. She opened her eyes wider to keep them from fluttering shut at the decadent pleasure of his lips on her skin. *Get it together, Chloe.* They were supposed to be having a "romantic" weekend. He was just playing his part.

"Based on my research, we'll float nice and easy," she said to hide that she was *this* close to swooning because he was now rubbing his lips back and forth on her knuckles. "Except for a short whitewater section."

"We're going down some rapids in a floaty?" He shrugged and grinned at her. "We only live once, I guess."

His smile, combined with the fact that he still held her hand, might've made her whimper just a little.

Mistaking the sound for nerves, Anthony said, "Don't worry. I'll hang on to your tube. We can go down together."

She managed a small nod. When she tested his grip by subtly wiggling her fingers, his hand tightened around hers. He brushed a kiss on her temple and spoke into her ear, "We'll have some privacy on the river, but let's keep up the act for now."

Even though she'd known it was an act, his reminder annoyed the hell out of her—probably because her body's response to his touch was all too real. She shouldn't be the only one suffering.

"Sure," she said with a saccharine smile.

She wrapped her arm around his waist and pressed her body against his side. Her other hand slid up from his stomach—rock hard as she'd suspected—and came to rest on his chest. Half-naked Anthony was a feast for her eyes but touching him felt infinitely better.

He made a little choking sound, making her grin widen…until he snaked his arm around her and slid his hand into the back pocket of her shorts. Using the hand on her ass, Anthony pulled her closer to his side, and her traitor of a body melted against him. They were acting like lovers who couldn't keep their hands off each other. Which was precisely the point.

They somehow moved in sync up the line so they remained pressed against each other the entire time. His breath ruffled the top of her hair. If she tilted her head back slightly, her mouth would be inches from his. But she refused to make the first move. If he wanted to fake kiss her, then he was going to have to fake initiate it.

When his finger grazed her chin, Chloe raised her face toward his, licking her bottom lip as though she could already taste the kiss—as though she couldn't wait for it. It didn't matter that he technically didn't apply any pressure to lift her chin, because nobody cared about technicalities.

His lopsided grin was playful but the gaze that dropped to her mouth held enough fire to burn her panties into cinders. She pushed up on her toes and his head lowered until his beautiful face blurred—

"For two?" said a friendly voice.

Chloe stepped back from Anthony, red faced and flustered. "Yup. For Two."

"Unless you have one that'll fit both of us," he said with a teasing wink, pulling out his credit card from the back pocket of his board shorts. "We won't need much extra room since she'll be on my lap."

"Hilarious, isn't he?" Chloe forced an awkward laugh and slapped Anthony's arm hard enough for her palm to sting. "We'll take two tubes."

"Ow," he said, rubbing his arm—his twinkling eyes belying his wounded expression.

The cashier giggled at their antics and directed them to the safety demonstration. But Chloe hardly heard a word as something niggled at her mind. She got a glimpse of Anthony's wicked sense of humor whenever his guard was down. It was like he couldn't repress it deeply enough—like there were so many interesting things about him that it couldn't be contained despite his very best effort.

Why would he purposely bleach his personality of color? It made no sense. It was as though he was trying to… A thought planted itself in her mind and her fury grew as it took root. She knew *exactly* why.

Once they were on the river, Anthony kept a loose grip around one of the handles on her tube so they floated side by side. It took all of Chloe's willpower not to slap his hand away. She didn't want to get into an argument with him right now because she couldn't exactly storm away from him. The tube was so big that her fingers barely skimmed the top of the water and she would have to push off her butt to even touch the water with her feet. Her only option would be to float slowly away from him, inch by agonizing inch. It would be frustrating and mortifying. The kind of argument she planned to have with Anthony definitely required a dramatic exit.

"I'm glad you suggested this," he said after floating in silence for a while. "It's quite scenic."

She gave a noncommittal grunt. But it really was beautiful. With lush trees lining both sides of the river, she almost forgot that she was in the middle of a city. And they were the last ones in the water, so they were pretty much alone except for an older couple past shouting distance from them.

"Is something wrong?" he asked hesitantly. "You seem quiet."

"Everything's fine." Her tone was terser than she'd intended, so she added, "Just enjoying the experience."

"I guess I'll leave you to it, then," Anthony said, tilting his face toward the late-afternoon sun.

Chloe leaned back on her tube and breathed in the

nature surrounding her. Her mind was a comfortable blank until she saw a bridge up ahead. She didn't realize they had already come so far.

"I think we're coming up on the rapids," she said, anticipation shimmering through her.

Anthony studied her face. "Will you be okay?"

"Absolutely." She grinned. "I'm so psyched."

She hooted when her tube picked up speed as she approached the rapids. The white water seemed to suck her in, spin her around and around and spit her out at the other end. She laughed as she glanced around for Anthony. He shot out right behind her, smiling broadly.

"Let's do it again," she shouted.

She paddled with one arm until she reached the left bank of the river and climbed out, dragging her tube behind her. When Anthony joined her at her side, they followed the signs to the start of the rapids. She forgot all about being angry with him as they rode the white water at least three more times.

Chloe was still giggling as they floated languidly down the river again. "That was so much fun."

"Maybe the first two times," Anthony teased. "Were you that kid who rode Space Mountain at Disneyland only to get right back in line? Five times in a row?"

"Well, obviously." She scoffed and rolled her eyes but her silly grin refused to be subdued.

"I bet you don't even know that there's a whole new world beyond Tomorrowland." He shook his head sadly.

"Are you about to burst into a song?" She swiveled around, checking her surroundings with narrowed eyes. They were floating past an area with idyllic cottages on both sides of the river. "Oh, God. Am I about to get flash mobbed?"

Anthony threw his head back and laughed, and the sound seemed to echo through her like the vibrations of a tolling bell. Her smile wavered as her heart thumped in her chest but she glanced away to regain her bearings. As a comfortable silence fell between them, a contented sigh left her lips. She couldn't remember the last time she had so much fun.

But her last thought snagged on the jagged edges of her suppressed anger. This was *fun*. Anthony was relaxed and playful—teasing her, charming her—and he hadn't mentioned classical music even once. Her chest began to rise and fall quickly. The arrogant, patronizing *bastard*.

She fumed as the current gently carried her down the river, and fumed some more because Anthony hadn't even noticed that the comfortable silence between them had turned positively radioactive. She couldn't take it anymore. With a roar of fury, she kicked Anthony's tube away from her.

"What the—" He bolted up and stared at her as though she'd lost her mind.

"You. Are. Not. Boring," she yelled, pounding her fists on her tube.

"I'm not?" If she wasn't so angry, she would've thought the flummoxed expression on Anthony's face was hilarious. "Wait, you thought I was boring?"

"Yes, and I'm calling your bullshit." She pointed her index finger at him with as much menace as she could muster. "Every time we meet, all you talk about is classical music, expounding on its many virtues. On and on. Nonstop."

"Look—" Anthony scrubbed his face with both his hands "—all I was trying to do is maintain some semblance of a professional relationship between us."

"No, *you* look," she said. "You thought that if you didn't turn off all your personality, I'll fall for you because you think you're *that* irresistible. You're trying to keep a gaping distance between us so I won't cross whatever invisible line you drew between us."

"Chloe." The pained look on his face confirmed her suspicions. "That's not true at all."

"You, my sisters and my brothers-in-law might think of me as a child who needs to be protected, but I'm a grown woman more than capable of making my own fucking decisions. This is actually all about you and what you *shouldn't* want." At some point in the conversation, she had started crying. She scrubbed impatiently at her cheeks and took a shuddering breath. "*I* decide what *I* want. No one else. I don't need to be *protected* from you."

"You got it all wrong—"

She was done with this conversation. Spotting the tube drop-off point at the right bank, she jumped into the river, gasping at the biting chill of the late-spring river, and swam toward the bank with long, smooth strokes. She was grateful for her childhood swimming lessons, which was the only reason she was able to make this much-needed dramatic exit.

Chloe was nowhere to be found when Anthony reached the shore, lugging two tubes behind him.

He walked up and down the small park, hoping for a glimpse of that sinful red bikini, but he was out of luck. He grabbed his T-shirt from his dry bag and pulled it on over his damp body. Hoping she was back at the hotel, he got on a bus to the start of the river float where he'd parked their rental car.

On his short drive to their hotel, he tried to figure out what the hell happened out on the river. All this time, he'd been so focused on keeping himself in check that he hadn't considered what Chloe was going through. He told himself that he would keep things strictly professional between them. He gave his word that he wouldn't hurt her. But what about her?

What did she say on the river? She said he'd drawn an invisible line between them. But it was more than a line. He'd erected a wall between them. And every day, he had to add more bricks at the top so he wouldn't try to climb over it to reach her.

He'd insulted her intelligence by assuming that she wouldn't notice how hard he fought to maintain that distance between them. But she'd misunderstood the reasons behind his actions. It wasn't to keep her away but to hold himself back. She had no idea how much he wanted to scale that wall to claim her.

Anthony hesitated in front of the hotel room before he let himself in with a keycard.

"Chloe?" He walked deeper into the suite and discovered the bedroom door closed. He knocked softly and repeated, "Chloe."

He started when he heard the handle rattle as she opened the bedroom door. He honestly thought she would tell him to fuck off, but it seemed he really didn't know her at all. She stood before him wrapped in a white terry robe that looked as soft as clouds. Her hair fell past her shoulders in damp waves and her eyes were red as though she'd been crying.

"I'm sorry." He couldn't remember a single thing he'd planned to tell her. He just wanted her to stop crying. He never wanted her to cry again—especially because of him. "I'm so sorry."

"About what?" Her shoulders slumped as though she was exhausted as she stepped into the living room.

He opened and closed his mouth several times but he couldn't articulate a single coherent sentence to explain himself.

"I thought so." She scoffed and settled into an armchair. "Would you like me to tell you what you should be sorry about?"

Anthony nodded numbly.

"You're using me to rehabilitate your reputation but you don't want to end up with a lovestruck girl on your hands. You don't want the mess. You don't want *me*," she said, clasping her hands together. His chest twisted at the slight tremor in her words. "But how do you know I want *you*? Or more of you than you're willing to share?"

"You're right," he said, coming to stand in front of her. "I don't know what you want. All I know is that I want you so much that I can't think straight."

Chloe's lips parted on a soft gasp. She was so beautiful that he had to take a step back to not reach for her.

"But I shouldn't want you," he continued. "It's wrong to want you."

"Why?" She rose to her feet.

Because he was cheap and promiscuous—he couldn't change the past no matter how ashamed he was of his actions. Because he had nothing to offer her. Because he couldn't betray Rachel's memory. Because he didn't deserve her—didn't deserve to be happy. Yet, he still wanted her, and that scared him shitless. But he didn't say any of that.

"I promised Daniel I wouldn't break your heart." His voice sounded as though his throat was lined with gravel.

"And *that*," she spat, fire sparking in her eyes again, "is why you should be sorry."

He blinked in surprise. "I should be sorry for not wanting to break your heart?"

"No, for your utter arrogance and disrespect for my agency." She shook her head and closed the distance between them. "And you should be sorry for the presumption that my heart could ever be yours to break."

Her words cut into him like shards of glass. It made no sense. He didn't want her heart. He would never forgive himself if he hurt her. Then why was he gutted by what she said?

"You don't need to worry about me falling in love with you—" she lifted her chin in challenge "—because I'm not foolish enough to trust my heart to a man like you. Someone who could never offer me anything lasting."

He stopped breathing as something inside him roared with pain. She made to walk away from him but he gripped her arm to stop her.

"A man like me? A man-slut, you mean?" He ran the back of his fingers down her soft cheek. He felt a vicious jolt of satisfaction when she shivered in response. "Your mind might not want me but what about your body?"

"What my body wants is none of your business." She shook her arm out of his grasp. "All you need to know is that I won't fall in love with you."

He nodded wordlessly as exhaustion swept over him and watched her walk into the bedroom, closing the door behind her. He stretched out on the couch and threw his arm over his eyes. A huff of humorless laughter escaped him. She was right. He had been an arrogant ass. In hindsight, it was pretty embarrassing. Had he really thought someone like her could fall for someone like him?

On the bright side, he didn't have to try so hard to keep his distance anymore. Hiding his desire for her had been about as sustainable as holding his breath. Now he could breathe and let her see what she did to him because it wouldn't matter one way or another. He couldn't have her even if he wanted.

Eleven

Chloe wasn't proud of lashing out at Anthony—for all but telling him that she thought he was beneath her. God, she didn't mean that. She would never think that. In her defense, she was humiliated and would've said anything to hold on to even a scrap of pride. That was a lousy excuse, though. She seemed destined to lose all common sense where Anthony Larsen was concerned.

And her big mouth might've gotten her into big trouble. She seemed to have unleashed something in Anthony… He'd gone from very attractive to absolutely irresistible. She was used to the polished professionalism that emanated from his posture, his expression and even the modulation of his voice. It was jarring to see the same man *draped* across the chair across from her in the hotel restaurant with nary a hint of professionalism to be found.

His eyes had taken on a heavy-lidded look that made him seem at once lazy and insolent. His lips seemed to have grown fuller and poutier overnight, and they had a sinful crook in one corner like he had a juicy secret to share. This was nothing like the time in Santa Monica when he had unleashed his inner man-slut on her—cruel and deliberate. He had worn his seduction like a mask that night. Something to hide behind. This... This felt like he'd lowered a shield, allowing himself to be seen. This was desire, free and unhindered. She could feel it in her very core.

She shifted in her chair and dabbed her mouth with a napkin in case she was drooling. It was only breakfast and she was already hot and bothered. The unnerving thing was that Anthony hadn't *done* anything. He was treating her exactly as he always had. *He* was different.

If Anthony had any idea about his effect on her, he didn't show it. He reached for his mimosa and took a long sip, and she watched his throat working with fascination. How had he kept all this animal magnetism under wraps? *Seriously? Animal magnetism?* But she couldn't think of another word for all the sex he was oozing. It was *obscene* how sensual the man was.

"Chloe?" Even the arch of his raised eyebrow was sexy.

"Yes?" she said weakly, staring at the lips that had just formed her name.

"Um, I asked what you wanted to do today." His voice was definitely deeper...like rich, dark chocolate. *Yum.*

"Hmm." She stalled to gather her thoughts. "We

should go see Tumalo Falls and take some sickeningly adorable selfies to post on Instagram."

"Hashtag Chlothany?" He smirked.

She almost snorted out some mimosa. After she managed to swallow, she wheezed, "Chlothany?"

"Catchy, isn't it?"

"Cringy is what it is." She wrinkled her nose. "It's not like we're celebrities. Well... Maybe you are. But I'm certainly not."

"Are you kidding? You're a rock star in the classical music world."

"That has to be some kind of oxymoron." But she couldn't hold back her smile. "So are we on for some waterfalls and selfies?"

"Sure." His shoulder rose and fell with fluid grace. Jaguar. He reminded her of a jaguar. "I'm rarely on social media but Tanner runs my accounts. He would love some pictures of us to post."

"All right, then." She pushed to her feet, eager to do something other than ogle Anthony Larsen. "Let's get going."

It was a lovely late-spring day, and she rolled down her window to enjoy the breeze in her hair as they drove to Tumalo Falls. She was proud of herself for only peeking at Anthony every five minutes instead of staring nonstop at him. He'd changed into a soft linen shirt with the sleeves rolled past his forearms, the white of the fabric contrasting beautifully with the golden tan of his skin.

His eyes were focused on the road but the knowing smile on his lips told her that he was very much aware of her greedy scrutiny. She cleared her throat and looked outside as they turned onto the unpaved road that led to the waterfalls. She had to close her window as dirt clouds billowed around them. The car rattled enough to make her teeth chatter.

By the time they parked below the lookout point, she felt more at ease. Anthony was still the same Anthony—a little less boring, perhaps, but someone she could handle. She had everything under control.

After parking their rental, Anthony stepped out of the car in one lithe motion. Chloe unbuckled her seat belt and reached for the door handle but he beat her to it and opened the door for her. He held out his hand and she took it gingerly, expecting an electric charge to surge through her. A tingle of awareness ran up her arm but it wasn't enough to make her want to throw herself at him. *Thank goodness for small mercies.* Even so, she withdrew her hand as soon as she straightened, not wanting to push her luck.

"Thank you." She smiled with relief, feeling like she'd passed a test.

He dipped his head toward her and replied in a low, intimate cadence, "You're welcome."

Gah. She'd let her guard down too soon. Her heart pounded out a wild rhythm and she definitely wanted to throw herself at him. How did he make something as dry and polite as *you're welcome* sound suggestive? *Like you're welcome to climb my delectable body.* The fact that he could do this to her without laying a finger on her was alarming. Her brief sense of control had been pure delusion.

She quickly sidestepped him and headed for the short trail up to the viewing platform. He caught up with her in a few long strides. It took all of her willpower to walk side by side with him when her survival instinct told her to run. She was grateful for the busy trail and the constant stream of people hiking up and down around them. It was a good thing they didn't have any privacy. If they were alone, it would only be a matter of time before she lunged for him.

When Anthony threaded his fingers through hers and threw a rakish smile her way, butterflies took flight in her stomach. On second thought, privacy might've been the safer option. At least in their suite, she could lock herself away in the bedroom before her self-control gave out. But in public, she had to play his besotted girlfriend, which gave her every excuse to touch him. In fact, it was her duty to paw at him. A deal was a deal.

Chloe dragged her mind away from her horny thoughts and refrained from groping him. She would pretend to be madly in love with him in public while pretending to not want anything to do with him—at least romantically—in private. *Help.* With a nervous gulp, she dimpled prettily at Anthony. She could do this. She just had to get through this *romantic* weekend without throwing herself at him. Only one more night.

Hand in hand, they walked up to the lookout point, the picture of a happy couple. She rose to her tiptoes and leaned this way and that for a glimpse of the famed Tumalo Falls. The fragmented pieces of the view between shoulders and above heads were underwhelming. But as people stepped back from the railing, the spectacular vista opened up before them.

"Oh, wow," she whispered, hurrying to claim a spot at the edge of the platform. Powerful streams of water, foaming white with speed, fell between emerald green trees onto a stream far below.

"Beautiful," he murmured.

When she turned to agree with him, Chloe found Anthony's eyes on her, blazing with blatant appreciation. She stared back at him, her cheeks flushing with pleasure. He thought she was beautiful. Even in the midst of all their pretenses, that much was true. Helpless against the lure of desire, their faces drew closer together. Her lips parted and her eyelashes fluttered—wanting to give in...to surrender.

With a sharp gasp, she turned away at the last second and focused her gaze on the view spread out before her. She blew out a long breath and inhaled the fresh air. She wanted to soak up the energy of the stunning waterfall and let it wash away the lust thrumming in her veins. This wouldn't have been their first fake kiss, but if she'd kissed him, it would've been all too real for her.

"Let's take some selfies." She pushed away from the railing and held out her phone in front of them. "That's what we're here for."

"Sure." Anthony put his arm around her shoulders, pressing his cheek next to hers, and grinned lazily at the camera. Her toes curled in her shoes as she fought the urge to breathe in his woodsy scent.

"You know what? This isn't going to work." She ducked out from under his arm. "I can't get us *and* the waterfall in the shot. Let's ask someone to take a picture for us."

"Come here. Let me try." He reached for her again and she stumbled away from him.

"No, no. We better do it right," she said louder than

she intended. She walked up to a young couple near them. "Excuse me. Do you mind taking a picture of us?"

"Not at all," the woman said with a friendly smile.

Chloe handed her phone to her and came to stand demurely by Anthony's side. Chuckling under his breath, he stepped behind her and wrapped his arms around her waist. His thumb somehow ended up under her shirt, skirting across the sensitive skin of her belly.

"We need to do it right, remember?" he said near her ear.

Temper flaring, she turned her head to glare at him and found his face hovering mere inches away. A sharp breath caught in her chest and she couldn't tell whether she was angry or horny. All she knew was she couldn't look away. His hazel eyes darkened to a near black, and she realized what she was feeling. *Hunger.* She was starving for him.

"Oh, that's perfect. Just keep staring into each other's eyes like that," the woman cooed, clicking away. "Okay. I took several."

Anthony's arms dropped from her waist as Chloe went to retrieve her phone. "Thank you so much."

"Do you want to check if they're okay? I can take it again if you don't like them."

"That's all right," Chloe hastily averred. She didn't know what would happen if Anthony touched her again. "I'm sure they're great."

She blindly headed down the trail, not bothering to check whether Anthony was following her or not. Even the beauty of Tumalo Falls couldn't keep her there a second longer. All this time, she thought she was smart enough and mature enough not to let him get under her skin. She thought she was strong enough to resist the attraction between them...

Chloe yelped as the dirt road slid out from under her. She would've landed on her ass if it weren't for a pair of strong arms that shot out to steady her. She didn't have to look up to know whom they belonged to. She felt it in the quickening of her pulse and the heat spreading through her body.

"Are you okay?" Anthony asked, turning her to face him. The reckless, seductive gleam in his eyes had dimmed with concern.

"I'm fine." She glanced up to find him scanning her from head to toe, making sure she wasn't hurt. "Thank you."

He waved aside her gratitude and stuck close to her side as they made their way back to the car. Anthony seemed to sense that she needed space and didn't attempt to start a conversation. Once they were in the car, Chloe leaned against the headrest and closed her eyes.

No, she wasn't strong enough. The only reason she'd been able to resist him so far was because he'd held himself in check—because he'd erected a wall between them. But now that she'd torn that down, she didn't think she could resist at all.

It was for the best.

But no amount of repeating would convince him of that. Anthony cursed under his breath and stood from the sofa. He saw no upside to the fact that Chloe was locked away in the bedroom because he'd been a total creep this morning. He paced back and forth in a tight ten-step length. Their hotel suite in Bend was quite a bit smaller than his suite back in LA.

He was angry even though he had no right to be. He was angry that she didn't want to be with him—even though he *couldn't* be with her—and he taunted her with the very real attraction between them. It had nothing to do with her heart or mind. It was pure chemistry. But he pushed her to *react* to him. He wanted to *feel* her react to him.

When they got back from Tumalo Falls, Chloe had suggested they rent a cabana at the pool. After snapping a few obligatory selfies of their fun in the sun, she spent the entire afternoon with her nose in a book. He deserved the quiet torture of her red bikini, which had forced him to swim lap after lap to keep his board shorts from tenting. Nothing like cold water and lactic acid to douse a hard-on.

Tired of pacing back and forth, Anthony walked up to the bedroom door and lifted his hand to knock. He imagined their conversation when she opened the door.

Yes, she would say. *What is it?*

Duh, he would respond.

Instead of knocking, he shoved his hand through his hair and stomped back to the sitting area. The poor woman said she was beat and needed to rest. What good reason did he have for bothering her? He couldn't exactly apologize because that meant he would have to admit to deliberately baiting her in the morning and explain why he did that… There was no way he was going to tell her that he was hurt as hell. *Wait.* Hurt?

Being angry was one thing. Anger was such a basic, straightforward emotion. He wanted her—even though he had no intention of acting on his desire—but he was angry because she didn't want him. Simple. But feeling hurt? Being hurt was messy and complicated. It meant he'd already given more of himself to her than he ever intended. It meant he'd started to *hope* to be with her. He was well and truly fucked.

If he knew what was good for him, he would stay far away from that door. But it was past eight o'clock. She must be hungry. He could offer to order room service. That would be a perfectly legitimate reason for disturbing her. Before he could talk some sense into himself, Anthony rushed back to the bedroom and knocked.

"Yes," she said, cracking open the door. "What is it?"

"Are you hungry?" He grinned like a doofus. It was good to see her face even though a part of it was hidden behind the door. "I was going to order some room service. Do you want anything?"

Her lips scrunched to one side as she considered him with wary eyes. He wanted to kick himself for putting that look there. He wouldn't be surprised if she shut the door on his face.

"I'll have a cheeseburger," she said to his relief. "Thanks. Let me know when it's here."

His relief fizzled out when she closed the door on him after all. He decided with a sudden vehemence that he hated doors. They were awful, isolating torture devices. Shaking his head at his pathetic self, he picked up the hotel phone and ordered their dinner.

When their food arrived, Anthony laid out the plates on the coffee table and even poured some ice-cold local beer into a couple of glasses. He wanted to make it obvious that he went to some trouble to set the table so she wouldn't disappear back into the room with her burger in hand.

After a deep breath, he knocked once more on the hated door. Chloe's eyes dropped to his empty hands as soon as she opened the door, and her eyebrows drew together in confusion.

"Room service isn't here, yet?" she asked.

"No, it's here." He stepped back and stretched his arm toward the coffee table.

"Oh." She worried her bottom lip. "I was going to eat in my room—"

"Wouldn't it be easier to eat out here? It's all laid out already." He hurried toward the sitting area, praying that she would follow him. "I hope you like IPA. I poured you some. But if you don't, I could get you something else."

"The thing is—" she lingered in the doorway "—I'm in my pajamas."

She'd opened the door all the way and he saw for the first time that she was only wearing a long T-shirt that fell halfway past her shapely thighs. He struggled to swallow past his dry throat. Her faded lavender shirt said *Ninja unicorns kick ass* on it. It was the sexiest piece of clothing he'd ever seen.

"There's...um..." He cleared his throat and waved a hand at his plain white T-shirt and gray basketball shorts. "There's no dress code tonight."

Chloe huffed a small sigh and pattered into the sitting area. He restrained himself from pumping his fist. He took a seat on the couch in front of his Philly cheesesteak sandwich and she sat down beside him. Now that he'd convinced her to have dinner with him, Anthony had no idea what to do. With his heart thumping, he reached for his sandwich.

"Wait." Chloe grabbed his forearm. Her graceful, long-fingered hand burned an imprint on his bare skin. But her tone was all business. "Put it back down for a minute."

When he arched an eyebrow at her, she disappeared into the bedroom and reappeared with her phone in hand. She arranged their dinner closer together and placed their beer in front of the plates.

"Okay. Put your feet up by your food," she said and lifted her legs onto the coffee table, crossing her legs at the ankle. She wiggled her toes, which were painted a bright pink. "This is going to look so cute."

Angling her phone to capture their bare feet with their dinner, she snapped a couple of shots. Once she got the pictures, she scooted away from him, leaving a respectable distance between them. The clear reminder that she was only there for their fake-dating scheme deflated his excitement at having lured her out of the bedroom.

He gulped down half of his beer and reached for his cheesesteak sandwich even though he'd lost his appetite. They ate in strained silence and the food tasted like ash in his mouth.

"Do you mind if I put the baseball game on?" he asked to break the silence. "The Yankees are playing."

"Right. You're a New Yorker," Chloe said dryly. "Go right ahead. Root for your Yankees."

"You're a Dodgers fan, I take it?" He flipped through the channels until he found the game.

"Through and through." Chloe placed her crumpled

napkin on top of her half-eaten cheeseburger and stood up. "Enjoy the game."

"You're not going to watch?" He couldn't hide his disappointment.

She hesitated a moment before she shook her head. "You couldn't pay me to watch a game between the Yankees and the Giants."

"Can I bribe you with more local beer?" He wanted to kick himself for suggesting the game.

"Tempting, but no." A ghost of a smile played around her lips. "Good night."

"Good night," he murmured as he watched her leave.

He lowered the volume and kept half an eye on the game as he finished his dinner. After he cleared away the plates, he clicked the TV off. His heart wasn't in it, especially since he blamed the Yankees for Chloe's retreat into her room.

He poured himself another beer but it wasn't enough to distract him from the long night ahead. He stood from the sofa and rummaged through his suitcase. With his laptop in hand, he settled back on the couch, stretching his legs out on the coffee table. His feet looked lonely without the company of a certain beautiful woman and her pink toes. His morose mood brightened as he booted his laptop. He knew exactly whose company he wanted if he couldn't have Chloe's.

Twelve

"Shit."

Chloe heard Anthony curse from the living room. Maybe the Yankees were losing. She leaned closer to her laptop to focus on her game, the point of which was to distract her from the gorgeous man on the other side of the door.

"Goddammit!" he roared.

She frowned. SerialFiddler was hit yet again. His head wasn't in the game tonight. The rest of their team was already out. He had to carry his weight for them to have a chance at winning this match.

Hey, focus! she chided.

Maybe I can focus if someone wasn't distracting me with their messages, he replied.

Excuses, excuses. She rolled her eyes before she

spotted a player on the other team sneaking up on Se-rialFiddler. Watch out!

"Fuck. Fuck. Fuuuuck." Anthony shouted as Serial-Fiddler barely managed to retreat behind a crumbling building.

Why was Anthony shouting every time SerialFid-dler got shot? Weird. He must really be invested in that game. But it sounded like the Yankees were getting their ass handed to them by the Giants. She shook her head and messaged her frenemy:

Hey, I got an idea. When I attack from the top of the roof, I want you to round the building and blast them from the side.

Without waiting for his response, she maneuvered her character up the stairs and climbed out to the roof.

Roger that, NightMusic.

She smirked. Of course he'd agree. It was a badass move and he knew it.

Go, she ordered as she brought hell and brimstone down on the losers from the other team. SerialFiddler shot out from the side of the building and finished off the ones she didn't get.

"Hell yeah!" Anthony's hoots of excitement carried past the wall.

Her heart thudded against her rib cage even before the thought fully formed in her brain. It couldn't be. An-thony and SerialFiddler? The same person? Her fren-emy…her friend…was Anthony? What the hell kind of *You've Got Mail* universe was she living in? Setting aside her laptop, Chloe swung her legs off the bed and headed for the door.

Grinning from ear to ear, Anthony tapped out something on his keyboard. His smile waned as he stared at his screen and waited. He seemed to hesitate before typing out a short message. His eyes didn't leave his laptop even as a groove deepened between his eyebrows. He was waiting for her to respond.

Something sweet and sorrowful flared in her heart. In some ways, they were the most open and honest, even to themselves, in that game world. And without meddling family, emotional baggage and fake relationships to bog them down, they were friends. Real friends.

"Where did you go?" he mumbled to himself.

"Anthony?"

He jumped even though her voice was no louder than a whisper.

"Oh, hey." He snapped his computer shut and placed it next to him on the couch. A smile spread across his face. "I didn't know you were still up."

She padded across the living room and sat down on the edge of the sofa next to him. His gaze dropped to her legs and his Adam's apple worked as he struggled to swallow. Her shirt had ridden up until most of her thighs were laid bare. A couple of inches more, the triangle of her panties would have peeked out. She gasped and tugged on the hem of her T-shirt, and Anthony's eyes shot up to her face.

"Sorry. I'm sorry," he said in a husky voice. When she didn't say anything, he continued in a rush, "And I'm sorry about this morning."

"You want me." It was neither an answer nor a question. It was simply the fact.

"Yes." The word left him in a rush of breath. A long awaited exhale. "I wanted you from the moment I saw you in that rehearsal room. But that's no excuse for how I behaved at Tumalo Falls—"

"Where you behaved like a man who wanted a woman," she interjected.

"I…" He raked his fingers through his hair.

"Where you were finally honest with me." She reached for his hand. "Like I'd asked."

"I still shouldn't have…" He stared down at their entwined hands, resting on top of her thigh. "You made it clear last night that you didn't want me."

"I never said I didn't want you," she whispered.

His eyes flew to her face. "But you said you would never give your heart…to a man like me."

"Were we talking about love?" She arched an eyebrow. "I thought we were talking about desire."

"Why would you want me knowing I can't offer you anything lasting?" His voice was low, disbelieving.

"Maybe I want to listen to my body instead of my mind," she said with conviction she didn't feel. "Maybe this is all I want."

"It isn't. You deserve more." Even as he said this, his eyes turned hungry again—reckless again—and he cupped her face in his free hand. "But I can make you feel good. So fucking good."

Did she still want him when it would only be a sliver of him? Only for a brief moment? Yes, she wanted him.

"And when feeling good isn't enough—" his chest rose and fell as his thumb smoothed across her cheekbone "—you can tell me and I'll leave. I'll leave when it's not enough."

When I'm not enough. He didn't have to say it. She still heard him. When she grew weary of having just a shadow of him, then he would leave her. She didn't know who it was sadder for—for him or for her. But it didn't have to be sad.

"For how long we have, it'll be enough," she said, rubbing her cheek against his palm. "Once you go back to New York in a few weeks, everything will naturally come to an end. The fake dating and…this. Until then, feeling good will be enough. Don't you think?"

His hazel eyes deepened into an indescribable color that reminded her of stormy seas and rain-soaked forests. And in a voice as rough as gravel, he said, "Yes, it'll be enough."

She didn't know who moved first but they were devouring each other, open-mouthed and desperate. He lifted her by the waist and she swung her leg around to straddle him on the sofa. God, he was already hard. She swerved her hips, grinding her center into his arousal. He groaned into her mouth and bit her bottom lip, hard. She moaned deep in her throat as he licked away the sting.

As her desire spun out of control, Chloe tore at his shirt with frantic hands and whimpered in frustration. Anthony chuckled with pure male satisfaction as he ripped his shirt over his head, which quickly morphed into a guttural growl as her mouth, tongue and hands found his bare torso.

"Shit, Chloe."

She hardly heard him as she divested herself of her

T-shirt and pressed her naked breasts against the hot, hard wall of his chest. *Finally*. But her need outgrew her brief relief at the meeting of skin against skin.

"More," she said, pushing away from him.

Sliding off his lap, she gripped his shorts along with his boxer briefs and tugged roughly. Panting, he lifted his hips off the sofa and let her undress him completely. She dropped to her knees in front of him and greedily wrapped her hands around his cock that jutted proudly toward his stomach. Her lips stretched around him and she took as much of him as she could into her mouth.

"Fuck," he hissed.

She dipped her head up and down and swirled her tongue around his length, tasting his salty arousal. She moaned and slipped one hand into her soaked panties. His hips jerked helplessly as she toyed with him and she slid one finger between her folds. Her muffled moan of pleasure seemed to jolt Anthony out of a trance. With one hand under her arm and the other fisted in her hair, he hauled her up and kissed her with punishing intensity.

"Enough," he growled against her lips.

In one powerful, fluid motion, he stood from the couch with her in his arms and strode to the bedroom. He laid her on the bed and stared at her like a man starved—the light in his eyes told her he was way past the point of control.

"Wait here."

"What?" she cried.

Without answering, he strode out of the bedroom. The sight of his perfect ass distracted her from her outrage. He stalked back in before she could pound the mattress with her fists. He was already tearing open the condom packet and stopped at the foot of the bed to sheath himself. He was on top of her before she could tell him to hurry the hell up.

"After," he said, the veins popping out on his forehead. "I'll taste every inch of you after."

She spread her legs and dug her fingers into his ass. "Now."

His mouth closed around her nipple and sucked hard as he pushed himself inside her—far too gentle for her current state of mind. Even with his control on the verge of shattering, Anthony was taking care to ease into her. To spare her even the slightest discomfort. But she was wet and aching. She needed all of him. He rocked in and out, inch by delicious inch until her eyes started rolling back in her head. *Fuck this.* She threw her legs around his waist and thrust her hips up, arching her back off the bed.

"Oh, God," she gasped as she felt him enter her body to the hilt.

He was right to take care. If she'd taken him in all at once, there would've been pain. But now, he just *filled* her. He felt so *good*.

"Chloe." He stilled over her, eyes darting around her face. "Are you okay?"

"Anthony." She glared at him. "I need you to fuck me. *Hard*."

To demonstrate how hard she wanted it, she grabbed his ass and drew her hips back before thrusting herself back against him. He groaned, his head falling back. Then he slid almost completely out of her and slammed into her to the hilt.

"Yes," she moaned. "Yes. Please."

He didn't need any more encouragement as he pounded into her again and again. Pleasure, hot and intense, gathered low in her stomach. Her head thrashed back and forth as the waves rose and peaked. He slid his hand between their slick bodies and pressed his thumb down on her swollen nub.

"Anthony," she shouted as she climaxed hard enough to see stars. His fingers and hips slipped and teased, prolonging her pleasure to the last shivering drop.

"Get up," he rasped. Her heavy eyelids fluttered open and she dizzily sat up, helpless against the command in his voice. "Turn around and hold the headboard."

She got to her knees and gripped the bedframe. Grabbing her hip with one hand and placing the other on the headboard next to hers, he drove into her from behind. He thrust again and again—without rhythm, without control—just with wild desire. She thought she was spent from her first orgasm but she felt waves of pleasure whirling and soaring inside her once more.

"Chloe," he groaned, his fingers digging into her hip. The headboard creaked and shook as he pounded into her.

Her name left his mouth in a guttural shout as she fell apart again, joining him in his climax. They stayed connected, panting and hanging on to the bedframe, slippery bodies pressed together. After a while, Chloe's eyes started drooping.

Anthony pressed a kiss to her temple and gently guided her onto her back. He pushed himself off the bed and strode to the bathroom in all his nude glory. As tired as she was, she greedily took all of it in. Once he came back and lay down next to her, he tucked her under his chin and folded her body against his.

It felt so good. She yawned, limp and satiated. It felt so right.

"You're a man of many talents, SerialFiddler," she mumbled and fell into a deep slumber.

Thirteen

Anthony had been drifting off to sleep when Chloe's mumbled words reached his ears. His eyes flew open as his postcoital mush of a brain registered what she'd said.

"What... What did you just say?" He leaned back to look at her but she was fast asleep.

How? What? Did she just call him SerialFiddler? How in the world would she know his gamer name for *League of Legends*? Did he ever mention in any interviews that he played *LoL*? He didn't think so. It was someplace he could maintain anonymity and just be one of the players. It was where he let off steam—where he happily kicked ass without worrying about offending his fan base. Even Tanner didn't know his gamer name.

Maybe she was a gamer as well and somehow figured out he and SerialFiddler were one and the same. But how could she? Unless... This couldn't wait. He reached for Chloe's shoulder but pulled back. She looked so angelic in her sleep. Did he really want to wake her up over some silly computer game? *Hell, yes*. If she was NightMusic, he needed to know. Besides, it wasn't like he was going to let her sleep for long. He wasn't finished with her. Far from it. His blood rushed south with anticipation, but first things first...

"Chloe," he whispered, planting kisses on her bare shoulder and down her arm. "Wake up."

"Mmm," she mumbled, tugging the covers toward her head. God, she was adorable.

"Come on, kitten." He nibbled on her earlobe. "We have unfinished business to take care of."

Her eyes stayed stubbornly shut but a smile spread across her face as she stretched languidly in his arms, pressing certain parts of her body closer to other parts of his body. At his muffled curse, her eyes finally opened, sparkling with mischief and sensual promise. She purred low in her throat as she dragged her fingernails down his chest to his stomach and lower...

"Whoa." He grabbed her hand and pinned it over her head. For good measure, he did the same with her other hand and pressed her down on the bed with his torso. He traced the side of her body with his free hand, her skin like warm silk under his palm. "We have something to discuss, but you are very distracting."

"Call me kitten again." She bit on her lower lip, her teeth dragging on the plump skin.

"I..." He cleared his throat. Maybe *League of Legends* could wait until after he called her kitten and did some very dirty things to her body. "No."

She pouted. He might have whimpered.

"I mean, not yet," he clarified. "What did you call me before you fell asleep?"

"What did I call you?" Her eyebrows drew low over her eyes. "What do you mean?"

"You don't remember?" Maybe he misheard...

Her mouth rounded into a perfect O.

"You do remember." Unable to resist, he planted a quick, hard kiss on her mouth. "Now tell me what you called me."

"SerialFiddler," she said slowly.

"How?" He released her wrists and rose up on his elbow. "How do you know I'm SerialFiddler?"

Chloe sat up beside him holding the bedsheet to her chest. Clucking his tongue in disapproval, he divested her of the cover with a swift flick of his wrist. She gasped and stared open-mouthed at him.

"What?" He swirled one finger around a dusky pink nipple and watched it tighten under his touch. "It'd be a shame to cover such perfect breasts."

"I thought you wanted to talk." She sighed in exasperation but one corner of her mouth quirked up.

"I'm multitasking." He circled the other nipple so it wouldn't feel left out.

"Like I said, you're a man of many talents," she said in a slightly breathless voice. He couldn't hold back his cocky grin. *SerialFiddler.*

His mouth went dry as his blood pounded in his ears. He swallowed after several tries and said, "NightMusic?"

"Yes?" she answered much too innocently.

"Are you fucking serious?" He shut down his thoughts before they could whisper words like *fate* and *meant to be* in his reeling mind. "How is that even possible?"

"Payback time." Chloe suddenly flipped back the covers over his lower body, revealing his painfully hard dick. She blinked. "You seriously want to have this conversation right now in *that* condition?"

"I do." He grabbed her wrist before she took him in her hand. "How long did you know?"

"What time is it?" She glanced at the alarm clock. "For fifty-three minutes."

He gaped at her.

"Did you know you scream when you play *League*?" He nodded and she continued, "Well, I heard you spout expletives every time SerialFiddler took damage. I didn't make the connection for a long time. I mean, what are the chances, right? But you went wild when we won the game, and the realization hit me like a ton of bricks. That's when I came out and found you on your laptop."

"That's why you didn't respond to my messages," he said as if that was what mattered. He shook his head. "What does this mean?"

"It means I know you're sarcastic, arrogant and funny as hell." She took his hand in hers. "It also means we're friends."

"And it means I know not to get on your bad side because you're as ruthless as you're smart." He brushed her hair back from her forehead and tapped her on the tip of her nose. "But yes, it means we're friends."

"I still can't believe you bored me to tears rambling on and on about the intricacies and nuances of chamber music—" she narrowed her eyes at him "—because you were afraid I'll fall for you."

"That's not true." Or it was only partly true. He gave Daniel his word that he wouldn't break her heart. But they were both idiots who didn't know that Chloe's heart would never be Anthony's to break. "I was trying to keep our interactions professional to stop myself from grabbing at you like a caveman."

"Well, that didn't work." She snorted.

"No, it didn't." He grabbed a fistful of sheets to stop himself from rubbing at the strange ache in his chest. He was lucky he got to have this much of her. So lucky. "And I want you to know that I really do love talking about classical music, especially with someone who understands. Just not all the time."

"Yeah." She giggled. "Sometimes you play *League of Legends* and talk trash to other players."

"And sometimes—" he pushed her onto her back and slid down her body "—I like to do this."

Her laughter caught in her throat as her eyes widened. He arched his brow and smiled wolfishly at her, licking his lips in anticipation. Holding her gaze, he drew her knees apart and settled himself between her legs. He slid his thumbs into her folds and opened her up for him to taste.

"So pretty," he murmured as he bent his head and smoothed the flat of his tongue over her swollen sex.

"Oh, God." The guttural tone of her voice made his groin tighten.

He began to lavish his attention on her in earnest, chorusing her moan of pleasure. Needing to see her, he glanced up to find her head thrown back against the pillow with a hand trailing down her throat. Before he became mesmerized by where that hand was headed, he returned to licking and teasing her until her hips bucked off the bed. He held her down and pushed a finger inside her.

"Fuck," she said almost viciously as something seemed to snap inside her. He would've chuckled if he wasn't concentrating so hard on not coming on the sheets.

She proceeded to ride his face and hand, writhing and bucking like a wild thing. She'd come undone and it was the hottest thing he had ever seen. He added a finger inside her and scraped his teeth lightly over her clit.

"Anthony," she whimpered. "Don't stop."

He smiled and twirled his tongue in circles before he said, "Stop what?"

"That. Everything." She buried her fingers in his hair and swiveled her hips. "Don't stop. Please."

"Fuck," he hissed.

At that moment, he would've done anything she asked of him. He feasted on her until she was ready to explode. Knowing she was close, he sucked her swollen nub into his mouth and she screamed. Her climax wracked through her body and he felt her clench around his fingers again and again. He almost lost it then and there.

He slowly withdrew his fingers once she grew limp and crawled back up the bed. She watched with drowsy eyes as he sheathed himself with a condom. Then he kissed her deeply on the mouth, smoothing his hand across her forehead. When she wrapped her arms around his neck and kissed him back, he placed himself at her entrance and drove home.

"God, you feel so good," he growled. He fought for control as he started moving inside her slowly. So slowly. When Chloe dug her fingers into his ass and lurched her hips against him, he stilled against her.

"What the hell, Larsen?" She scowled at him and tugged at his hips.

He chuckled and leaned his forehead against hers, but he didn't give her an inch. Their first time had been a wild coupling born of weeks of suppressed desire. This time, he wanted to draw it out and savor every second.

"What's your rush?" He dropped a kiss on the corner of her mouth. "We have all night."

"Do you want me to go crazy?" she demanded.

"Yes. As a matter of fact, I do." But he knew that he would go mad as well. Mad with want for her.

He moved against her once more, setting a pace that might very well destroy him. Sweat dripped from his forehead, down the tip of his nose. He drew out of her and pushed back into her, shuddering from the pleasure.

Noticing his control slipping, Chloe smiled wickedly. "Well, then. I'll make sure I don't go alone."

She matched him thrust for languid thrust, swerving her hips as he pumped in and out of her. He put his lips against her ear and gritted out, "Are you trying to kill me?"

"You started it." With a husky laugh, she circled her hips again. "Ready to give in? Ready to take me hard and fast?"

Anthony broke then. Every cell in his body screamed for release and he gave in to the primal call. He drove into her with wild, hard thrusts. When her head started thrashing back and forth, he pulled out of her and flipped her onto her stomach. Understanding what he wanted from her, she got to her hands and knees, thrusting her round, sweet ass toward him.

He sunk into her again and they groaned in unison. He rode her, his thighs slapping against her ass—the sound obscenely loud in the quiet hotel room. He was close but wanted her there with him. He gripped her hips and tilted her up. The keening wild noises she was making told him she was close. So close.

Anthony came with a shout as her internal muscles clenched around him. He bucked into her once, then twice, his climax shuddering through him in waves. For a moment, it was silent in the room except for the sound of their panting. As soon as he pulled out of her, Chloe's knees and elbows seemed to give out and she collapsed into a heap. He rushed to the bathroom and cleaned himself up, so he could hurry back to her.

When he joined her again, Chloe was stretched out on her side, facing away from him. Thinking she might be asleep, he carefully curled up behind her and wrapped his arm around her midriff. With a sigh, she snuggled back against him and linked her fingers through his.

"You okay?" He kissed her bare shoulder.

"Better than okay." Her words were slurred around the edges. "But I could use some sleep, Larsen."

"Sure, kitten." He smiled as he settled his head on the crook of his elbow. "You can take a catnap."

He waited for a sassy retort but the rhythm of her deep breaths told him she was already asleep. He buried his nose in the crook of her neck and inhaled. Even beneath the tang of sweat and sex, he could smell her sweet scent, which he couldn't get enough of. His arm unconsciously tightened around her waist.

As fatigue tugged his eyes closed, he realized all of this felt…right. The thought might alarm him later— he smiled drowsily, letting the warmth of Chloe's body seep into him—but it only made him happy for now as sleep blanketed around him.

Fourteen

Chloe fidgeted in her seat as she waited for the concert to start, tugging on the hem of her dress. The cut and fabric of the designer dress ensured that it was tasteful enough for a classical concert, but her white asymmetrical dress was one of her more risqué outfits. It hugged her curves in all the right places, ending halfway down her thighs, and made her look every bit her age.

Some of the comments on the pictures she posted of her and Anthony were getting to her—like the ones about ditching the "teenage girl" to date a real woman. She had to admit that she looked youthful in their pictures from Tumalo Falls with her hair in a high ponytail and not a stitch of makeup on her face. But it wasn't like Anthony looked that much older than her. A ten-year age difference wasn't a big deal.

Besides, most people thought they made a cute couple. She bit her lip to hold back her smile. They were a cute *fake* couple even though they were sleeping together. A lot. Chloe's cheeks flooded with heat as her pulse picked up. She exhaled slowly and reminded herself for the umpteenth time that they were having a summer fling. He still loved his late wife and she was supposed to be too smart to fall in love with someone emotionally unavailable. She was certain that was the only reason Anthony agreed to their fling, because superficial and temporary were all he had to offer.

She swallowed the rush of emotions that rose up inside her. They weren't in a real relationship but their friendship was real. They were friends with benefits—with the benefits set to end once he returned to New York—but she wanted to believe that they would remain friends. They would remain in each other's lives. They would always have *League of Legends*, right? That was enough. That had to be enough.

Chloe listlessly glanced down at the program in her hand. For tonight, she wasn't a performer but an excited fan. Anthony had cleared his schedule to join the Hana Trio during Megan's maternity leave but kept one concert with the LA Philharmonic. One of his dear friends was guest conducting that evening and he said he enjoyed working with her too much to miss the opportunity. Besides, the concert was scheduled for a Tuesday evening when the Hana Trio wasn't performing.

She hadn't seen Anthony perform live—not counting their rehearsals and concerts as the Hana Trio—in a long time. She couldn't wait to hear him play, especially his performance of the Sérénade mélancolique by Tchaikovsky. Just the thought of Anthony infusing the rich, dark piece with his power and passion made chills run down her spine.

When the lights dimmed and the concert commenced, Chloe had to repeatedly remind herself to breathe. She was a chamber musician and she believed that there was power in a smaller, intimate performance, but the grandeur of a full orchestra couldn't be denied. The music filled the Disney Concert Hall—the acoustically flawless architecture embracing and amplifying the sound to perfection—and vibrated in her chest.

She blinked and it was time for intermission. Her knees felt weak but she forced herself onto her stiletto-clad feet and headed backstage. Anthony promised her an introduction to Fumi Tanaka, the renowned conductor. She was the first Asian-American woman to become the music director of a major American orchestra. The woman was a legend.

Chloe found him waiting outside the backstage entrance, craning his neck to peer over the people. They had no idea that *the* Anthony Larsen actually stood among them and rushed about for the restrooms and/or refreshments. She knew the exact moment he spotted her because his face split into a grin that warmed her heart.

"What are you doing out here?" she said even though she was pleased by his thoughtfulness. "You better get inside before you get mobbed by your fans."

He arched an eyebrow at her. "I'm a violinist, not a member of BTS."

"I thought we were rock stars of the classical world." She tugged on his arm as heads started turning their way.

Chuckling under his breath, Anthony held open the door for her and followed her inside. "Of course we are. I think #chlothanyforever is trending right now."

She winced at his joke because... There was no forever for them. What was the matter with her? Of course there wasn't. That was part of their deal. She pasted on a smile and turned toward him. "So where is she?"

"I'm hiding her from you." He pinched her chin between his fingers and planted a kiss on her lips. He pulled back just enough to meet her eyes. "Life is so much simpler now that I can do that without pretending to be pretending."

And yet, here she was pretending that this was nothing more than a fling to her. She turned her head away just as his smile faded. She didn't know what he saw in her expression but it wasn't something she was ready to discuss.

"Anthony, are you going to introduce me to your lovely girlfriend or spend all intermission kissing her?" an amused voice said from beside them.

"Can I get back to you on that?" he drawled, putting his arm around Chloe's shoulders. "Chloe, this is Fumi Tanaka. Fumi, Chloe Han."

"It's such a pleasure to meet you, Ms. Tanaka." Chloe shook the older woman's hand. "You're an inspiration."

"Thank you, my dear. And stop it with the *Ms. Tanaka* nonsense. Call me Fumi," she said with a hearty laugh. "Anthony has been talking my ear off about what a talented and dedicated musician you are. As if I'm not familiar with your work. You and your sisters inspire *me*."

"Oh, my God. I could hug you," Chloe said, tearing up. "What the hell? I'm gonna hug you."

She launched herself at her idol, who hugged her back tightly and patted her back. "He also mentioned that you are the sweetest person alive. I'm going to have to agree with that one."

Chloe stepped back from the embrace and glanced at Anthony. He rocked back on his heels with a sheepish grin on his face. She was suddenly on the verge of ugly crying. She didn't know if it was because Fumi thought she was the sweetest person alive or if it was because Anthony thought so.

"I might have oversold you a bit," he said. She punched him in the arm but she was grateful for the levity he offered. "Ow. That hurt. Fumi, I think I'm out of commission for the rest of the night."

"See what I have to put up with?" Chloe heaved a sigh.

"You're a saint." Fumi watched them with an indulgent smile. "But it truly warms my heart to see Anthony so happy again. I haven't seen that spark in him for far too long. And I have a feeling it's all thanks to you, Chloe."

"It's... I..." Chloe had no idea what to say. She realized she would do anything to make Anthony happy and chase away the bleak light that sometimes stole into his eyes. But by the wary expression on his face, now was not the time to broach the subject. She wasn't sure if he would ever be ready. With an inward shake of her head, she put on a cheeky grin. "I guess I just add a bit of color to his humdrum life. There are only so many Barbies he could date."

The brilliant conductor bent over with a belly laugh. "While I could carry on chatting with you all night, we do have a concert to finish. But I would love to take you out to dinner tomorrow night."

"Yes please," Chloe said without hesitation even though she had a term paper due at the end of the week. Having dinner with her idol was more important than a mere master's degree.

After exchanging numbers, Fumi excused herself to prepare for the second half of the concert. Chloe sighed dreamily once she was out of sight.

"Do I get to come, too?" Anthony said with convincing puppy-dog eyes.

"No boys allowed." Chloe shot him a warning glance.

"Okay, okay." He laughed and kissed her on the temple. With his mouth close to her ear, he whispered, "Will you wait for me after the concert? You're killing me with that dress."

Her toes curled and heat gathered low in her stomach. "I have a term paper to write… But you can drop by my apartment when you're ready."

"Keep that dress on." The heat in his eyes almost made her whimper. "I know exactly how I want to strip it off of you."

"Focus more on the concert ahead of you, Larsen," she said huskily, "and less on getting me naked."

"I'm quite good at multitasking." He planted a soft kiss on her neck, making her knees go weak.

"Hmm. We'll see about that." She glanced at the orchestra members finding their way back to their seats. "You should go."

He placed a lingering kiss on her lips. "I'll see you soon."

Chloe liked the sound of that too much for her own good.

Anthony tapped his foot as he waited for the rickety elevator to reach the third floor of the graduate housing building. As soon as the doors began inching open, he squeezed past the narrow gap and ran for Chloe's apartment. His breathing already fast and uneven, he pounded on her door like a madman. If she didn't open in the next five seconds, he might start shouting her name—

"What took you so long?" Chloe opened the door with one hand and dragged him inside by his lapel with the other.

"I—" He didn't even know what he was about to say but she didn't let him finish.

Her mouth crushed against his, hot and hungry, teeth nipping and tongue swirling. "God, Anthony. Your music makes me *wild*."

With his fingers digging into her waist, he spun her around and pressed her back against the door. He swooped in for a hard, possessive kiss. "You want to talk about music? Right now?"

"I thought it was your favorite topic." She ground her hips against his aching hardness. "Hearing your solo in Sérénade mélancolique made me so wet…"

"Are you still wet for me?" he growled, sliding his hand under the short hem of her dress and between her thighs. "Fuck."

"My panties were soaked." She licked the side of his neck. "I had to take them off as soon as I got home."

"That was my job." He drove two fingers inside her and she clenched around him.

"It's your fault for being so sublimely talented," she said between short gasps of pleasure as she rode his hand. "The sound of your violin felt like a caress against my skin. It vibrated *inside* my body. I don't think I've wanted anyone as much as I wanted you in that moment."

"And I want you more than anything." He fumbled for his wallet and grabbed his condom as Chloe unbuckled him and slid his pants down to his thighs.

She took the condom from him and covered him with trembling hands. He hoisted her up against the door by the back of her thighs and drove into her. Shouting her approval, she wrapped her arms and legs around him. He pounded into her, the door rattling behind her, driven by a need he couldn't even comprehend. He needed this—he needed her—like his next breath. He wanted her so much it hurt. Even as he was taking her and giving himself to her, he wanted more. *More. More. More.*

"Anthony," she panted. "Harder."

He spun them around and carried her to her couch. He dropped her beside it and bent her over the arm. "Hold on."

Anthony grabbed her tightly by the hips and pulled her toward him as he pushed into her. She threw her head back with a moan, titling her ass to take him in deeper. He gritted his teeth to hang on to his control but he felt his climax blazing toward him.

"I need you to come." He was jerking in and out of her frantically. "Come for me, kitten."

His release came a split second after her hoarse cry and they rode their orgasm out together. Slowly, the small but cozy comfort of Chloe's apartment came into focus. He was still fully dressed with only his pants and boxer briefs pushed down to the middle of his thighs. And he'd pushed her dress up past her waist. He tenderly set her clothes right before pulling up his pants.

"Are you okay?" he asked.

Chloe trudged around the side of the sofa and fell onto it before she nodded, looking a little dazed.

"I need to clean up," he said, still out of breath. "I'll be right back."

He returned to the living room and crashed down next to her. She brought her feet up and tucked them under her bottom. He leaned his head back on the sofa and she leaned hers on his shoulder. Limp and satiated, they took a moment to catch their breath.

They'd been sleeping together for weeks now but they still went at each other like they hadn't had sex in a decade. At first, he thought it was his pent-up need for her surfacing after the long, hard weeks of resisting her. But his need for her hadn't waned—he still wanted her as desperately as the first time he had her. And he didn't know if he would ever stop wanting her like this. Something dark and sharp clawed at his insides. He only had a few more weeks left with her. Everything inside him clenched.

Anthony inhaled deeply through his nose. He would get her out of his system by then. Hadn't the plan been to *not* let her *in* his system at all? But that had been wishful thinking from the start. She got in his blood, in his very cells, the moment he laid eyes on her. And that was why he had to quit her when the time came. Until then…

He shifted to the side and nuzzled her neck where it met her shoulder—a corner of paradise—and breathed her scent in.

"What are you doing?" she mumbled even as she tilted her head to give him better access.

"Take a wild guess." He scraped his teeth along her collarbone and had the pleasure of hearing her breath catch. "I told you I'm taking that dress off. I missed the mark on my first try, but I plan to succeed this time around."

"Anthony, I can't." Her obvious reluctance took the sting out of her rejection. "I have a term paper to write, remember?"

"Now I do." Heaving a forlorn sigh, he stopped his delectable exploration and sat back up. Pressing her hands on her thighs, Chloe heaved herself to her feet and stared pointedly down at him. But for the life of him, he couldn't make himself stand to leave her apartment. "If I sit here really quietly and promise not to bother you, can I stay?"

Something tender entered her expression and her mouth curved into a soft smile. "You're hard to ignore even just sitting there."

He grinned like an idiot. "I'll even make you tea and give you shoulder massages on your breaks."

"You must be tired after your concert…"

"Not at all." He could feel her swaying. "Besides, I'm a night owl. Even if I go back to my hotel right now,

I'll stay up reading for hours. I might as well do it here and take care of you."

She stood nibbling on her bottom lip, ready to cave, so he got up and took off his tux jacket and started rolling up the sleeves of his shirt. "You won't even know I'm here."

"You doing things like that—" she watched his arms with glazed eyes "—will wreck my concentration."

"What?" He frowned. "I'm just rolling up my sleeves."

"Ugh." She threw up her hands. "You're so clueless. That's forearm porn."

"Forearm what?" He paused in the middle of pushing up his other sleeve past his elbows.

"Goddammit. You can't stop." She stomped her foot. "Finish your strip tease and be done with it."

"Oh—kay?" He did as she ordered and bent down to remove his shoes. "Is... Is it okay to take my shoes off or is that distracting, too?"

"What? Don't be silly. I don't have a feet fetish." She scoffed. "Besides, I'm Korean. If I was in my right mind, I wouldn't have let you in here with your shoes on in the first place."

"Wait." He held up his hand, a shit-eating grin taking over his face. "So does that mean you have a *forearm* fetish?"

"Oh, shut up." She turned around and stomped into her bedroom. "I'm going to change into my comfy pajamas then ignore you for the rest of the night. Because I'm a responsible graduate student."

Anthony wisely said nothing else and sat back down on the sofa. He pulled up his current read on the phone and settled in for a quiet night of being ignored. He decided not to question his soft, contented sigh or the happy smile that lingered on his lips. It didn't matter what any of this meant. He just wanted to *be*. It would all be over in a few weeks anyway.

Fifteen

Anthony was a world traveler who hadn't *seen* the world. When you traveled for work, you hardly had time for sightseeing. He might be an expert on various concert halls around the world and which hotel suites offered the best views, but he hadn't seen much of the beautiful cities he'd visited.

Chloe wanted to fix that—at least for her neck of the woods.

"Where are we going?" he asked from the passenger seat.

"I told you it's a surprise," she said, keeping her eyes on the road.

She had sequestered his car for the night to take him on a surprise visit to the Getty Museum. If traffic cooperated for once, they might even make it there for the sunset. She had a feeling he would appreciate the stunning view.

When she pulled into the parking lot, he turned to her with a cocked eyebrow. "A museum? You put on the cloak-and-dagger show to bring me to a museum?"

"What?" She smiled coyly, not bothering to explain that the Getty was not your typical art museum. "You don't like museums?"

"I love them." He shrugged. "You just raised my expectations way high."

"Ingrate," she huffed, secretly enjoying herself. "I bring you out for a surprise date night and this is the thanks that I get?"

"God, sorry. I am an ingrate, aren't I?" He leaned over and kissed her cheek as she parked the car. "Thank you for planning this. I'll be sure to thank you properly later tonight."

She went hot all over at the sensual promise in his voice. It scared her a little that he could affect her so much with a few murmured words. Before she could jump him, she hurriedly stepped out of the car. She had to hang on to some semblance of pride even though he made it clear again and again that he wanted her just as desperately as she wanted him.

Anthony joined her at her side and linked his fingers through hers. Her heart dipped when he smiled at her. She tugged him toward the elevators that would take them to the trams. "Your chariot awaits."

Summer evenings at the Getty were popular and they had to move through a labyrinth of humans for their turn on the tram. It was crowded inside but brightly lit and air-conditioned to the point of chilly, so the ride up to the top of the hill wasn't uncomfortable. It didn't hurt that Anthony stood behind her with one arm wrapped around her waist to hold her steady.

"Come on." She led him up the outdoor stairs as soon as they piled off the tram. "I know the perfect spot to watch the sunset."

She was able to squeeze in between two couples for a spot against the balcony railing. Anthony stepped up behind her, resting one hand on the railing and the other on her hip, and pressed his cheek against hers. She breathed in the woodsy scent of him and closed her eyes on the spectacular panoramic view to feel his warmth against her.

When she finally opened her eyes, the sky above Los Angeles was saturated with impossibly vibrant colors in shades of pink, orange and purple. It was one of the prettiest things she'd ever seen—even though she'd seen it a thousand times. This one would be unforgettable because she was seeing it with Anthony. She was a fool.

Forcing herself into her tour-guide mode, she said, "They say smog is what creates the distinctive color palette of the Los Angeles sunset."

"That's the most romantic thing anyone has ever told me." His laughter tickled her ear.

"Romance is overrated." She elbowed him in the ribs. "Random factoids. That's where it's at."

"Shush." He smacked a kiss on her cheek. "Let me enjoy this."

After a moment, Chloe turned around and leaned back against the railing to look up at him. With his eyes still on the view, Anthony resettled his hands on each side of her waist. His face was soft with wonder and his full lips were curved into a smile. This was who he was behind all his masks—someone gentle, kind and happy. An aching tenderness twisted in her chest. She reached up and cupped his cheek. His gaze finally shifted to hers as he leaned into her touch. Placing his hand over hers, he turned his head to kiss her palm.

Chloe smoothed her hand up his jaw and around to the back of his neck. Burying her fingers into the soft locks of his hair, she tugged his head down and pressed her lips against his—light and curious. It was a question. *Is this you? The real you?* He kissed her back, warm and tender. An answer. *Yes, this is me.*

She should pull back. This was the Anthony that she should guard her heart against. The one she couldn't resist. But she melted against him with a sigh because this Anthony was worth risking everything for. He was the one she would do anything to make hers.

He deepened the kiss with a low growl, tilting her head as his tongue drove into her mouth. And she opened wide for him with a shudder—tenderness giving way to yawning hunger. His fingers fisted in her hair and his other hand, spread wide on her back, pulled her flush against him.

She rose onto her tiptoes, gripping his shoulders hard enough to leave a mark, and kissed him with unfamiliar desperation. And she realized she was scared—scared that when this kiss ended, the real Anthony would be hidden behind his mask again.

So even when she heard the indignant huffs and uncomfortable coughs around them, she didn't stop kissing him. Even when she felt Anthony's hands wrap around her shoulders and gently push her back, she gripped his shirt in her fists and held on. Only when his lips left hers to laugh softly in her ear did she stop.

"I'm not sure if dry humping you against the railing will help rehabilitate my image," he drawled, all traces of his vulnerability locked tightly away.

Chloe gathered herself as she smoothed away the wrinkles she'd created in his shirt. "I was just trying to thin out the crowd so we could get a good selfie with the sunset behind us."

She busied herself with her phone to hide the tears that were just beneath the surface. There had been nothing in her mind but him when she kissed him. She didn't kiss him as a show for the crowd. She kissed him because she cared about him.

"All right." He wrapped himself around her from behind. "Let's go, Chlothany."

She let her head fall back on his shoulder. She didn't know if she was taking any decent pictures. She just let herself exist in the moment. *Click.* Anthony licked the side of her face. She scrunched up her nose and scrubbed at her cheek. She turned to glare at him and he leaned over to rub the tip of his nose against hers. *Click, click.* She couldn't hold back her smile and he grinned back at her.

Soon, the sun set behind the horizon and the dark city below lit up with twinkling lights. Chloe tucked her phone in her purse and turned her gaze toward the view once more. Anthony leaned his elbows on the railing and stood quietly next to her, the soft smile back on his lips. She glanced sideways at him from under her lashes, memorizing the details of his beautiful face.

Without meaning to, she had been storing away moments like these because she was going to need them to survive losing him. It didn't matter she didn't have all of him. Far from it. But even the little she had of him would be dearly missed when he was gone.

And if she wasn't more careful, he might end up leaving with her heart...which was the last thing he wanted. She dug her nails into her palms as fiery pain flared in her chest. She could almost see the hairline fractures forming across her heart—glowing an ominous red like lava pushing up to the surface.

Chloe was a smart woman. Giving something as precious as her heart to someone who didn't want it was not a smart thing to do. Nope. Not smart at all.

Be smart, Chloe.

Her heart seemed to huff a wise, sad laugh...already knowing it was a lost cause.

Anthony rubbed his damp palms down the front of his pants and pushed up his sleeves past his elbows. It didn't feel right that Chloe was the one planning all their romantic dates. He didn't care that she was just doing it to help rehabilitate his public image. He wanted to do something for her in return.

He hummed as he cooked, excitement bubbling up at the prospect of surprising Chloe with a home-cooked meal. He was making poisson en papillote with a Mediterranean twist. She loved olives so she should enjoy this dish.

She probably developed a *system* for their publicity dates. He grinned. The woman took her responsibilities very seriously. *Fucking adorable.*

But his amusement turned to chagrin as he stood in

her cramped kitchen. Suddenly, he wasn't at all sure what he'd gotten himself into. What would she think of all this? A private, romantic dinner technically didn't help rebuild his reputation. *Shit*. Maybe he could tell her that it was for the lovely selfies they would get.

Chloe seemed to have strict categories for all the times they spent together—music, publicity and sex. It was as though she didn't want to share any other part of herself with him. *I'm not foolish enough to trust my heart to a man like you.* Her angry words rang through his head and an odd ache gripped his chest.

Their nights together were incredible. Making love to her often left him wrecked in a way that was impossible to describe but Chloe always held a part of herself back. She was quick to tease and make jokes the moment things veered toward the serious. She loved to mention how *fun* the sex was. A little too often. But wasn't that what he wanted? Wasn't he the one who told her that was all he had to offer?

Even so, he couldn't deny the growing panic inside of him. Every time he took a step toward her, she seemed to step back. He hungered to have as much of her as possible—more than just music, publicity and sex—but she kept twirling out of his reach. Had the sense of wrongness begin chafing at her? Was feeling *good* not enough anymore? Did she want to be with a man worthy of her heart?

The tomato he'd been holding became pulp in his fist. He cursed under his breath as he tossed the mess into the trash can. He grabbed the extra tomato and sliced it for the salad. It would've been nice to have two but he mistook the other one for a stress ball.

He took a deep, calming breath and forced himself to face the facts. Their fake-dating scheme and their… fling would soon come to its natural demise. He should be grateful for the parts of her she shared with him— not be greedy for more. He had to accept that eventually some lucky bastard would realize that she was the most amazing woman in the world and hold on to her for dear life. He was *not* that lucky bastard.

Something inside Anthony screamed and raged. *Chloe is mine.* The thought of another man claiming her made him want to punch a hole through the kitchen wall. The *facts* fucking sucked. Deliberately placing the kitchen knife on the counter, he stepped out onto the small balcony before he destroyed the rest of their dinner.

It wasn't like him to overthink their relationship. When his image was rehabilitated and the funds from the Soleil contract were secured, his life would return to what it had been. Something bleak and empty—made even more meaningless by the beds he shared with women whose faces became an unrecognizable blur.

He pressed the heel of his hand into his chest. Bleak or not, he would return to that life. His time with Chloe was fleeting. It was nothing more than a stolen moment. But didn't that mean he should make the most out of every second he got with her? Even if he didn't deserve happiness, didn't he at least deserve some memories to hold on to?

"What are you doing up there?" Chloe stood outside the graduate housing building—three stories down— with her hands cupped around her mouth. "Weren't you going out to see your friends tonight?"

"Busted." His surprise dinner was ruined but he couldn't hold back the smile that lit up his face. He welcomed the rush of happiness that filled him because it was only temporary. He didn't have to be afraid. It would all be over soon. "Oh, well. You might as well come upstairs."

"What?" She jutted her hips to one side, planting her fists on her waist. "You weren't going to let me inside my own house?"

"Just come up here." He needed to taste that smile—touch those sassy hips.

He couldn't wait for her to come to her apartment, so he rushed barefoot to the elevators. When the doors slid open and her eyes widened, he stepped inside and backed her into the wall.

"Anthony—"

He didn't let her finish her sentence. He crushed his lips against hers and demanded entry. She complied with a moan and he swept his tongue in, swift and possessive. She grabbed onto his shoulders as he wrapped her leg around his waist and ground into her.

"Um… Are you guys getting off?" someone asked with a nervous laugh. "Getting off the elevator, I mean."

The elevator must've been called back to the lobby. He took one step back from Chloe and turned around so his back covered most of her. "No, we're going to the third floor."

"Are you…" A striking black woman stood with her mouth hanging open, no longer laughing. "Are you Anthony Larsen?"

"Yes." He coughed into his fist.

"This is unbelievable." She rushed into the elevator

and pressed the buttons for the third and fourth floors. "I'm a huge fan. I heard you were dating Chloe, but wow."

Chloe peeked out from behind him and said with a little wave, "Hi, Ava."

"Hi, Chloe." Ava held out her fist and Chloe bumped it. Then eyeing Anthony with a sly smile, she said, "You go, girl."

"Yeah, I know." Chloe shrugged without a hint of modesty and pushed herself off the wall. "Okay. See you in advanced composition."

"See ya."

Anthony was so fascinated by the exchange that he hadn't realized they were back on the third floor. Chloe tugged him out of the elevator. He stared at her as they walked down the hallway.

"What?" She stopped in front of her apartment. "I'm not above capitalizing on the popularity being your *girl-friend* gives me."

He frowned at the air quotes she made when she said *girlfriend.* Chloe missed the look, taking her shoes off at the entryway. "Now, tell me what you're doing here."

"I am here—" he pushed his fingers through his hair "—botching up a surprise romantic dinner."

Her lips formed a perfect, plush O and he had no choice but to swoop in to kiss her. When he pulled back, she studied his face with a tender expression that made his heart hammer. *More, more, more.* He was starving for her affection. For any sign that he was more than a hookup to her.

"Tanner is going to get a kick out of posting all about it," he said to remind himself that it couldn't be.

Her lashes fluttered and he thought he saw a glimpse of disappointment in her eyes. But she flashed him a cheeky grin and said, "The surprise part is blown but will there still be dinner?"

"Yes." He pushed away the tumultuous thoughts that had stopped him from cooking. "I just need to throw it in the oven for a few minutes."

"And will there be—" she ran the tip of her finger down his chest, wiggling her eyebrows "—romance?"

Something about her brash tone made the ache return to his chest.

"In case I'm not being clear, I mean *sex* when I say *romance*." She pouted when he didn't respond right away. "Hey, Larsen. Are you going to salvage this romantic dinner or what?"

"Or what," he said hoarsely. He cleared his throat and gave her a playful wink. "Dinner and romance—by which I mean sex—coming right up. In that order."

"You're such a dork." Chloe laughed. "Let me change and help you."

"No help necessary." He gave her a firm push toward her bedroom door. "You're going to put your feet up and have a glass of chilled chenin blanc while I finish up."

"Careful." She threw him a sultry smile over her shoulder. "A girl could get used to this."

He stood staring after her, mesmerized by the sway of her jean-clad ass. Then he snapped out of it to finish making their dinner. He placed a filet of sea bass onto a piece of parchment paper and added olives, red bell peppers and seasoning before folding it into a little envelope. Once he made the second pouch, he placed them in the oven and set the timer.

Then he opened the wine he promised Chloe and brought out two glasses. As he was pouring, she came out of her room dressed in a cream wraparound dress that draped tantalizingly over her curves.

"Whoa." She rushed over and righted the wine bottle. The glass was filled to the rim. "I do love a generous pour but it'll be a shame to spill good wine."

Clicking her tongue, she carried both glasses to the sink and split the wine between the two. He stalked after her and pushed up against her. He ran his lips down the side of her neck and growled, "You're very distracting."

"What?" She tilted her head to the side, exposing more of her neck to him. "All I did was walk out of my room."

"In that dress." He lightly scraped his teeth near the base of her throat and she shivered against him.

"This dress?" She sounded perplexed. And breathless.

"Yes." He smoothed his hands down to her ass and squeezed. "It's begging to be stripped off of you. Now."

"So…" She placed the wineglasses on the counter by the sink and turned around in his arms. "Does this mean romance before dinner?"

"What dinner?" He cupped her full breasts, his mouth watering to taste their peaks—to feel them pebble against his tongue. He cursed when the timer for the oven went off.

"*That* dinner," she said with a smirk but her hands didn't stop roaming his chest. Then she sighed and pushed him back. "Let's see this romantic dinner you planned for us."

He hesitated for a full five seconds before he went

to retrieve the poisson en papillote out of the oven. The pleasure of feeding her a delicious meal would have its own rewards. He shooed her out of the kitchen and grabbed the salad from the fridge. They could eat that first while he let the fish sit for a few minutes to redistribute the juices. He served the salad with some crusty bread and sat down across from her.

"Ooh, fancy," she said, doing a little shoulder dance. She took a bite of her salad and moaned. "Oh, my gosh. This dressing is so good. Where did you get it?"

"I made it." He took a sip of his wine to hide his smile when her eyes doubled in size.

"You made this?" She shoveled two forkfuls into her mouth. "Mmm. It's delicious. How come you didn't tell me you're such a good cook?"

"It's just a salad," he said modestly but was inwardly thrilled at her reaction. "Let me bring out the main course."

He set the plate in front of her and sliced an opening at the top of the paper pouch to let the steam escape. Her mouth dropped open and he almost laughed out loud.

"Did you secretly train as a French chef or something?" She gave him the side-eye.

"I did take a couple of classes years ago when I was in Paris." He shrugged but he kept his eyes glued to her face as she took her first bite of the fish.

"Fucking hell." Her eyelashes fluttered close. "Sorry, but…fucking hell."

He burst out laughing. Making dinner for her was such a small thing, but damn if it didn't make him happy. "I'm going to take that as a compliment."

"When your looks go and people stop coming to your

concerts, you should open a restaurant." She winked at him as she took another bite.

"I'm not sure how to unwrap that compliment within an insult within a compliment." He mock scowled at her. "I'm tempted to take that fish away from you."

"Over my dead body." Chloe folded her upper body over the plate, then she grinned. "All right, all right. You're a fine chef. And you're *fine*. Period."

"That's more like it." He nodded. Sometimes she was so adorable he couldn't stand it.

He paused with his wineglass halfway to his lips. They couldn't remain friends. When this ended, it *had* to end. All of it. He couldn't be with her—in any capacity—and not want her. He wanted her more and more every day, and he thought less and less about Rachel… No, this couldn't go on.

"Anthony?" Chloe peered at his face. "Is something wrong?"

"No. Not at all." He forced himself to take a bite of his fish. "This really is good, isn't it? I'm awed by my own culinary prowess."

She rolled her eyes at him as he'd hoped and he relaxed into his seat. He had the now. That was all he would allow himself to have. So he would cherish it—cherish her—and be grateful that he had this much.

Sixteen

Chloe tucked her chin and giggled quietly as Anthony stepped out to make a quick call. But not quietly enough.

"Aren't you guys taking this fake-dating thing too far?" Angie asked, rifling through the sheet music on her stand. "I mean, you don't have to put on the lovebirds act in here. There's no one in the practice room to see but me."

"We're not acting like lovebirds." Chloe made pooh-poohing noises. "Don't be silly."

"Oh, no?" Her sister arched an eyebrow. "As soon as he whispered something in your ear, you literally giggled like a schoolgirl."

"What? He's funny," she said a tad defensively. "Besides, I'm technically still in school so it's entirely appropriate for me to giggle like a schoolgirl."

"Is there something you want to tell me?" Angie's exasperation was replaced by genuine concern.

"No, not particularly." Chloe felt guilty about keeping a secret from her sisters but she didn't want to deal with their overbearing protectiveness at the moment. She also didn't want them to worry unnecessarily. "Look, Unni. I know Anthony and I lay it on thick, but we just want to make sure that this faking dating thing sticks. He wants to do right by those kids. And besides, when have you ever seen me do anything half-assed? Hmm?"

"I guess so," Angie relented.

"This is only me doing my best." Chloe squeezed her sister's hand. "There's nothing between Anthony and me. Stop worrying."

"Yeah, sure." She rolled her eyes. "I'll just turn off my big-sister mode."

"Sorry about that," Anthony said as he walked back to his seat. "Tanner couldn't wait to share some good news."

"No worries. We were due for a break anyway," Angie said graciously.

"What good news?" Chloe demanded.

"Soleil wants to proceed with the campaign." Anthony's smile brimmed with relief. "We're scheduled to shoot the next commercial in a month."

"That's great. Congratulations." Chloe restrained herself from throwing her arms around his neck and kissing the hell out of him. She didn't need to give Angie confirmation that her worries were actually warranted.

"That *is* good news." Angie cast a meaningful glance

between Chloe and Anthony. "You guys did such a great job selling your *fake* relationship that you fooled the whole world."

But not her sister. Nope. She definitely didn't buy Chloe's reassurance that nothing was going on between them.

"Thank you," Anthony said, shooting Chloe a questioning glance. She gave him a small shrug.

His role as Soleil's spokesperson was no longer in danger. That was the whole point of their fake-dating scheme. She should be thrilled for him. But after tonight, they only had one more concert left in the season. Then he would return to his real life. Their fake relationship as well as their real one—did a fling even count as a relationship?—would come to an end much too quickly.

How had she allowed herself to forget that he would be leaving soon? The room began closing in on her. She'd forced herself to forget. She hadn't wanted to think about it—what his leaving would do to her and what that meant. But Chloe wasn't dense. She might've proved herself to be the queen of avoidance, but she was a smart woman.

She was in love with Anthony. Brilliant, kind, funny Anthony. Anthony who still loved his late wife. Anthony who thought it felt *wrong* to be with anyone who wasn't Rachel. Despite knowing *all* of that, she fell in love with him. Chloe's heart was not smart by any standard.

"All right. Break time's over," Chloe announced. She couldn't fall apart right now. She needed music to hold herself together. "Shall we run through the adagio movement once more?"

She lost herself in the music—in the sublime harmony the three of them created. She missed playing with Megan but Chloe was now so accustomed to Anthony's sound that she knew that was yet another part of him she would miss—painfully so. She poured her confusion, love and heartache into the music, because there was no one else she could tell. And the sound echoed back to her, soothing and healing.

This was what she had to do. She would hang on to her music to survive all that was about to come. Her love of music helped her cope with her mom's illness and death. It would help her through this loss as well.

"Chloe, that was exquisite," Angie whispered when they were finished, unshed tears and understanding glistening in her eyes.

"Thank you," she said with a sad smile.

Anthony squeezed her shoulder, his searching gaze roaming her face. She ducked her chin and let her hair fall like a curtain across her face. Yes, she loved him, but she couldn't let him know how she felt. It would gut him to find out that he'd hurt her.

Her heart would break when he left. But her love for him was true and beautiful, so her heartbreak would be, too. And it would be hers alone.

The three of them walked off the stage with their faces shining with joy. The performance had been a huge success and the audience was still clapping on their feet. There was no feeling quite like it—connecting so deeply with the audience. It was like spinning something beautiful from the strands of your heart and handing it to them, and watching them cradle it in their arms, cherishing your gift.

"God, that never gets old," Chloe gushed once they were backstage.

Angie laughed. "No, there's no feeling quite like it."

"It's addicting for sure," Anthony added. "I don't think I could ever quit."

Chloe smiled at him and he winked at her. The rakish slant of his lips told her that he wasn't just talking about the performance. Even as her toes curled at the sensual promise in his eyes, his words cut deep into her heart. Because he *could* quit her and would very soon. She turned away from him before her expression betrayed her thoughts and saw Johnny rushing toward them.

"Johnny?" She frowned. He was out of breath and dressed in jeans and a T-shirt. Not exactly concert attire. "I didn't know you were coming tonight."

"I didn't come to watch the concert," he said in a rush. "Your father sent me to take you and Angie to the hospital. He didn't want you guys driving."

"Hospital?" Angie picked up her skirt in one hand and started walking toward the exit. "Is it Megan?"

"Yeah." Johnny nodded. "She said she'll kill me if I interrupted your performance, so I waited until you finished. She's been in labor for almost two hours now."

"I'm going to kill you for not interrupting us," Chloe said through gritted teeth. "What if she already had the baby?"

"She hasn't." Johnny held up his hands. "Mr. Han said that you guys had plenty of time to get to the hospital."

"Where did you park?" Chloe retrieved her case and

put her instrument away while Angie and Anthony did the same. "Come on. Let's go."

Chloe turned to follow Johnny to his car when Anthony pulled her into his arms and kissed her on her forehead. "Everything's going to be fine. I'll meet you at the hospital."

She rose on her tiptoes and kissed him squarely on the mouth. She was excited and terrified and didn't have the emotional capacity to hold herself back. Besides, there were other people present to witness the kiss so she had a solid cover.

"I'll see you there," she said and hurriedly caught up with Johnny.

"I thought you were in a rush." Her friend didn't slow down even as he grumbled, "You guys were clinging to each other like you weren't going to see each other for days."

"Oh, give me a break." Chloe threw her hands up. "I can't give my boyfriend a goodbye kiss?"

"I'm just saying the hospital is less than half an hour away." Johnny shot her an exasperated glance. "If you can't stand to be apart from him for thirty minutes, I don't know how you're going to handle a long-distance relationship when he goes back to New York."

Chloe opened and closed her mouth. She had no idea where all this was coming from, but the reminder of Anthony's impending departure hurt like hell. She didn't understand. Johnny was the most easygoing, laid-back person she knew. Why was he doing this?

"Enough bickering," Angie interjected. "Let's focus on getting to Megan."

Chloe insisted that Angie sit up front with Johnny

because he was being too weird tonight. He had no idea that he'd buried a dagger in her heart with his words. There would be no long-distance relationship for her and Anthony. There would be no relationship at all. Now that she knew she loved Anthony, she wouldn't be content being his friend. Being in the periphery of his life would never be enough. It would hurt too much.

She squeezed her eyes shut. Something threatened to shatter inside her. Taking a deep breath, she pushed it all away and focused on the present. She was going to become an aunt. Her throat tightened with tears. She would have another person in this world to love.

But… Would *she* be someone that her nephew could love and look up to? Or would she become a bitter shadow of herself, unable to move on from the past? Someone who forever regretted burying her love inside her, too afraid to rock the boat.

For every endeavor she'd taken on in her life, Chloe had given her 100 percent. She was never satisfied until she knew that she had done her best, no matter the result. If she failed at something, she didn't want to spend sleepless nights wondering if she could've done more.

How was this any different? If she let Anthony go without telling him how she felt, she would wonder for the rest of her life if they might've had a chance if only she had confessed her love to him. The *what-if* would eat away at her—break whatever was left of her after she lost him. Yes, she was taking the risk of hurting him—because it would wreck him to hurt her—but she would be risking her heart as well. And if anything was worth risking *everything* for, it was love.

So Chloe would risk it all. She had to rock the fucking boat.

* * *

Anthony rushed toward the waiting room in the labor and delivery wing of the hospital. His friend was about to become a father but all he could think about was getting to Chloe. She'd gone pale and wide-eyed when she heard the news that Megan had gone into labor. He needed to be there for her.

He found her handing hot, steaming paper cups to Angie and her father. It was just like her to take care of her family before she thought about her own needs. *He* would have to take care of her.

As he stepped into the room, someone called out from behind him, "Hold the door please."

It was Johnny holding another pair of hot drinks. He nodded his thanks to Anthony as he walked past him and handed Chloe one of the cups. "I got you hot chocolate."

"Ooh, perfect. Thanks, Johnny." She blew at her cocoa and took a sip. "I'm already jittery enough without adding caffeine into the mix."

"I figured as much." Her friend grinned.

"Chloe." Anthony joined them and put his hand on the small of her back. When her father frowned at the gesture, he stopped himself from dropping a kiss on top of her head. "Mr. Han, how are you? Are you ready to become a grandfather?"

Minsung Han's stiff posture relaxed and he smiled widely. "I'm ready to spoil the little rascal. That's for sure."

"Joshua got held up in a meeting." Angie glanced at her watch, biting her bottom lip. "But he should be here soon. I'm going to check in with Megan."

Angie glided out of the waiting room, her sapphire

formal gown flowing behind her. None of them had stopped to get changed. Chloe looked good enough to eat in her figure-hugging gown, the same color but a different cut from her older sister's. Anthony made a concerted effort not to run his eyes over her body and busied himself with loosening his bow tie.

Chloe guided her father to some empty chairs on the other side of the room, laughing at something he said. Anthony was about to join them when Johnny came to stand beside him.

"You must be looking forward to going back to New York," he said. "Traveling and staying in hotels must get old quick."

"I'm enjoying my time in LA," Anthony said curtly. He didn't appreciate the reminder that his time here— his time with Chloe—was running out.

"I'm sure you are." A muscle jumped in Johnny's jaws. "But all good things must come to an end."

The fuck? The man was jealous, Anthony realized with a jolt. Johnny was jealous because he was head over heels for Chloe. Anthony had sensed as much the last time they had met but now he saw it with crystal clarity. He barely kept his lips from curling into a snarl.

But another thought struck him squarely in the chest. Johnny would be worthy of Chloe's heart. There was such easy affection between them. It could blossom into something more than mere friendship. Johnny could give her something true and lasting. Chloe was just too blind to see it.

The irony didn't escape Anthony that he could give Chloe her happily-ever-after by nudging her into the arms of another man. But if they couldn't be happy together, wasn't it better that at least she could be? It was for the best but he didn't have to like it.

"Not all good things come to an end." Anthony bared his teeth in a mimicry of a smile and left the other man seething.

He sat down beside Chloe and took her hand in his because he could—because she was still his for now. Then he noticed how cold her fingers felt and frowned.

"Hey, how are you holding up?" he said, leaning closer to her.

"I know Megan and the baby are going to be fine." She blew out a slow breath through her mouth. "But this waiting thing is pretty terrifying."

"She's your sister. Of course you're scared." He didn't care that her father was sitting right next to her. He pulled her toward him and kissed her forehead. Then he tucked her head under his chin and held her tight against him. "But like you said, they're both going to be fine. This hospital has some of the best doctors in the country. There is nothing to worry about."

She burrowed into his chest and he closed his eyes, breathing in her scent. He would lend her his strength and comfort her tonight. He would allow himself that much before he set her free. He tightened his arms around her as his chest twisted painfully.

Angie rushed back into the room and said breathlessly, "The doctor said she was ready to start pushing."

Chloe jumped to her feet and pulled her sister into a hug. Together, they walked back to the chairs and sat on either side of their father. The three of them held each other's hands and stared at the wall clock with unblinking eyes.

After a while, Joshua burst into the waiting room. "Did I miss it?"

"No, honey." Angie waved him over. "You're just in time. She's pushing right now."

"It's been thirty minutes," Chloe said. "Shouldn't the baby be here by now?"

"The doctor said it could take up to two hours for first-time mothers," Angie reassured her. "But it should be soon."

Joshua nodded his greeting at Anthony and Johnny and sat with the rest of the Han family, hardly breathing. It was approaching two hours when Daniel came to them, beaming despite his red eyes.

"You can come and see them now," he said huskily.

The waiting room exploded with sounds of relief and harried movement. Anthony and Johnny stayed back to allow the family to see the new mom and baby first. By an unspoken, mutual agreement, they sat at the opposite ends of the waiting room.

Angie, Joshua and Mr. Han returned half an hour later. Angie and her father were talking over each other about how adorable the newest member of their family was, both breathless with happiness.

"I like this grandpa business," Mr. Han announced. "Angie, you're the eldest. Don't you think you have some catching up to do?"

"And that's our cue to exit," Angie said, hurrying toward the door. "Joshua, you coming?"

Joshua bowed to his father-in-law with a grin that promised to get right on that and caught up with his wife.

"Daniel said you two can come in." Mr. Han covered

a yawn with his hand. "And I've been ordered to go home by my daughters. I guess some sleep won't hurt."

"Good night, Mr. Han," Anthony and Johnny chorused. The older man left with a nod, still smiling dreamily.

"All right." Johnny clapped his hands together. "Let's go and pretend the baby is cute."

Anthony arched an eyebrow at him.

"What?" The other man shrugged. "My niece looked like a squished potato when she was born. All newborns look like that."

Shaking his head, Anthony followed him out of the waiting room and headed for Megan's labor and delivery suite. His breath caught in his chest when he walked into the room. Chloe was holding a bundle wrapped like a burrito in her arms and the love shining on her face was breathtaking. He was shocked by the sudden aching desire to see her holding their baby someday, glowing with happiness. His steps faltered. The thought had come out of nowhere and blindsided him.

When Rachel was alive, he'd been too focused on his music to even think about having a baby with her. And when she died, he had no intention of committing himself to another relationship…to another woman. He had never thought about becoming a father.

But in that moment, he saw what his future could be with Chloe so clearly that it almost felt real…terrifyingly real…as terrifying as the hope that burst inside him.

"Congratulations, man." Anthony walked up to Daniel and gave him a one-armed hug. "You're going to be a great father."

"Thank you." Daniel swallowed. "I sure as hell am going to try."

Anthony approached the bedside where Chloe was standing with the baby. He focused his attention on Megan. "Hey, how are you feeling?"

"Like I pushed a ten-pound baby out of my vagina," Megan said wryly, but a beautiful smile lit up her tired face. "But mostly, I'm incredibly happy and grateful."

Taking a deep breath, Anthony put a hand on Chloe's shoulder as he looked down at his friends' newborn son. He was so tiny and precious that his heart ached. And the way Chloe was gazing at the baby as she cradled him against her chest... Anthony couldn't get enough air in his lungs.

"Isn't he the most perfect baby in the whole wide world?" she cooed. "I think I'm in love."

"Oh, great," Johnny grumbled jokingly. "More competition."

Anthony couldn't stop himself from stiffening at Chloe's side. Megan's sharp eyes searched his face, and he quickly turned away from her probing gaze.

"You're such a dingus." Chloe snorted. "Come hold the baby."

"Hells no." Johnny raised his hands in front of him like a shield.

"Anthony?" Chloe looked into his eyes and his world seemed to tilt.

He cleared his throat and held out his arms. She placed her nephew into his arms like the precious cargo he was. The baby was so small and light that Anthony was afraid of breaking him. After a minute, he returned the newborn to his mother.

"He's beautiful," he said.

"Thank you," Megan answered, still watching him. Her expression was kind but there was concern in her eyes.

"Chloe, are you ready to leave?" Anthony asked, putting his hand on the small of her back.

She leaned her head against his shoulder for a moment before she nodded. "Yeah, Megan needs to rest. And Daniel doesn't look much better."

"I'm fine," the new father insisted. Megan raised an eyebrow at her husband. "Maybe I'll take a little nap. That armchair in the corner reclines into a bed."

"Yes." Megan yawned loudly. "We all need a nap."

Johnny parted ways with them at the hospital parking lot with one last lingering look at Chloe. Anthony's hold around her waist didn't loosen until the other man was out of sight. He got into the car after he helped Chloe into the passenger seat and pulled out into the late-evening road.

But no matter how hard he tried to hold on to Chloe, she wasn't his to keep. Guilt rushed through him. He shouldn't *want* to hold on to her in the first place. He was sullying Rachel's memory with his infatuation with Chloe. Yes, he admitted it. He was infatuated with Chloe, but he needed to end it.

Maybe he wouldn't even be the one to end it. He was convinced that Johnny was the perfect match for Chloe. The two of them were the same age and her family already loved him while they didn't even trust Anthony. After spending the last decade drifting from one woman to the next, he didn't deserve their trust.

But most importantly, Johnny could offer Chloe something lasting and good.

Once she found out that Johnny was in love with her, she would probably run into his arms without a backward glance at Anthony. His hands tightened around the steering wheel but he forced himself to relax. This had gone on for long enough. Playtime was over. It was time to let go of Chloe.

After tonight…after just one more night to last him a lifetime…he would let go of her.

Seventeen

Chloe loved Anthony with her hands, her mouth and her body, willing him to hear her. To hear that she was offering him her whole heart. Even before she understood that she loved him, she'd been telling him that she loved him every time they made love. It had never been just sex for her. It had never been only about feeling good. It had always been everything. He was everything.

Tonight, she told him with her eyes, too. She let her love shine from them. She held nothing back and bared her soul to him. But he seemed lost in his own world. His every touch and kiss held a note of desperation that made her quake with fear. His hands were everywhere—as though to claim every inch of her—and he brought her to the brink of release again and again until she was writhing underneath him.

"Anthony...please," she moaned.

"Please what, kitten?" he drawled in a dark voice, his fingers sliding down her folds again. He pressed his thumb down on her clit. "You mean this?"

Her hips jerked against his hand. "Yes."

"And like this?" He rolled his thumb in a slow, maddening circle.

"Anthony." It was a warning and a plea.

"Or maybe this?" He made a leisurely trek down her body, stopping to kiss the peak of her breasts and to scrape his tongue across the sensitive skin of her waist. She was wild by the time his hot breath tickled her center. "I think this."

He licked her with the flat of his tongue like she was ice cream, melting in the hot sun. She hissed and shamelessly ground her hips into his face. He held her down with a firm grip on her hips as his wicked, talented tongue explored every throbbing inch of her.

"And this." He slipped his finger inside her while he flicked her swollen nub with the tip of his tongue.

His hand and lips moved on her simultaneously and she began seeing stars behind her eyelids. But she was afraid he would stop again. She buried her fingers in his hair and breathed, "Don't stop. Please don't stop."

He didn't stop and she shattered into a thousand pieces with his name on her lips. He guided her through the waves with gentle licks of his tongue and she finally melted into the mattress, utterly spent. Anthony rose above her and kissed her deeply. Again, she had that sensation of being claimed. It was thrilling but something niggled at the back of her mind. Something felt off.

"Are you okay?" he asked, brushing the hair out of her eyes.

"Yeah," she croaked. She could feel his hard length pressing against her entrance and she found that maybe she wasn't spent at all. Desire curled in her stomach again. She wasn't surprised, though. It had always been like this between them. She reached between her legs and wrapped her hand around him. "Are *you* okay?"

He groaned as though in pain as she smoothed her hand up and down his erection, his hips jerking helpless against her hand. She smiled as she reached for his nightstand to retrieve a condom. She pushed him onto his back and rolled it slowly onto him.

"Fuck, Chloe," he growled.

"That is kind of the plan," she said saucily as she straddled him. Giving him one last hard squeeze, she rose to her knees and poised her entrance over his proud length. He stared at her with wild eyes, control a thing of the past.

She smiled again. She did this to him.

Biting her lip, she sank into him, taking his whole length inside her. They groaned in unison. God, it felt so good, so right…because it was right. He was the man she loved. And as she rode him, she showed him just how much she loved him. Another climax was rising inside her but she fought it. She wanted to come with him. She was panting and her hair stuck to her slick face and neck, but she still rode him hard.

"Time for you to come for me, kitten," he said and surged into her, hips jutting off the bed.

She screamed as her orgasm slammed into her, even stronger than the first time. She had wanted him there with her but she couldn't complain. Just as she was floating back to earth, Anthony flipped her onto her back and wrapped her legs around his waist. He pistoned in and out of her, so deliciously rough, until he tipped his head back with a roar. Her inner muscles clamped around him as she joined him in the climax. Just as she'd wanted, he finally came with her.

As soon as they were able to breathe again, Anthony climbed out of bed and stalked to the restroom. He usually came back to join her in bed as soon as he cleaned himself up, but she heard the shower turn on. That uneasy feeling began roiling in her stomach again. She swung her legs off the bed to look for her clothes. An annoyed huff left her when she saw her sapphire gown on the floor.

They hadn't had time to change before running to the hospital, and they'd come straight to his hotel afterward. But she had a feeling she needed to be dressed for what was about to come. Chloe pushed down her anxiety and firmed her resolve. She wasn't leaving the hotel until she told him she loved him. She wasn't giving him up without a fight.

She tugged on her panties and bra, and stepped into her dress. With some acrobatics, she was able to pull the zipper up all the way. While she was at it, she made the bed because the evidence of their frantic lovemaking might become distracting. She didn't know exactly what she expected to happen but the butterflies in her stomach had turned into piranhas that were gnawing at her insides.

Chloe blew out a long breath and sat on the edge of the bed, facing the bathroom. By the time the shower stopped running, she'd wrung her hands raw. Anthony stepped out with a towel slung low on his hips and she couldn't stop her eyes from devouring him—from the top of his damp hair to his sculpted chest and stomach.

She dragged her eyes up to his face, but he wasn't looking at her. He walked over to his dresser and pulled on a pair of black shorts and a gray T-shirt. Throwing his towel over the back of a chair, he finally faced her.

"Do you want some tea?" Without waiting for her answer, he strode out of the room and into the sleek modern kitchen.

"I could actually use some hot chocolate," she murmured, following him. She needed something sweet and comforting.

"I can't even get your drink right." His laugh didn't hold much humor. "Johnny knew exactly what you needed at the hospital."

"It's not a big deal." She frowned at his back. "Johnny's known me for a long time. That's all."

"I think there's much more to it than that." He busied himself with turning on the teakettle and emptying a bag of Ghirardelli's hot chocolate into a mug.

"Anthony, I don't know what you're getting at." She went to stand beside him and peered up at his stony face.

"He's in love with you," he said in a flat monotone.

"Who's in love with me?" she asked in a bewildered voice.

"Johnny," he bit out. He pushed away from the counter and shoved both his hands into his hair. "He's the perfect man for you. Someone who could give you a lasting commitment. Someone you could…trust your heart with."

Chloe felt her blood drain from her face. Was he actually shoving her into the arms of another man? Was he that eager to be rid of her? "You're out of your mind."

"Am I?" He stalked up to her. "Anyone could see it. You're the only one who seems blind to Johnny's feelings for you."

"Why are you doing this?" she whispered, her voice hoarse with impending tears.

"I'm trying to help you find your happily-ever-after." Sarcasm dripped from his words.

"Why are you angry at me?" Her voice rose as her apprehension morphed into anger.

"Who says I'm angry at you?" he gritted through his teeth. "We're friends, aren't we? I'm just trying to be a good friend."

"By throwing me at the first man who shows interest in me?"

"I'm trying to *help* you." He threw his hands up.

"You're only trying to help yourself." Her chest rose and fell. *The coward. The goddamn coward!* "Are you so afraid that I would try to cling onto you? Is the possibility of a real relationship with me that abhorrent?"

Anthony stopped his agitated pacing and stared at her. He was suddenly so still that she couldn't even tell if he was breathing.

"I lied," she confessed in a quiet voice. "I told you I could never trust you with my heart but that's not true. I trust you, Anthony."

"You…lied? Why?" His stillness wavered at his softly spoken words but soon settled back. It felt as though he was listening to her with his whole body, afraid to miss a single word.

"I was angry and humiliated." She turned her face away. "My family decided that you were *bad* for me. Like I'm a helpless child. They thought they knew better than me. Even *you* thought you were bad for me."

"I am bad for you," he choked out.

"You don't get to decide that for me. I make my own choices even if they're mistakes. I'm strong enough to live with the consequences. It's my life...my heart." She sucked in a shaky breath. "You are all I want. I love you, Anthony. My heart belongs to no one but you. And I believe with everything in me that this—*us*—is not a mistake. It's *right*."

"No." He shook his head and stumbled back from her. "No."

"I'm not asking you to forget Rachel." Chloe felt her heart cracking but she couldn't stop now. It was her last chance to give her everything to him. "I know you still love her and a part of you always will. I don't want to take her place. I just want a chance to love you. To make you happy."

"I don't deserve to be happy." Agony replaced the stunned expression on his face. "Rachel died alone because I put my career ahead of our marriage. Because of my selfishness."

"How could you think that? What have you been putting yourself through?" She couldn't stop herself from cupping his cheek. He was hurting and she needed to comfort him.

"We were supposed to go out to dinner. To celebrate our anniversary," he began in a hollow voice. "But I was in the middle of recording an album and I didn't want to leave the studio until everything sounded perfect. I played the same piece again and again, wanting to get it right. I didn't even call her to let her know that I'd be late. She must've left me seven messages.

"When I got home three hours late, the house was… it was…a wreck. Someone had ransacked our home. There was overturned furniture and broken glass everywhere…" Anthony swallowed hard. "I found her on the floor of our bedroom. Her body was already cold. So cold.

"She was still wearing the pretty pink dress that I'd always liked. She hadn't given up hope that I'd be home for our anniversary. I can't imagine how scared she must've been. She bled out from a chest wound. Alone. She died waiting for me. Rachel died alone because of me."

"Oh, Anthony." She wrapped her arms around him and pressed her head to his chest. *Take solace in me. Please don't hurt.* "That was no one's fault but the robber's. The gunman pulled the trigger. Not you."

"If I'd kept my promise, she wouldn't have been home. If I'd gotten home earlier, I could've gotten her help before she bled out." Anthony's voice cracked. "She died because of me. She was only twenty-five. So full of life. And that life ended because of me. Don't you see? I can never forgive myself."

"No, please." She tightened her arms around his waist but he pushed her away.

"This is over," he said with cold finality.

"That was ten years ago." She was begging and she didn't care. "You can't keep punishing yourself for something that wasn't your fault. Rachel would never have wanted that."

"Don't—" he held up a finger "—talk about Rachel like you knew her. *I* knew her. Better than anyone in the world. And I know how best to keep her memory alive."

"Anthony." Hot tears streamed down her cheeks. They were for Anthony. They were for her. For them. "It doesn't have to be like this."

"I didn't want to hurt you." Anguish laced with anger flashed in his eyes. "*You* made me believe I couldn't hurt you. Now I have one more thing to hate myself for."

He lurched toward her when her legs gave out but he stopped himself and let her sink to the floor. She couldn't breathe. The kitchen swam around her. She needed to breathe. Digging her nails into her palms, she slowly sipped air into her lungs. A little more. Just a little more. When the room stopped spinning, she grabbed onto the counter and lifted herself to her feet. Anthony stood rooted to the spot, his fists clenched at his sides.

"I'm sorry I lied. And you don't need to accept my love." She lifted her chin and was proud of how steady her voice sounded. "Like you said, that was all my doing. My choice. I can live with the consequences, because I'm stronger than anyone believes me to be. Even stronger than I believed myself to be.

"But Anthony…please. Don't live the rest of your life in pain." Her voice broke at last—splintered with anguish. "Forgive yourself. Be happy."

Chloe walked to the living room and gathered her belongings. Anthony orbited around her. Like he couldn't bear to let her out of his sight but was afraid to get too close.

She didn't let herself think about that. She didn't let herself think about anything. All she could do was stave off the pain that was about to crush her. She couldn't fall apart here. Not in front of him.

Without a backward glance, she left the hotel room even though she felt him standing behind her. She left without saying another word even though she wanted to scream and rant. She did all she could. Chloe had fought for him with everything in her.

Now it was over.

Eighteen

Chloe didn't know how she'd gotten there, but she was home. She didn't know what time it was—sometime in the early hours of the morning—and she didn't have the strength to check. She knocked on the door until her knuckles felt raw, forgetting that she could ring the bell. She didn't think she could take another breath, live another moment. She was crumbling like a sandcastle being washed away by the sea.

Then there he was, holding open the door in a rumpled navy pajama set. Only then did she know that she would be okay. Not now. Not tomorrow. But he would do everything in his power to make sure that she would be whole again. His love would hold her together.

"Appa," she cried and fell into her dad's arms.

"It's okay, sweetheart. You're okay." He held her close and smoothed his hand down the back of her head.

He didn't ask what happened. He just loved her unconditionally now and forever. "Appa has you. I've got you."

For the next two days, she cried and slept, and ate when her dad cajoled her to eat. When she opened her eyes on the third day, she found the sun streaming into her old room. Someone had changed her into an oversize T-shirt and sleep shorts. Probably Mrs. Chung, their housekeeper extraordinaire.

Her teeth felt fuzzy so she trudged to the en suite bathroom to brush her teeth. She winced at her reflection in the mirror above the sink. Her face was a ghostly white and her eyes were nearly swollen shut. *Right.*

Chloe rummaged through her closet for some old sweats. After changing into them, she headed for her dad's study. She didn't remember what or how much she told him, but he had to be worried sick. She took a fortifying breath and knocked.

"Appa," she said through the door. "It's me."

"Come in. Come in."

Her dad was already getting to his feet when she opened the door. He came around his desk and wrapped her in his arms. She sighed with her whole body, going limp for a second. She was so lucky to have him. But she stepped back before she started crying again and wandered over to the sitting area.

"How are you feeling, baby?" Her dad took a seat beside her and squeezed her hand.

"Better," she croaked.

He waited patiently for her to speak but she didn't know where to start. She quietly cleared her throat.

"If I ask you who broke your heart, will you tell me?" His voice took on an edge that she rarely heard. This was the icy, formidable side of her dad that allowed him to build a successful electronics company from the ground up. It was also the side that would allow him to destroy anyone who dared hurt his daughters.

"No, Daddy." She smiled sadly. "I love you too much to see you go to jail."

"But someone did break your heart." It wasn't phrased as a question.

"It was the last thing he wanted to do." She was so quick to defend Anthony. But in the wake of her utter misery for the last two days, there was a burning anger inside her. "Maybe he didn't have to break my heart. He could've given us a chance."

"Anyone who doesn't fight for you isn't worthy of your love," her dad said with fierce loyalty.

"I know, but it seems my heart has a mind of its own." Her laugh turned into a sob.

"Your heart *is* you." Pride shone in his eyes. "Strong, kind, determined. It'll take time, but it'll heal. You will heal."

"Thank you, Appa." She threw her arms around his neck. "I'm so sorry for worrying you."

"That's what I'm here for, baby." He patted her back and she finally allowed her tears to fall. "I want to take away all your pain. I want to hurt *for* you, but I can't. When it comes to love, you need to feel all of it. Sometimes love hurts. Maybe *because* of this pain, the absolute joy, the fullness and the sense of coming home you'll feel when you find your other half will mean…everything. And you will find that love. I know you will."

Chloe nodded into her dad's shoulder. Even though Anthony gave up on them, she couldn't give up on him.

She would love him the best way she could—the only way he would accept—by getting through this. She would heal, then thrive, so he could be happy for her.

But that would take time. For now, she would concentrate on getting through their last concert without falling apart. She had to pretend that she was okay, because it would gut him to see her hurting. He had enough heartache in his life. She would send him off with a smile.

Anthony had done nothing as the best thing that ever happened to him walked out of his life. But he didn't have a choice. He couldn't betray Rachel's memory even if it meant breaking Chloe's heart. It hurt him, though. God, it hurt. It felt as though he was dying—drowning in his pain. If he felt this way, how much worse must Chloe feel? He wasn't even the one with the broken heart.

When darkness threatened to overwhelm him, he thought back to the brief moment when he had felt joy like he'd never known before—incandescent and glorious—because Chloe Han loved him. In that moment, he'd imagined that he was someone who could accept the love of an amazing woman like her. But he wasn't. He didn't even deserve that burst of happiness that her love had given him.

Anthony adjusted his bow tie in his rearview mirror and got out of his car. He trembled to his core at the thought of seeing Chloe again after the long, hellish week. He thirsted for the chance and dreaded it at the same time. It was their last concert. It might even be the last time he saw her. His steps faltered and he pressed the heel of his hand into his chest.

Time and distance. That was what he needed. He never thought he would survive losing Rachel but he did. He would survive this as well. He just had to fight his deepest instinct to kneel at Chloe's feet and beg her to take him back. That would be a disaster. He was broken and scarred. She would find someone better than him. Someone who deserved her love.

When he walked backstage, time seemed to slow. Chloe looked pale and a little tired, but she was as beautiful as ever. Angie leaned toward her and whispered something that had her throwing her head back and laughing. He smiled like an idiot as he stared at her. He loved the sound of her laughter even more than he loved the sound of the violin.

Unaware of what he was doing, he took a step toward her, drawn to her like a sunflower to the sun. He knew the moment she sensed his presence. The laughter died on her lips and all her warmth seemed to fade away. The stark pain in her eyes when they finally met his nearly brought him to his knees. But she blinked, then it was gone to be replaced by a small smile.

"There you are, Larsen," Chloe said lightly when his feet carried him the rest of the way to her. "Cutting it pretty close, aren't you? We're taking the stage in less than twenty minutes."

It was as though that night had never happened. It was as though their time together had never happened. He should be relieved to see that she was okay but his stomach lurched. Had she meant what she said about being in love with him? He stopped his ragged thoughts. He was a bastard for feeling anything but relieved to find her well.

"Yeah, Anthony." Angie glanced between them with obvious concern but forced herself to smile. "You should go warm up."

He realized Chloe hadn't told her sister what had happened between them. Was she trying to protect him? He had half expected Daniel to burst into his hotel room at any moment to beat him to a pulp. But his friend never showed up. Anthony wished he had. It would've been a relief to have Daniel knock him out.

"I warmed up at the hotel," Anthony said stiffly. His violin had been his only solace for the past week. He felt as though he would go mad every time he stopped playing, so he lost himself in his music every chance he got.

"That's good." Chloe glanced around the room listlessly. Maybe she wasn't as unaffected as she appeared to be. "I'm going to use the restroom and grab some water. I'll see you guys back here when it's time for us to go on."

"I love my sister," Angie said quietly when Chloe was out of earshot. "But sometimes she's too quick to put others ahead of her."

Anthony shook his head, not knowing what she was trying to say.

"I don't know what exactly happened between you two, but I know you hurt her." Her eyes flashed fire at him. "Don't fool yourself for one second that she's okay because she is hurting more than you can imagine."

"Angie..."

"We'll get through this last performance." She took a deep breath, fighting for composure. "Then, you can either make this right or get the hell out of her life."

Their performance that night was technically flawless but riddled with tension. The audience applauded them warmly nevertheless and they walked off the stage smiling their gratitude toward them.

"Good job tonight." Angie hugged Chloe and shook

his hand stiffly. "I'm going to find Joshua and grab some dinner. I'll see you guys later."

Angie strode off after a pointed look at him. Anthony stared at Chloe, helpless to look away. Her brave smile wobbled at the corners. And he didn't know—he just didn't know how to make any of this right.

"Chloe—"

She threw her arms around his waist and hugged him tightly. Just as suddenly—before he could wrap his arms around her warm, perfect body—she stepped back. "Goodbye, Anthony."

Just as he had done at his hotel, he stood frozen to the spot and watched Chloe walk away. For the last time. He felt pain shred through his soul. Angie was right. Chloe wasn't okay. She was hurting, and it gutted him utterly and completely. He would give anything to have her not hurt anymore.

Even your heart? he thought without volition.

That was impossible. He'd buried his heart with Rachel. Only a scorched, hollow cavity remained in his chest. Since she died, he'd dedicated his life to keeping her memory alive. If he devoted his time to accomplishing what she'd cared about most, then it would be as though a part of her had never died. She lived on through him—through his efforts to support Life Village. Rachel deserved at least that much from him.

Anthony would leave tonight. He would go help build the housing community for the children with his own two hands. If he worked hard enough, exhausted himself enough, maybe he could forget who he was…whom he loved.

Nineteen

Chloe packed the last of her boxes and looked around her bare apartment. It had been her home for the last two years while she attended graduate school. It was also the last place that held the most intimate memories of Anthony and her.

She clapped her hand over her mouth, muffling the sob that escaped. It had been over a week since she'd cried, but she'd spent nearly a month struggling with her pain. It had to stop. She would fight harder to move on.

She'd finally told her sisters about…well…everything, and they didn't keep secrets from their husbands. So Megan had to tackle Daniel to the ground to stop him from flying out to New York to pummel Anthony. But it turned out he wasn't even in New York. He'd been spotted in Arizona at the Living Village housing community's construction site. Yes, she still stalked him on social media. Yes, she knew it wasn't healthy, but she just wanted to make sure he was okay.

Her sisters insisted that Chloe should be more concerned with her well-being since Anthony was the one who ended the relationship. They knew his reasons for ending things and deeply sympathized with him but Chloe was their sister and she came first for them. And that was one of the things that made her more worried about Anthony than herself.

Sure, she was hurting, but she hadn't let it fester. She cried when she wanted to. She vented to her sisters. She let her dad coddle her and let Mrs. Chung feed her. And she sometimes indulged in fantasies of her fierce brothers-in-law beating some sense into Anthony—they certainly had volunteered their services often enough. Her favorite self-care was to hold her baby nephew, Peter, in her arms and breathe in his sweet baby scent. She could get through this. But Anthony had no one. Especially not in Arizona.

Once Daniel's temper cooled enough, he became worried about Anthony and reached out to him. Anthony politely refused to accept the olive branch. Chloe knew why and it broke her heart. He didn't think he deserved Daniel's forgiveness.

"Hi, guys. Please come in." Chloe waved in the two moving guys. "It's all ready. You have the address, right?"

"Sure do," one of them replied, hefting a box onto a dolly.

She was moving back home at her dad's behest. He said he was lonely without any of his girls at home. But she knew he just wanted to take care of her. She didn't mind that one bit for now.

"We've got this, miss," the other man added. "We'll meet you over there."

"I should help," Chloe insisted. But when her attempts to help only slowed the guys down, she finally decided to get out of their way. "Thank you so much."

She shouldered her purse and picked up her viola case. After a lingering glance around the apartment, she walked out with her shoulders back and chin held high. Despite the chaos that Anthony Larsen had brought into her life and her heart, she'd succeeded in finishing graduate school with her master's degree. It might not feel like it at the moment, but a bright, new chapter was about to start in her life.

Anthony had done everything he could to distract himself from missing Chloe. He drank himself into a stupor. He worked himself ragged on the construction site. And every time he wanted to run to her, he reminded himself of how he cut Rachel's life short— how he didn't deserve to be happy—because being with Chloe would make him happier than he'd ever been. But even the guilt couldn't outweigh his longing for the incredible woman he'd left behind, which made him feel like the worst kind of bastard. And on and on, the vicious cycle of guilt, resentment and regret spun around and around.

He gazed blearily around the construction site. He'd hardly gotten any sleep the night before and he was exhausted from working all day in the sun. So when someone called out in warning, Anthony reacted too slowly—realized too late that a wooden beam was tumbling down toward him.

"Anthony!" He heard people yelling his name. "Anthony!"

"Sir, can you hear me?" a man said close to his ear. He winced as a bright light flashed in his eyes. "Did you lose consciousness?"

"No, I don't think so," he croaked.

Or had he? He wasn't sure what happened. He hurt everywhere. No, he hurt significantly more at one specific spot. God, was it his hand? His arm? Would he ever play his violin again? He tried moving his arms and legs but he couldn't move anything. Something was pinning him down.

The ambulance…the emergency room…the lights hurt his head. Too many people peered into his face, asking too many questions. Then something warm seeped into his arm through his IV and blessed oblivion claimed him.

His eyelids felt weighed down by iron ingots. He forced them open with Herculean effort. After taking in the hospital room, his gaze finally focused on the big, angry man sitting by his bed.

"You're a fucking bastard," Tanner roared as he shot to his feet. "A stubborn, reckless fool."

"Good to see you, too." Anthony smiled weakly. He felt drained and light-headed.

"Do you realize how fucking lucky you are?" His friend scrubbed his face with his hands and Anthony finally saw how exhausted Tanner looked. "That beam could've crushed your hand or your arm. Your career could've ended. Just like that. You. Could've. Died."

Anthony sighed in relief as he raised his hands and looked down at them. Other than a few scrapes and cuts, they were intact. Next, he moved his arms and shoulders. They were a little sore but otherwise fine. But his right leg was encased in a cast up to his knee and raised above heart level. He pushed his upper body off the bed to get a better look but settled back with a groan, grabbing his right ribs.

"Fractured shin and a few cracked ribs," Tanner muttered. "Like I said, fucking lucky."

Anthony couldn't say anything as he caught his breath.

"You had no business being on that construction site in the first place." His friend had donned his manager hat. "I told you—no, begged you—to reconsider."

"I wasn't thinking clearly," Anthony said hoarsely.

"No, shit."

He laughed, then moaned. "Don't make me laugh."

"I wasn't trying to." Tanner finally cracked a smile. "But I probably should torture you for putting me through this."

"When can I get out of here?"

"They're going to keep you here overnight for observation to make sure you don't have a concussion," his friend explained. "I told them you had a hard skull but they won't take my word for it."

"God, you asshole." Anthony laughed and hissed through his teeth. "That really hurts."

"Good." Tanner sat back down and leveled him with a stare. "Did that accident knock some sense into you?"

"Yes." It really had. He'd been running away from himself for the past month—for the past ten years—and it had taken this accident to force himself to stop and face his fear. "I know what I need to do."

"And what is that?" Tanner asked softly.

Anthony had known all along that he was in love with Chloe but he thought loving her was *wrong*. He had begun to resent Rachel, thinking she was the reason he couldn't be with Chloe. But no. *That* was where he was wrong. She lived and loved with abandon and would've hated seeing him hurt like this. *I'm so sorry, Rachel.* She would be heartbroken if she knew how he'd been punishing himself for the past ten years.

It had always been him. He had been afraid to let Rachel go because he'd felt too guilty to move on. And he refused to let himself fall in love because he was terrified of losing someone he loved again. He'd allowed guilt and fear to engulf him—to propel him into leaving the person he loved before he could lose her, too. When he looked at himself with clarity, it absolutely made no sense. But no one ever said fear was logical.

"I can keep Rachel's memory alive without denying myself a life worth living." Anthony stared at the ceiling as tears seeped out of the corners of his eyes. "I need to be true to myself and my love for Chloe. That's what Rachel would've wanted. Chloe and I can honor her memory together by celebrating her life and her dedication to children."

"Damn straight." His friend's voice was thick with emotion. "That's the smartest thing you've said in ten fucking years."

If he'd died without telling Chloe that he loved her

with everything in him…if she had lived her whole life believing that he didn't love her… He couldn't even finish the thought. How could he have risked that? How could he have broken Chloe's heart, the most precious thing in the world to him?

More than anything, Anthony hated himself for hurting Chloe. But he had to show himself the same grace he showed the people he loved. If he'd been the one to die, he would never have wanted Rachel to torture herself with guilt. The last thing he wanted was for people he loved to suffer. And maybe Chloe didn't want him to hurt either because she loved him.

But what if it was too late? After what he did, she might not love him anymore. She might not take him back. *God, please no.*

"Hey, do me a favor." Anthony turned to his friend. "Book me a flight to LA for tomorrow."

Anthony was done letting fear rule his life. He fucked up. He might not deserve her forgiveness. But he would fight for it. He would fight for Chloe with everything he had.

Twenty

Chloe would have recognized that sound anywhere. Anthony was outside her window, playing his violin for her. She tried ignoring him for an hour. Then she finally relented and tiptoed to the window and cracked it open a sliver. But she didn't look outside. She wasn't ready to see him, yet.

She pulled up a chair beside her window and leaned her head against the windowsill. She closed her eyes and let the music seep into her veins, into her bones. She wiped a hand across her face and found it wet. She didn't realize she was crying.

Chloe vaguely noticed her dad hovering in her doorway. Then with a sigh, he was gone. She didn't know how much time had passed when Mrs. Chung brought a tray with tea and sandwiches and placed it on a small table next to her chair. The sun faded into night and the music did not stop.

Musicians spoke truer with their music than with words, and she understood exactly what Anthony was saying to her. There was a lightness to his music that she hadn't heard in over ten years. A weight that had muffled his music had at last lifted. The melody took flight with unhindered wings. Sobs wracked her body. Finally…finally he'd forgiven himself. He'd stopped punishing himself for Rachel's death.

But more than anything, she heard his love for her. His pain and regret made her chest clench tight but the sweet tenderness of his hope soothed her. He loved her. Anthony loved her. If she let him, he would stand outside and play until the moon took its place in the sky. With a shaky hand, she pushed open her window and looked outside at last.

She rose to her feet with a horrified gasp, knocking her chair over in the process. She raced down the stairs with her hand over her heart and threw the front door open. She didn't bother with shoes as she ran to where Anthony stood, leaning against a tree.

"Anthony," she said raggedly. She grabbed fistfuls of his shirt and shook him. He wrapped his free arm around her waist and tugged her to him. "What happened to you? Why are you hurt?"

"Construction accident, but that's not important right now," he murmured into her hair.

"Why didn't you say anything?" She sobbed into his shirt.

"Shh." He smoothed his hand down her hair.

"You've been standing out here for two hours."

"I would've played for you until the next morning if I had to," he said. "I would've come back every night until you forgave me. I would play for you every night for you to love me again."

She pulled back from his embrace but reached out to grab his waist when he swayed. She raised panicked eyes to his. "Come inside with me."

"Chloe, please," Anthony entreated.

She jutted her chin and poked her index finger into his chest. "I'm not saying another word until you're safe inside the house and sitting beside me."

"Would you mind?" He handed her his violin with a grimace as though lifting his arm caused him pain.

"Of course." She crouched by the case leaning against the tree and carefully placed his instrument inside.

By the time she stood up, Anthony was leaning against a crutch, breathing through his mouth as though he was bracing himself for something. Before she could ask him what was wrong, he wheezed, "Let's do this."

She had to skip to keep up with him as he hobbled to the front door and inside the house. She closed the door and hurried to his side as he stood with one palm planted on the foyer wall, chest rising and falling rapidly.

"Are you okay?" She peered at his face and realized that he was far from okay. He was alarmingly pale and his forehead was beaded with sweat.

"Just…give me…a minute." He winced as he straightened. "Can… Can we sit down somewhere?"

"Oh, my God. I'm so sorry." She glanced frantically

around. She wasn't sure he would be able to make it to the living room.

"I'm fine." He nodded encouragingly. "Just lead the way."

When they finally got to the living room, Chloe helped Anthony onto the sofa and sank down next to him. "What else is wrong with you?"

"I don't even know where to start with that one." He grinned sheepishly.

"Don't even try to charm me." She narrowed her eyes at him. "Tell me where else you're hurt."

He held up his hands. "I just have a few bruised ribs. Well...maybe they're fractured?"

She promptly burst into tears. It was too much. He loved her and he was hurt and it was too much.

"I'm sorry." He pulled her into his arms. "I'm so sorry."

"I know." She sniffled.

"And I love you, Chloe." He kissed her on the temple. "I love you so much."

"I know." She hiccupped.

"You know?" He leaned back just enough to look into her eyes.

"Only a man in love would serenade a woman for two hours on a broken leg." She arched an eyebrow at him with more bravado than she felt. Her insides were quaking because Anthony was sitting across from her with love shining from his eyes. "With broken ribs."

"That's true." He chuckled, then groaned. "But you have to stop being adorable and making me laugh."

"I think you planned it this way," she said with a decisive nod.

"Planned what this way?" His head cocked to one side. God, she'd missed that.

"You came here all injured so you wouldn't have to grovel as hard for me to take you back." She leaned in and kissed him on one corner of his eyebrow.

"Did it work?" He kept his tone light but his eyes searched her face frantically.

"How can you not know?" she whispered. "I love you, Anthony, and I'm going to make you so happy."

At last, he pressed his lips against hers in an achingly tender kiss, his fingertips brushing against her cheek.

"*We* are going to be so happy." He drew his lips across her jawline, drawing a shiver from her. "I love you, Chloe. And I want to show you how much every day of our lives."

With a moan, she clasped his face between her hands and kissed him with everything in her. He responded by deepening the kiss, the familiar passion sparking to life between them. She tried to pull away when he grunted with pain but he drew her back with a low growl.

"You're not going anywhere," he said.

She let him kiss her again but she slowed it down until he sighed and rested his forehead against hers.

"We still have a lot to talk about." He buried his fingers in her hair like he was afraid she'd pull away.

"We have time," she said softly.

"Time to talk and figure everything out." He kissed her lightly on the mouth as though he couldn't stop himself.

"And time to be happy." Her heart stuttered in her chest. "Together."

"Always." Tears filled his beautiful hazel eyes. "I love you."

"That's music to my ears." She sighed against Anthony's lips as happiness sang through her veins.

Epilogue

Chloe grinned with a hint of viciousness. She rubbed her hands together then checked in on her teammate.

Are you ready to serve a major dose of ass kicking to these suckers?

You're as bloodthirsty as ever, NightMusic.

And you're starting to sound soft in your old age, SerialFiddler.

A crumpled piece of napkin bounced off her head.
"Hey, watch it." She glared at Anthony, who was sitting across from her at his dining table.
His eyes were already back on his laptop and he

typed rapidly into his keyboard, You're the idiot who's in love with this soft, old man.

Anthony bought a house in LA six months ago. They sometimes stayed at his place in New York when he had concerts in the East Coast, but sunny California was definitely their home base. It was where her family was and he would never take her away from them. While it took some convincing—Anthony groveled like a pro—her family had forgiven him. And though he liked to pretend otherwise, even her dad adored him.

She chortled with delight and responded, And you're the lucky bastard who's in love with this idiot.

When you're right, you're right, my dearest NightMusic.

SerialFiddler, are you ready to get serious? The game's about to start.

Anthony cleared his throat and his chair scraped against the floor as he adjusted his seat. He tugged on the collar of his shirt, then smoothed a hand down his hair.

"What's going on?" Her eyebrows furrowed in worry. "Why do you seem nervous? It's been a while since we played, but you know you're good."

He answered as SerialFiddler, You said to get serious. I'm just getting ready.

Jeez, I didn't mean to make you nervous. It's just a game.

Actually, it's my whole life. You're my whole life.

Chloe's eyes shot up from her screen but Anthony had his head stubbornly lowered. Then the next message from SerialFiddler came in.

NightMusic, will you make me the happiest man alive and marry me?

She clapped her hands over her mouth but soft sobbing noises escaped through her fingers.

Anthony finally looked up at her and his hazel gaze bore into her soul. "*League of Legends* is where I first met you. It's the place where I was my real self even before I figured out who I really am. Something I didn't figure out until I thought I lost you."

She dropped her hands to the table and took a shuddering breath. "And who are you, Anthony?"

"I'm yours, Chloe. That's who I am."

Her fingers shook and slipped off the keys as she typed, And who are you, SerialFiddler?

Your archnemesis.

She snorted.

Your frenemy, he continued. Yours. All yours. Now and always.

Chloe didn't bother to wipe away her tears because more would replace them anyway.

As I'm yours, she typed. Forever.

"Is that a yes?" His voice broke on the last word. He rushed to her side and knelt beside her. "Will you let me show you how much I love you—how much you mean to be—for the rest of our lives?"

"I'll never try to replace Rachel." She gently took his face in her hands. "I know she'll always have a place in your heart."

"She will." He nodded solemnly and pressed his hands over hers. "But *you* are my heart now, Chloe."

"Oh, Anthony." *Can a person die from too much happiness?* "Nothing would make me happier than to be your wife."

"I love you." With tears in his eyes, he pressed his lips reverently against hers. "I love you so much that I can't breathe sometimes. I don't know what I did to deserve you but I'll never let you go."

"Anthony, you deserve me, my heart and all the happiness you can handle because you're you." She wrapped her arms around his neck. "I love you because you're you. You're my everything."

Chloe squealed as he picked her up from her chair and headed purposefully to his bedroom. She kissed the side of his neck and his arms tightened possessively around her. He was going to claim her—she could see it in the intensity of his handsome face—and she was going to enjoy every moment of claiming him right back. She had found her true love—her happily-ever-after.

Rocking this particular dreamboat had been the best decision of her life.

* * * * *

Anne Marsh writes sexy contemporary and paranormal romances, because the world can always enjoy one more alpha male. She started writing romance after getting laid off from her job as a technical writer—and quickly decided happily-ever-afters trumped software manuals. She lives in North Carolina with her two kids and five cats.

Books by Anne Marsh

Harlequin Desire

The True Love Experiment
The Inheritance Test

Harlequin Dare

Hookup
Have Me
Hold Me

Visit the Author Profile page
at Harlequin.com for more titles.

You can also find Anne Marsh on Facebook,
along with other Harlequin Desire authors,
at Facebook.com/HarlequinDesireAuthors!

Dear Reader,

Too-romantic Wren Wilson is a dating disaster. She believes Mr. Darcy 2.0 is just around the corner—or the next date. Her grumpy best friend, Nash Masterson, is her unromantic polar opposite, dismissing love as mere chemistry. He's a successful scientist, so he should know.

When Nash's acquisition of a new chemical company hits a snag, he reluctantly turns to Wren for help. He must convince the CEO that he's a likable family man, while she may have told her sisters a tiny white lie about her amazing new boyfriend. She'll bid for him in next week's Martha's Vineyard bachelor auction, and in exchange he'll fake date her at an upcoming family wedding.

But as one fake date leads to another and the wedding draws nearer, Wren's feelings for Nash start to look a whole lot less friendly, and Nash is beginning to realize that feelings might not be so terrible after all. Maybe it's time for a true love experiment. I love a friends-to-lovers, opposites-attract story, especially when the hero is stern and grumpy to the heroine's sunshine—and I hope you do, too.

Here's to happy endings!

Anne Marsh

THE TRUE LOVE
EXPERIMENT

Anne Marsh

One

Wrenley Wilson was a dating disaster.

That last breakup made it official.

Relationships ended all the time, but her endings somehow always turned out to be the beginning of someone else's happily-ever-after. She was the Father Christmas and Cupid of relationships, delivering true love to everyone but herself.

The proof was right in front of her on her laptop: a save-the-date e-card from her last boyfriend. After she and Noah had broken up six months ago, vowing not to let their short romantic relationship affect their long-term friendship, her cousin May had promptly asked him out. As Wren had just returned from watering Noah's plants and taking his absolutely adorable French bulldog for a walk, she'd known Noah was away. She'd even known, quite academically, that he was away with

May, her replacement. What she hadn't seen coming was their engagement. Noah hadn't been Wren's one and only, but part of her regretted she wasn't the woman in the e-card, standing on a Maldivian sandbar while the love of her life knelt with a truly spectacular ring.

You couldn't get the guy to bring you flowers even once. He never even tried to romance you.

"Third time's the charm," Emily snickered on Wren's laptop. Even through the screen, she could see how sunlight flooded the kitchen in the gorgeous Napa Valley house Emily had built with her wife so that they had room to grow their family.

"You should open a matchmaking business," Amelia chimed in from her San Francisco office. "Your slogan could be 'I break him, you buy him!'"

Wren loved her older sisters, but they were ruthless when it came to Wren's love life. This wasn't the first time they'd pointed out how Wren's ex-boyfriends went on to fall madly in love with the very next woman they dated. Instead of leaving a string of broken hearts behind her, she'd left diamond rings and Instagram-worthy proposals.

Her mother frowned at the camera. "Are you seeing anyone now?"

Amelia rolled her eyes. "There's a great new dating app. I'll send you a link."

Either Amelia or one of her engineer friends had probably developed the app during their weekend downtime or something equally overachieving. Amelia ran the engineering division at a hot, new software start-up. The Wilsons were all happy and successful and Wren loved them to bits, but while she believed there was room for one more person in their happy circle (her very own person), she was never finding him through a family setup.

"No," Wren said. And then because she was a polite person, a *nice* person even when she wasn't trying to be, she added: "Thank you. I'm good."

Emily snorted. "No one finds the perfect man on a dating app. Dick pics, yes. Romance, no."

Her family considered this with varying expressions of amusement. The teasing was good-natured. Academically, Wren knew this. She liked a laugh and a joke, too. It was just that, seeing yet *another* of her exes go on to find true love stung. How hard could it be to find someone to fall in love with and who would actually love her back?

Hard, the obnoxiously honest voice in her head said. *You should consider a cat as a lifetime companion.*

"Whoever she meets, he'll need to be very romantic," Emily continued. "The reformed Mr. Darcy kind of man. A chivalric knight who sweeps her off her feet, white horse optional but highly recommended. The problem is that men like that simply don't exist, not outside the pages of a book."

"I'm not looking for Mr. Darcy 2.0—"

Her mother interrupted before Wren could explain that she just wanted a nice guy, someone a little sweet and who didn't require hours of executive coaching to pay attention to her. "You really are too romantic for your own good."

Amelia flashed her phone with her own save-the-date electronic card. "Let's focus."

"Who," Emily asked, blunt as always, "are you bringing to the wedding? Lola?"

Lola was lovely, but as Wren's best friend, she'd ranted rather creatively about Noah's shortcomings directly to Noah himself. There was no way Wren took her to the wedding. She reached for the name of a nonplatonic date…and came up empty. Surely there had to be someone?

Wren had gone out on coffee dates after breaking up with Noah. In fact, the consumption of caffeinated and alcoholic beverages occupied far too much of her social life. She'd met up for drinks with the cousin of a friend's dentist's accountant's…well, with someone. She'd chatted with guys on her phone. But none of those brief encounters had been exciting and none of the men had felt right. She was just going through the dating motions, and both she and her dating candidates deserved better. So she'd stopped dating. Temporarily.

"I'll find you someone to take." Amelia rolled her eyes. "Someone charming, tall and successful enough to stick it to Noah. A better kind of doctor."

This was quite unfair to poor Noah, who was a urologist. Urology was an important medical field, even if it was a conversation killer at family get-togethers.

Her phone buzzed on the desk next to her laptop and she gave the screen a quick, guilty check. A series of Stetson emojis filled the messaging app—Nash had texted. Even though he was the least country person ever, he had a cowboy name and so she'd saved him in her contacts with a string of cowboy hats. His contact photo was a shot she'd snuck of him lecturing her chemistry section eight years ago in her senior year of college. The photo filter gave him horns and a curly moustache because he was far too serious for his own good. Or so she told him regularly at their friendly Tuesday taco meetup. Hopefully, he wasn't about to cancel on her today.

Nash was busy taking over the world of chemical engineering, so everyone wanted to talk to him and he often had last-minute meetings.

His text turned out to be even shorter and pithier than usual: SOS.

Which meant…it meant…

Had he fallen down a well? Perhaps space aliens had invaded and beamed him up to the mother ship? Nash wasn't the type to run out of gas on the freeway or get lost in the rabbit's warren of their local IKEA. Still, even for Nash, SOS was annoyingly cryptic.

Of course, cryptic was terribly on-brand for him. Nash was closemouthed and curt and did a masterfully broody, stern look, usually in response to some playful foray of her own. She couldn't remember the last time—or *ever*—when he'd asked for help. It was a nice change, and a shockingly warm, pleasurable feeling bubbled up inside her. Usually, they just ate lunch together on Tuesdays while she overshared about her life and tried to pry the details of his out of him. They'd known each other eight years: her senior year of undergraduate, the six years of her doctoral program and now this last year she'd taught at Pomona College, near his company headquarters. But never once, in all that time, had Nash asked for *her* help. Nash didn't let his guard down easily and it had taken three years to progress from friendly acquaintance to their weekly lunches.

She could ask Nash to go with her to the wedding. He was single, she was single, and he'd probably help her out. Except that she didn't want a platonic date or a friendly assist. She wanted the real deal, not sympathetic smiles from her friends and family as they realized that she'd brought a guy who had friendzoned her on the very first day of their acquaintance.

She forced her attention back to the conversation her sisters and mother had been carrying on—entirely without her, thank you very much—about her dating life. They'd resurrected the usual stories, including the one where her five-year-old self swore she'd marry the King of England and not some second-rate European prince.

"So," her mother asked, "are you bringing someone to Noah and May's wedding? Because if not, we could be each other's date for the big day." She smiled encouragingly. "It would be lovely, being the Wilson girls all together."

Amelia pointed through her screen. "Let's focus on the real issue. Wren. Do you, or do you not, have another boyfriend?"

Wren's mouth was dry, her heart beating too fast. This wasn't… Well. She blurted out some very wishful thinking. "I…do."

Ouch. The silence that followed was less disbelieving and more *Oh God, here we go again*. The dating sea was full of fish and she'd just pluck one out for the wedding. No big deal. She'd tried dating apps and those horrible six-second speed-dating meetups and even a year of saying yes when someone said "My dentist is single, would you like his number?"

"You're seeing someone?" Emily restated. "Seriously?"

Was that a "seriously, are you seeing someone?" or a "are you seeing someone seriously?" It was best, Wren knew, to be very clear with her family.

"I am. Seeing someone. Quite seriously and in all seriousness."

"Isn't this rather fast, Wren?" her mother murmured.

"Of course it is," Amelia snapped. "But it hardly matters, does it? The wedding isn't for six weeks. Wren will be single long before then."

"I will not be."

"You could find someone perfectly nice," Emily cut in. "You know you could. Just take your time. No rushing in, certain that whatever new guy you've met is the one, only to give up after a few days or weeks. Relationships aren't paint colors that you slap on the wall to see which one you want to try today."

Embarrassment hit her in a dizzying rush. Did she hurry? Or did she just seize the moment and commit to it wholeheartedly? And was that such a character flaw?

When in doubt, brazen it out. "Perhaps I've already found him."

"Bet me," Amelia said. "Prove it."

"You're betting that I fail at another relationship?"

Amelia sighed. "I want you to be happy, Wren. We all do. You're twenty-nine years old, nice, smart and a junior professor, yet you're a serial dater when you claim you're looking for Mr. Right. You never give anyone time to prove that he could be the one."

"That's not true." Was it?

"You get bored, Wren," Emily piled on. "It's all fun

and games in the early days, but then you move on before there's any chance of something serious really developing. You want someone to be with you, to care, but that takes time. You're too impatient."

She'd tried. She had. Well, maybe not so much with Noah—they'd never been right for each other—but all those other times. Which just made it all her fault, didn't it? She wasn't enough, hadn't done enough. She blinked back angry tears. Of course they thought she dated too fast, too often. That she should have settled for someone years ago.

"I'll take that bet," she snapped. "I bet that I'll still be in a happy, serious relationship when Noah and May's wedding rolls around."

"You'll bring your mystery man to the wedding?" Emily asked.

Wren doubled down. "Absolutely."

Emily nodded. "I bet you won't."

"I wish you wouldn't," her mother hedged.

"Too late," Wren said at the same time that Emily asked, "What are we betting?"

"The usual five?" Wren and her sister had traded a single five-dollar bill back and forth since they'd been teenagers. The winner of their latest bet got the framed bill and family bragging rights.

"Ugh. No. Not this time." Emily's face took on a gleeful look that did not bode well for Wren. "If you lose, I get to pick your next boyfriend."

Danger. Danger.

"And when *you* lose, I'm naming your firstborn child. Robin tops my list."

The rest of the conversation devolved into good-natured insults about Emily's ideas on a proper boyfriend and Wren's avian-inclined baby-naming skills. Wren held her breath, hoping they wouldn't ask the name of her secret boyfriend. She was afraid that if they kept talking too long, she might break down and admit there was no wedding date. Or cry. And then Emily would demand she concede their bet now and would probably proceed to fix Wren's love life with the well-intentioned tenacity with which she had steered her baby sister through public school and beyond.

"I have to go," Wren said. "Nash needs me."

Amelia groaned. "The one who does a stellar impression of a grumpy iceberg?"

"He's lovely," Wren lied. Nash was an acquired taste, like blue cheese or durian. She felt a twinge of guilt for lying to her mother and sisters. Not about Nash—like the prickly Southeast Asian fruit, he *was* wonderful, once you peeled back his cold, hard outer layer—but about her wedding date. She'd just have to find someone fabulous to go with her.

And then convince him to act wildly in love.

It could happen, she told herself.

"Send proof of life," Emily yelled as Wren lowered the lid of her laptop. "I want a picture of this wonderful mystery man you're seeing."

She was doomed.

Two

"He's a hottie, isn't he?" This came from a cheerfully rounded, middle-aged woman in a white lab coat who was staring intently at something on her desk.

"If you like them tall, dark and stormy. Very Heathcliff." The unfamiliar, twenty-something man in a suit sounded doubtful. Wren didn't recognize him, which meant he was the newest personal assistant in charge of manning the gate to the castle. That position turned over almost monthly for what she called Nash reasons.

The third member of the trio clustered around the desk frowned. "Very broody. Does he know how to smile?"

Ooh… That *did* sound deliciously Heathcliff-worthy and romantic to boot. Wren was an expert in English Gothic novels, so this eavesdropping was strictly professional curiosity.

She snuck closer, an action made considerably more difficult by the way her flip-flops squeaked on the linoleum floor. She was, she realized looking down at her very cheerful, pink-painted toes, in violation of lab rule number one: thou shalt wear closed-toe shoes only. Dr. Nash Masterson, ruler of the chemistry lab, was a stickler for rules. People had been known to cry when he explained their infractions, possibly because the man was a total Eeyore who made Genghis Khan seem like Martha Stewart. Since he was also CEO of the very successful Masterson Chemicals and filthy rich to boot, he got away with it. Such were the perks of money and looming at the top of the organizational chart.

She, however, got away with nothing, as evidenced by the way Nash's trio of employees looked up as she flip-flopped nearer. Busted, she waved. She recognized two of them, now that they weren't hunched over the desk. Martha was senior vice president of development, while Jenn was in marketing. The young guy remained unfamiliar.

The lab was through a set of doors behind the desk, beaker-filled tables, shelving and mysterious, shiny equipment stretching away in sterile white rows behind the floor-to-ceiling glass windows. It was like a stainless steel Arctic Circle, minus the cute penguins. Nash himself was nowhere in sight, but he'd pop up on time. Tardiness was also against lab rules.

"Is it Tuesday already?" Martha asked.

"Please tell me you're here to kidnap our evil billionaire boss for lunch." Jenn said this as if she were joking, but her fingers stress-clenched on the laptop clutched to her chest.

"He's all mine," she agreed cheerfully. Really, she didn't know why no one else got along with Nash. Sure, he could be arrogant and bossy and his default facial setting was *glare*. And, yes, he had a bad habit of discovering any hole, no matter how small, in one's logic—and also one's presentation, experiment or patent application—and then pointing out the omission in front of an audience. He was closed off, performed an amazing imitation of a hungry polar bear trapped on an iceberg and had stubbornly rebuffed her efforts to get to know him better for years. He accused her of wanting to crawl inside his brain and make herself at home there, while she knew he needed more people in his life.

After eight years, he'd succumbed to her friendship wiles to the point that they had a standing taco date every second Tuesday of the month. Well, not a *date* date. It was more of a friendly appointment. Between taco-eating friends who shared a compatible meal schedule. She wasn't certain what Nash had told his team about their lunch plans—no. Wait. The answer was nothing at all because Nash operated on a need-to-know basis, sharing zero details about his life with anyone.

"Is Nash in the lab?" She angled closer because her day could only be improved by seeing this Heathcliff look-alike.

"The ogre is, indeed, in his lair," Suit Guy reported nervously. Nash's assistants generally left for stress-related reasons quite quickly.

"Hasn't left in thirty-six hours," Jenn added. "So if you could please drag him out, you'd be doing us all a favor. Something about *very important research* and *blah blah blah*."

Wren winked. "He begged me to come help him out."

SOS counted as an urgent request for help, didn't it? Plus—tacos.

At least one of them made enough to pay for lunch. It turned out that college professors did *not* make a living wage in Southern California, especially once student loans were factored in. And while Wren loved her job teaching at Pomona College, some days she fantasized about buying a house or even a pair of shoes that were not on sale. Maybe she could scrounge up enough money to rent herself a professional boyfriend before Noah and May's wedding. Would that make her win or lose the bet with her sisters? Oh God, she'd have to attend the wedding solo and smile as if she was absolutely thrilled to be dating herself or whatever it was *Cosmo* called the single life these days.

"What are these?" She snagged the laminated set of cards from the desk before anyone could stop her. Although to be fair, based on the giggling, she doubted she'd just nabbed Nash's secret corporate plans for world domination. Nope. She held in her hand a deck of laminated cards of…she flipped…some extremely attractive people. A gorgeous face smiled out from each card, paired with a brief name and description like a birding guide, or those horrible chemistry study cards she'd been married to that one semester in college. She reminded herself that despite her recurring stress nightmares that she was late to the final exam and couldn't find it or the bathroom, she'd passed that class—barely and thanks only to Nash's tutoring—and flipped some more.

"Bachelors," Martha said.

"And bachelorettes," Jenn added.

"All single and available. For a price." This caused general snort-laughing.

"So it's…a guide to prostitutes?" Were these pretty people *cheap*? Because if so…hello? Solution to her wedding dilemma. She'd buy one and fall in love.

"It's a bachelor menu," Suit Guy said, as if you could order single people like ordering Chinese food or an in-flight movie.

And— "Okay?"

"For a bachelor auction. You bid on hot dates and the money goes to a nonprofit on Martha's Vineyard that runs accessible summer camps for children. This is the menu of your choices."

That seemed fun, if a bit archaic. And possibly raising issues of consent and power, although she assumed the bachelors had volunteered and not been voluntold. If only she'd possessed a small fortune to contribute to a good cause, perhaps she really could have purchased a handsome hottie to be her plus-one for her cousin's wedding. She flipped some more, her gaze catching on a card halfway through the deck. Unlike the other pictures of charming people smiling at the camera, this bachelor was half-turned away. The bits she could see were impressive, though. He was broad-shouldered and built like a lumberjack, dark-haired and scowling sideways at the camera. He totally gave off Mr. Rochester vibes, if Jane Eyre's Mr. Rochester had spent every moment not devoted to hiding his wife and romancing Jane to working out. She'd bet this guy had chiseled biceps and a six-pack and, honestly, why not just have the bachelors take their shirts off and eliminate a source of speculation and potential disappointment? If you were going to host something as ridiculous as a bachelor auction, you might as well go all in on the cheesy goodness and, wow, it was inexplicably quite hot in Nash's lab. He should get that checked out.

"Do you think anyone will bid on Mr. Masterson?" Martha tapped the glowering hottie Wren was drooling over.

Wait. What? Apparently the universe wasn't done messing with her. She refocused on the bachelor she'd been ogling—this time starting with his face—and realized that the sexy, brooding cutie was, indeed, Nash. That was—*weird*, her brain supplied. *Off-limits. Delete and erase all mental backup tapes.* Nash might have lab rules, but she had friendship rules—and they included never, ever lusting after the friend she might, once upon a time, have had a teeny-tiny crush on in college. Fortunately, that crush had died a tragic death after the first time she read his scathing comments on her chemistry exam.

"Ladies. Gentleman. Are we having an unscheduled team huddle?"

She looked up in horror, dropping the bachelor menu. Because, of course, that was Nash's voice, all low and rough and quite authoritative. She'd bet he'd only have to say *stop, thief!* once and the culprit would beg to be taken into custody.

Suit Guy squeaked and dropped into his desk chair. Judging from how he smacked his hands on his keyboard, he was trying—badly—to pretend that he was working and not part of the bachelor-menu-reading crowd. It wouldn't work. Nash was painfully observant. He leveled his arctic gaze at the gaggle of people at the desk and, sure enough, his employees fled like ducks before a storm cloud.

"Dr. Masterson," she crowed.

"Dr. Wilson."

She rolled her eyes at his perfunctory chin dip. One of these days she'd scandalize the man and his lab with a full-bodied hug.

"Have you gotten taller?" She tilted her head back, trying to mentally measure him. Thirty was too young for her to have started shrinking, so he must have had a growth spurt.

He snorted. "No."

"Shoe lifts? Heels?"

"No."

He turned and headed for the door to the stairwell. She followed him with a skip and a little wave for her fellow co-conspirators.

"Who's the new guy?"

Nash lifted one shoulder. "A temp."

"How come you're in a bachelor auction?" She had to trot to keep up with him because he had such long legs.

"Declan," he muttered, as if that explained everything.

Which it did. Declan was Nash's older brother and very, very good at tormenting his younger brother. Wren had suggested that fraternal teasing was man code for *I love you*, but Nash had only growled that even flowers would have been better. Which was saying something because Nash thought floral bouquets were, firstly, a waste of natural resources and, secondly, a meaningless gesture because words, chemical symbols, or a nicely written lab report were all clearer than a bunch of dahlias or, God forbid, roses. The language of flowers, he liked to argue, was as well-articulated as that of a toddler still learning to speak.

Wren beamed at him. This story was going to be awesome. "He hates you so much that he's selling you to the highest bidder? Is he branching out? Is moviemaking no longer interesting enough?"

"No." Nash scrubbed a hand over his face, the Nash equivalent of running around in a circle panic-shrieking.

"Can I have a bonus word? Maybe an explanatory sentence?"

"Not here." Nash pushed the stairwell door open and scowled, mostly because he wasn't a Hollywood fan despite his brother's box office success. She made her own face at the prospect of taking the stairs. Nash hated small spaces and adored exercise, so he never used the fancy, mirror-lined elevator in his building. At least his luxury sports car compensated for the lack of speed in exiting the building. It was definitely, she thought a few minutes later as she sank into the buttery-soft seat, the closest thing to a rocket ship that she'd ever ride in even if Nash steadfastly refused to drive over the speed limit.

Thirty minutes later, they had collected a paper bag of tacos from a Mexican food truck and parked by the Malibu beach. While Wren kicked off her flip-flops and tossed them onto the passenger seat, Nash methodically removed his laboratory-approved steel-toed boots, tucked his socks inside them and rolled up his dress pants. Ladies and gentlemen! The differences between them summed up.

"How was your day?" she asked after they'd wandered down to the sand and mainlined a taco as if they hadn't eaten all day. She had, of course, but tacos this delicious demanded eating.

"Later." He tilted his head, his eyes scanning her face. "Tell me about yours first."

She handed him her phone so he could see the picture of Noah proposing to May. "Romantic, right? This guy breaks up with me by text because he's not ready to be in a relationship and he thinks we should be just friends, but six months later he's secreted a diamond ring into the Maldives. My curse has struck again. He's madly, truly in love with the next woman he met."

"You have no idea if she was the next woman he met," Nash pointed out. "In fact, it's entirely unlikely, unless, hypothetically, she was present when he sent that text."

"Not helping," she muttered.

Nash shrugged and reapplied himself to his taco.

"But he's in love. For real."

"He was pitiful," Nash interjected.

"You weren't the one dating him!"

"This is the ex-boyfriend who texted you from somewhere over the Indian Ocean this week to ask you to feed his dog? Because he assumed you'd say yes and he was too lazy to bother to find someone before leaving on vacation?"

"That would be the one." She took the phone back and shoved it into her pocket. Okay, so Nash had a point and she hadn't exactly been heartbroken when Noah had mostly excused himself from her life. Noah wasn't her one and only, so she'd moved on. Quite easily.

"I—" Nash stopped. "Do you want me to just listen or to fix things?"

They'd established this rule early on because Nash was a doer and methodically took problems apart until he found a solution. Her life was not his personal Rubik's Cube, she'd explained on multiple occasions. And while a small part of her wondered how he would fix Noah, she mostly wanted to vent.

"Listen, thanks," she said. "I'm thirty, I run through boyfriends faster than you do personal assistants, all of whom go on to find true love with the very next woman they date, and now I'll be attending yet another wedding solo and enduring my family's well-meaning but embarrassing attempts to fix me up with their dentist or the UPS driver."

That said, she threw herself back on the sand, or rather she tried to. A large hand arrested her midflop. Nash shook his head and slipped his suit jacket onto the warm sand beneath her so she wouldn't be shaking half the beach out of her hair. She'd chopped it off to her chin a couple of months ago and then ignored it, so it was fast reaching the unmanageable stage where it was too long to stay put but still too short to twist up.

"So that's me, but," she reminded him. "I got a text this morning from someone who was very grim and mysterious."

"Did you? Perhaps we should introduce your ex-boyfriends to my ex-assistants."

"All he said was SOS." She ignored the matchmaking dig—one of Nash's many character flaws was his refusal to believe in true love—and winked. "Could you expand on what you need rescuing from? And also on whatever horribly embarrassing stunt your brother has cooked up? Is there any chance he's related to my sisters and we're all one happy, dysfunctional family?"

She waited a minute. Then another. But he didn't seem to be in any rush. She looked up at him and then up some more. He had that familiar, steely-eyed look going on, the one that said he was very unhappy with someone and that heads would roll. One of his jobs as her college chemistry TA had been to post the exam scores on a piece of paper on the professor's door. He'd march out like an executioner, slap it up, and everyone around Wren would burst into tears. He'd failed half her UCLA dorm and single-handedly crushed hundreds of medical school dreams.

She'd snuck into his lab once, at the start of the semester, to ask him out because he was a science god and she'd thought his grim glowering was romantic. There might have been a hot professor fantasy involved, too. At any rate, she'd blurted out an invitation to go somewhere and he'd lifted his head from his chemistry bench and destroyed her illusions. "No," he'd said. Followed by: "Do I know you?" He'd had the most adorable frown puckering his forehead, except then she'd realized that he'd been confused about her presence in his lab and not her name. Then he'd told her when the chemistry extra help group met. Her crush had died a sad, swift death.

"Still waiting," she prompted, when he didn't answer.

He frowned. "I'm flying to Martha's Vineyard this weekend."

"That's great." Who didn't like a nice vacation? "Unless you've got one of those flights that lands in six different airports with twelve-minute layovers and you have to crazy-run dragging your suitcase behind you while better-prepared travelers judge you from their barstools."

He grunted. "Private jet."

"Perks of being a billionaire?"

"Absolutely," he said dryly. "Not all of us work for peanuts and teach young minds about the joys of English literature."

"Hey, you commercial sellout," she said. "Literacy is important and Jane Austen is the best. If you ever read the books I gave you, you'd know why Mr. Darcy gets the girl."

He slanted a glance at her. "You made me watch the movie. The man was a farmer and had too many antiques. I had no idea that was a factor in sex appeal."

"Mr. Darcy is the best," she said happily. "But, you were saying—private plane?"

"My brother's fiancée is raising money for her nonprofit and I've agreed to participate despite being in the middle of a very important acquisition."

Nash was always buying other chemical companies. In fact, he was almost always working.

"So out of the goodness of your heart, you're flying across the country in a private jet to spend the weekend at the Martha's Vineyard home of your brother, the famous movie star. I'm still not seeing how being a nice guy is a hardship."

This earned her a grouchy look. "There's an event."

"Uh-huh." Wait. *The bachelor menu.* "Would the participation portion of this charity weekend be an auction type of event?"

"Yes." He looked more disgruntled than ever.

"You're letting your beautiful sister-in-law-to-be auction you off for charity?"

"I don't know why Charlotte just won't take cash."

She burst out laughing. "Because this will be *so* much more fun."

"For you maybe."

"Please tell me there's a livestream. Or internet bidding! The world absolutely needs to see Nash Masterson posing onstage. Do you plan on smiling, or will you just glare someone into buying you? What do they *do* with you? Wait. Don't tell me. I've read this in a book! Two middle-aged ladies will fight viciously over your beautiful body and you'll be won by the awkward wallflower who accidentally raises her bidding paddle to swat at a fly. Do they still use bidding paddles? Do you strip down? Are there wet T-shirts? Just how classy is your future sister-in-law and can she be convinced that less class is a moneymaker?"

The faintest hint of a smile quirked his lips, barely there and just for her. "Smart aleck. It's black-tie with a fancy dinner beforehand."

"Dinner and a show." She grinned at him. "So there you'll be in your tux—"

"And there you'll be, sitting in the audience," he interrupted. "Because you're the one who's going to buy me."

Three

With the bachelor auction four days away, Nash was running out of time. He had no idea why he'd agreed to participate, but Charlotte refused to let him make a cash donation in lieu of attending. And then there was the further complication of his acquisition of Durant Family Chemicals, which had a very nice portfolio of patents that would complement his own research.

Durant Senior was a self-avowed, old-fashioned, family-values-loving kind of man who thought everyone should play happy families. Nash would have ignored the sentiments and focused on the business contracts, but his was one of three competing offers to buy the company and Durant was currently deciding which one he liked best. Liking was a terrible way to do business. Worse, Durant had strongly intimated that his company would go to someone who prioritized family values (ones that matched Durant's, of course), and the Masterson family was a byword thanks to a recent scandal where a written contract between his adoptive father and his brother had been leaked to the public. The agreement had stipulated that, in exchange for proving himself to be a good guy worthy of the Masterson family name, Declan would inherit the company. The gossip websites had had a field day. So it was an uphill battle already, convincing Durant that Nash was the ideal man to take over his beloved company, and that was before Durant had announced that he'd be attending the bachelor auction because he loved a good cause.

Since Durant was bringing his three twenty-something single daughters, Nash could foresee exactly how that night would end and he didn't have time for that kind of romantic drama.

Why did everyone else seem to have this need to add people to their lives, to search for love and romance and happily-ever-after? He was busy and, according to Wren, he had the emotional intelligence of a rock. It worked well for him.

Wren tilted her head farther back. Her eyes were hazel, the second most common eye color of them all, a rich brown flecked with green and gold. Indecisive eyes, Wren claimed, but he liked them. The color seemed to shift with her mood, even though he knew it was simply an effect of the light. His own were a brown so dark they appeared almost black. Black like his mood. His soul, if you asked one of his subordinates at work after a particularly contentious meeting. He didn't have time to worry about what they thought; there was always too much to do.

Taco Tuesday was an indulgence, one he didn't have time for. He should move it to taco-once-a-month. Or semiannually.

And yet, here he was, parked on a beach, eating tacos that got grittier with each bite. Something about Wren moved resisting temptation to the bottom of his to-do list. Right now, she stared up at him, completely incredulous. Scandalized? She certainly didn't look like *100 percent on board with the plan*, although he was no emotions expert.

She had sand on the side of her nose. He brushed it off carefully, ignoring the way her nose scrunched and her hand came up to bat him away.

He should make a joke about free vacations or the open bar at the bachelor auction. Instead, he just watched her back. Thunder. That's what his brother Declan's team called him, inevitably in comparison with Declan. Declan was lightning, the charismatic brother who charmed where Nash growled and was courted by absolutely legions of people who, valuing his opinions and presence, dogged his heels, stalked him with cameras and generally invited themselves into every moment of his brother's not-so-private life. It was horrifying.

He had felt a bit like an ass this morning, texting Wren for help peopling. But she was the perfect solution to his auction dilemma. They were friends, or so she'd assured him more than once, and friends helped each other out. Despite her unabashed romanticism, she wouldn't read anything into it and he liked hanging out with her. Still, it was a big ask even if it was summer and she wasn't teaching. She probably had research papers to write or lectures to plan.

Something better—*more fun*, his brain supplied—than an unplanned jaunt to Martha's Vineyard with him. He'd have to make it up to her.

She blinked up at him. "Did you just ask me to buy you?"

Maybe? Yes. Definitely yes. "I did."

Perhaps the expression on Wren's face was *weird*? *Weird* covered how her forehead had puckered, lips parting as if she had intended to say something and then lost the thought in her surprise. She looked one part surprised, one part—he tried and failed to decipher the expression on her face. He needed to get back to his lab.

"You're absolutely, totally, one thousand percent serious?"

"Yes." He paused. "One hundred percent so."

"Oh my God. You're the *worst*."

And then Wren's happy laughter bubbled up, warm and fizzy, as effervescent as baking soda and vinegar meeting. An answering if reluctant amusement tugged at the corners of his mouth, but he waited for her to finish. He could almost see the thoughts chasing each other, one after another through her brain. He had no idea how Wren's mind worked but she was good people. Loyal. Funny. Devilish and tremendously smart. She routinely undersold herself and the dating world had been unkind, but he had no idea why. Her ex Noah was an idiot to break up with her.

He looked down at her. "Are you refusing?"

She rolled over onto her stomach, stacking her hands under her chin as she grinned at him. New grains of sand streaked the sun-flushed curve of her right cheek. "Please. Say it again. This is the best thing I've heard all week."

He fought not to reach out and brush the newest sand away. She'd only acquire more. It was a losing battle and he needed to focus his efforts elsewhere. "Come with me to Martha's Vineyard. Attend the bachelor auction. Place the winning bid on me."

She hooted again, rummaging in her bag. For a brief second, he let himself believe she wasn't looking for her phone. Which was in her pocket, but no way he pointed that out. "I'm going to need video evidence this conversation happened."

"Not a chance."

"Please?" She pouted, but he refused to be swayed.

"Remember who drove three hours in the dark to a surf shack south of the border because someone else had accidentally and quite illegally gone on a romantic sailing date?"

"Yes?" she said cautiously.

"Yes," he agreed. "Me. I had to break into your condo, committing felony B&E, search for your passport, and then use that stupid phone app to locate you. I did not record you for posterity when I arrived."

"It wouldn't be for posterity," she argued. "Just until you did something more ridiculous."

He gave her a look and she sighed.

"Right," she said. "You are Mr. Anti-Romance and would never, ever take a girl on a surprise trip to Mexico."

He certainly wouldn't get lost while sailing his own boat, which was what had happened to Wren's date, but he didn't think she wanted to hear that. The guy hadn't even called her again after Nash had driven him back to Los Angeles, although that had been no loss. Some things were best buried in the past.

Since she probably knew this, too, even if she'd never admit it, she let him close his fingers over hers and tug the phone away. He slipped it into his pants pocket for safekeeping. Wren loved a good joke, and he'd end up starring in a slide deck for one of her freshman writing seminars. Or one of those literature conferences she'd dragged him to over the years "to double her audience numbers." Participating in a bachelor auction was embarrassing enough without becoming an internet meme.

"We're in the cone of silence," he said, borrowing one of her favorite phrases. "This is just between the two of us."

She sprawled on his jacket, grinning up at him. "It's not against the rules for you to fly in a bogus date who will snap you up in the bidding?"

Nash spent a lot of time trying to determine the properties of various compounds, because he liked to know how things worked. And also because then he could reassemble them into new, more useful compounds. He'd attempted more than once to break down what it was about Wren that made her voice so nice to listen to. So far, he hadn't figured it out. Her words flowed—and flowed and flowed—and she sounded confident. Not too loud, but sure.

"It's a bachelor auction," he said dryly. "There are very few rules."

"Oh." She laughed again, the loud belly laugh that made her face scrunch up, carving happy lines around her eyes. Not laughing at him, he decided after making a careful assessment, but with him because it truly was a ridiculous situation that he'd found himself in. He'd much rather that his brother's fiancée hadn't come up with this ridiculous fundraising idea. Then again, he'd also rather not be forced into socializing, fly across the country when he was in the middle of a very interesting experiment, be forced to wear a tux and parade onstage in front of an audience that was absolutely not interested in his *chemistry*.

"But *why*?"

"Why not?"

She made a face. "Give me the words. Pretend I'm your brand-new junior research assistant fresh from college."

"Wren." He gave up and reached over, brushing the sand from her face. "We both know I would never hire you as a research assistant. I know what your college chemistry grades were."

She stuck out her tongue. "Yes, because *you* gave them to me. You were stingier than Scrooge and twice as grumpy."

He shrugged because it was mostly true. Grades weren't gifts; they had to be earned. On the other hand, grades could be quantitative, too. The more daily grades you had, for example, the more you could raise your overall score.

She made a get-on-with-it gesture. "Right but there must be some parameters. I mean, it's a bachelor auction, not a wedding ceremony. You're not making a lifetime commitment to your lucky winner."

He sincerely hoped not, but Durant had overshared

a story about how he had met his wife at some kind of retro box picnic social and fallen instantly in love with her. Then he'd mentioned the auction and his daughters. Nash had refrained from saying anything, but it had been difficult.

"I have to commit to one date." Was there any way to make this sound reasonable?

"One night with the billionaire? Your sister-in-law-to-be has met you, hasn't she? And she realizes that you're not Mr. Romance?"

He stared at her. "One night is hardly romantic. Even I know that. Also, I know how to date."

"When is the last time you had a date?" she said dryly.

He shrugged. "More recently than you."

She groaned. "Don't go there. You're going to have glamorous Martha's Vineyard types throwing cash at you for the chance of one night with you. Whereas I've been reduced to contemplating Craigslist-purchasing myself a date."

This was new. "Excuse me?"

"I told you that I've been invited to a wedding," she said. "*Noah's* wedding, to May. It's going to be a huge family affair. They're getting hitched in September— although she should have held out for a May wedding on principle—at some super-romantic Napa Valley vineyard."

He pulled out his own phone and did a quick Google search when she muttered the vineyard name with the same distaste most people reserved for discovering a deer tick stuck on themselves. Huh. He wasn't sure the vineyard even made wine—certainly not world-class wine—but it did come with a pond, an inordinate number of roses and a candle-filled wine cave. The photos would be nice, although lighting might be a challenge.

If not the challenge that Wren was worried about.

"You'll be grilled over champagne and canapés in the wine cave about your dating prospects," he said, stating the obvious.

He'd met her family very briefly. It had not been a successful meeting. They'd attempted to pull some kind of practical joke that involved them standing in their front yard and, possibly, singing (he still wasn't quite sure what the noise had been intended to be) while Wren made pained noises and accused them of being an embarrassment to humankind. Wren's family had a weird sense of humor and no boundaries. They'd be all over her single state.

"Worse," she said glumly.

"Perhaps you could work on establishing some boundaries before this big family event."

"Right." She snorted. "Says the man who's letting his future sister-in-law auction him off for cash."

"You're going to buy me. And how is it worse?"

"Because I panicked. And I told my mother that I was bringing a guest, so now she wants to know who I'm seeing and why she hasn't met him before."

"So," he said. "You buy me, and I'll date you. You can take me. To the wedding."

Take. Nash.
Date Nash?
Win her bet by bringing a fake date to the wedding?
Wren's college self would have squealed with glee,

and not just because present-day Nash wore suits that did amazing things for his shoulders. He had an entire wardrobe of dark, custom-tailored, cost-an-absolute-fortune three-pieces that hugged his muscled form and were completely wasted beneath his lab coats. Right now, sitting there in his shirtsleeves, he should have looked ridiculous on a beach, but didn't. He was just so *big*. And calm. How did he do it? He'd lobbed the most ridiculous idea at her and he didn't look bothered. Or worried. Or really anything regular people might feel if they were about to star in something as cringewor-thy as a *bachelor auction*. Maybe it was all a practical joke? Had Nash been working on his sense of humor?

"Your next words will be *gotcha*."

"That's one word." He shrugged his broad, dress-shirt-covered shoulders. "And no."

"You're completely serious."

He nodded.

Here on the beach, without him towering over her, it was easy to forget just how imposing he was and yet he was medieval-knight-sized, with roughly the same height and broad-shouldered build as the Beast. Not that she was Belle. Although she did have brown hair and there *might* be a yellow sundress hanging in her closet just in case she ever got the chance to waltz in an en-chanted library. His voice matched his outsides most unfairly, a beautiful, smooth tenor that was also some-how masterfully cold and biting. The decisiveness with which he approached life came through in his words, along with a seemingly effortless *rightness* as he laid down the law to lesser mortals.

Right now he was eying her calmly. Nash was always

calm, ruthlessly, preternaturally so. As she'd told him on multiple occasions. "It's a good plan, Wren. Admit it."

"It is not! Your definition of *thinking things through* generally involves a twelve-hour strategy session with whiteboards and three-ringer binders, so you can't have spent any time on this." This plan was so bad that it didn't even qualify as a *plan*—more of a Hail Mary, a desperate launching of the football at the end zone as the clock ticked down and the buzzer rang on her sad, sad excuse of a life. "No one will believe we're a couple."

"Why not?" He set his uneaten taco back in the take-out container.

And gave her his undivided, annoyingly *calm* attention. Ugh.

"Is this where you decimate me with logic?" She failed to keep the suspicion out of her voice. They'd had similar discussions before. She'd lost all of them.

And there it was—that crooked hint of a grin, here and then gone on his beautiful, stern face. "You bet."

Those were currently her two least favorite words, and far more motivational than he knew.

"Okay. Hit me with why you think this could work."

"People date to not be alone. To practice for finding a long-term mate. For sex." He shrugged. "But mostly people just see what they want to see. We've been friends long enough that some people wonder why we're not romantically involved, while others know that we're the last two people who would ever be attracted to each other. My brother will fall into neither camp and will just be happy for us, while your family will enjoy telling you all the reasons why I would make a terrible partner. Also, I'm expecting there to be some competition for me at the auction and it would be more efficient to prevent that."

"Mate?" She made a face. "FYI, true story on the opposites thing and this is why you're single, Mr. Romance. Who's the competition?"

"The Durant family."

"An entire family wants to date you?"

"*I* want to buy Durant Family Chemicals. Durant Senior only wants to sell to a family man like himself. He's attending the auction along with his wife and three daughters."

She sighed. "And you don't want to date three women? You don't think you might, just possibly, be struck with Cupid's arrow and fall in love—or at least in like—with one of them?"

He had that expressionless look on his face, but she knew what it meant. No. He did not. Plus, having three competing candidates meant there would be two losers and loads of hurt feelings Nash would have no idea how to deal with.

"Is it a yes?"

"Why not get yourself a real girlfriend?" She poked his thigh with her index finger. "Have real sex. Practice those *un*real social skills of yours. You could meet someone—maybe one of the other auction attendees would be perfect for you."

He shook his head. "No."

Paused.

Leaned toward her. An enormous, frowny, warm mountain of billionaire scientist blocking out the California sunshine, his fingers inches from her arm. *It's not a big deal.*

"Are you looking for a real boyfriend?" His voice was a deep rumble. "Think of how much easier it would be to not have to fake things at your family wedding."

"Point taken," she said hastily. "Reality is highly overrated."

Since the details of her breakup with Noah were well known to her entire family, in addition to winning her bet, she'd also like to head off the sympathetic glances and pity matchmaking. Nothing quite said *I'm completely over him* like bringing home a tall, dark and handsome billionaire who would… Right. *That* was worth double-checking.

"Will you pretend to be at least semi-smitten with me? Or are you going to skulk around my cousin's wedding looking all dour and unhappy?" She poked playfully at the corner of his mouth. "Smile!"

"Like this?" He eyed her and then, oh gosh, he gave her a completely smitten smile, a little loopy, the corners of his mouth soft and 100 percent tilted up, if slightly crookedly on one side. It was no less devastating for being a con job. In fact, perhaps it was more so? Because it made her realize what she'd been missing out on all these years.

"Good job," she said hastily, cutting those useless thoughts off. "You pass."

"Is that a yes?"

What was the worst that could happen?

"Yes," she said.

They finished their tacos while they finalized their plan. She'd fly with Nash to Martha's Vineyard on Friday night, attend the auction on Sunday and then hang out with him for two weeks, doing the pretend-dating thing. This, he suggested, would give them plenty of time to practice for the wedding. Hmm. Well, it would, although she'd rather he'd pitched it as a free trip to the beach.

Which reminded her that bachelor auctions were unlikely to be *free*.

"Are you going to be hideously expensive?"

He frowned. "I'm paying for the weekend. And the next two weeks."

"So it's like a *Pretty Woman* script and I'll be your kept woman?"

He arched an eyebrow, a talent she desperately envied. "Except that there will be no romance, no sex and absolutely no serenades from a limousine."

She'd made him watch that movie, too.

"Right. This is strictly a friends-with-not-sexy-benefits deal."

That was a pang of…*something*. It wasn't that she lusted after her friend anymore, but no guy seemed to want her, the super-smart academic who was fun and funny and who probably (definitely) ate too many baked goods. She was apparently the kind of girl you asked to feed your dog while you were away on a romantic weekend with the woman of your dreams.

Her phone cut her pity party off. She glanced down and then turned it so Nash could see the screen. "See? My mom. Again. And…my sisters. They want the details about my plus-one for the wedding."

"So tell them."

She still wasn't convinced it was a good idea, but since it was the only idea that she'd come up with and she wished with embarrassingly juvenile fervor to not lose her bet with her sisters, she went with it. Bringing my SERIOUS boyfriend.

There. That wasn't a lie, not at all. Nash was preternaturally serious. It took mere moments for her phone to blow up with texts.

Amelia: You really do have a boyfriend?

Emily: She's lying.

Mom: GIRLS!

Amelia: Bet or no bet, she'll have broken up with him by the wedding.

Emily: Give us a name, Wren.

Amelia: Details now plz!

Emily: Or you forfeit.

Mom: Is this the boy you said you were "very serious" about?

Wren: I'm bringing Nash.

This triggered an avalanche of follow-up texts and three new group chats, one of which she was fairly certain she'd been added to by mistake.

Emily cut right to the chase. You're dating the automaton?

Amelia piled on: Nash, the hot cardboard cutout who is not nice at all? Or do we know more than one Nash?

Emily: You told him about your curse, didn't you? He thinks you're going to introduce him to The One. I think I'm totally winning our bet. This can't be for real.

Wren: Shut up.

Emily: Every. Single. ONE.

Amelia: At least you're already friends with him!

Amelia: I thought we didn't like him? Isn't he the rude one?

Emily: Very rude.

Mom: This is the one who's built like Conan the Barbarian?

Amelia: MOM

Wren: Objectifying my boyfriend is rude.

Emily: Don't go there. He's like one of those cardboard cakes in the bakery case. All frosting on the outside and nothing edible on the inside.

Amelia: Ice, ice baby...

Mom: Isn't he the one with all the money? So he's smart, rich and handsome. *Shrugging woman emoji

Wren: NOT talking about this.

She looked up at her hot, automaton cutout of a fake date. "You made quite the impression on my family."

Her phone buzzed again, said family clearly not done questioning her (admittedly fake) taste in men.

Does he send you flowers and love notes? Take you out on dates? Do NOT settle. Wrenley Wilson, I'm talking to you!

That last one was from her mother.

"This is going to be a hard sell," she told Nash.

He frowned—thoughtfully, not angrily—and then reached over and plucked the phone out of her hand. And then—well, *then* he plucked her up as easily as he had the phone and somehow settled her in the curve of his arm. She was squished up against him, half on his lap, and he had some seriously muscled thighs. Which she tried to ignore, but he made it hard, no pun intended.

"Smile," he ordered, holding the phone out in front of them.

What?

"There." He handed the phone back to her, reestablishing some distance between them. "Send that."

He'd taken a selfie of the two of them. She looked startled (no surprise), her face sun-flushed, her lips parted. It was actually a good photo, not least since Nash had his face pressed against hers and was staring steadily at the camera, wearing his almost-smile.

She sent it because, why not? And what else was she really going to do other than admit the truth that she was single and stubbornly proud? Plus, she liked winning a bet as much as the next person.

He started picking up their picnic lunch, sorting out the recyclables from the trash. "You shouldn't need to fake a boyfriend to keep your family happy."

Wren stiffened and gave serious consideration to throwing her leftover taco at him. "It's not to make them happy. I just don't want to answer the questions. Or deal with the pity."

"Because it's okay to be single," he continued. "Especially if you're happy. Not everyone has to be partnered up."

She eyed him suspiciously. "Are you seriously going to suggest I date myself? Because I'm doing that now and the battery budget for my vibrator is killing me."

Pink tinged his cheekbones. "If you're happy, you're happy. Fuck them."

"Wow." She stared at him. "You're Mr. Romance, aren't you?"

He stood up, offering her a hand. "I don't believe in romance. Do we have a deal?"

"Yes," she blurted out. "It's a deal."

She had a date to buy herself a billionaire.

Four

Billionaires did not stand in line or wait their turn at airline check-in counters.

Wren had agreed to meet Nash at the private jet terminal at John Wayne Airport on Friday night, as he'd had business to take care of—chemical companies to buy, the dreams of his subordinates to crush, just your average everyday CEO stuff. She herself had had last-minute edits for a journal article that two hundred people would read, fifty of whom would email her to point out all the places where her scholarship was flawed. At any rate, after an afternoon with her head in Jane Austen land, it was disorienting to find herself at the private terminal, which was modern and sleek, with enormous glass windows that let in incredible amounts of sunlight and looked out on the small commuter jets and private planes lining the runway. She could practically smell the money.

This must have been how Elizabeth Bennet had felt, arriving at Pemberley for the first time. It was one thing to know that Nash had money, and another thing altogether to realize that she had a ten-year-old MINI Cooper and he had a plane. They'd never, she realized now, so much as road-tripped together, other than her one ill-fated, hours-long jaunt south of the border. Nash was a workaholic, and as no one earned a graduate degree without an obscene amount of work, she hadn't had copious amounts of spare time herself.

The Lyft driver had dropped her in front of the terminal with a low whistle, while she swallowed the urge to explain that her real life involved lines and mass airport chaos and absolutely nothing exotic or luxurious. How had Cinderella gone from the ball straight back to the kitchen?

She was still contemplating this new and luxurious lifestyle as she made her way through a brief security check and her bags were whisked away. There were no pesky luggage restrictions, no barked orders to remove as much of her clothing as possible so that her stripped-down self could be processed like a cow in a cattle chute. Even the waiting lounge was serenely beautiful, decorated in tasteful beiges and blacks. There were what looked like some trillionaire technopreneurs (jeans, Birkenstocks, and carrying sleek, space-age laptops), but she spotted no movie stars. Bummer.

"Fake it until you make it," she reminded herself.

Fortunately for her self-esteem, Nash materialized behind her, seemingly out of thin air and looking rather like a grim, suit-wearing thundercloud. He was pulling a roller bag that probably cost more than her entire monthly salary, but otherwise he looked familiar. Familiar was good.

"Wren." He took her carry-on bag from her, slinging it over his own shoulder.

She thought about protesting, but why? It wasn't as if she actually wanted to carry her own things and he was so big.

"Lead on," she told him, trying to pretend that she flew private all the time and had a clue about what she did next.

Nash knew what to do, of course. He got them both outside and onto the tarmac, leading the way to a small, sleek jet plane. A steward whisked their luggage away and then the pilot and her copilot stepped forward to greet them and share the night's flight plan with Nash.

Flying private did not disappoint. It was a luxury cocoon of cream leather and chrome. If her Instagram account had been followed by more than her family and a few friends, she would have posted a picture. Hashtags #livingthelife and #bossgirl.

They were offered drinks and then she'd barely had time to get settled into the seat across from Nash's before the plane took off. Nash promptly got busy with his laptop, while she gave up on any semblance of productivity and dived into the stack of glossy magazines she'd picked up just in case she needed to buy $400 pants or draw a perfect cat eye with her liner. This was a fake vacation! Self-care time!

When her stomach rumbled some hours later, he looked up and gave her that almost-smile of his, motioning for the steward. The steward came bustling forward with lobster tacos and what turned out to be champagne margaritas. Having a billionaire fake boyfriend, she thought as she dug in, had its perks.

Eventually, Nash closed his laptop and looked at her. His outstretched legs made her feel like a tiny hill next to an Alp-sized mountain.

"Right," he said. "We should discuss the schedule."

"The schedule." She felt like a bad echo. Wasn't there a Greek nymph who'd been turned into an echo for distracting the goddess Hera from the affairs of her husband? She tried to remember if those had been business affairs, or something more carnal, but drew a blank. It was getting late and Nash was still talking, laying out times and places and events in a neat series of crisp sentences. God bless the man, but he loved his plans. Also, he was still talking. Oops.

"So we're agreed?" He looked at her.

She looked back. "Sure."

"Were you listening?"

"Mostly?" She made a face. "Recap me?"

"The auction is Saturday night. We'll need to go out on our date. I've scheduled that for Sunday."

"A date?"

"The winning bid is for a date with the bachelor." He frowned. "We established that."

Had they? "So I've got to do two public things with you, but you only have to attend one wedding with me?"

"You get two weeks in a fancy romantic hotel," he pointed out. "Complete free of charge."

"Except for the auction. And the *date*. I'll have to

pretend to like you." She gave a huge, mock sigh. "It will be hard."

He blinked. His lips parted. She almost thought—but no. Nash was terrible at puns and double entendres.

"I'm sure you'll be quite convincing," he said carefully.

"We should ease into it. You wouldn't run a marathon before you could jog around the block. I can do that."

His phone buzzed and he glanced down. Frowned. "Excuse me."

She guessed that the rule about turning off your phone just in case a spam phone call caused the plane to nosedive in a fiery crash must not apply to private flights because Nash answered, stepping away to the back of the plane. His frown deepened. Uh-oh. Her work interactions with Nash had been limited to retrieving him from his lab for their taco not-dates, but he had a reputation, one that he'd clearly earned. He barked out a handful of words at the luckless person on the other end of his call. Mostly, those words consisted of *no, fix it* and *now*. She wondered what the job descriptions for his team looked like and if potential candidates knew they'd be working for Oscar the Grouch, albeit in much more upscale surroundings.

"Send me a status report in an hour," he snapped, ending the call.

He strode back down the plane and dropped into the seat beside her, still frowning. He didn't immediately start talking, probably because he was busy glowering at his poor phone, fingers tapping on the armrest of his seat.

"Did you shoot the messenger?"

His fingers stopped, midtap. "Wren."

Admonishing. How cute.

She grinned at him. "Maybe they waited to call until they knew you'd be in the air and couldn't march down to their office and yell at them."

He fixed a stern gaze on her. "I don't yell."

No, she didn't suppose he did. Yelling implied a lack of control. Or that he was a bully. Nash was neither of those things. He was, however, coldly disappointed, disapproval radiating off him. Being a perfectionist, she'd come to realize, was terribly challenging when he had to live his best life surrounded by the less-perfect people. Fortunately, he had her to shake his life up. She was his own personal snow globe. Or something.

She leaned into his shoulder. The plane was chillier than she'd expected and he was warm. He smelled good, too. Maybe it was his cologne, or the soap he used. His dry cleaner. She didn't know what, but it was unique to him, and she had to fight not to inhale him greedily.

"What went wrong?" she asked, forcing herself to sit up and break the contact between them.

"What?"

He'd already forgotten the call and moved on to the next obstacle in his path to world domination or whatever it was he thought he had to accomplish before he turned thirty-five in a few years.

"The work guy who called?" she prompted.

"Oh." The frown returned. "A patent application was rejected because of an issue with the drawings."

She'd thought it before, but it was still true that she was deeply, deeply grateful she was not one of Nash's employees, even if it seemed as if chemistry was quite the lucrative profession. Private planes weren't cheap. This one came with posh leather seating for twelve, bathrooms at the back that were probably gold-plated and what looked like a separate room. Perhaps a bedroom? It made sense, what with all the business traveling Nash did, what with the money he'd made and the deals he'd landed, that he couldn't show up at a meeting red-eyed and stupid with exhaustion. He probably earned five or even ten thousand dollars a minute like the world's richest men, so waiting in line at the airport like regular people did was an inefficient use of time. Her last business trip, on the other hand, had included a three-hour flight delay and two stops because that had been the cheapest ticket she could find and even then her grant had only covered half of it.

Literature was definitely a labor of love.

"So we're on the same page about Martha's Vineyard?" he asked her.

She wrapped her hands around her drink and considered.

"About us," he clarified.

"Us." The word felt strange. Off somehow. She tried to imagine the two of them as an actual couple. Even during her brief college-days crush, she'd recognized that they'd been an unlikely pairing, an American Akita or an exotic Kangal to her teacup poodle. And yet here they were. Friends about to pretend to be lovers.

"Problem?" he prompted.

She pulled her mind out of the wormhole it had detoured into. She could imagine what kind of dog Nash would be later.

"No one will believe that we're actually a couple unless we act like a couple."

"Right." The frown returned. "I don't see how that's a problem."

"We're friends," she said.

"And?" he asked dryly. "Friendship is generally considered an excellent basis for a romantic relationship, is it not?"

"Yes, but—" She waved a hand. The champagne-free hand, fortunately for him and his expensive suit. "There are other things."

"Other *things*."

"Like spending time together and shared interests. Talking about things that matter, like what scares you and what you want to accomplish. Dreams and stuff. Plus—" she felt her face color "—*sex*."

"Sex." She had no idea how he could say the word so calmly. He was a scientist and practical, what with all the experiments he ran, but honestly—the S-word was loose in this very small cabin space with them and there was no taking it back because *of course* she was now imagining Nash. And sex. Possibly with her, or at least with her watching him get it on with some nameless but beautiful woman and really—she had no idea *how* she felt about that.

Oh, God.

"People will expect us to have sex," she hissed. "To touch. Hold hands. Random hugging and personal space incursions."

He shrugged. "All right."

"All *right*?" There was simply nothing *all right* about the words *sex* and *friends* in the same sentence. Except, well, possibly there was the whole friends-with-benefits thing? Which could never work for the two of them. Ever. Just because. Which was absolutely as much as she was ever going to allow herself to think about sex with Nash.

Who lifted his arm and then paused.

"What?" she snapped.

He wiggled his arm. "May I?"

What had she ever done to deserve this? *Perved on him in college,* her brain supplied. *Deducted your Cheeto and romance novel purchases on your income taxes as charitable donations. Self-care is not IRS-approved.*

She sucked in a deep breath. Be strong, she told herself. "Okay?"

Nash promptly draped his arm along the back of her seat, his fingers brushing the side of her neck. "See? Touching is covered."

Right. While she couldn't *see* anything, she could feel.

Stupid, sexy shiver.

So she went on the defensive. "Now I understand why you haven't dated in over a year."

Frowning, Nash retrieved his arm. "I can date just fine."

"Really?" She smiled. "You, my friend, need to work on your technique. Also, your delivery."

Nash glared. "Do not."

Now it was her turn to shrug. "A pretty face will only get you so far."

"Pretty?" His glare deepened.

"Sure." She grinned at him because it was true. Objectively, Nash hit the handsome ball right out of the ballpark of attractiveness. He had the whole tall, dark and built thing going for him, for one thing. Plus, the man had a fortune. *A single man in possession of a good fortune must be in want of a wife,* her brain suggested. Why *was* he single? "Cheekbones, the sexy stern thing, money. You're almost the complete package."

"Almost?"

"A noble title or an estate would seal the deal."

"I'll get right on that."

"Romance," she sighed. "It's like you've never heard of the concept." She paused. Made a face. "Or you've *heard* of it and banned it from your life entirely. I get that it might not come naturally to you, but there are thousands of books and movies out there you can borrow from. It's a big plus in the dating world."

"Romance is a waste of time."

All right, so maybe it wasn't so surprising the man was unmated, bereft of a girlfriend, forced to fake-date a friend and bribe her to buy him at auction. It made perfect sense. Nash possessed not an ounce of charm or even a single romantic bone in that big, muscled body. His steely forearms and even steelier gaze are one enormous caution size: *Warning! No heart inside!*

"Mmm-hmm," she said. "Remember that when you're stuck in a sexual drought longer than Queen Victoria's reign."

He nodded like a fencer acknowledging his opponent had scored a hit. No one had ever accused Wren of not dating enough. "Let me rephrase. How long has it been since you felt some stirrings of romance that lasted longer than the first date?"

"Nash Masterson, are you asking me about my sex life?"

A flush painted his gorgeous cheekbones. "It seemed relevant."

To give herself credit, she tried to do the math in her head. She'd much rather not know. Plus—math. "It's not like graduate school left me with any free time to invest in long-term relationships. Mind-blowing sex doesn't just fall out of the sky."

And if it did, she wanted a map and precise GPS co-ordinates, please and thank you.

"You graduated over a year ago," he pointed out.

"And?"

"So maybe you're the one who doesn't remember how a satisfying date goes."

Embarrassment and panic flooded her. Her dates with Noah had been memorable only for their sheer and utter boredom.

"Practice would be good for you," Nash concluded.

"You know what?" she said glumly. "It's entirely possible that it's practice that I'm missing in my life. Not romance, not sex, not someone to save me a seat on the train by throwing his body across it. Not that at all."

They both sat there, thinking it over. The plane kept moving toward Massachusetts, its flight path remarkably smooth. Surely, this would have been a good moment for turbulence or at least snacks. Instead, she'd somehow been tricked into a postmortem of her very unsatisfying dating life.

She sighed. "God, we're pathetic. Unkissed, unloved."

"Right," he said briskly. "So we'll practice."

The idea of *practice* did not seem any less ridiculous. Romance and dating weren't like yoga or daily affirmations. Or...or flight hours! Her dating life wasn't a pilot's flight book, where logging hours spent made her more valuable and more experienced. *Because you have* zero *successful dating experience.*

Which explained the truly horrifying words that fell out of her mouth.

"You want to practice kissing, then?" The words hung in the very small air space of the private plane cabin, quite possibly loud enough for the flight attendant, the pilot and all of their friends to have heard. And that wasn't even the worst of it. Nope. Because not only had she suggested *sexual activities* to her *friend*, but that friend's mouth seemed to have somehow acquired its very own gravitational pull and she couldn't stop staring at it. At *him*. At Nash's firm but very male and possibly super-sexy lips. Had she just asked him to kiss her? What was *in* those champagne cocktails? She tore her eyes away and redirected her hopeless staring at the half-empty glass on her tray.

There was a metaphor there.

"Probably not," she said hastily to the sad, lonely ice cube dying a slow, cold death at the bottom of her glass. "No kissing."

He made a sound. Or possibly his mouth re-exerted its strange fascination for her because her eyes bounced off the ice cube and back to Nash's face. Which was inscrutable, giving nothing away. Mostly that was just how Nash was. And if she occasionally—very, very occasionally and absolutely no more than once a week— wondered what it would take to shake him up and elicit a stronger reaction from him, she always shoved that recalcitrant thought deep down and ignored it.

Mostly.

"You want to kiss." He blinked. "Me."

"Well, yeah." Lean into it, Wren. *Own* the bad mistake. "Not the steward. That would be on-the-job harassment."

"Me."

"Yes." She waited for Nash's brain to catch up.

And then he shrugged and turned to her, his big hands coming up to cup her face and his own was coming closer and closer and really she hadn't thought this through at *all*, had she? Because he just went for it with the same direct approach he did the rest of his life and kissed her.

Her brain sheeted white—more from panic than anything—and then when it came back online after a full emergency reboot, she was aware only of his mouth pressing against hers, his warm fingers gently cupping her cheeks. He had to bend over and she had to angle herself up to fit their mouths together. She wasn't quite tall enough to reach him otherwise, but his hands urged her closer and her own—well, her own were reaching for him, her fingers somehow wrapping themselves around his suit-clad biceps and holding on because either the plane was plummeting out of the sky or Nash's mouth on hers made her stomach jump and set her nerves on fire.

The man could kiss.

His lips pressed against hers, his hands steadying her as the plane dipped ever so slightly, or perhaps that was her stomach. Heat flushed her face, set her throat on fire and then moved in a southerly direction as her body came alive. He felt so solid. Strong. Not in an overwhelming, caveman way, but simply present. He kissed her deeper when she didn't pull away, his tongue tasting her lower lip, coaxing.

As kisses went, this kiss was entirely PG, barely there—just his lips on hers, and the places where her hands touched him or his steadied her because kissing on a plane wasn't entirely smooth. The plane moved up and then down, dipping with the wind or whatever technological magic kept them up in the air rather than nose-diving toward the ground. She was sure that Nash could explain it, probably in excruciating detail. This kiss, though, was entirely, completely inexplicable. She'd had no idea he would feel like this, warm and solid, utterly dependable and dangerously safe.

And, and—*unrestrained*. Because really, if she'd stopped to think about it (which she never, ever did because friends did not imagine how their friends kissed), she'd have thought Nash would be quite firmly in control of the kiss. One of those sexily domineering types who knew how to position them both and turn the fireworks on. Possibly a bit of a dirty talker? But this Nash, this kissing Nash was absolutely a surprise. He was kissing her with no control whatsoever, his mouth devouring hers, firm, demanding, giving back as much as he took.

She could feel the flush building on her cheeks, the heat in her stomach and lower, all of her warm and squirming with this desire that had come out of nowhere, setting up an absolute drumbeat in her chest as her heart endorsed this kiss 100 percent.

His lips parted and her own were on board with this next step in their kissing plan and her tongue slicked his bottom lip, tracing the surprisingly plush curve and teasing a damp, wet path into—

She pulled back. Wow, her brain supplied. Whee! Her body answered.

She yanked herself back, putting all of five inches between them. Six inches. Enough room to breathe on her own, at any rate. For one moment, Nash was still leaning toward her, ridiculously long, soft lashes dusting his stern face. His hands fell away from her face and his eyes opened. He stared at her. He looked—

She had—

This was bad.

"Well," she said, buying time. "That was interesting."

"Was it?" He folded himself back into his seat in a very neat piece of billionaire origami.

"Explanatory," she corrected. And then, when he gave her a look, she said teasingly, "Not romantic or push-your-buttons hot."

"Push-your-buttons hot," he said thoughtfully. "Is that a thing?"

"Totally." She winked at him and silently blessed the pilot who came on to announce that they'd begun their descent. "And you don't have it. No wonder you're single."

Five

After crash-landing out of that kiss and then landing much more safely at Martha's Vineyard Airport, Wren had let Nash's team shepherd her off the plane, into a Range Rover and to a darling boutique hotel that screamed *romance*.

Trying not to remember how Nash's mouth had felt in that terrible miscalculation of a practice kiss, Wren had gone to sleep with her balcony door ajar so that she wouldn't lose a single moment of her time on the island. If peace had a smell, it would be the ocean. Seabird racket filtered through the open door, a bright counterpoint to the lower notes of waves rushing in over the sand. Even better, there was no California traffic noise, no people rushing from point A to point B and then back again. The island had a rhythm of its own and it was deliciously, wonderfully slower. Less focused on getting things done and dots in her bullet journal. In. Then back out.

As a child, she'd gone to the beach during the summer months, but those trips had lessened as she'd grown older, dwindling to a few stolen hours when she and her friends had ditched their classes and stuffed themselves into a single beater car and run off to the beach for the day. Los Angeles beaches were nothing like Martha's Vineyard, being wider, more peopled and dotted with volleyball players and Rollerbladers. Plus, the parking. The hard-to-find, enormously expensive parking that made California beaches more challenging than summiting Everest.

Fake-friend-dating had its perks.

She staggered out of the bed, trying to shake off the jet lag, which was less welcome. Still, the ocean felt close enough to touch when she pushed the door all the way back, stretching away into what seemed like an eternity of blue-gray waves, a New England breeze bending the seagrass and whipping up the tops of the sand dunes. The hotel was so oceanfront that it practically had its front doorstep in the water and she loved it. People dotted the sand, splashing in the surf, poking at potential treasures in the flotsam that had washed up overnight on the shore.

She let herself pretend for just a moment that she was a Jane Austen heroine, visiting Bath perhaps or even the unfortunately fictional Sanditon, a seaside resort and her entire future life stretching out in front of her, with its possibilities of love and romance, happily-ever-after and an English country estate. Except, well—

No.

Because she wasn't here on vacation. Not precisely. She was here to buy herself a billionaire and then use him as a decoy boyfriend so her friends and family wouldn't pity very single self at her at her *cousin's* wedding.

She peeked out into the living room that presumably connected her bedroom with Nash's, but Nash was gone. His laptop sat on the work desk, however, along with a headset and his suit jacket. He didn't know how *not* to work.

Or at least she'd very rarely seen him in any kind of an off mode.

She made a victory lap of the living room, taking in the shiplap on the walls, the vintage-looking crystal chandeliers and the cleverly layered rugs in front of an actual fireplace. The decorator had gone with white-and-blue percales full of tiny chinoiserie patterns, the kind that told entire stories, and rattan furniture. She wanted to tuck all of it into her suitcase and bring it home with her. Her own shed-sized condo partly (a very, very small part) looked at the San Gabriel Mountains through some very large trees, but mostly just faced the parking lot and her neighbors' cars. That was California for you.

She grabbed her phone and FaceTimed her best friend. Lola was in the Comparative Literature Department and they'd met at a faculty seminar where a professor emeritus had mansplained domestic literature to them. Lola was stunningly beautiful, which she considered a severe professional liability as people stared at rather than listened to her. Right now, all that beauty looked rather rumpled and half-asleep, her blond hair in a messy twist and her usual cotton and recycled cashmere separates replaced by a ratty Brown University T-shirt.

"Wren." Lola squinted at her. "Why is it daylight where you are?"

Crap. She'd forgotten about the three-hour time difference.

"Oh, God. I can grovel now. I'm sorry."

"How about you just tell me where you are?" Lola's face pulled down in a frown that rivaled Nash's. "Because I'm concerned and, so far, this conversation is *not* allaying those concerns."

"I'm in Martha's Vineyard. With Nash. Helping him out."

The cone of silence didn't extend to Lola.

"Wow." Lola hesitated, which was unusual for her. "You two flew across the country just because you could? Or did Nash have deeply interesting reasons for spontaneously relocating to the other side of the country?"

"He has a thing," she groaned. "A bachelor's auction kind of thing."

Lola's glee radiated through the phone. "This, my love, is worth waking up for. Tell me all about it."

Just rip the Band-Aid off. Admit the truth. "He's up for sale tonight. I promised to buy him."

Okay. So that was half of the truth.

A sleepy beat. "Okay. Congratulations on your altruism."

"Also, you see, Noah and May have their wedding soon," she said quickly, before her natural good sense could convince her to keep those details to herself. She was so not inviting Lola to her pity party. "They 'can't wait' and 'when you find the one, you know' and all the other sentiments you'd find printed on the bridal decorations at Dollar Tree."

"Wren," Lola said sternly. "Either your grammar is horribly poor for an English professor or there's a connection between your purchasing your hot billionaire friend at a freaking auction and this upcoming wedding. Explain."

That word *explain*, a word that was really uttered as an order and a direction, a demand for complete and total accountability on her part, reminded her of Nash. He didn't take shit from people.

"We made a deal." She wandered over to the window—the ocean was truly spectacular, no view of the dumpsters or the parking lot for Nash—and gave up trying to conceal the truth from Lola. "I'd buy him and he'd date me. Just once. For the wedding, obviously. Just to get everyone off my back and so I can win a bet with my sisters."

Lola sucked in a breath. "You're kidding."

Wren hated pity. And accepting help. Looking stupid was also not on her list of favorite things and therefore showing up at Noah's wedding with a smoking-hot, fabulously successful "boyfriend" seemed ideal. "It's easier this way."

"Right," Lola said. "Because this way you can just pretend that your entire life is Instagram-worthy? And stick it to your sisters?"

Well. Yes?

"You do not need to prove anything to them," Lola continued.

"Yes, but—"

"There are no *buts*," Lola said severely. "You are perfect whether you are part of a couple, a throuple, a reverse harem—or solo. Single is fine. It's great. It means you get to focus one hundred percent on the most important person in the world—Wren Wilson."

"But—".

"But I get it," Lola sighed. Loudly and obnoxiously because she did have a point. "Broccoli's good for us, too. As is cardio. And investing in our retirement plans. We should have been the other kind of doctor, the practical kind."

She rolled her eyes. Nash was actually a very practical doctor, one who made ridiculous amounts of money and commanded the kind of respect usually reserved for presidents of entire countries. Arts and Letters professors were all well and good, but they usually were fairly broke. Lola herself taught sections to very reluctant undergraduates on how Russian poets responded to the English Byron. The only thing less popular, she'd pointed out, would have been if she actually *wrote* Russian poetry and then forced people to listen to it.

"Have you ever thought of *not* faking it?" Lola went on.

"What?"

Wren felt rather like Emma Woodhouse, learning that Frank Churchill had been sewn up by her nemesis.

"You could date Nash. He could date you." Wren could *hear* the shrug in Lola's voice.

"This is a fake-dating relationship. We're friends. We're *Tuesday* friends who share a love of tacos and not much else. No one would ever believe that we were dating for real."

"But you expect them to believe you this weekend."

"That is the point, yes."

"So actual, genuine belief is possible. Think about that," Lola demanded. "Your dating is, in fact, either entirely believable or you're about to have the world's most awkward forty-eight hours where everyone tries not to call you a liar to your face."

"I'm not getting into this," she said weakly.

"Because you know you'll lose. And that I'm right," Lola prompted. "Like I often am. What on earth is wrong with dating Nash for real?"

"We're friends."

"And friendship is a fantastic basis for a relationship."

"He doesn't believe in romance."

"Oh." A pause while Lola regrouped. Then, "Look. I love you—"

"I hear a *but*."

"Yeah. *But* you always tend to fantasize about the really unobtainable men, the kind that are closed off or commitment-averse or just ten thousand percent not available for a relationship."

Nash's head would explode at that math. She sort of wanted to repeat it just to see what he would do.

"You should be open to possibilities," Lola continued. "Focus on that, not some pie-in-the-sky romantic guy who doesn't really exist."

"There are good guys out there," she protested. "I read. I watch Netflix. Romance isn't dead."

"Are you still holding out for Mr. Darcy to be reincarnated?" Lola asked suspiciously. "Because we've discussed this. It's not happening and, if it did, we'd have to duel each other."

"I'd settle for Colin Firth to stop by for a cup of Earl Grey," she muttered.

"Colin who?" Lola said. "I'll take Matthew Macfadyen. But either one of them is better than the fantasy guy. You can't kiss a made-up man."

Nash either had a well-hidden Disney princess fetish or Wren's accusing him of being the anti-Mr. Romance had stung because he'd gone all out on the dress he'd sent her for the charity auction tonight. It was spectacular.

"Way to stand out," she muttered to herself, snapping a picture of the dress and texting it to Lola.

Not that she was a hermit (much) or anti-center stage (although a lectern was more in her comfort zone). Mostly, it just seemed sensible to fly under the radar at what was bound to be an event full of rich people and celebrities. Also, she suspected that she wouldn't be the only guest interested in purchasing Nash, so there was no point in sparking a bidding war before she absolutely had to.

The dress was not low-key. Not in the slightest. The setting sun pouring in the windows of their suite bounced off the yards and yards of crystals and shiny things sewn into the fabric. It was a Michael Cinco, according to the label, floor-length and made from armfuls of airy, beautiful tulle. Calling it gray was like calling mist wet; the dress sparkled and wrapped itself delicately around her fingers. Both the sleeves and the skirt were sprinkled with pale flowers and delicate fern fronds. It was a dress fit for Titania or a princess royal.

OMG, Lola texted. Did he give you a diamond parure? The crown jewels? Is he secretly Prince Harry???!!!

Harry is married, she texted back. They'd watched his wedding on YouTube and toasted him with champagne when he'd gone off the market.

Nash, on the other hand, refused to so much as stick a toe in the market. Tonight was going to be quite educational for him. Or rather, she looked forward to teasing him a great deal and teaching him that bachelor auctions could be fun. Probably. And if the night turned out to be a complete and utter debacle, at least they'd be supporting a great charity. She'd installed the mobile bidding software on her phone and tucked an emergency lipstick charger into her clutch because it would be just her luck for her phone to die before she could seal the deal and buy her billionaire.

Her phone dinged, but it was just Lola: Live text me!

This was followed by a picture. In the shot, a golden latte in a paper cup from their favorite coffee shop sat on a big rock in front of Stoddard Canyon Falls. This had always been their stopping spot in Angeles National Forest, and if Wren squinted, she could make out the water cascading down the flinty cliffs in the artfully blurred background. It was their favorite way to spend a Saturday.

Almost, she wished she were there. Sure there was graffiti scrawled on the rocks, but the water was icy cold even in the hottest of California summer months. Despite the way she jumped feet-first into relationships, she'd never worked up the courage (or defied sanity) to take the literal plunge and slide down the waterfall into the canyon. Putting on that magical dress and admitting she was going out on a date with Nash tonight felt too much like finally making that blind leap of faith, like letting going of everything that had held her back. The second she launched herself down the path, there would be no going back, just those handful of seconds, terrifying and exhilarating, exciting and fleeting, that separated the start from the end.

And then she and Nash would be over. Done. Burned out and finished, like all her relationships.

Friends, on the other hand, were forever.

Don't have too much fun without me! she texted, then wished not for the first time that the message app on her phone had a take-back feature. It was good if Lola had the best, most adventurous, exciting night ever. Wren didn't have to be there for it—it was about Lola. Just like tonight would be about Nash. It would all turn out all right.

She went into the bathroom, determined to relax and stop feeling sorry for herself. How hard could it be to shake out of her funk when she had a place like this to relax and she didn't even have to foot the bill?

The bathroom looked like a dream come true, or at the very least like the fantasy suite in some dating reality TV show. Vintage subway tile covered the floor, the kind found in slick Pinterest pictures or glossy design magazines. The walls were white and there were a ton of gold fixtures and Turkish towels. The star of the show, though, was the deep soaking tub in front of a floor-to-ceiling window with what the hotel manager had assured her was one-way glass overlooking the Atlantic Ocean. She dumped an irresponsible quantity of the hotel's foaming bath salts into the tub and started the water. Nash was a shower guy, so he'd never noticed that she'd taken more than her fair share.

When the tub was full, she sank into the hot water, letting the heat soak into her. She had two hours until the auction fake date, and she planned to enjoy every one of them. So there. She even lit the double-sided fireplace because who cared if it was summer? This was New England, where the beach never completely warmed up. She'd crank the AC if she had to and pretend she'd never heard of global warming.

Bliss. Utter bliss.

Bath water chaser for her ocean water? Yes, please. She let herself sink deeper, pretending that she never had to get out, that there was no bachelor auction to get through or crowd of strangers to make nice to. That she never had to go back to work, with its endless undergraduate papers and peer-reviewed journal edits, or her own rather quiet personal life. Which she liked. She *did*. She closed her eyes and let the audiobook playing on her phone lull her into a half-asleep state.

There was a straitlaced English Duke striding through her random, drifting thoughts, muscled from wrangling horses in just his linen shirtsleeves, and he'd found someone—who looked suspiciously like her shinier, prettier doppelganger—to kiss passionately in front of a roaring fire. Better, dreaming Wren acknowledged, than her usual stress dreams of searching endlessly for a bathroom or her teeth falling out. In her dream, she wasn't alone. She'd checked in—to the fantasy, to the hotel, to wherever she was—with someone special, someone she trusted and who held her close and whose hands moved confidently over her body.

She woke up aching and disoriented, the water still warm.

She slipped her hand between her legs, letting her fingertips drift over her folds and press down gently on her clit. There it was, the slow beat, the unfurling of something sweet and dark. She loved touching herself. She didn't need a duke or anyone else for this. She was enough. The guys in her life had loved watching, but she'd realized that made it about them, what turned them on, a secret shared that they enjoyed but then forgot. She always knew what she liked.

Her fingers continued to move, dipping deeper, gathering the slick moisture and the warmth of the water. Drawing circles around her clit as she told herself a story. Not a duke this time, but the hero of her favorite Jane Austen movie, the surly, unlikable but eminently lovable Mr. Darcy. He came striding through the mist in her fantasy, overcoat billowing around him, his eyes so dark they seemed black, that stubborn frown creasing his forehead.

For a second, she lost her rhythm, jolted out of her make-believe. That… That wasn't Mr. Darcy. That was Nash. Her big, grumpy, indomitable friend and fake-date buddy. A white linen shirt stretched over his broad shoulders, his unfastened cuffs making her want to seize his hand, place it on her body and then undo every last button. She leaned into dream Nash, her mouth reaching for his, feeling his hands seize her. His own mouth pressed an openmouthed kiss against her throat and she...

She melted.

Her stomach lurched, her eyes flying open. She didn't. She couldn't possibly. Lusting after a friend was weird, a violation of the friend rules that you could never, ever quite take back. She'd never felt like this for Lola, so she shouldn't be craving *Nash's* touch. And yet. She was wet.

For Nash.

Nash was off-limits.

And yet again... Her fingers made another pass over her clit.

Fantasy Nash was muttering things, rough, dirty things. *Don't open your eyes. Let me touch you here. You're so wet. Good girl.*

Her breath caught, her body on fire. Anticipation had her pussy liquid. What else would he do? What would she let him do?

A sound from the living room connecting her space with Nash's jolted her out of the fantasy. She wasn't alone, and even though he'd never come in, not without an invitation, she froze. If he did come in, he'd find her with her hands between her thighs, her fingers skimming over the sensitive flesh there, teasing and pressing deeper. Just the thought of that was enough to send her over the edge, the pulse of greedy need making her pussy contract. She wished...she wished.

She didn't quite know how she'd ended up here, but it didn't feel wrong. Not really. But then she was coming, her senses flying and every part of her focused on where her fingers pressed hard, holding herself together as she came apart quietly, barely breathing, her body on fire.

A door shut somewhere in their suite. She sat up, falling back into reality.

Six

After the Bathtub Incident, Wren got ready for the bachelor auction, certain of just one thing. This was not her world.

Scratch that. It wasn't even her universe.

But even if English professors rarely attended gala balls in couture dresses, she was happy to pretend to be someone a little more Cinderella than her everyday self for this one night.

The shoes helped.

Okay, the shoes were the gold star, the sprinkle of pixie dust, and single-handedly made flying across the country worthwhile. She swore undying affection for these shoes.

Even if they might kill her. Wren slipped on the delicate stilettos and got gingerly to her feet. Woo-hoo. Gravity defied, dose of reality applied, she was almost completely upright. She only hoped tonight's event included zero dancing.

As she took tentative steps to get her sea legs, someone knocked briskly on her bedroom door. Undoubtedly Nash, having braved the no-man's land of the ridiculously large living room connecting their bedrooms. Rooms. Thinking of Nash and *beds* in the same sentence was certain to lead to disaster. Or unseemly thoughts. There was an entire auction agenda to conquer, beginning with cocktails, followed by a fancy plated dinner and then the auction itself. She pulled the door open and her jaw dropped. Nash was—

There were no words, really, for what Nash was.

His obsessive working hadn't stunted his growth any. He was just as massive as always, his shoulders blocking out the room behind him. The jacket he wore, however, was a suit jacket in the way dragon fruit was a member of the fruit family. He looked exotic and expensive, absolutely delicious and stern. The black emphasized the aura of power clinging to him, and what woman wouldn't want more? He was drop-dead gorgeous. Ruggedly handsome. His big, muscled body wrapped up in the world's most devastating black tuxedo. Holy *shi—*

No. Be classy, Wren. Refined. At the very least, friendly and not drooling. She reached out and poked him in the center of his hard, white-shirt-clad chest.

His brow furrowed. "Wren?"

"Just checking to see if you're real," she said. Because honestly the only men she'd seen wear a tuxedo with that degree of appeal had been entirely imaginary. Movie stars. English princes. Models lounging around French palaces advertising luxury perfumes. Not that those weren't actually real people, but still. They were hardly going to knock on her door and ask if she was ready.

Which she was.

She totally was.

The furrow deepened. "What?"

"Never mind." She pointed down at her feet in their sparkling torture devices. "I'm charging extra for wearing these. You owe me at least one holiday meal with my family. Thanksgiving. Possibly Christmas. Both if I can't discreetly kick my shoes off under the table tonight."

He nodded. "Noted, you certainly should, and I expect you can. Worst-case scenario, we recreate our last hike together, without the actual ankle injury."

That would be the Runyon Canyon hike where she'd rolled her foot and he'd had to carry her out, piggyback style. Her stomach was doing the pitter-patter thing. Or maybe that was her heart? Indigestion, almost certainly. She simply had heartburn from her expensive foray into the hotel minibar earlier.

"Then our bases are covered," she said lightly.

Nash nodded again, wrapped her fingers up in his free hand and tugged her after him.

The valet had a sleek sports car waiting for them outside the hotel. Nash handed her in—look at the two of them, acting as if they had manners and this was really, truly a date—before tipping liberally and sliding into the driver's seat. He seemed even larger in the small confines of the car, those perfect shoulders filling up the available space. She redirected her attention out the window and up at the night sky. Despite the harbor lights and the more distant twinkle from the Massachusetts coast seven miles away, stars dotted the inky black above them. The moon rose over the ocean, almost full, luminous and beautiful.

She looked over the dunes to the ocean, waves breaking on the sand, rhythmic and soothing. "It's beautiful here. I can see why your brother likes it."

"He likes Charlotte," Nash said. "His fiancée."

"Do you think they'll stay here?"

"Maybe." He lifted one shoulder. "He walked away from Masterson Entertainment and J.J. He started his own film studio. He could run it from here. Mostly. With some travel."

"How did they meet?"

She'd looked them up on the internet, the details of their charity work and his film career almost buried in the more scandalous recent reports. She had no idea what a *good-guy contract* was or why Charlotte's first fiancé had been a world-class asshole, but she'd stopped reading quickly. It felt rude and she was just glad the other woman had gotten a happily-ever-after.

"They were partnered together in a charity boat race."

"Not your usual first date," she said.

He nodded, his face a little closed off. Probably, everyone asked about his famous brother, looking for stories or gossip. She focused her attention on Edgartown as the silence stretched on. Edgartown was pretty, the sort of place where you'd be constantly pointing out something new to your companion. There were white-timbered shops, flower boxes spilling geraniums, bicycle rentals, galleries, candy shops…

"The boat wrecked," Nash volunteered abruptly.

"*Very* unusual. We're not sailing tonight, are we?"

"Absolutely not."

"Was it romantic? Were they trapped in a cabin, forced to share body heat?"

He shook his head. "It was risky, cold and expensive. His insurance shot up."

"Mr. Romance." She slid him a look, but his attention was focused on the road. "So. Where are we going, mountain man?"

He flicked her a brief glance and named an iconic resort hotel. At least the food should be good. Nash drove with the same smooth confidence that he did everything, although he stuck precisely to the speed limit.

She sighed. "Are we really going to drive like a granny the whole way?"

"Speed limits increase safety and reduce the risks caused by drivers making their own speed choices."

She grinned at him. "So that's a definite yes."

"Smart aleck."

Lights from the sailboats moored at the private dock glinted on the water and she caught a glimpse of a lighthouse on the sand dunes that stretched out into the Atlantic. Lola had claimed she was too closed off to possibilities. Not that it was true, but perhaps she could be more adventurous tonight.

"Can I bid on two bachelors?"

He pulled to a careful, controlled stop by the valet parking stand. "Starting a harem? One guy's not enough?"

She shrugged. "Maybe I'd like a girl."

He slanted her a glance. "Whatever you want."

See? There was absolutely zero romance or romantic comedy possibilities in this evening, she realized even as she grinned self-consciously back at him. Of course he didn't see her as a romantic partner. He'd never imagine sex with his friend. In fact, he probably fantasized about beautiful, witty technopreneurs or world-class fencers. Some kind of exotic, ferociously intelligent woman who could have been a supermodel but instead decided to devote her life to curing cancer or something practical. Their practice kiss on his private jet had been just another piece of theater and not something he'd actually felt.

So maybe she wasn't closed off to possibilities, but she did seem to have a type. An unobtainable, impossible type. Had Noah been like that? Not that she'd felt all that strongly about him. He'd seemed like a good idea, liked by her family, employed, nice to her and willing to both text and call. He'd always been a bit distant and standoffish, coming over when it was convenient for him or, she realized now, wanting something. Dating him had turned out to involve quite a lot of work. Lola was right; she didn't put herself out there when there was actually a chance of someone reciprocating.

She gave up trying to solve her dating life and just watched Nash drive, steering the car with his big, competent hands, the pull of his tux jacket over his arms and shoulders as he moved. Objectifying him seemed weird but, on the other hand, they were on their way to a bachelor auction where presumably an entire ballroom's worth of people would be staring at him and deciding if he looked like someone they wanted to go on a date with. They'd weigh him up based on his face and his body, possibly the four-sentence CV in the bachelor menu. No one would know who he really was when you got past the face, the job title and all the money. They were missing out.

Maybe it was a good thing she was under a dating curse. They'd fake-breakup and then he'd go on to meet the love of his life.

Nash was a good guy, even if he made Mr. Darcy look like a ray of sunshine. Sure, he wasn't much of a talker, but he was good at listening. Plus, he came in that supersized body and he always looked all stoic. He'd be the guy commanding you not to panic as your airplane nosedived, right before he crawled out onto the wing and fixed the engine with a bobby pin and duct tape. Nash got things done and he took care of the people in his life.

The whole not-caring thing was, now that she thought about it, just a cover story. Rather like that nonexpression he liked to wear, when he was really closely monitoring everything around him, ready to spring into action. Of course he cared. If he didn't, he'd never have agreed to let his future sister-in-law auction him off. There was, in fact, no more wrong with his insides than his outsides. He listened, he came fully equipped with moral integrity, and all that gruffness hid some really genuine kindness. Of course she'd noticed his good looks, Exhibit A being her fleeting crush on him when he'd been her chemistry TA. The stern face, the grumpiness, the love of barked commands and annoying logic didn't change his fundamental attractiveness.

All it did was make her want to take a second look. And then a third, a fourth and right on to infinity looks. Ha. Nash would hate her math.

The iconic resort hosting the bachelor auction was a five-story hotel, white, with a gabled roof and a fabulous view of Edgartown Harbor and the coast. Nash brought them to a slow, precise stop in front of the valet parking stand. Someone immediately trotted toward them as Nash opened his door and strode around the car to help her out. He was Gentleman Nash tonight, his hand cupping her elbow to steady her as if she was a newborn baby elephant that couldn't be trusted on its feet yet.

She could feel the warmth of his hand on the bare skin of her elbow, smell the pinesy scent of him as he waited patiently for her to move. He smelled like an entire forest, something crisp and clean. Had he changed colognes? How had she not noticed this before?

"Is this what your brother's life is like?" she whispered as a swarm of photographers snapped their picture together. "He'd better invest in a castle with a moat."

The corner of his mouth twitched. "Smart aleck."

He steered her briskly past the photographers, ignoring them like he did most people in his path, and then they were walking through the hotel lobby and outside into a wonderland.

A stately, white Sperry tent stood just behind the hotel and overlooking the ocean. Tiny pennants that flapped in the ocean breeze topped the stiff canvas peaks. White fairy lights looped along the edges and through masses of peonies and roses. She grabbed onto Nash's arm, steadying herself as she hopped up trying to take it all in. A formal garden stretched away behind the tent, the shrubberies lit up with lanterns.

We're not in Kansas anymore.

Nope, she was on a white, candle-lined carpet that led into the tent.

"You're sure this isn't a pop-up wedding?"

"Very," he said dryly.

"Do you have hives? An allergic reaction? Because, news flash." She snuggled up against his arm. "This is extremely romantic. Beats boat racing any day. I had no idea bachelor auctions looked like this."

"Wonderful," he muttered.

"I imagined something much more like a heifer sale," she said, then skipped ahead of him with a laugh when he threatened to swat her butt. And then she stumbled in her ridiculous, fabulous shoes and he had to steady her, but never mind. He loomed by her side in a truly gorgeous tuxedo and looking like he was the movie-star brother with those broad shoulders and confident grip…

Nope. She was not going to think of him that way. Never again. Think of the periodic table. Something boring and entirely unsexy. Unfortunately, she only remembered that it started with single letters (the story of her life) and then rapidly became letter pairs, a capital letter and its lowercase friend. But. Still.

Unaware of her inappropriate interest, Nash steered her toward a table at the very heart of the tent and closest to the stage. A million eyes turned their way. Nash was big, he was rich and he was an all-round impressive guy.

He was a gentleman, too. He held out her chair for her and helped her sit down, even though she'd been sitting successfully on her own for almost thirty years now. More heads turned their way, people flipping through the same slick bachelor menu she'd first seen in Nash's lab. "Billionaire identification in three, two, one…"

He winced. "I have no idea why I agreed to do this."

Because he cared about his brother's fiancée. It was cute.

"It does seem unlike you," she agreed. "So. I installed the auction app on my phone. I assume I just wait until they call your name and I spot you on the stage. And then I throw money at you?"

"You bid."

"I throw money at you," she agreed.

"On your phone."

"Potato, potahtoh."

He gave her a look, then took her phone from her and added his credit card information to the app.

The dinner portion of the evening went surprisingly well. Their table sat eight, two of whom were Nash's famous movie-star brother and his fiancée. Nash had introduced them, but they'd barely sat down the entire evening as a bachelor auction required hands-on supervision. Whatever. Their other tablemates were Durants. The elder Mr. Durant was bearded, white-haired and pleasant, while his wife was more of a mischievous free spirit. Wren liked her immediately. The three daughters were pretty, fiercely entrepreneurial and entirely oblivious that their father was holding out hope that one of them would fall instantly in love with Nash and he with her. The oldest daughter ran an Etsy wallpaper business, while the youngest was a successful social media influencer who'd just bought her first house. The middle daughter was Durant's corporate attorney and, all in all, Wren thought they were too plain busy to even consider dating Nash, let alone marrying him. He could have saved his money.

Still, a deal was a deal, so when Mr. Durant turned toward her, she was ready.

"I'm Theo Durant, husband to this fabulous woman on my right, and proud daddy of the world's most amazing girls." She nodded, but the man didn't need any encouragement to launch into a fabulously embarrassing summary of his girls' latest achievements, which was cute but also made two of them look as if they were giving serious consideration to hiding out in the bathroom until he finished. Which could take all night because Durant really, really loved his family. It wasn't until he'd spent ten minutes extolling their virtues that he concluded with: "And I'm the owner of a chemical company this young man here has offered to purchase. And you are?"

She was charmed that the successful company came last in his list. Durant sure loved to talk, but he also loved, openly, honestly and loudly. Good for him.

"I'm Nash's girlfriend," she said brightly.

Surprise!

Durant blinked. "A girlfriend?"

"Well," she winked. "We don't like to put labels on our feelings for each other, but that's a good one, right? It lets people know where we started and that we're on step one of our 'Be family!' plan. Right, Nash?"

Nash grunted something.

Durant, on the other hand, was examining Nash as if he'd never seen him before. Was that a good sign?

She beamed at the older man and told the absolute truth. "Nash is a very nice person. He's doing this auction for his brother and his brother's fiancée. She refused to just take cash, so here Nash is. Participating."

The ghost of a smile appeared on Nash's mouth. "With Wren."

"We've known each other for eight years," she added. "There's no one else he'd rather *participate* with. So. Here I am."

Durant's face softened. "Taking things slow, are you? But not too slow, I hope. You never know how long you'll have."

Wow. That was a downer.

"Slow is good," she argued. "Lets you appreciate a good thing. Plus, slow is Nash's natural habitat. He drives like a granny, he's an engineer and *methodical* is his middle name. He likes to be sure of his…facts."

"Theo." Mrs. Durant rolled her eyes. "Stop trying to matchmake."

"He doesn't need to do that for us." Wren wrapped her hand around Nash's amazing left bicep and squeezed.

"I don't?"

"Nope," she said cheerfully. "Because this is a very big weekend for us. Huge. The biggest milestone ever! Nash told me to expect something very soon. When you find your one and only, you know, right?"

Nash imitated a sullen iceberg beside her, but Mrs. Durant was giggling and Mr. Durant was nodding slowly, clearly having a conversation with himself in his head. Hopefully, it was going something like this:

"Is this Nash guy a total family man who will cherish my company the way I do? Why, yes! He totally is!" And then they could e-sign the contracts or whatever it was one did to transfer ownership of a multibillion-dollar corporation.

Fortunately, Mrs. Durant steered the conversation in another direction, and it was smooth sailing straight through the main course. She'd even managed to steal a selfie with Nash that she texted to her family: Look who's about to be off the market!

Are you quite sure? Emily texted back almost immediately. Is he going to growl and stomp around the wedding? Isn't he the one you called a bear?

Nash cleared his throat. "Did you?"

Dinner was being cleared away and the quiet Charlotte was muttering as she flipped through a stack of actual paper note cards while her movie-star fiancé lounged next to her, smiling and rubbing her back like a beautiful guard dog. Wren was deeply grateful that she wasn't the one getting up onstage.

She felt Nash stiffen as she leaned up to whisper in his ear. She should probably give him his space but they had to maintain the illusion of their fake date, didn't they? "Would I have called you a bear if I'd known we'd be in this situation? A bachelor auction? An entire fake relationship? No, of course not, Nash. This was not how I foresaw the future when I signed up for Chemistry 101 in college. I could have prepared. You could have told me some things about yourself. I would have stored up some really great material, stories to tell my sister and my mother. Now they think you're this big, unfriendly guy I sometimes have lunch with and they wonder if it's Stockholm syndrome rather than true love. You're hard to get to know. We eat lunch together and we hang out, but that's not the same as dating."

So there. She sank back into her seat. There was a hint of a flush on Nash's cheeks and the pink made him seem ever so slightly more approachable.

She risked a quick glance around, but no one was paying attention to them. The volume of excited chatter in the room more than drowned out her quiet whisper. It was so loud that he had to bend his head closer to hers, close enough to reinforce their dating cover story, that was for sure.

"You would have tried to be my real girlfriend?" A momentary look of surprise crossed his face before it hardened back into its usual stern lines. "This is something you would have done?"

"Would I have striven for more authenticity? For you, yes." She stole the decorative cookie from his plate. Was it classy? No. But hey, people had been eating with their fingers for thousands of years and who wasted a perfectly good cookie? "It's not such a hardship, Nash. Plus, I do have some pride and I do not need anyone at the wedding knowing—or hinting, guessing or Instagramming—that I was so desperate that I bought myself a boyfriend."

He tilted his head. "Is that so?"

"Plus, the better I do here, the better you'll do. I'll hold up my end of our bargain. You don't have to worry about that."

"Are you worried that I'll back out on you?" he asked calmly.

It wasn't that. Not precisely. More like *humiliation*

galore being in her future if he recanted, not least of which would be Emily's crowing over winning their bet and then having to date a man her sister had picked out for her.

"I... I need you to do this, all right? I told them you were coming and so now if you don't come, it will be a thousand times worse. Which is probably only fair since I'm not exactly telling them the truth. But still. Please."

"I told you I'd come, Wren. I won't break a promise." She thought she heard him mutter, "not to you."

"All right, then." She stared at him, not sure what to say next. This wasn't tacos or friendly conversation. It wasn't even the easy relationship where she teased and he sat there like the Grim Reaper, scaring off everyone but her. He was, now that she thought about it, a bit of a rock in her life.

But there was no time to think about it further because a woman in a black suit with a headset and a badge around her neck was discreetly touching Nash's arm and motioning for him to follow her. Across the table, Mrs. Durant was laughing and clapping as Nash stood, while her bevy of gorgeous daughters suddenly perked up. Crap.

"Showtime!" Wren tugged his sleeve, forcing him to bend down to her level. A good girlfriend would probably send him off with a good-luck kiss. Or goose his butt. Paint some lipstick on his cheek. She settled for brushing a quick kiss in his direction, an air kiss that almost, not quite landed on his mouth. They should have practiced more. She was still debating whether she should come in for the kiss landing on his cheek or his mouth, when he turned his own head, his lips brushing hers.

"Don't forget me," he murmured against her mouth. She felt his lips curve ever so slightly upward as he… he *kissed* her and then he was pulling back and she was sitting there, probably looking like she'd been hit with a two-by-four.

Seven

Declan flashed a discreet but rude gesture at Nash from the emcee's podium. Since Nash was on hour three going on eternity waiting in the wings for his onstage debut, his answering response was less subtle. And given the amusement on his brother's face, he'd get no sympathy from that quarter.

The auction guests were laughing and finishing their meals, champagne flutes raised, smiling at the bachelors onstage… Nash felt like the prize lobster in a restaurant tank, waiting for some hungry diner (or Durant) to pluck him out. It was the first time in…well, almost forever that he'd waited for someone to choose him. The feeling was every bit as horrible as he remembered, although if he leaned to the left he could see out past the stage to Wren and their table.

Smile, Wren mouthed from her seat. *Play nice with the other kids.*

Smart aleck, he mouthed back at her.

She waved her phone at him. *Ready to go, boss!*

The bachelor lounging next to him, wearing a Stetson and a bad-boy grin, pointed at her. "Do you know her? Is she bidding on you?"

"Yes. Less risk in the known," he said, eying Wren. Was she bidding on the current bachelor?

The cowboy considered that for a moment. "Smart."

"You have no idea."

Truth was, Wren was more than smart. She was funny and protective, her beauty outweighed only by the tenacity that had gotten her through graduate school and into a tenure-track position.

"I appreciate smart. Perhaps I should beg her to bid on me."

The cowboy flashed a slow, lazy smile at Wren, adjusting his Stetson as he did so. The thought of Wren smiling back made Nash bristle.

Nash choked down an unexpected urge to throttle his fellow bachelor. Charlotte wouldn't thank him if he made the guy less pretty before she'd had a chance to auction him off. He settled for glowering, which must have got the message across just fine because the cowboy readjusted his hat and then nudged the woman in the suit who'd been hovering near him.

"Take one for the team and bid on me, sweetheart."

Looking unimpressed, Suit Lady crossed her arms over her chest. "If I win, I'll have you cleaning out my garage, Bowen West."

Nash was rooting for her to win.

Bowen's grin deepened. "I've had worse dates."

"I'll just bet you have," she huffed. Then nudged him forward. "You're on."

Bowen sauntered onto the stage to whoops from their audience as Declan announced that Bachelor West was a poker player, cowboy and star of an upcoming reality TV show. Apparently the network executives had decided it would be a good idea to house a bunch of poker players in a Las Vegas mansion and have camera crews follow them around while they lived the *high-roller lifestyle*. Nash had a good idea how that would turn out.

But then, there was tonight.

The crowd greeted Bowen with enthusiasm and more than one loud wolf whistle that almost, but not quite, drowned out the horribly cute rhyme with which Declan summarized the guy: *this poker whiz is in the movie biz.* Bowen seemed to eat it up, tipping his Stetson one last time at Wren's table, so that Nash bit back a growl.

Whoever had written tonight's script needed to be fired. He bet Wren would have something to say about the overuse of alliteration, too.

Still, all the bad poetry didn't seem to put off the bidders. The auction app made a clicking sound whenever someone placed a bid, and an enthusiastic wave of sound swept through the ballroom. Of course everyone liked a cowboy, and this one was shooting a reality TV show. From the number on the screen positioned behind the stage to show the current high bid, that was worth a lot. Like ten thousand dollars' worth of appreciation. Huh.

His phone buzzed and he looked down discreetly at Wren's text.

I'm bidding! How could anyone pass on a charismatic cowboy?

Focus, he texted back. Wrong bachelor.

Wren looked positively gleeful as she hunched over her phone. Perhaps we have an open relationship?

There was only one possible response. I would be more than enough.

Wren grinned at him across the distance. *Are you sure?* she mouthed.

He nodded.

His phone promptly buzzed again. He hoped she could bid as fast as she could text. Do you come with cowboy accessories? I'll bet he has a HORSE. Unless you have a pony or a unicorn, you're beat.

He'd never been much of a smiler, but he could feel the corners of his mouth curving upward. "Jesus. She's such a smart aleck."

"I know the feeling," the minder beside him muttered. "Imagine trying to wrangle *that*."

She gestured at the cowboy, who was sauntering in a lazy circle onstage, gesturing for his audience to "go all in on him" and "bet the farm."

Look at his dimples! I'll bet he has the cute butt dimples TOO, Wren texted.

He leaned back against the wall. Best not to feed the beast when it came to Wren's sense of humor. Plus, she was right. The cowboy did come with an amazing set of dimples. The face kind, not the butt kind. Nash wasn't going to speculate about the guy's hidden assets. He also looked fun and baggage-free, which were good qualities in a date. Wren deserved to meet someone like him.

Wren narrowed her eyes, but fired one last shot. There's no rule against buying two bachelors, right? I mean, a lucky girl gets two desserts. This is the same thing.

Waiting his turn in the wings to go on the block, Nash radiated dark and dangerous. Wren knew the glower painted all over his handsome face meant that he was deeply unhappy about his current situation, but hadn't figured out a way to extricate himself. Yet. Of course, he could turn and walk away. But since he seemed to genuinely care about his brother's fiancée and making her happy, Wren didn't think he would do that. It was kind of cute, really. And absolutely sweet.

It was also the first time, she suspected, that those words had ever been used to describe Nash.

But he was.

Onstage, bidding wrapped up on the cowboy, and he sauntered off to meet his lucky winner. Nash strode onto the stage and took his place. The sheer ludicrousness of the situation must have sunk into his super-brain because he caught her eye and there was an actual, honest-to-god smile on his face, a sighting that was rarer than a nene goose in Hawaii.

Declan rested his chin on Charlotte's shoulder. He'd pulled his fiancée onto his lap behind the emcee's podium, and it was too stinking cute how he had his arms wrapped around her waist.

"Bachelor Nash," Declan intoned, and there was no missing the humor in his voice. "Ladies and gentlemen, please welcome my baby brother to the stage. This thirty-four-year-old bachelor owns and runs his own billion-dollar chemical company. He may not have the family charm, but he definitely got the brains."

The ensuing devilish pause did not bode well for Nash's dignity. If it had been her up there, she'd have turned and run.

Sure enough, Declan winked and delivered the corniest line of the evening. "He's smart—and might have a heart."

Whatever zinger he might have planned to land next was drowned out by a wave of clicking as every single person in the tent started bidding. Whoa. She had one job and she was failing.

Wren looked down at the phone in her hand. A deal was a deal.

Then she started bidding frantically, certain she'd sprain her thumb or worse. Because who knew that billionaires could be so expensive?

She forced herself not to look up and check on Nash. He'd be fine, the big baby. All he had to do was stand there and look hot and unattainable, stoking the crowd into a bidding frenzy. From the crazy numbers popping up on the auction app, he was going to cost a fortune. Cars were cheaper and at least you got to keep those. Still—she risked a look at the stage, thumb tap-tap-tapping away on her screen—and eyed her prize. Perhaps the price was per pound or something? He was freakishly large, muscled and strong, all wrapped up in that black tuxedo like a very sexy, glowering package.

Honestly, it was a good thing he seemed constitutionally opposed to smiling. If he actually broke out a grin or a wink or any one of those charming gestures his cowboy predecessor had wowed the audience with, he'd break the app. His dark hair was cut ruthlessly short. Smoldering eyes, so dark they appeared almost black. Ridiculously long lashes. Broad shoulders that made her think of Vikings, either the medieval invaders or the football team. He was just so big everywhere she looked, and not even the urbane sophistication of his tux could soften the impression he made. This was the guy you wanted to fight for you.

Onstage, Charlotte crowed, clearly delighted by the constant stream of bids. She was probably wishing that Declan had a dozen brothers she could raffle off for her charity foundation.

Nash's frown deepened. His gaze lasered in on Wren. *Bid,* he mouthed. There was another word after that, but she couldn't quite make it out.

I've got you, she mimed back.

The bidding hit fifty thousand. Sixty. Wren gave up thinking logically about all the things one could do with sixty thousand freaking dollars and worked her phone like it was a video game controller. A quick scan of the faces around her told her she wasn't the only one who wanted to add a broody bachelor to her life.

Seventy thousand.

Eighty thousand.

Charlotte couldn't spit the numbers out fast enough and Declan just kept egging everyone on.

The crowd picked up on his chant. "Ninety thousand, one hundred thousand."

Wren clicked and tapped like a woman possessed. Thank God she was using Nash's special billionaire credit card because her own would have burst into flames like a vampire in the sun.

The bidding hit 150. 160. This had to be the home-stretch, right? She was the jockey and Nash was the racehorse and the finish line was right there so it was time to let 'er rip. Or perhaps boxing would have been a better sporting metaphor? She bid faster, eyes glued to the screen, no longer looking around. This was it. This was the moment where she brought it home, scored the winning goal, saw her victorious self hoisted up above the cheering crowd on a pair of sexy, broad shoulders. Nash was hers.

"Going once," Charlotte called.

Wren stared at the phone. Then the stage. Then back at the phone again. Just to be sure, she tapped the button a few more times. It was for charity after all and Nash was rich. Generous. About to be relived of the awful burden both of dating a total stranger and $300,000.

"Going twice," Declan intoned beside her. Nash crossed his arms over his chest, looking like a man who had somewhere important to be.

You're going home with me.

"Sold!" Charlotte's announcement was almost drowned out by Wren's celebratory whoop as the app dinged and digital confetti burst across her screen.

"Gooooaaal!" she shrieked. Did it make sense? Not at all. But… She'd *won*. She wanted to rush the stage. To throw her arms around Nash and do a little victory jig right there. Take that! She'd won!

A wave of laughter and applause rippled through the audience, starting with Mr. and Mrs. Durant. Nash didn't look as if he minded. He strode off the stage, down the steps and straight toward her.

She stood up to greet him. "You're all mine."

Mr. Durant was busy announcing to their table that true love had won and slapping Nash on the back with enough vigor that Wren was tempted to ask him if he'd confused camaraderie with the Heimlich maneuver.

"Can we go now?" Nash asked her.

"Go?"

"Now that you own all of me," he said.

"Body and soul?" She batted her eyelashes at him. They did have an audience, after all.

"Smart aleck," he said, but he was laughing silently. She was sure of it.

After the auction, Nash stuck by her side for the brief remainder of the evening. Wren wasn't sure how long they were expected to stick around, but even she knew their fake-date charade wouldn't pass muster if she bid and then they immediately fled out the door. At the very least, people would wonder if her credit card had been declined and she was absconding with the goods. Or decide that she couldn't wait to get him naked, except that it hadn't been one of those sell-your-virginity auctions that Lola was always trying to get her to read about and that she thought sounded far too much like Almack's and the nineteenth-century marriage mart.

But they got through the night. The Durants liked her or at least weren't holding a grudge at her having cornered the market on Nash. She probably should have told him that she was a good-luck love charm and that Nash would undoubtedly fall madly, passionately in love with one of the Durant daughters quite soon. The thought of him dating one of their dinner companions felt inexplicably off: her chest twinged thinking about it, although that was probably just too much free food.

In the end, it was a good thing she wasn't really Cinderella because by the time they were back at the hotel, it was long past midnight, most of the island's residents gone to bed and the moon painting long, silvery strips on the surface of the ocean. A sleepy desk clerk nodded to them as they came in, but otherwise the hotel was quiet.

Nash leaned against the side of the elevator, hands jammed into his pockets, head tipped back. He looked pained. Or tired. Definitely not as if he wanted to relive tonight over and over. At least she'd scored an amazing dress out of it.

"Mission semi-accomplished!" she announced cheerfully as soon as the elevator doors closed behind them and they were on their way up. "It went well, don't you think? Durant thinks we're madly in love."

"You told him you were sure I was about to—and I quote—'put a ring on it.'"

"I went with the flow and it was genius. You're obviously a family kind of guy now, right? You're thinking forever and babies and he knows it. His company will be utterly safe in your family-friendly hands. And then you can live happily ever after with your true love, Durant Family Chemicals, and fake-break up with me." The elevator doors slid open. "In fact, that just proves that I'm totally a love charm."

"What?" He tilted his head.

"Anyone I date goes on to find true love right after breaking up with me." She shrugged. "It happens every time. You'll just get matched with your ideal patent portfolio rather than a flesh-and-blood person, but details! Or you could branch out, date for real, find your one."

His jaw twitched. Right. Nash was an unbeliever when it came to love. That was fine. It would happen for him, no matter what he believed, because he was a surprisingly good guy.

They'd gone out on a fake date. They'd kissed—once on the plane, and did that half kiss at the auction count? It should, although she should probably double-check the definition of a kiss on the *Merriam-Webster* website later. Just to be sure. *Two* kisses. Not that it mattered.

She got to the door first.

"Wren?"

"Yeah?" She rummaged in her bag, looking for the card key. Her purse was a key-eating black hole. It was a new scientific phenomenon that would be named after her.

"Let me help." His arm came around her, the rest of him moving closer. Just to open the door, of course. Nothing more, and yet she was disappointed when he simply slid his own card key over the lock pad and the green light flashed.

Go in, night over, all done. That was not her first choice. Instead, she stared at his hand. Okay. So his hand wasn't her first choice, either. She wanted to turn around, to pretend that she'd won him for real and that this was the ending to an actual, honest-to-God date. She had no idea why. Perhaps it was a side effect of the open bar and outbidding his fan club?

"Let me?" A rough catch in his voice. His mouth brushed her ear. As if he'd leaned into her, as if his mouth was right there, close enough to whisper. *Or kiss,* her brain suggested.

Curious, she turned around, back against the door. She felt it give slightly as he turned the handle. Instead of going in, she looked up—and then up some more— at his face. At his mouth, specifically.

"I'd like a second chance," he said.

She forced herself to look up farther, to meet his dark eyes, focused on her. Intent. Warm. That was new. She thought. Maybe? It wasn't as if she'd spent much time inventorying her friend's face.

Liar.

"At kissing you," he clarified. "You said our plane kiss wasn't fire."

"Why on earth would that be a good idea?"

"Because I can do better. *Be* better," he said and gently pulled her toward him. The door was open, she could step back, walk away. Instead, she let him tug her nearer and then he kissed her. Thorough. Deliberate. As if *he* were making an inventory of *her.*

Heart racing, pulse pounding, she fisted the lapels of his jacket. She really, *really* wanted to lean into this moment. She wanted it enough to pull him nearer.

He met her more than halfway, wrapping his arms around her, bringing their bodies flush together. His jacket brushed against the bare skin of her back, his big hands wrapped around her ribs and waist. Chest to chest, thigh to thigh, and all his best parts touching hers. No. Fitting hers, like puzzle pieces or the key to a lock. He kissed her, and she kissed him back, long and slow, hungry and eager.

A first kiss.

The first that was for just them and not for this... game they'd made up, the joke they were playing on the world. It started so slowly. With how she watched him coming closer, his mouth discovering hers, breathing her in, giving her back that same breath. It was almost painful, the intensity in his dark eyes, the heat with which he watched her. Standing this close, no space between them, she could feel his chest rise and fall with each new breath, the heat of him, the small tensing of his arms as he moved. Heat pooled in her stomach, moved lower.

"Wren."

He kissed her then, his mouth closing that last small distance between them, and it felt like everything. Soft and determined, then firmer, his teeth nipping at her lips as everything in her demanded *openupopenupopenup*. His tongue slid into her mouth, his hands pressing her closer while her own moved over his arms, up, digging into his shoulders, his neck, his scalp. Marking him as hers. He uttered something, a rough, half-a-word, pleased, surprised, and her body unfurled, aflame with wanting this man. She threw herself into the kiss, holding nothing back.

"Wren—" He groaned her name, nothing more, but that was good. She was too desperate for more, moving against him, kissing him back, trying to show him how he made her feel. That it was almost, not quite, enough. She was dizzy on him, body on fire, head spinning and Nash drunk. The world shifted—

Not the world. The door. Pushing open. She staggered, off-balance, but he steadied her.

"Good to know," she told him, pulling back just the smallest amount, still close enough that her lips brushed his with each word. "That you respond so well to criticism."

He laughed, nipping gently at her lower lip. "Suggestion. But—"

Hello, her good friend Reality. She'd just—she'd kissed Nash. She'd fallen completely, entirely off the friend wagon. It had taken eight years—*years*—to get this far and she liked him. She loved their friendship. She'd forgotten how much their friendship mattered to her, and she'd risked it all. Because he was staring at her thoughtfully, the heat in his eyes banked. Because they weren't really boyfriend and girlfriend. Boy and girl. They were friends.

"Wren?" She looked up. Okay—that was concern painted across his beautiful face. Ugh. He didn't seem swept away anymore or wowed or as if that kiss had been anything more than a sexy exercise. He didn't seem any different than before. "I can't be your one and only."

"Of course not." She hadn't—

She'd never thought—

"You deserve that."

"I do."

She believed that. She really, *really* did, but the thing was, he deserved it, too, even if she seriously doubted that he thought true love and happily-ever-after were fairy tales. Made-up things. Fake.

And then he said the last thing that she expected.

"Good night."

And then before she could regroup and say anything,

he turned and walked his fine ass down the hallway and out of sight.

Fake date, fake kiss, totally fake expectations.

It sucked.

Eight

"Is there a reason why my beloved baby brother is asleep on my sofa?"

Nash pulled a throw pillow over his eyes, not ready to face his brother without coffee. Especially not when the way Wren had kissed him last night kept looping through his head. The needy whimper she'd made. For him. It made him want to rethink his conclusion that he couldn't be the man Wren needed and go straight back to their hotel suite, and that was a bad idea. No matter how quickly they ended, Wren went all in on her relationships while they lasted and she deserved someone who could meet her wholeheartedly.

Hearts were for blood flow, not feelings.

"He's smart—and might have a heart?" he counter-asked, rather than considering that he might, just possibly, have experienced a few unexpected feelings last night. There was no room in his life for anyone, himself included, to have actual goddamned feelings.

"The jury's out on that one. You've got a lock on the role of curmudgeon, but sometimes you can't just typecast."

For fuck's sake. Was that a metaphor? Poor use of symbolism? Figurative language was wasted on him. "This is Martha's Vineyard, not Hollywood."

"Also true," Declan said. "And you still haven't answered my question."

The truth was, he'd borrowed Declan's couch because he hadn't wanted to make Wren feel awkward or as if he expected anything from her, even though they'd both agreed that last night's kiss had been a mistake. Declan had just bought an enormous waterfront place in Edgartown because Charlotte was a year-round Vineyard resident. And since sleeping somewhere other than his hotel suite had seemed like the right thing to do and Declan owned an enormous mansion, here he was.

"I don't have a heart," he said. "Not that kind, at any rate."

His was just the normal four-chambered organ, not the greeting-card kind.

Declan snatched the pillow away and Nash gave up hiding from reality. It was more efficient to face problems head-on anyhow.

Declan smirked. "You have a heart, you bastard."

"Well, obviously." He sat up, scrubbing a hand over his head. He should have thought his overnight out better because all of his things were in his hotel room and absolutely none of them were here. "It's a basic circulatory requirement. Mine just doesn't do all that other stuff people mistakenly attribute to hearts."

"You mean happiness, sadness, fear, anger?" Declan wandered away from the couch and Nash followed him, hoping there was coffee somewhere close by. "And let's not forget about your favorite, love!"

Emotions came from the brain and from the limbic system in particular, but even Nash knew that wasn't the point here.

"The jury is out on my having a heart," he said. "Permanently."

"Because you refuse to have one," Declan argued, leading the way into a modern kitchen the size of Nash's laboratory.

"Overrated," he countered. "And why would I even want one?" He hated the chaos and uncertainty that came with the sort of feeling people liked to label as love. Hated the coming and the going, the arguing and the completely unsettling sensation of not knowing what would happen next or when. He had no idea why anyone would want that.

"Lots of reasons," Declan groaned. "So many reasons. You have to trust me on this."

"Name *one*."

"It makes the sex way better."

Nash shot him a look. "My sex life is not open for discussion."

"Love," Declan said firmly. "It makes the sex better. You can be honest, open up, share what you really want."

"I do those things already." In bed, obviously. Communication was important. He *knew* that, thank you very much.

"Right." Declan eyed him. "We're not getting anywhere."

Nash knew most people were convinced he was a scary asshole. That reputation, however, hadn't stopped their adoptive father, J.J., from trying to convince Nash to take over the family film business when Declan had refused to play their old man's games. The ask had been futile because Nash hated the overly emotional film world. The personal drama. The emotions everyone flaunted for the whole word to see. He kept the emotional side of himself private.

For J.J., Masterson Film was everything. It meant a seat at important Hollywood tables and being acknowledged as a player in the industry. It meant money. Power. He couldn't understand why Nash didn't want to be more like his adoptive father. Nash, on the other hand, had put himself through school, launching his own company, building its portfolio of patents and products, even if it meant sacrificing a personal life and living in his laboratory. He'd worked, and then worked more to build a thriving company. He'd expanded to new sites and built his patent portfolio to record numbers. Even better, he liked what he did. Masterson Chemicals had developed some life-changing products, including a new synthetic fertilizer that was both green and inexpensive. And the money was good. Great. He had more now than J.J. had ever had, and he'd earned it on his own.

He was dependent on no one.

He *needed* no one.

After the chaos of his childhood, being moved from

one foster placement to the next until J.J.'s unexpected adoption, he'd vowed to be in control of his life. No one would make decisions for him, however benevolent. And yet somehow he'd allowed a real friend to turn into a fake girlfriend, all because a potential business partner thought Nash needed to be a different kind of person and more like the partner. Worse, having Wren in his life like that felt nice. Natural. And not wrong. He might…like it.

"I had high hopes when you said you were bringing someone. You've never done that before." Declan eyed him over his coffee cup. There was an uncomfortable amount of hope and encouragement in his brother's eyes. "How long have you had a girlfriend?"

"Are we back to the love-and-feelings thing?" Nash downed half his mug. This was ridiculous.

"Tell me about your girlfriend. Then, yes, I'd like to hear about love and your feelings. In the girlfriend context."

As a scientist, Nash was all about accuracy and veracity. He knew the value of an experiment where the data had been rushed or fudged and it was worthless. He would never cheat on his results or record anything other than facts. He could identify patterns and follow a set of protocols without a single deviation. But none of that helped him now.

"Wren is not really my girlfriend."

Declan looked at him suspiciously. "Are you going to argue she's some random stranger? Because you've mentioned her before."

Of course he had. "We're friends."

Declan continued to look suspicious. "Just friends?"

"What the hell does that even mean? Wren is my friend. She's also the kind of person who's extremely helpful and who has no boundaries. She's constitutionally incapable of saying no."

"You've never brought someone before," Declan repeated. "You always come to my things alone."

He could feel the flush creeping up his face. "Well, this particular *thing* seemed *particularly* awful, so I asked Wren to come. As a friend. A very helpful friend."

Declan shook his head. "I don't even know where to start with that."

Nash did.

"Did last night go well? Is Charlotte happy?"

"Ecstatic," Declan said. "Last night was amazing. So amazing that she's still upstairs, sleeping. Completely worn out, but she's smiling in her sleep."

Nash held up a hand. "Overshare."

Nash was not going to ask how much of that ecstasy had come from the auction results and how much from his brother. He did not need to know. Plus, it made him think about Wren, which was inappropriate. Was she still asleep? Was she smiling? Intimacy had never been something he overthought. He had sex, he adhered to the Golden Rule (make sure she comes first and most) and he enjoyed himself. Sex was great. Who wouldn't like it? But it turned out that sex in a relationship was entirely different from dating app hookups or conference sex. People wanted to hear about your feelings. Worse, they insisted that you have them and got upset when you didn't.

Declan sighed, put his coffee mug in the dishwasher

and pointed toward the beach. "Come on. We'll run and I'll get it out of you when you're too breathless to resist."

There was no *it* to get, so Nash wasn't worried. He changed into a pair of borrowed shorts and strode down to the long strip of private beach that fronted his brother's new home. The ocean was calm today, the cloud cover minimal. The sun was out, too, burning off the remnants of the early morning fog. Good. The blue sky was good, although he'd already counted an inordinate number of seagulls that would shit on them.

"So where are you taking Wren on your date?"

"My assistant booked something."

Declan groaned. "But what does Wren like?"

Nash shrugged. "It doesn't matter."

Wren and he had a deal, and she'd keep her end of it. He could take her on the world's worst date, a voice in his head reminded him, and she'd laugh at the joke of it and go along. Romance was not required for a fake date. Who really wanted romance anyhow? Sure, lots of people—apparently including Declan—thought they did but love affairs almost always seemed to end badly with hurt feelings and dramatic scenes where people moved on only after explaining all the ways the other person had failed to live up to expectations. Just look at Wren's dating life. It was like the world's worst performance review at work, only over and over again and without the possibility of a raise.

And yet Wren claimed to like romance. No, she completely and 100 percent believed that she did, and he did try not to scoff at her opinions even when they were completely ridiculous. He picked up their pace, laying in a neat, straight course above the high tide mark.

"Fuck's sake," Declan groaned, falling into step beside him. "This isn't Coronado. We're not training to be a Navy SEAL."

Since there was no point in doing something if you weren't going to be the absolute best at it, Nash ignored him. If Declan still had air to waste on talking, they weren't running fast enough.

Undeterred, Declan kept right on going. "She obviously likes you just fine."

Nash kept his gaze focused on the horizon. It was safer.

"There was plenty of chemistry between the two of you."

"Wren is a friend."

"Nope," Declan said, popping the *p*. "You can't convince me of that."

"Sorry," he gritted out. "But it turns out you're not the only actor in this family because Wren is a friend of mine, a friend who agreed to help me out in exchange for a favor. She agreed to come here as my fake date and buy me."

"Why wouldn't you ask her out for real? She sounds like she's great."

"Seriously? Are you fronting a dating app now?"

"Don't knock the matchmaking potential of charity events," Declan replied, although he was smirking. "Remember how I met Charlotte."

"You fell out of a boat and were shipwrecked," Nash said dryly. "This is not an easy scenario to replicate."

"The important bits are easy," Declan argued. "Alone time, a common cause, some kind of sticky relationship glue to hold you together while things set."

"Sticky like a shipwreck."

"What's wrong with you?" Declan asked.

They'd been over this. Repeatedly. "I'm not relationship material."

"Who told you that? Look, all I want for you is a partner and happiness, a family and a place where you belong."

"Christ," Nash muttered. "You sound like a greeting card or one of those self-actualization mantras."

"I sound *right*," Declan countered. "And you know it. Completely, totally right. I want you to have it all. I think you've spent so much time proving that you don't need anyone, that you're doing just fine on your own and that you won't let J.J. play us off against each other, and that just gives you another reason not to take anything from him."

"So I prefer to take care of myself. Last time I checked, independence was a good thing. We're family. J.J. doesn't get between us."

"Is that your issue? It was always the two of us against the world. We looked out for each other. You protected me, I protected you. It's a good thing. Important." Declan waved a hand. He clearly expected Nash to do all the heavy lifting here and fill in the blanks. Boy was he in for a surprise. "The most important. Nothing comes before family. I'm just saying that it's okay for families to get bigger."

He rolled his eyes. "I thought that auction was more like a one-night loan rather than a permanent sale?"

Declan put on a burst of speed as the house came back into sight. He'd probably spotted Charlotte at one of the hundreds of windows. He certainly couldn't argue that his brother appeared to love his fiancée. Disgustingly, wonderfully, quite alarmingly so. He felt something twitch in his chest.

"I'm just saying it's okay to try for something more," Declan said, sounding disgustingly upbeat.

Wonderful. Just wonderful. Nash's brother had turned into a matchmaker.

Nine

Fake Dating 101, as Wren had dubbed this ridiculous night out on the town, was not a success. They needed Remedial Dating. Possibly Social Skills for Academic Nerds.

After last night's explosive if impulsive kiss, Wren had expected—

Well, she didn't know what she'd thought would happen next.

Not romance, or even a steamy hookup.

More kissing, probably.

Hotel-room sex, almost definitely.

Words strung together into actual sentences and a mature, adult conversation about where Nash's tongue had been? You betcha.

Instead, she'd gotten that growled good-night and the sight of Nash's admittedly fine backside hightailing it down the hallway of their hotel and away from her as fast as all those muscles could take him. She knew he hadn't come back because she'd eventually given in to temptation and checked his room. He'd stayed gone all day Sunday and while, yes, they were just friends, surely it was only friendly to be concerned when you'd received no proof of life in over twelve hours? And then said friend had texted that he was downstairs and ready for their date, and she'd considered looking up the Massachusetts laws on felony murder. Instead, she'd put on a sundress and then thrown herself into his car, and now here she was.

Be a better friend, she exhorted herself. Better fun. Better company. Next month at Noah and May's wedding, she needed to convince her family that she was in an actual relationship. She and Nash would have to get their flirt on and share cute, well-memorized stories about each other. Tonight's fake date was just to fulfill the terms of a ridiculous bachelor auction that no one really cared about anyhow.

The restaurant was fancy and the seafood probably straight off one of the cute little fishing boats bobbing in the harbor, but no one looking at the two of them would have sighed about the romance of it all.

"This isn't working," she told him.

"This—"

"This fake-dating extravaganza." She waved a hand at the absolutely darling but entirely ridiculous white tent-for-two they sat under. The tent was in the middle of a garden, making them the cynosure of a billion other dinner-eating, fun-having parties, including the anniversary-celebrating Durants, who'd waved, winked and were now surreptitiously staring at Wren and Nash. They clearly expected a showy proposal to go with their overpriced seafood.

Perhaps she'd oversold the romance of their Beauty and the Beast relationship the night before.

"Do you not like your entrée?" Nash started to catch the waiter's eye.

His soft-looking white cotton dress shirt had been rolled up to expose his forearms and Wren was temporarily sidetracked by the sun-bronzed skin on display. Unlike his movie-star brother, Nash had no ink, but now that she was paying attention, there was no *not* noticing the muscles. He had actual lines carved into his forearms. No wonder he had an iron grip on his life. The man was made of curls.

"It's not the food." She brought her brain back online before he could order a replacement banquet or, more on brand for him, make the food and beverages manager cry. "It's this tent."

"The tent." He blinked. "So you want to sit inside?"

Inside sounded great, but only because she'd have to go inside in order to get back out again and to their car. "Are you team romantic white tent and fairy lights?"

He sighed. "It seemed—"

Since she was allegedly the romantic half of their fake couple, she supposed he might, just possibly, have picked the world's worst dating site for her. Plus, most people liked—or at least ate—dinner and he *had* promised her her weight in free food. Then she remembered that he hated romance, feelings and anything that could possibly smack of a long-term relationship. Which was undoubtedly why he was weighing his words so carefully.

"Appropriate," he finished.

Appropriate?

She'd show him appropriate. "For what?"

He gave her what she was fairly certain was his mock glower. He was all frowns tonight, more reserved and closed off than over. She took in his dark suit, the immaculately ironed dress shirt and the powder blue tie and had to appreciate the effort even if he looked as if he should be attending a very important boardroom meeting.

"For a date. Someone told me I had no dating game and not an ounce of romance in me."

"So there," she prompted.

He tilted his head. "Excuse me?"

"What you forgot to add to that sentence is *so there*. As in, *So there, I do* too *have an ounce of romance in me*."

"But only an ounce," he said gravely. "Since you're measuring."

They both contemplated the private dinner setup. The waitstaff had drawn a large, loopy heart around their tent with white rose petals. There were lanterns—candle-filled—plus crystal and tulle draped in enough places that she worried about the proximity to the candles. Going up in flames was definitely unromantic.

"You randomly picked this, didn't you?"

He flushed. "Do I look stupid? I'm not answering that."

Stupid was not the adjective that came to mind. Grim, hot, big enough to swing a huge Viking sword… Those things came to mind, sure. Stupid wasn't a contender.

"So this isn't your typical date?" he asked.

"Well," she hedged.

She had been on quite a few first dates, rather fewer second dates and then almost no dates after she'd been in a relationship. Certainly no one had ever tried to take her on a fantasy date that looked like it had been birthed in a Pinterest board. Nash deserved an A for effort.

"Well?" he prompted.

"What do you want to know about my dates, Masterson?"

"What's the benchmark? What did you do?"

"Coffee? Maybe dinner." She frowned. "The movies. Hanging around at his house."

"Seriously?"

"What's wrong with—"

"Boring," he said. "Also far too close to a job interview, right? You swap questions, spend a lot of time staring at each other panicking over your response. Or you go to the movies where no one talks. And hanging out at his place just means he couldn't be bothered to think about what you'd like to do."

When he put it that way, he was annoyingly right. Any other time, she would have teased him about that smugness and then pranked him, but he might just possibly be onto something.

"All right, then, hotshot. Tell me about your first dates."

She was a good person. She was going to learn from Nash and master these first-date secrets he seemed so certain of. Except. Well—

"Are you including tonight in your list of first dates?"

Should she have dialed down the note of horror in

her voice? Maybe. A dose of humility would be good for him, though. She told herself that no one gave him pointed feedback because he was a billionaire and scary smart, in addition to the whole thing about him usually being right. Anyhow.

"No," he said firmly. "Fake dates don't count."

"So tell me the secret, Date-meister. What do you do on your amazing first dates when you want to get to know someone?"

He looked nonplussed, but he nodded. The world's slowest, least happy nod. Rationally, Wren knew that he couldn't actually slow down time in order to not answer her question. Still, she felt as if it was taking about two hundred years for him to respond. She used the time to do a quick mental inventory of the women she'd seen him with over the years she'd known him. It was a very short list. Nash had always been very (very) focused on his work.

"Things." He crossed his arms over his chest and looked at her.

"Like?"

"Hiking," he said firmly.

"That's it?" He was impossible.

"Do you have something against hiking?"

"It seems very…aerobic."

"It was an entire mountain." His mouth curved upward. "Perhaps you'd like to rethink your position on having a nice dinner underneath a tent?"

She did and she didn't. She hadn't been on all that many first dates herself, including this not-date, and they'd ranged from slightly boring to vaguely interesting. She'd been responsible for some of the planning, so it wasn't even as if she could blame the other person. She would have loved to have had more first dates—and second, third and four-hundredth dates—but it hadn't worked out that way. Maybe she was boring or just un-datable. Maybe it was all the stuff that people seemed to expect you'd be willing to do after dinner?

"Do you use one of the hookup apps? That seems very time efficient."

He sighed. "Smart aleck."

"So that's a no? No judging. Sometimes you want comfort food. I get it."

Nash didn't answer, which was answer enough. She'd always been slightly envious of people who could decide that, yes, they were in the mood for sex and then leave the house and actually find someone immediately to have it with. How did that even happen? Were there designated sections in bars or clubs? Not that she could remember the last time she'd been in a club herself, which was part of the problem. She'd always needed to really trust her partner, which meant getting to know him or her, and that took time and more than just a first or second date and people got impatient and—

Well, she didn't do hookups and that had whittled down her dating pool.

"Why are we discussing this?" Nash asked. There was just the slightest quirk at the corner of his mouth, so she didn't think he was annoyed. And at least she hadn't bored him on their fake date. So there.

"To be fair, *I'm* discussing it and you're avoiding answering the question."

He shrugged. "On a first date, I'd rather be doing something. Outdoors. Hiking. Sailing."

"Mountain climbing," she agreed, a smile curling her own mouth. "Which seems tremendously unfair, if you're going to rule out all the people who can't manage that. It's terribly short-sighted. Of course, that's why you look like that. Come on."

She stood up and grabbed his wrist, tugging him up with her. He let her, which won him plenty of fake-boyfriend points.

He shook his head, but let her lead him. "Is our date over?"

"For the sake of women everywhere, I feel like I should absolutely say no." She winked. "Let's do something you would enjoy."

Naturally, her brain flashed straight back to last night's kissing and the unexpected pleasure of it all. The kiss had been a surprise, but a good kind of surprise. Like finding a pristine second edition of a favorite author tucked away in the rare book collection of the library or $500 in your underwear drawer that you'd forgotten about.

"Do I get to pick what I enjoy?"

She laughed. "We're not going to run chemistry experiments or whatever it is you do on weekends."

She was running through possible places in her head when Nash paused.

"Wait for me," he said. And then, "Please."

She grinned at him. "You're the one with a car."

He shook his head. "As if that would stop you."

He went over to the hostess's stand and had a low-voiced conversation that she couldn't make out. She tried to feel ashamed of her nosiness, but failed. For some reason, she didn't think Nash would mind. He seemed to be okay with her weird interest in his life and what he was doing, even when it was this totally ridiculous date they'd gone on.

"Has he proposed yet?" The familiar voice behind her made Wren jump. Damn it—she'd been ambushed by the Durants. "I could give Nash some tips."

Reluctantly, she turned around. Yep. Both Mr. and Mrs. Durant were checking out her left hand hopefully. At least Mrs. Durant was elbowing her husband, presumably because *she* knew that her marital timeline was none of their business.

Except…business.

Oh. Nash wanted to do business with this man, even if his head was stuck somewhere in the early nineteenth century. Hopefully, the Durant patents were more modern.

"Nope," she said, "but we have one of those modern relationships. We're the fairy-tale 2.0 where Prince Charming gets proposed to."

"So you're asking him tonight?" Durant demanded eagerly. "Do you have a ring?"

She tried to look coy rather than murderous. "I can neither confirm nor deny."

"Theo." Mrs. Durant sounded exasperated. "Ask her how her meal was or how she's enjoying Martha's Vineyard. Do not grill her on her love life."

"I was just trying to help," he grumbled.

Mrs. Durant rolled her eyes. "We're leaving," she said. "Enjoy the rest of your night."

"Will do!" she said with forced cheer. There. *Please read into my handful of words that Nash is the perfect family man and sell him your company.*

She'd only just settled on where to take him for the rest of their not-date, when he came back, his gaze warming as he got closer. Which was weird. Except for his eyes, he looked like Nash, her good friend, always-grumpy, super-dependable Nash, who had made her a deal so that they could both minimize the embarrassment in their personal lives. It was a good deal.

"Ready," he said. He had a lavender-colored paper bag with cute little twine handles and the restaurant's name printed in a retro font.

"What is that?"

"You're not good with secrets, are you?" He made a sound of disapproval.

"Did you just tsk me?" she asked in mock outrage.

Now he definitely smiled at her, that barely there, reluctant twitch of his lips that lit her up inside like a supernova. She did her best to ignore the feeling and followed him outside and to the valet parker who had brought around his car. She was trying to decide if it was magic or just his supersized tipping habits that made everything come together so seamlessly, when he slid into the driver's seat and looked at her.

"Where to?"

She beamed at him, shaking off her thoughts. "Am I officially in charge of our not-date, then?"

"We can do whatever you want to do," he said patiently.

"So I am." She thumbed through her phone notes trying to decide what he might enjoy. She'd come across a couple of possibilities…yes! That one would work. "Although I am sorry/not sorry to derail your fairy light fantasy back there."

He shrugged and got them onto the road. "It's fine."

She read him directions from her phone and he nodded, taking them away from town and out along the outer edge of the island.

"Here." She frowned, double-checking the directions with their current location. She wasn't convinced her phone hadn't frozen ten minutes ago thanks to her spectacularly poor cell phone plan, but it was also hard to judge where they were. One dark, sand-dune-covered beach looked pretty much like the next one. Oh well.

"Definitely here." She pointed to a sandy sliver of shoulder by the road, deciding to own it.

"Are you sure this is a parking spot?" he asked doubtfully, but parking nonetheless.

"If the car fits, absolutely. Come on." She hopped out. "We're going to do outdoor things."

Sure, her preferred outdoor activities involved imitating a lizard horizontally in the sun, but she also—take that, dating-profile cliché!—loved long walks on the beach. Sunsets were, fortunately, totally optional since the sunset opportunities on this beach were currently nil. She grabbed Nash's hand and pulled him after her.

He let her do it, but then Nash always did what he'd said he'd do—and he'd agreed that she was in charge of directions tonight. After a second, which she attributed to the shock of having his hand held like they were old-fashioned sweethearts, he curled his big, warm fingers around hers.

The beach was really just a sliver of the absolutely miles of beach that ran around Martha's Vineyard. The dunes made a neat little barrier against the road, the sand stretching away on the other side to the water. It was unexpectedly private, quiet and dark, in contrast to the noisy, brightly lit restaurant. Nash raised his eyebrows and looked at her.

Right. She was in charge. Except she sort of liked his bossy look, as if he had a plan, a backup plan and a backup backup plan just in case she couldn't find something to do that made her happy.

"Do I get to find out what's in the box now?"

He handed it to her wordlessly—it turned out he'd organized an entire picnic for them during his brief pit stop at the hostess's stand. It was impressive. Two kinds of cheese and red grapes, plus a little chilled bottle of champagne that probably broke a million rules about not bringing glass onto the beach. Just like their Tuesday lunches, he took off his jacket and she sat on it, feeling nostalgic as they shared the bottle back and forth and pointed out the lights coming from the Massachusetts shore. Really, she had to be single-handedly responsible for doubling Nash's dry cleaning bills, and if she'd been a better friend, she'd have offered to go halves.

"So," he said, when they'd decimated the champagne level in the bottle, "what do you like to do on a first date?"

She scowled. "Something without too much talking."

"Right," he mused. "Because you hate talking so much."

"Hey. There's a time and a place. Plus, first-date talking is so high-stakes. Everything has to be fun and memorable, full of meaning without sounding too heavy. It's a lot."

"New question, then. What were your best first dates?"

She eyed him suspiciously. "Are you planning to steal my ideas?"

"No," he said calmly.

"Will you put your machine-learning, enormous robot brain on it if I don't tell you?"

He nodded. "I'm absolutely going to solve the algorithm of Wren, so you should just tell me. It would be more efficient."

They'd been casual, help-me-move-this-weekend, I'm-having-a-BBQ, want-to-split-an-order-of-tacos friends. Fake-dating was all-new territory. Wren wasn't sure she should answer the question. Plus, she sort of wanted to hear about Nash's first dates. He was a billionaire, hot and surprisingly thoughtful in a gruff way, which meant he probably had amazing stories to tell. He did look like he'd give good date, not that she'd admit it to him.

"My last one was a setup, by a friend," Nash said unexpectedly. Oh my God, was he voluntarily *sharing*? "We went out to dinner, saw a movie, had drinks by the ocean. It was nice."

The word *nice* came out of his mouth the way other people said *root canal* or *paper wasps in my attic*. *Nice* was the kiss of death for him, apparently.

"So no second date? Did you sleep with her?"

He gave her that small, almost-smile, the one that was the barest tilt to his lips. "I haven't slept with as many people as you seem to think I have, Wren."

"No hot-for-the-billionaire supermodels or scary-smart CEOs or, or—" Her imagination failed her.

"Or curious, funny, really stubborn literature professors," he agreed. "Yet."

That last word was entirely unexpected. Stunning, really. She opened her mouth, found that nothing came out, and promptly closed it because the whole stunned-fish, parted-lips thing only worked for sexy social media models. Curious. Funny. Stubborn. Those weren't bad adjectives at all. Except—

Her brain tried desperately to power back on, knocked completely offline by that last word. Apparently, she'd been right about the beach being better date material. The waves continued to wash in and then back out. There was a nice breeze. Birds and some terribly romantic moonlight. Really, the entire world continued right on turning as if he hadn't said—

Well.

He'd just said *yet*.

It was one word. It didn't have to mean anything, and certainly nothing like *I regret not coming in last night* or *Can I have a second chance, you sexy, hot professor of literature?* Her brain briefly derailed and threatened to shut down again when she considered playing one of those sexy, stern professor and the mis-behaving-student games that she'd never quite got the appeal of but that heated her body up to volcanic temperatures. *Yet.*

Fortunately, there was a large body of ice-cold water close by.

"Come on, Mr. Athletic." She jumped to her feet. "Let's go swimming."

She pointed to the ocean, just in case his comment had been a throwaway or his brain was as stunned as hers.

Or he was nervous.

Did billionaire science hotties get nervous?

The answer seemed to be *not* because he looked at her, as calm, stoic and irritatingly impenetrable as ever. Right. That had to change.

"Strip," she said.

Ten

Nash tried to remember the last time he'd had fun. Maybe his last Taco Tuesday with Wren. Probably the whole series of Tuesdays. He didn't know why. He worked, he worked out, he spent quality time with his brother and some less-quality time with his father. Dating wouldn't have made his top five—or his top twenty. He disliked the expectations and it seemed like a waste of time when he knew that what he had to offer did not include a heart. The heartless state was a deal killer for everyone he'd met, and he didn't blame them.

There was no point in opening up to someone, let alone a more or less random stranger he was drinking coffee with, eating dinner with or about to have sex with. He didn't have a vulnerable side because he didn't have *sides*. It couldn't be helped. It was just how he was, and frankly, it made his life much easier. His dates had complained. Wren, however, wasn't a date, not a real one at any rate, so his dating rules didn't apply. And yet, as his *friend*, she pushed and poked, cajoled and smiled, and he suspected she wanted to look right inside him.

Whether or not she'd like what she found was immaterial.

Their Martha's Vineyard trip had been surprisingly not bad. He'd enjoyed watching her take on the auction and its roomful of socialites, power players and do-gooders. Okay, so some of the people had been there just to support a good cause and to have fun. But he'd watched Wren throw herself into the evening whole-heartedly, enjoying the cheesiness of the auction while still…well, having his back. She'd been there for him. Hadn't backed down or let go. She also wasn't apologetic about who she was or just how much she loved girlie things and a romantic night out. And every time she admitted that she'd been let down or left alone or not even close to a movie-perfect night out with a guy, he wanted to fix that for her. Hire an entire production company to give her the full Fred Astaire treatment with tap dancing, roses and a devoted man in black tie. If that was romantic. Hell if he knew.

And even though Wren could handle life just fine on her own, she was unabashedly looking for someone to share it with. And despite one dating disappointment after another, she kept on trying. It should have come as no surprise that she'd refused to let him shut her out once she'd decided that they would be friends. She was simply, inexorably, perfectly part of his life. Even his lab loved her. He couldn't miss how they included her in their conversations, smiled when she popped in to drag him out for their ridiculous Taco Tuesday lunches. Which he loved. Not that he'd told her that. He needed to work on that.

If she could be open to new experiences after getting knocked down more times than a punching bag, he could, too.

Wren, of course, didn't seem to have any reservations. She shimmied out of her dress and her shoes at the same time, letting everything fall in an untidy heap on the sand.

This left her standing there in just her bra and panties. Jesus. They were white, lacy and utterly, completely set his body on fire. His mouth was dry and he was so turned on being near her that a dose of cold ocean water seemed like an excellent plan. Was this a friendly swim? Or something else? Wren, of course, didn't wait for him to sort himself out. She ran lightly down the beach toward the water, laughing so hard that he couldn't make out the words she yelled back to him, words that turned into yelps when she plunged in up to her knees.

She threw her arms out, looking up at the night sky. "Why is it so cold in August?"

He could have explained about upswells and surface temperatures. Instead, he tried not to stare. He'd seen her in a swimsuit a few times on the Los Angeles beach and it had been no big deal. There'd been no urge to commit the sweet curves of her body to memory or the surge of hunger that roared through him now. There had been friendship, companionship. None of these fiery *feelings*.

He folded up her clothes, tucked them inside his jacket for safekeeping and then went back to grab a blanket from the car. He should have done that first, but she made him stop thinking. It was probably more of that feeling thing. Probably. Once he'd gotten the blanket, he undressed while he watched her splash around in the shallows. The bottom might drop off. There could be currents. Rogue waves. Prehistoric, tourist-eating sharks. Midnight swims were not his thing, and anyone who'd spotted him now would have had something to say. They'd have been surprised he wasn't already back in his lab or working through the mountain of emails and documents that had accumulated in his inbox. They knew he liked his loose ends tied up.

But he had a mermaid and free spirit to swim with. He wasn't a fool and he wasn't letting this night slip through his fingers.

He strode down the sand in his boxer briefs and into the water, fighting the urge to point out that the hotel had a heated swimming pool if she was in a water kind of mood. It wasn't the first time he'd swum in the Atlantic Ocean, so the icy water shouldn't have been a shock and yet it was.

Better all in than half out, he decided, diving beneath the next wave and then propelling himself toward Wren. She shrieked happily when he grabbed her ankle and surfaced. Her bra was so wet, he'd see her nipples if the water level dipped even an inch.

He forced his eyes to hold hers.

"Why, Mr. Masterson," she said, batting her eyelashes at him. "Fancy meeting you here."

"Wren." His voice came out more growl than not as he sluiced the salt water off his face with his hands. Thank fuck for cold water because his dick had decided

to redefine friendship. Friends, he reminded himself.
They were friends, and friends did not swim with—or
walk around with or talk about—their massive erections.

"Do you think there are sharks?" She threw out a
hand to use his shoulder as an anchor as she floated on
her back. Jesus, the ocean wasn't going to be enough.
The water skimmed the soft slope of her breasts, which
were barely, quite indecently covered by the translucent
fabric of her bra. Maybe sharks and a dose of reality
would be enough to deflate his interest?

"Usually not until August."

"Seriously?" She jerked upright. "Really, Nash?"

"Yeah." He gave up fighting the urge to touch her
and playfully nudged her side—her bare, water-slick,
soft side—with his closed fist. He might have, ever so
quietly, whistled the *Jaws* theme song. In the water,
she looked magical, more suited to one of those Shake-
speare plays with fairies and woodland sprites than his
practical, lab-coat-wearing world. She was his friend.
He didn't want to lose that, and yet something inside
him, some unfamiliar *feeling*, well, it whispered that
maybe they could be a different sort of friends.

"There are sharks in Martha's Vineyard?"

"There are shark sightings every year." He shrugged.
"Although usually not this close to shore or this early
in the summer."

"Usually?" Her voice rose. "It's *August*."

"Usually." He shrugged.

"Are you joking? Because your delivery needs improvement."

"No." He frowned, hunkering down in the water next
to her. They were barely six feet from the shore. If he

stood up, the water would be maybe waist-deep. "This was your idea."

"I have *terrible* ideas."

He laughed, spreading his arms to keep his balance as the next wave rolled in. She promptly wrapped her arms around his neck, clinging to his back, laughing harder than him.

"Why didn't you *stop* me?"

"Are we done swimming, then?"

"I might need to stick to pools. Jacuzzis. Really, really big bathtubs." She wrapped her legs around his sides, her heels digging lightly into his stomach, and his dick roared to life.

Jesus. This was not what she wanted from him. He stood up, taking her with him. He might be having a friendship crisis here, but she still wanted to be just friends. Didn't she? Sure, she'd fake-dated him and let him take her out to dinner, but that was helping out a friend in need and free food. And swimming had been an impulse, right? When she'd stripped down in front of him, it had been for fun. Everyone knew a bra and panties covered more than some swimsuits. She was comfortable. That was all. It didn't have to mean love or romance, did it?

No.

His bio dad had left before Nash had any memories of him, and then for a few chaotic years, it had been the three of them against the world: his mother, Declan and himself. The car accident that had claimed her life had triggered the turbulent years of foster care, followed by his adoption by J.J. Masterson. J.J. had picked them, Nash and Declan, and made them part of his family, and while he knew Declan had never felt as if he truly belonged and was a second-rate, runner-up Masterson, Nash knew the truth. They'd been loved enough to be chosen, and the odds of that ever happening again were miniscule. Lightning didn't strike twice.

So could he have fun with Wren, date her casually and not mess up their friendship?

Of course he could.

To prove it, he ran out of the water with her clinging to his back, laughing. Fuck, he loved the way she laughed, the sound as all-out and committed as the way she lived. Every so often, her breath would catch inelegantly, sounding more like a snort or a rasp than that merry-bell crap people talked about. There were no small, polite sounds for Wren. She filled a room with that laughter.

He swiped the blanket and his jacket from their pile of things as she slid off his back. Draped the jacket around her shoulders before she could protest that she was fine, that she wasn't cold and that she didn't need anything from him.

"My turn." He held the blanket out to her. "Strip."

Well, two could definitely play that game.

Wren clutched Nash's beautiful suit jacket around her in one fist, wriggling undercover until she could unhook her bra and slip out of it. It had to be her imagination, but the silky lining felt warm against her skin, as if he'd just slipped it off like some early nineteenth-century duke. She thought he might have meant to turn around because he seemed determined to be a gentleman, but when her bra fell to the sand, he froze. Well, then. Perhaps she hadn't misread his extremely subtle, almost invisible Nash signals after all.

"Wren," he said. And stopped. Stared as if he'd gotten stuck on the important part of his sentence, which was *her*. She didn't need more words from him—just to know that he really, truly saw her. That even if they weren't going to be each other's one and only forever, she was still the only one he saw right now.

Now was good.

His eyes were dark and warm, holding her own eyes before gliding over her throat, the V of her cleavage and then lower to where the jacket, huge as it was, failed to completely cover her thighs. She let the jacket slip lower, off her shoulders ever so slightly, and his breath caught, a muscle in his jaw ticking.

"Wren," he repeated roughly. Sternly. As if he truly believed that now was an appropriate time for following their fake-dating rules. "Get dressed."

"But you told me to strip," she whispered back, feeling playful and daring, slightly wicked and far too intoxicated by the moonlight and the man standing there so large and solid. His boxer briefs, wet from the ocean, clung to an impressive bulge and a massive pair of thighs.

She let the jacket slip lower still, taking another step forward. "I'm cold. Warm me up?"

He took a step forward, meeting her more than halfway, she thought smugly. Whatever this was between them, he wanted it—*her*—too, and it was magical.

So she dropped her panties, too, kicking them to the side with as much dramatic flair as she could muster up. All that stood between them now was his jacket and those silly, silly rules. She thought he must have agreed with this unspoken assessment because his hands slid beneath the edges of his jacket to cup her bare shoulders and pull her up against him.

"What are you doing?" he asked, more hoarse than calm. She'd got underneath his skin and she loved it. She wanted to undo the tidy package that was Nash Masterson completely.

Without waiting for an answer, he pressed his mouth against her forehead as if he couldn't resist and they were two particles attracted to each other that—well… she gave up on the bad chemistry comparisons because he was the science expert here.

"Kiss me better," she demanded, reaching right back for him. Her pulse was hammering in her ears and possibly her heart was leaping up and down in place. Possibly it was all of her beating in one big pulse of anxious awareness. Because as she slid her arms around his neck, his jacket fell off her shoulders and hit the sand and he cupped her face in his big, warm hands and now his mouth found her throat, tasting the skin there as if *this* was the moment he'd been waiting for all night.

Me, too.

This is what I want.

You.

Her heart beat to that one word, her blood heating and fizzing. *You you you.* An echo in her body. He moved closer, his hands tightening, his breathing rougher. All of him focused on her. *More,* her body demanded.

"Anything you want…"

"Promises," she said, pressing her mouth against his,

letting her tongue trace his lower lip and slip inside, tasting him. He groaned roughly and then he kissed her back.

Roughly, possessively and absolutely perfectly.

His hands slid upward from her shoulders to her hair, gathering the damp strands into his fist and angling her head so that he could kiss her more deeply. He kissed her and kissed her, completely abandoning all that iron control and surgical precision he wore like a suit of armor. She wrapped her own arms around him, leaning into him. Onto him. There was heat and a delicious warmth wherever they touched and she wanted more. For one precarious moment her brain wondered what this meant, this connection between them, but then her body took over and she forgot about any emotion but lust.

She moaned into his mouth, because it turned out that Nash was like whiskey or her beloved jeans and he only got better with time. She forgot about the beach and the ever-so-slightly chilly night air. Forgot that she'd done a completely, wonderfully ridiculous thing by swimming in the cold ocean after dark and that she was wet and her hair standing on end as her makeup ran down her face. All she could feel was Nash kissing her, devouring her mouth, his tongue playing with hers in a way that had her going up on tiptoe because this was not enough, wonderful as it was. He coaxed sounds from her she hadn't thought she could make, raw noises and greedy whimpers that he answered with rough tones of his own. They made, she thought with the 1 percent of her brain that was still functioning, a whole symphony together.

Somehow he got them both down onto the sand, the blanket spread out beneath her, his arms braced on either side of her head as he lowered himself onto her. She shifted, needing all of him, the perfect, heavy weight of his body blocking out the rest of the world. Sometimes, when she'd had sex, she'd felt almost disconnected, as if it was a choreographed dance where partners met in a careful sequence of touches but none of it really *touched* her.

Nash touched her. Oh God, he rested against her, pressing her down into the sand with a directness and a deliberation that was so him. One hand moved down her body, stroking over her ribs, along the curve of her waist and hips. Heat rushed to her thighs and between.

"Wren."

"That's me," she gasped, clutching at his shoulders—his beautiful, broad, absolutely muscled, bare shoulders—possibly, ever so not subtly, nudging him down. "Yes. This is great. Keep doing it."

The bastard laughed.

"This is not the time to develop a sense of humor," she hissed.

He pulled back, searching, but her hearty consent must have been written all over her face because he nodded. And then, oh God, he smiled. She was doomed.

"Just kissing, then?" he clarified.

She hesitated, suddenly nervous that she was jumping, vagina first, into a situation (*relationship,* her brain whispered stubbornly) that she hadn't quite thought through. At all. He didn't rush her, didn't demand an answer or a condom or that she at least go down on him like one of her now-ex-boyfriends had when she'd gently tapped the brakes on their sexfest. She looked down at his big, sexy, still-wet body. Well. That right there was more than enough motivation to keep going.

"Lots of kissing," she amended.

He pressed his mouth against her forehead. "Am I limited to one particular place? Do you have a favorite?"

And just like that she had her friend back. Her solid, warm—and yes, sexy—friend. She grinned up at him. "Would you like to perform an experiment with me, Dr. Masterson?"

His answering smile was slow, wicked and absolutely devastating. "Absolutely, *Doctor.*"

It felt completely natural to laugh with him—and then to lean up and press a kiss against the corner of his mouth. This led to more small kisses and then, why not, she licked him there. He tasted like salt mostly, but also sweet. Definitely very good. Possibly, she thought, very bad in the absolutely *very* best way.

"I'll start here." He took control like he always did.

"Will you? What if I want to go first?"

He went still, fingers gripping her hips. Then, "You can come first, Wren-bird. Could you do that for me?"

"I guess it depends on how good your research methods are."

She didn't wait for him to take charge. Maybe because he tasted so good that once she leaned in to kiss him, she kept right on kissing him. And then kissing him some more, running her hands over the muscles of his back, down his spine, over his butt. She loved this. *Yes,* she thought. *Yes, let's do this.* She loved the size of him, a bulwark between her and the world. She loved how his eyes darkened as he stroked the pebbled tips of her breasts with his big thumbs. She loved everything about him. She could be someone who had wild, crazy, romantic beach sex. She wanted to be that person, with him. Right now.

"Hypothesis," he whispered roughly, pulling back from their kiss. "You'll like this more."

His hands stroked lower and his mouth moved down her body, and he moved down. And down. And down. Until her thighs were over his shoulders, and he was right there, his mouth covering her.

"Hypothesis," he said again. She felt every syllable. "You'll like this most."

"Nash—"

One big hand cupped her butt, while the other opened her up. His tongue covered what he'd exposed. She made a rough sound. It wasn't a word. She couldn't— This wasn't... Oh. A new pulse detonated in her, an electric pulse that was so, so good. Her core tightened. Her heels dug into his back.

He groaned something. She had no idea what. The man didn't need language when he could do *this* with his tongue. His tongue that was licking her again, slowly and wickedly, sure and hungry. His other hand, the one not squeezing her butt, teased her clit. She was tensing. Pushing down. Reaching for more.

Nash being Nash, he gave it to her. He kissed her, his tongue making her feel all the things, pushing and coaxing, and there was no holding still, no worrying about what he could see or taste. Just the electric friction of his mouth on her.

"You are so goddamned perfect, Wren," he growled against her. "Fucking perfect." And she felt his words all the way through her, moving up from her core, bursting through her body in a bloom of heat that filled her chest, pushed at her ribs and her heart in a sticky, wet, absolutely perfect wave of feeling.

She'd always taken a long time to get there in bed, but with Nash, it felt okay. As if he'd happily kiss her all night and tomorrow, too. The pleasure washed through her, her body tightening, contracting in on itself, holding the sweet pulse tight before letting go. And the whole time, as she came apart, Nash held on to her, anchoring her, whispering words of praise and admiration against her.

"Well," she said, a long time later. There were no bones left in her body and she sounded dazed, but that was completely due to the world's best orgasm Nash had delivered. "Well. Wow."

"You," he said, "are amazing, Wren."

This felt a bit like the beginning of an explanation, the kind that ended with *but this was a mistake and I'm repenting and will be either donning my hairshirt and engaging in self-imposed penance or I'll just get up and leave and do the actual relationship thing with someone else.*

They hadn't even had actual sex yet, so she felt somehow cheated. It didn't matter. If they did go to bed together and she did, well, whatever this situationship—because it absolutely was *not* a relationship—was, then eventually they'd part ways. Break up. Everything would be over and done with and she'd have quite literally fucked up a friendship that meant a good deal to her.

"But?" she suggested carefully. Would it be easier

if she said the magic, sex-ending incantation? *But we should just be friends!* Those words shouldn't feel somehow less than, but that was how the people in her life meant them. Friends were less than lovers. Every time.

He looked at her. "But we shouldn't rush into this."

And there it was.

She disentangled herself from him with as much reserve as she could muster, which wasn't much since she was missing all of her clothes and most of her dignity. She'd ridden his face, if she was being completely blunt, and after that… Well, he'd certainly seen a side of her no one else had. Worse, she'd enjoyed it. At first it had felt safe and then amazing.

"Right." She sat up and cast a hand around for her panties. "We're fake-dating and sex is completely against our rules. So you're right. It's not as if we could be in an actual relationship. It would have to be just sex."

She gave up on her underwear and pulled on her sundress. Thanks to Nash, it wasn't any the worse for wear.

He frowned, but got up and pulled on his own pants. Over, she couldn't help but notice, a very impressive bulge in his boxer briefs. The wet cotton made his pants cling, but it wouldn't have been friendly to point that out.

Plus, she was pissed. It would serve him right if the entire hotel watched him march inside with a boner.

"Just sex," he said and then those two words hung in the air between them, taking on a life of their own, while they finished getting dressed, folded up the blanket together and tried to figure out what the appropriate transition was from sex on the beach to car.

"Yes. Well. We're agreed on that," she got out. "That's what this was."

"Except—" He opened the door to the car for her. "Well. We could be friends who have sex."

That was not the conclusion she had expected him to draw from this sex experiment of theirs. She got in the car, framing and abandoning responses in her head. This was the kind of conversation, she realized, for which the best response would come to her hours later. At some awkward moment in the horribly distant future, she would know: *that is what I should have said but there's no way to rewind time.*

Nash dropped into the driver's seat and picked up where he'd left off.

"We're attracted to each other and we're friends. That doesn't have to be a bad thing."

Parking tickets, a cracked tooth, broken AC in the summer—those were bad things.

She looked at him incredulously. "It was freaking amazing, you idiot."

He nodded once. Got them on the road. Lined up his ridiculous arguments in his head, unlike her. Launched them with military precision.

"I'd obviously never be your Mr. Perfect. We don't have a romantic future together. Romance isn't something I'm interested in. And it matters to you. You should get to have it."

"It's not a cupcake."

"What?"

"Love isn't dessert. It isn't something you tack on to the end of a meal as an afterthought or a guilty pleasure. It's not a joke or unimportant."

"That's not what I meant," he said calmly. "It's just that you value love and romance and you deserve to have it. I'm simply not the person who can give it to you. But of course I'd like you to have it."

"You don't think it's silly?"

"I don't understand it," he said carefully. "But that doesn't mean it's not worth having. It doesn't mean that you shouldn't get to have it. You should get everything you want. We'll add that to our friend rules, if you want, but what I really wanted to know was if you would like to add sex to that list."

"Friends with benefits," Wren said after she'd found her tongue. It was a ridiculous idea. Wasn't it? *Almost as ridiculous as fake-dating your billionaire best friend.* Well. That was also true.

"Yes." He flicked a glance at her. "But I had assumed it wasn't your thing."

"What?"

"You're a serial monogamist, Wren. You believe wholeheartedly in love, throw yourself in your relationship. Obviously, I'm not love affair material."

He was so insistent that he couldn't care. Couldn't? Or wouldn't? Sometimes, when she was with Nash, she felt very much as if he cared. In a friendly, deeply interested, very-different-from-anyone-else, eight-years-long kind of way. Their friendship had outlasted all of her boyfriends. Boyfriends always moved on to someone else.

"Anyhow," he said stiffly. "Perhaps think it over. Being friends with benefits with me."

Eleven

Fake-dating was complicated. Nash stared down at his phone. His brother had just invited him and his fake girlfriend to his wedding. To *Charlotte*. Nash had known that there would be an actual, formal event at some point in the not terribly distant future, but he hadn't expected them to decide on a surprise elopement a week after the bachelor auction. They were getting married on the beach at sunset. On Monday. Which was *today.* He checked the weather app on the phone and the weather was good, so perhaps that was it? They'd want to take pictures—people always did—and sunsets were better when rain didn't hammer down on the bridal party. He'd go and congratulate them. Easy. He was trying to decide if he needed to text anything more than a straightforward *I'll be there* when Wren landed beside him.

They'd agreed to take turn choosing activities and today was his turn. He'd had to insist that his working a half day did *not* constitute his choice before she'd agreed to a bike ride, not that he wasn't willing to do whatever she wanted. Rather, his problem was that he was *too* willing to do so, and while stripping off her clothes and having hotel sex with her topped his own list, she still hadn't given him an answer yet about adding sex to their friendship. So. Instead they were on a very public and quite athletic bike ride where he absolutely couldn't pull her over on the side of the bike path and kiss her. Or do other things. No, thank you. They were *friends*.

He looked her over with a frown, not sure about the pink flush on her face. It was hard not to step in and take care of her.

He settled for pulling a bottle of water out of his backpack and handing it to her.

"Here."

She took it, a little mulishly, the sun painting a golden nimbus around her hair. Really, she looked deceptively angelic for someone who'd had her tongue in his mouth and offered to put it other places on his body. He struggled not to think about that offer because riding a bicycle with an erection was guaranteed to be unpleasant if not downright painful.

His phone buzzed again, helpfully reminding him that he hadn't answered Declan's text.

Wren looked curious, but he'd learned that Wren had no boundaries when it came to questions. She liked to know details, and would check in with him about how his day was going when it had only been hours since they'd last seen each other. She'd gone full-on tourist this week while he'd holed up in their suite to work, filling his phone with campy shots of herself at various Martha's Vineyard hot spots. He'd saved them all.

She frowned at him. "Has your team blown up your lab or posted your IP on the internet where everyone can download it for free?"

"No." He shook his head. "Not this time."

"Huh." She pursed her lips. "So it's a totally new not-disaster?"

He wrenched his mind back from its detour into considerations involving tongues and favorite body parts. The explosion had been minor burn damage to a second-floor laboratory and the IP mishap had been swiftly handled.

"My brother's getting married."

He held out his phone so she could see the invitation. He'd forgotten how good she smelled. And felt. And the way her voice tugged at something inside him, something that wasn't *good* but was, rather—well… He wasn't going there. He hadn't forgotten anything about that night on the beach, and sometimes he wasn't sure why breaking it off had been the smart decision. He really wanted to kiss her again.

"He's getting married at sunset," he clarified. "Today."

"Oh. Wow." She looked him up and down, assessing. It turned out that his body reacted to looking as well. They were just biking, so no, he hadn't expected to receive a wedding invitation. If Declan had given him more notice, maybe he would have worn a suit. Or showered. Bought one of those fucking boutonniere flower lapel things that seemed to be obligatory at these things.

"Do you want to go with me?" he asked abruptly. *Very smooth. Compelling, even. That's the world's worst sales job.* "To the wedding?"

"Oh," she said, last week's intimacy and his offer hanging over them. "It seems like the kind of thing a good fake girlfriend would do, right?"

It occurred to him that people often complained about being invited to too many weddings, that other people's ceremonies could be boring, that she didn't know his brother or Charlotte and therefore wouldn't really be interested. He retrieved his phone from her.

She slid him a teasing glance. "I know you'd rather be holed up in your lab being an ogre and barking at hapless chemists."

He liked working, and what he did, frankly, made a difference in the lives of a great many people. He put in a sixty-hour workweek and then did more on the weekends. It was a habit of his, one he'd picked up as a kid. Work was good. Work got you ahead, made people happy, made sure you could take care of them in the ways that mattered most. But now, doing absolutely nothing work-related with Wren, he wondered if he'd missed out on something.

He allowed himself a moment to think about what Wren might do on her weekends, the little things like napping on a couch or surrounding herself with books and snacks. Rearranging the furniture in her tiny condo for the four hundredth time and then declaring an IKEA emergency. But she was already laughing and saying, "Of course I'll go with you. You know, there's nothing more romantic than a sunset wedding. Plus, a movie star!"

Her enthusiasm was cute. He tended to forget that people thought Hollywood was glamorous and liked spotting movie stars and other famous people. He'd never particularly cared for it, although he knew he'd been lucky to be adopted by someone who had a job that paid well and who'd done the best he could to raise the two boys who'd come to him from a very rocky start. It was just that so much of the Hollywood lifestyle felt like living in a never-ending production. It was artificial at best, fake at worst. Everything was about surface appearances rather than genuine depth.

But Wren was grinning, looking excited because of course she would be. It was a *wedding*. There would be romance galore. Amazing how little he seemed to mind going if she went, too. She'd be able to put into words for his brother all the things that Nash knew he should say, but that got bottled up inside.

"I can't guarantee romance," he said.

"Sunset. Movie star. *Wedding*," she countered. "Plus, your brother and Charlotte are obviously in love. I'm pretty sure they've cornered the market on romance."

He shrugged. "Maybe. I wouldn't know."

She sighed. "I would."

Not to make dramatic overgeneralizations, but perhaps love did exist and Nash's brother really had found that emotional unicorn with the woman who had just become his wife.

Nash had never been a believer in True Love (that was Wren's thing), but watching Declan and Charlotte promise to love and honor each other forever, starting today, he admitted there was new and compelling data standing there in front of him. As a movie star and producer who was the subject of intense paparazzi scrutiny, a secret elopement had seemed like a certain way for Declan to ensure he had privacy for his wedding day. Now, however, he thought that maybe his brother just hadn't been able to wait any longer. If heaven were real, why wouldn't you want to go there right away and enjoy all that?

The wedding was taking place on a private beach that belonged to a friend. The bridal couple had decided to arrive by boat—a nod to the night that had brought them together—and Declan had brought the keelboat right up onto the sand. Nash could just make out the name— *The Cake* (he'd never understand his brother's sense of humor)—but then the groom was prying his bride out of her life vest and swinging her up into his arms so that he could jump down into the shallows and wade dramatically to shore. Once an actor, always an actor.

Wren sighed loudly beside him. "That man right there knows how to create memories."

He slanted her a glance. "How do you know this was his idea?"

Declan had probably had a wedding planner. Or a producer. He'd certainly had *help*, although judging by the faces of the wedding guests, it had been expert, amazing, really good help. Everyone loved the entrance.

Ignoring him, Wren tugged on the sleeve of his linen jacket. "Look at the flowers!"

Banks of flowers surrounded the clergywoman waiting to marry Declan and Charlotte, hydrangeas in shades of lavender and white, long stalks of lark-spur and fat, ripe peony blossoms. The sun beat down on the white canopy protecting the seats where they waited with the handful of guests, turning to watch the happy couple come up the beach serenaded by a cellist. He supposed it was nice. Somehow, though, he found himself dragging a glance—and then a second and a third—over Wren, who was enthusiastically watching the bridal couple approach.

Wren's eyes were suspiciously damp as she clutched her hands to the center of her chest. Was she even breathing? Was she regretting breaking up with that asshole Noah and imagining it was her getting married? He patted his jacket pocket, double-checking that he'd brought tissues.

Declan set Charlotte back on her feet when they reached the makeshift aisle. A gauzy white veil billowed around her straw hat and the white sundress that stopped at her knees. When he looked back at Wren, he caught her mouthing *perfect*. He didn't know about perfect, but Charlotte radiated happiness. As did his brother.

And Wren. It seemed painfully fucking obvious to him that weddings were her jam and her happy place. She beamed as the couple walked up the aisle. There was already a tear on her cheek, he noticed with a sigh and handed her a tissue. Had he told her that she looked pretty today? He couldn't remember now, which seemed to his usual condition around Wren nowadays and it was disturbing. His inexplicable attraction to her pushed all of his usual thoughts right out of head.

Well. Not *inexplicable*. He knew exactly why he

wanted to carry her straight to bed. Her yellow dress nipped in at her waist and cupped her tits, which were unfortunately completely covered up. The dress clung to her hips and her thighs, swirling around when she hopped up to see something better. She'd tried on three different dresses in their suite in a five-minute window, while he'd stood there trying to come up with three different and persuasive ways to tell her she looked gorgeous. "I don't want to wear the wrong thing," she'd said. He'd been pretty certain that as long as she'd shown up mostly clothed, it would be fine—and naked worked for him disturbingly well—but she'd worried. She didn't need to. She was gorgeous and that yellow dress of hers would drive any man crazy. He wasn't stupid and he wouldn't have told Declan this for anything in the world, but she was more beautiful than Charlotte. There was something in her smile.

The clergywoman smiled and got started. Apparently Declan and Charlotte had opted to put their own creative stamp on the traditional wedding vows and semi-write their own. There was a lot of promising to love each other forever and then some rather detailed lists that overshared the reasons behind that love. And yet... Yet. Those words, as silly and sentimental, as clichéd and recycled as they were... They meant something. Fuck, he could practically see them being knit into a single unit, one couple, a synthesis reaction where two different become one and new. It was startling. He'd been off base to think that there was nothing more between his brother and his wife than lust, attraction or even basic attachment. Testosterone, dopamine, oxytocin couldn't explain the emotions written on Declan's face when the clergywoman declared them wife and husband.

The new pair kissed, everyone applauded and then Declan and Charlotte ran down the aisle as the guests pelted them with rose petals.

"That was unbelievably romantic," Wren sighed, leaning into him. "Best wedding ever."

"Okay," he said. "There's also a seafood barbecue and champagne. An ice cream cake."

Charlotte was not a traditionalist when it came to cake.

Wren groaned. "It's a wedding, Nash."

He knew that. He'd been there. "And?"

"Doesn't it make you think about what you want for yourself? Who you want to spend your life with?"

"That would be like attending a housewarming and assessing your real estate portfolio," he argued, steering her toward the reception.

"Exactly!" she said happily.

Okay. So he hadn't grasped her point, but he wasn't going to tell her that. Not now.

"Someday my prince will come," she hummed.

"Literally?"

"I'm not planning on discriminating against royalty, Nash, but no. I doubt that the man I walk down the aisle with will be a literal prince."

She motioned for him to stand beneath a tangled arch of purple wisteria. Right. They needed appropriately romantic pictures for her family. He stood where she pointed and then she squeezed in beside him, her head on his chest, one hand around his waist, the other holding out her phone for the photo. Was this kind of casual contact supposed to feel so sexy? He shouldn't be fantasizing about carrying her off, pushing up her dress and tasting her again. Followed by more touching, kissing and, honestly, whatever she'd like him to do. He'd have asked if they weren't sharing a hotel suite—he didn't want her to feel awkward or trapped.

She sent the photo to her family and then linked her arm through his.

"Food?" He steered them both toward the tables set up outside the house on the bluff. Maybe if they were eating, he'd think less about getting his hands on her.

"This was such a magical wedding." Her tone was dreamy, but when he looked at her face, she seemed a little mischievous. "Are you really, truly sure you don't believe in love?"

"The jury's out," he said lightly. "But you know me."

"All facts."

"No romance," he agreed.

"Do you ever think you might be missing out?" She nudged his shoulder with hers. "Or that you could just be wrong? And there's all this love out there and you're not getting any of it because you won't ask for it?"

"Don't make love sound like asking for a raise or an extra day off at work."

"You and work," she said, skipping along by his side. "You need something more in your life."

"Smart aleck. And I do believe in love," he continued firmly, ignoring her last comment. "I do have family, you know."

"Declan's amazing and now you have Charlotte, too."

"They are."

"And just think," she said. "After we break up, my dating curse means that you'll fall in love yourself. You'll go meet an absolutely perfect person and live happily ever after."

"And what will you do?" he asked, tugging her a little closer. His fingers brushed hers, which were tucked into his arm.

Her mouth twisted ever so slightly. "I suppose I'll do what I always do. Be happy for you and try to convince myself that it's time to try a new dating app. Go meet someone new. Figure myself out. Cut myself some revenge bangs or book a solo trip to hike in the Andes and meet a hairy, fit man looking for a new start."

You should get someone. Someone should look out for you. Nash slid his arm out of her bear hug and wrapped it around her shoulders. She let him, sighing as she did that thing where she melted into his body and he tried to pretend as if he hadn't noticed. Didn't care.

Which he was, alarmingly, starting to think he did.

The science of curses was quite thin. Mostly, people's belief gave the curse life, made them think that the ill-wishing had an effect. And it wasn't that Wren actually believed in curses, more that she had a not insignificant pattern of behavior that bore out her belief that men broke up with her and then committed to the next woman they dated. She joked about a love curse, but all Nash saw was idiocy. She was quite lovable.

Obviously, he had the usual friendly feelings for her. He enjoyed her company. In a friendly way. He didn't want to see her get hurt or taken advantage of, which meant he'd be helping her negotiate her next lease or check on her car insurance and make sure she was fully covered because insurance companies were known to sneak all sorts of clever loopholes into their policies and Wren trusted everyone.

So no, he absolutely couldn't kiss her again. Or ask her if he could, please, take her to bed.

Twelve

Weddings made people horny. It was a known fact. You watched two people at the peak of their physical attraction march down an aisle (or up a beach) and immediately your own hormones started jumping up and down in a pick-me dance. Wren found herself staring ferociously out the window at the ocean, trying to keep the stupid tears from falling. It was angry crying. Technically. She wasn't sad because of the wedding—she blamed the hot, moody man standing *all the way across the room* from her. It was Nash Masterson's fault.

Iceberg.

She glared some more at the ocean. Look! There was a wave and another and another. Plus seagulls, undoubtedly pooping and doing disgusting bird things. She needed everyone else—except for the happy newlyweds, obviously, because she wasn't a horrible person—to feel her pain. To descend to this unexpected, really embarrassing low with her.

It wasn't that she wanted Nash to witness his brother's obvious happiness with his new wife and then decide that he must have that for himself. It was just that—well, every so often she wondered what was wrong with her, if she'd been the reason why her past relationships hadn't worked out, if she had a character flaw or just lacked the happily-ever-after gene. Nash seemed perfectly happy as he was, having meaningless sex and not pledging his eternal love to one person. So. There was that.

Nash sighed.

An obnoxious, loud, totally put-upon sigh, too.

And then he crossed the room—she watched him come, reflected in the window—stopped right behind her and draped the throw blanket from the sofa around her shoulders. Damn him.

"What can I do?" he asked.

"There is absolutely nothing wrong with me."

"You look sad." Window Nash frowned and she recognized that tone in his voice. She was on his fix-it list now.

"I am not looking for a solution, Nash Masterson."

He nodded. Hesitated for a nanosecond before making the observation anyway. "But you're unhappy."

"And?"

He cocked his head, meeting her eyes in the window. "You've eaten a king-sized bag of M&M's. Taken a two-hour bath. On a scale of one to 'worst day ever,' you're at least an eight. Possibly a nine."

"I had a bad day! It's no big deal."

"We went to a wedding." His brow furrowed.

"Exactly."

"Weddings are happy."

"Yeah," she muttered. "Mostly. Except for the FOMO part."

He was clearly trying not to smile. It was adorable even though she knew him well enough to know that he wasn't a smiling sort of person. It would pass.

He cocked his head. "So. No fixing?"

It was an invitation to slip back into their friendly, familiar relationship, the one where he'd never put his fingers and his tongue inside her. Gah. She was the one who couldn't forget. He knew her well enough to figure out that she wouldn't be able to stop poking at their not-quite-a-hookup on the beach. It was the sore tooth in their friendship.

"You don't want to fix my single state."

"Wren." She hated that calm tone.

Make a joke of it. She swung around from the window and almost slammed into him. Oh well. He was a grown man and he could take care of himself. She dropped to her knees in front of him.

Wait. Two knees were for blow jobs.

She shifted to one bent knee, wondering if people actually did this in real life. Nash froze. Perhaps he thought she'd passed out at his feet? Ha. She had a point to make here and, no, she didn't care that she was wearing just the hotel's terry cloth bathrobe (white!) and a pair of cotton panties (also white!). She'd probably flashed him, but it couldn't be helped.

She grabbed his hand and tucked it under her chin.

Stared up at him through her lashes. "Nash Masterson, will you marry me?"

He pulled gently free. "What did you drink?"

She flopped over onto her back and glared at the ceiling. "See? This is the problem."

"Explain it to me." He turned away, striding over to start the fire in the electric fireplace. Probably, he wanted to put a safe distance between them.

"Maybe it was just a legal ceremony to you, but Declan and Charlotte's wedding was gorgeous and I'm jealous. Completely, totally, stinking jealous." She held out an arm. "Look. I'm turning green."

"Are you?"

"You bet," she said glumly. "The world's supply of perfect men was reduced by one today and it was already an endangered population."

That got his attention. "You think my brother is perfect?"

"Well, not for me, obviously. So mostly perfect? Charlotte's welcome to him."

"So to recap, you're upset because—"

He seemed slow. Maybe because true love was so not his area of expertise. "I should have demanded you marry me rather than just fake-date me."

"Too late."

"I know. I'm regretting my life choices. But mostly I'm horny."

Nash made a choked sound.

"You heard me. Fix that, buddy." She turned her head to the side to look at him. Since she was starfished on the floor with no intention of getting up from her pity party, she had an excellent view of his feet in a pair of glossy black dress shoes that had probably been handmade in Paris or Venice. One thing was certain: they were the nicest shoes she'd ever seen. She tried to imagine Nash in some place as mundane as a Walmart and smiled. Nope. He was a high-maintenance man.

A very quiet, mute man.

She bit her lip. Had he stroked out? She should check on him since it was, sort of, her fault. She tilted her head back, hoping she looked sexy and carefree rather than desperately nervous and turned on. He was watching her, looking thoughtful. She squinted. Was there just a shade of lust in his eyes, or was that merely wishful thinking on her part?

"So why is horny a problem?" he asked.

She shut her eyes again. "Hello. Because I'm single, lazy, and there's no one attracted to me in a zillion-mile radius?"

That was only a slight exaggeration. It shouldn't have mattered that Nash had re-friend-zoned her. She was an ungrateful wretch to want more. Still, she was going to keep her eyes firmly shut because looking at what she couldn't have—or taste, touch and ride like a cowgirl—was torture.

"That's not true." His calm voice had her considering ever-so-accidentally knocking him into the ocean. Martha's Vineyard was an island; it would be easy to do.

"Is, too."

"I'm here," he pointed out.

Uh-huh. Hence, her problem. "There is zero chemistry between us."

"Is that what you believe?"

"It's what I know. *Facts*, buddy."

"Right," he said thoughtfully. "So the whole sex-on-a-beach thing was—"

"An aberration," she suggested. "A one-time-and-never-again thing. Driven by proximity. Like a drunk hookup in college."

"A drunk hookup," he repeated.

"In fact," she continued, "you're the champagne of drunk hookups." And then morosely because if you were going to throw a pity party for yourself, you might as well go all in, "I'm that cheap pink wine you buy in a can at the gas station and let roll around in your car for a week before you finally bring it inside your house, wondering what on earth you were thinking."

"And my suggestion last week that we rethink our plan and have sex?"

"You never asked again."

"I was waiting for a response."

"*What?* I wasn't sure."

"And are you sure now?"

"More so." She waved a hand. "But not entirely. No. I'm confused. Would it be worth the risk?"

There was a pause. One of those pregnant, thinking-type pauses. Or maybe Nash had fallen asleep? She was not checking, she decided. She'd started this conversation and she'd stay right here, on the floor and with her eyes shut, until it was over.

"Come here." His voice, low and stern, rough and delicious, rolled over. She only wished he'd said something more flattering, or less sexy-sounding. She knew one thing for sure—

"No way. I'm never leaving this rug. You can roll

me up in it and cart me onto your private plane just like this."

He barked out a laugh—Nash *laughing*—and then she felt rather than saw him stride across the room toward her, at which point she risked cracking her left eyelid ever so slightly and discovered him tugging off his suit jacket. It went flying stage right and then he lay down beside her on the rug. No. Wait. Because he wasn't done rearranging her life yet, big, warm hands snugged her waist and lifted her up and…down. Down onto his *chest*. Her breasts were pressed against his muscles, her thighs nestled on his. And between his…

Wow.

Weddings did, indeed, make everyone horny.

The heat that radiated off him threw the poor fireplace firmly into the shade. His body was strength and steel against hers, sending a pulse of pleasure through her. She'd found her new favorite spot. He'd have to pry her off him. It—he—felt familiar and safe, and yet somehow neither of those things.

"Nash?"

She opened her eyes. Oh, God. Rookie mistake. His beautiful, stern face looked down at hers as he linked his arms around her, his palms locking at the small of her back. She gave a small wriggle, losing her train of thought. Could she go anywhere? Did she even want to?

"Yeah?"

"Do you have an identical twin?"

"No." Amusement softened his gaze. She was sure of it.

"Amnesia?"

"No."

"Because I'm confused."

"You said that there's no real attraction between us." His thumb rubbed a small circle around the base of her spine. "I disagree. We should test your hypothesis. Conduct an experiment."

"We should—"

What?

"Test your attraction hypothesis."

He unlinked one of his hands and ran it up her spine to cup the back of her head. This was so good, so exactly what she needed. She'd known he was a genius, but he exceeded expectations. Her body felt hotter than the Serengeti or Earth's core, and that followed absolutely everywhere he touched before migrating to other places. Well, one, possibly two other places, one of which was most definitely her core.

"You want to run an experiment?"

"For science," he said gravely.

"That wouldn't be weird? Because it seems weird to me."

His mouth softened, the corners quirking up. "It doesn't have to be weird. Tell me what you want."

He was just so *Nash*. God, she—

He was touching her again, his fingers stroking gentle, soft circles on her back. She'd just focus on these sensations, not the feelings he might or might not arouse in her. No head feelings—only below-the-belt sensations.

"Then it would *totally* be weird. I need you to never, ever find out about my secret fantasies."

A questioning look this time. "Why not?"

"Well, we already came this close to having sex on

the beach. In fact, some people would argue strongly that I sullied you."

A definite smile from him this time. "Or vice versa."

"Also true! One mistake between friends is awkward but it can go away. Twice seems like a pattern. And we are friends and I don't want to lose that. I like hanging out with you. We're good together. That's way better than sex."

It had to be because sex would be a one-night thing, but friends were forever. And with the heat pooling between her thighs, her body aching for his, the rulebook was suddenly shut up and off the table, possibly tossed right out the window...

She wanted him.

His hand stroked the side of her face, calling her back. "Can I kiss you, Wren?"

It was funny how fast everything could change. One minute she was sad, turned on and lonely, and now here she was, in Nash's arms and he was holding on to her. Not quite roughly, she decided, but firmly. With purpose. This wasn't an accident or even naked swimming on the beach. So she nodded.

He reached for her with both hands, sliding a hand into her hair so he could tug her face down to meet his. His other hand pressed flat against her back, a sweet, heavy weight and the best kind of anchor. He touched her as if he were memorizing her—learning this curve, that dip, so he would always recognize her. *This hip, this waist, this rib and that one and then this breast.* Desire pooled in her core. He had them all mixed up together, arms and legs, hearts. No. Not hearts. But something sweet and almost as good.

His lips brushed hers, carefully, a little hello. She kissed him back, just to say *Welcome. Come on in. I'm glad to see you.* He nipped gently, biting ever so tenderly into her lower lip for a taste.

"Nash?" She grabbed at his shoulders with her hands.

"Let's try this again." He kissed the corner of her mouth. Moved eastward. "Can I kiss you?"

"Yes," she said faintly. *This is Nash. Yes, you can kiss me. Yes, please do whatever you want. Yes, make me feel good.*

"I've thought of so many different ways to kiss you. Tell me which one you like best."

I like all of you. If she'd been standing, she would have melted because all of her quivered, going liquid at the sweetly dominant tone in his voice. His confidence was gorgeous, as was his big, strong body laid out beneath hers, the chiseled muscles of his chest leaping when she ran her fingertips over the thick lines, the cut planes, and down to the enormous ridge in his pants. His eyes were darker than she'd ever seen them, his lips parted on a rough sigh. He looked like her fantasy man, but he was hers.

"Can I take this off?" he asked roughly, hands smoothing back the bathrobe.

"If you take yours off," she countered, eager to see him. She hadn't seen him, had she? Not completely, not that day on the beach. The boxer briefs hadn't concealed much, but still. She rolled away, shedding her own clothes as he stripped his own off. He was as amazing as she'd imagined him to be, muscled and strong and sun-bronzed, with a six-pack that drew her attention down to the thick ridge of his penis.

"Come back here," he rasped. Then added, "Please."
And he pulled her back on top of him.

"You're so cute." She laughed, then giggled as his
fingers skated up her ribs, tickling in mock punishment
before they settled into a more soothing stroke up and
down her back. She'd never been so aware of her own
body before, of her bareness, the erotic press of his skin
against hers.

"And you're beautiful," he added softly, but as if he
saw through her skin and somewhere deep inside her.
She loved the way he looked at her.

Loved how his hands moved patiently over her body,
in no rush. As if they had forever to get this perfect. And
somehow it turned her on more, sending her body soaring from zero to sixty, this slow, sure way he mapped
her body, found her breasts with his hands, his thumbs
stroking first the undersides and then the plush curves
and the sensitive tips.

Yes.

"You're so quiet," he murmured, his thumbs rolling
her nipples. "You're never quiet. I think I imagined
you'd have more to say about this."

Each pass of his thumbs wound her up, had her body
tightening, heating up. "Why are *you* such a talker
now?" she gasped, leaning down to kiss him. This shut
him up, but only for long, delicious moments.

"Is that a yes?" he asked, in that stern voice of his.
"You have to give me that word."

"Yes." *Oh.*

"So you'll let me—"

"Yes," she said, rather more desperately. "Less talking, more kissing. Please."

He laughed, the bastard, but he kissed her mouth, her throat, placed openmouthed kisses along her shoulder and the slope of her breasts. Perched on top of him, she somehow felt safe and delicate, as if she was the absolute, most important—possibly the only—person in his world. All of his fierce focus, his drive and his concentration were on *her. Thank you so much, universe, thank you thank you.*

He eased her farther up his body, kissing his way lower.

Like that. Yes. Please.

He lifted her, moved her effortlessly up, not giving her time to worry about what he saw, the soft curve of her thigh, the wet, slick heat of her folds. He just kept right on shifting her until her knees were pressed against his neck and face and then, God, he was kissing her, right there where she wanted him so badly, and—

"Nash—"

"Let's see if you like this," he whispered, his tongue opening her up. She whimpered, making a sound that was half squeal, half greedy demand. She fell forward, catching her hands on the floor, caging him in.

"You're so beautiful," he said, kissing her again, slow and deliberate, absolutely and maddeningly methodical. His tongue was everywhere, licking and teasing as the sensations coiled tighter and tighter inside her until she trembled, clenching down on nothing.

She bit her lip, because otherwise the words would have fallen out of her. Words of praise and demand, promises, half words and something suspiciously like a scream. He felt so good, so good, but then he'd reversed their positions, pulling her underneath him, swinging himself over her. There was a crinkle, the small sounds as he rolled a condom on, her finger smoothing it into place along with his.

"May I?" he asked.

"Don't stop," she said. "Yes."

"I've imagined this." He pressed a kiss against her forehead, her cheek. Her mouth.

"Me, too."

"Good," he growled.

She couldn't believe this was happening. Or that it was so good. He pushed carefully inside her, a fraction of an inch at a time, breathing heavily, and she wrapped her arms around him and held on to him. Next time, next time she'd be creative and bold, do something different. Vacation sex or a hookup or whatever label they'd put on this tomorrow, for right now it was perfect.

She hadn't known it could feel so good. He made a sound, as if he agreed, and then he was moving and she was amazed and on fire, feeling everything at once, because this person, this absolutely perfect man worshipping her body with his was the reserved, stern man who was out to save the world one chemistry experiment at a time. His finger dug into her hips, holding on to her, anchoring her with a sure grip that said *here I am and so are you*. And it was a surprise, better than anything she'd imagined.

"Look at me," he ordered.

She couldn't look away, but that was a problem for later. She lost herself in his gaze and his hands, letting him touch her inside and out. He pushed deeper and deeper, making a space for himself inside her, sending heat and excitement spiraling through her body.

And it was absolutely enough and so exactly what she wanted—*him*—that she was coming long before she thought it possible, crying out, yanking him closer still as he thrust inside her, holding still, giving her everything as they both found release.

Thirteen

Was it weird that Nash had just had the best sex of his life with a friend? It wasn't as if Wren was his only friend, but she was the first he'd gone to bed with. Well not to bed precisely, since they hadn't made it past the rug in front of the fireplace.

Wren had fallen asleep, but Nash had never been one to sleep for long. The two hours he'd spent being the bottom slice in a Wren sandwich had been enough. He should catch up on work. Maybe check his email.

But he did none of those things. Instead, he got them both off the floor, Wren cradled in his arms, and carried her into her bedroom. She'd somehow managed to put her stamp on the room even though they'd been on Martha's Vineyard for only a handful of days: a pink kimono draped over a chair, two and a half pairs of shoes on the floor by the bed. A stack of books and a Diet Coke can on the bedside table.

The hotel had turned down the bed, so sliding her between the sheets was simple. They'd always had a fun but casual relationship. She teased and he pretended not to like it. But from that first day in college, when she'd bounced into his office he shared with two other graduate students and announced that she was there to learn and she'd read Oliver Sacks but nothing had prepared her for this week's lecture, he'd been ever so slightly off-balance.

Instead she'd become his friend. He could explain it a dozen different ways, could pinpoint the moments when they'd stopped being TA and student, graduate student and undergraduate, two people who had at best a professional relationship—and they'd become more. They'd become themselves. As she'd worked through her PhD program at UCLA and he'd started his company, they'd spent more time together, sneaking into J.J.'s Hollywood mansion when the AC went out in her place and it was 110 degrees even in the shade. Swimming beneath the stars with a bottle of four-dollar sparkling wine and the girlfriends with whom she shared a two-bedroom rental that abutted the highway. Talking her down when she'd freaked out about her dissertation and debated scrapping the whole thing. Practicing questions with her when Pomona College had invited her to interview because, she said, he did an awesome scary face.

Wren was simply there. She'd sent him a cookie "the size of your head!" when his company turned its first profit. She'd come over to help him eat it, too, because *sharing is caring.* She mailed him funny vintage post-cards because she thought it was important that some-one remind him to "have a nice day" and she always put fresh coffee creamer in his fridge when he was coming back from a business trip even though he swore he'd just add some to his grocery delivery order.

So he didn't want to mess that up. Not in a million years. Not for anything.

He slid her into the bed, then… He had no idea what he should do next. His heart was doing something un-familiar in his chest. Something more than its usual, routine beating. He could lie down on the empty half of the bed. He could leave. His phone buzzed, vibrat-ing on the hardwood floor in the other room, but he ig-nored it. Whatever it was, it could wait.

He pulled the covers up, but Wren was asleep, sound asleep, and there was nothing else he could do for her, was there? He gave up and went out into the other room.

It was J.J. calling. In the picture Nash had used for his contact, J.J. had his favorite power suit on, his arm raised, his focus entirely on some movie scene he was directing because merely running a successful film stu-dio and production company had never been enough for J.J. He'd pushed himself every bit as much as he'd pushed his adopted sons. There was always an award to win or box office numbers to beat, higher revenues, better ticket sales, more spectacular effects.

They were more alike than either of them cared to admit.

He muted the call. J.J. would want to know if Declan had gotten his head out of his ass yet about the produc-tion company and repented. That would never happen.

Nash retrieved a T-shirt and jeans, then started checking his work emails. There were fires to put out and feedback to provide, but he couldn't stop thinking about Wren and last night. How had he not realized that finding someone really mattered to Wren, that deep inside her romance-loving soul, his best friend wanted nothing more than to meet someone and fall in love? And after that she'd have a life that wouldn't have as much—or any—room in it for Nash. He didn't think she'd appreciate his expectation that she'd remain single. Which was statistically unlikely, anyhow. She'd find someone. Someone else.

Around dawn he ended up a call with his head of product development. He and Dan were working out a tricky bit of chemistry for a new polymer when Dan froze. Not because of a bad network connection—a red flush crawled up his cheekbones and his eyes did a panic-stricken dart—but… Nash turned at the sound of bare feet on the floor behind him.

Wren padded toward him and, shit, she was on his camera, wasn't she? She had a very sexy case of bed-head going on, which paired beautifully with the haphazardly tied pink kimono. Holy cleavage, Batman. She was sleepy and rumpled, and he wanted nothing more than to peel the lacy edges away and kiss her from head to toe.

He shut the lid on his laptop and swung all the way around, the better to give her his undivided attention. "Hey."

Was he supposed to…? Did she want him to…? What was the morning-after script when you'd just had sex with your friend? Whatever that script was, Declan needed to green-light it ASAP. His brain suggested he should apologize or ask her how she felt. Say *something* other than a three-letter hello. But this was Wren and everything felt strangely…okay.

He thought she would stop when she reached his chair, but this was Wren so of course she kept on going, plopping herself down in his lap. She sighed, relaxing into him.

"Did I just photobomb your work call?"

"Best part of the meeting."

"Oh, good." She curled up like a cautious cat. She might have stretched a little. Hell if he knew. His brain didn't work 100 percent when she was around. Wren liked to touch. The problem was, they'd always been friendly touches before. A quick hug hello, a squeeze of his shoulder. He'd look down and there she would be, arm brushing his, leg pressed against his thigh as they watched a movie or whatever, as if he were just such a comfortable part of her space that there were no boundaries between them. He hesitated, then wrapped his arm around her. She was warm and smelled like Wren.

He liked this and he didn't want to lose her.

The sun was coming up outside. Perhaps an early morning walk on the beach, some coffee? And then they could go back to being the way they'd been before last night. Friends. Partners. People who had each other's back because it was only practical to look out for each other.

She tilted her head back, using his armpit as a pillow. "Thanks."

Great. He had no idea what for. "Anytime."

Her smile, while slow, was glorious. Better than any

fucking sunrise. "You don't have any idea what I'm talking about."

She had him there. He shrugged. "You know me well enough to fill in the blanks."

She'd used him as a chair before, mostly on boats, or crowded cars, or on one memorable wet-bench occasion when she'd claimed that only one of them had to walk away with a wet ass and he was too big to sit on her. Which had been fair enough and yet it felt wrong to pretend that this was just a friendly gesture and nothing more.

"Who were you talking to?"

"No one important."

"So not your scary dad? Or Declan?"

"Declan is on his honeymoon, smart aleck. But no, not my dad, either. My head of product development."

She groaned. "Our hooking up is now common knowledge in California. I need to eat my feelings. Do you want to grab breakfast? There's an awesome-looking café just down the street."

What was the correct answer here? "Breakfast?"

She grinned. "Don't people get breakfast the next morning if they hook up? If the sex was good?"

The sex had been amazing. Better than good. He probably should go find a Hallmark greeting card that spelled out exactly how amazing it had been. If she thought it was merely good, though, he'd be tempted to prove to her that it could be better and that wasn't a good idea. They were a one-time deal. Fake.

She angled her head so she could see his face. "FYI, we had amazing sex. I owe you two breakfasts." And then she looked away, biting her lower lip. "Also I'd like to know that we're okay."

"We're always okay. That's a promise."

"Then let's get breakfast. I want a stack of pancakes as big as my head. My treat." She bounced off his lap.

"I should…work…"

She was already gone, back in her room, the door not quite closing behind her. He heard the shower turn on a moment later. This was a problem because his brain immediately suggested that he follow her and fuck her in the shower. Go down on his knees and eat her out again. Press her hands up against the glass enclosure, cage her in with his body as he drove into her from behind. Honestly? All of the above. *Respect her boundaries,* he told himself, standing restlessly. *This was just sex. Be detached. Polite. Respectful.* He wasn't supposed to be obsessed with her.

Thirty minutes later, he was this close to inviting her to come back to his room as they were seated at the outdoor café she'd picked. The hostess had taken one look at them and seated them side by side on a bench on the same side of the table. Did they look like a couple? He was supposed to be all casual about this, but he wasn't. He was this close to saying something, but she was beaming, snapping pictures of the café excitedly, and he wasn't going to make her unhappy by suggesting they leave, was he? The café was sandwiched between a street popular with tourists and the water; their table looked out on a logjam of boats, yachts, dinghies and assorted watercrafts. Seagulls hovered opportunistically overhead. It was all complete chaos and therefore exactly Wren's jam.

"So," he said, after the waitress brought a black Americano for Nash, a cinnamon latte for Wren and an absolutely towering stack of pancakes. "We should talk about last night."

She dug into her pancakes. "Do you think so?"

Great. He wasn't sure if that was sarcasm or not. "Yes."

"You realize that *we should talk* is usually the opening line in a breakup conversation, right?"

She offered him a bite of her pancake, though, and he took it, even though he was more of an egg-white omelet kind of person and they both knew it. Her eyes danced as a hundred grams of sugar attacked his teeth.

"We can't break up if we're not really a couple," he pointed out.

"Fake break up, then." She shrugged. "If you want to get technical."

What he *wanted* was to get naked. *Again.* Which was a bad idea, certainly without having some kind of discussion to solidify what they were and were not doing. Together. Her arm brushed his, her knee touching his under the table. He'd kissed both last night. He knew what she looked like naked. He'd touched and tasted all the parts of her that she covered up.

"Are you okay?"

She put her fork down. "Really? You're asking me that?" And then when he just waited, because this question was important to him, even if she thought the answer was obvious, she said, "Yes. I'm good."

Then she sighed. "Are you okay?"

That was a very basic question, but surprisingly he

had to think about it. Last night had been fantastic, but not if it came at the cost of their friendship apparently.

"Excellent," he said awkwardly, when what he wanted to ask was *Can I see you again? Can we go back to the hotel and do it again? Am I really okay for you and would you like to make a casual thing of it and—*

She made a face. "We're such liars. Of course this is awkward. We've seen each other naked. On the other hand, most of my friends have seen me naked!"

"Really," he managed. He had no idea he'd been, well, missing out.

"Although getting changed around someone is more like noticing the beach outside the car window and thinking it's really pretty and maybe taking a picture on your phone. Whereas sex—" she shrugged, digging back into her pancakes "—that's going for a swim. In your case, a gold-medal-worthy swim. Did that make your head explode?"

"My head is fine." He started on his omelet.

She beamed at him. "So we're totally good. We had amazing hookup sex and we can talk about it. We're still friends! Were you expecting a ring and a declaration this morning?"

"No," he said carefully. "But I don't think you're a casual-sex kind of person. Which is not me judging. Or saying that casual sex is good or bad or anything other than a choice that some people make—and others don't."

Even as he said that, he had an idea, a choice that he selfishly wanted her to make.

"Because I still believe in romance and love?" She

made a face at him. "Unlike the barbarian sitting at this table?"

He toasted her with his Americano and she laughed. "That coffee is as black and bitter as your soul, Dr. Masterson."

"Guilty as charged," he said easily, wondering how best to bring up his idea. Because perhaps last night hadn't been as amazing for her as it had been for him. Except—she'd *said* she was lonely. And horny. And looking for someone to be there when she got that way.

And he could be that someone, couldn't he?

She still hadn't gotten back to him on his friends-with-benefits offer.

They finished up their breakfast while he tried not to think about all the ways he could be there for Wren. He also did his best not to check his phone too often. It was a weekday and even though it was barely seven in the morning on the West Coast, his team was already working. They had an important deliverable coming up and he needed to contribute. Of course, he shouldn't ask Wren his question. Because it couldn't work. She was beautiful and funny, so full of life, and he just sort of sucked it—life—out of other people. Rained all over their parades like an Eeyore. He tried not to look at her or think about sex with her. How it felt to be inside her.

Fuck. These were feelings.

Sex feelings, but still.

He marshaled his arguments while he halfheartedly fought and lost a battle over who got to pay for breakfast. Wren insisted it was her treat, and he found he didn't like saying no to her.

"So," he said, "we've established that I'm not capable of love and romance."

"Right," she deadpanned as they headed out. "You're an automaton. A very sexy but unemotional Data."

The *sexy* part seemed promising, but he wasn't sure about the comparison to the Star Trek android who had to use an emotion chip to feel human emotions. He seemed to recall that it had been untried technology and ultimately faulty. Which gave him an idea.

"We should keep doing this."

"If I eat any more pancakes, I'll explode." She mimed something that he assumed was the threatened explosion, but it could have been anything.

"Smart aleck. Not the pancakes. Us. Maybe we should keep having sex."

"What?" She stared at him, clearly shocked.

"We can keep having sex. You said you were lonely and sad that you didn't have someone to have sex with. We don't have to stop right now."

"We'll just keep hooking up forever?" Her voice went up on the last word.

"As friends. Until you meet someone better. The perfect-prince guy you mentioned at the wedding yesterday."

"So you were listening to me?"

"I always listen to you, Wren." He forced himself to try and smile. Be nice as whatever half-assed plan he'd cooked up over their breakfast seemed to have flown out of his head.

She raised her eyebrows. "To be perfectly clear, you still want to be friends with benefits?"

"Yes," he said. "Why not?"

* * *

There were reasons why not. Wren was sure of it. Not that any came to mind at the moment, other than the absolute certainty that if they did the friend-sex thing, eventually she'd forget he was only a friend and start thinking about him as someone more. She'd screw it up and then she'd lose him. Nash might be a bit of a sex god, but was that enough to risk their entire friendship? It was why she had yet to give him an answer.

"We're just going to hook up over and over like some kind of sexual Groundhog Day?"

He blinked. "Well—"

Her brain helpfully supplied some very lovely memories of what he'd been like last night, memories that made her even more aware of the lazy, slow throb in certain parts of her anatomy that were deliciously sore and quite happy that she'd shamelessly jumped her friend. It was her very own Nash brand on her body.

And yet—

She told herself it didn't matter. That it was none of her business. She barely knew the real Nash, the man beneath the surface, and she didn't get to know him any better. He was grumpy and reserved, far too wealthy and quite horribly work-focused. He worked eighty-hour weeks and never took a holiday. She'd never come first, except, apparently when he wanted sex.

"You still don't want to try and find a real girl-friend?" she asked.

"No."

"Because you totally could." There. That was extremely fair of her. She was a saint. A good person. And also, a very jealous person.

It was silly to wish that he might consider being her boyfriend. To wish that he'd see that he did, in fact, have the qualities that would make him an unqualified success in the boyfriend arena. All he seemed to want was friendship—and sex. Sex was a good thing, right? Or at least it was enough of a thing? Still, someone who looked like him could, quite obviously, get all the sex he wanted, probably with acrobatic twins or a porn star. Someone super creative and much more flexible than her, at any rate. Yeah, Nash could be a bit of an asshole, particularly when it came to work, and the same focus that made him a miracle in bed would drive most people nuts anywhere else because he inevitably turned it on work but… Still. He was barely past thirty (if you rounded down), hot, rich and had actual six-pack abs.

So.

"What's in this for you?" she asked suspiciously.

He shrugged. "The same thing that's in it for you. Good sex with someone I trust." He hesitated for a moment. "A known quantity. Not an experiment or a hypothesis."

"The fact that you're calling potential girlfriends an *experiment* is part of your problem."

"Probably." He didn't sound concerned. "Is that a yes?"

"This is a bad idea." Her voice sounded weak, even to her. *Grow a spine, Wren.*

"It's practical," he countered. "We've already done the hard part. We survived our first date."

Oh God, this man. There was really only one answer, wasn't there? She'd just have to say what she felt.

"Yes."

Fourteen

A few days after the Let's-Be-Friends-That-Have-Sex decision, Wren was demonstrating her maturity by hiding in the bathroom. Nash himself had demonstrated earlier that shower sex was absolutely not overrated and that having a not-so-fake boyfriend built like a football linebacker was useful. When he'd kissed her knees to water, he'd been more than capable of holding them both up until they'd crossed the finish line. He'd given her that small, just-for-her smile she loved. She'd have broken the internet if she'd taken a picture of that Nash, wrapped in a towel, a smile softening his harsh features, water droplets on his fine chest.

"So," Wren mouthed to the bathroom mirror. "I did this thing, Lola." No. That didn't capture what had happened since she'd told Nash yes to his crazy proposal.

Lola would see straight through what was absolutely the understatement of the year.

Take two. "Nash and I had sex."

Mirror Wren made a face. That was more accurate, but still missing something. She and Nash had spent their daylight hours playing tourist on Martha's Vineyard and then at night they'd had amazing, fantastic, mind-blowing sex. Okay. So clearly that activity had leaked over into the daylight hours, too, this morning's shower shenanigans being Exhibit A. He'd totally ruined her for anyone else, and she wasn't sure she minded.

With a sigh, she went out, kissed Nash hello and goodbye (he was, of course, working although they'd compromised on half days) and headed for the beach and to make her own SOS call.

"Are you tired of living the life of luxury?" Lola asked after they'd exchanged the usual pleasantries. "Because I could be convinced to switch places with you. News flash—never assign a ten-page paper that's due the day after a holiday weekend. The undergraduates phone it in. Assignment Billionaire's Fake Girlfriend sounds like the better deal. Your Instagram updates are amazing."

This was not news to Wren and she was grateful not to have summer classes to teach this year.

"Well, about that—"

"Tell me you didn't sleep with him after your fake date," Lola demanded.

"Why would that be so bad?" Wren asked, even though she knew it was—it was, after all, the whole reason she was calling.

"Because no one ever successfully goes back to being truly just friends after having sex. No matter how fine that man is, you value your friendship. He's been in your life for *years*, Wren. No sex is that good."

Before Nash, she would have agreed. She'd always been able to take or leave sex. But now she had some very sexy memories of Nash imprinted on her mind, stripped, muscled, watching her with hot, needy eyes because he wanted her. She couldn't imagine ever getting tired of that. Or being in his arms. His bed. His life.

"Hello?" Lola prompted. "Tell me you didn't have sex with him."

"Pretty sure lying is against the friend code," Wren said.

Silence.

"You slept with him."

"Yeah."

"Was this a one-time kind of thing due to alcohol poisoning or orange aliens with skin like a basketball holding a ray gun to your head?"

"It's an ongoing kind of thing," she admitted. "We've decided to be friends with benefits."

Lola sighed. "This is such a bad idea, Wren. Did you walk into it with your eyes wide open? How is this fake dating if it involves a real penis?"

"Look," she grumbled. "After a gal's seen Nash naked, she's not going to shut her eyes."

"He's that good?"

"Better." Another sigh escaped her mouth. Damn it. She needed to hold it…this…herself together better. Why did this all suddenly feel so real?

"So he's not all delicious frosting on a cardboard

cake? Because we both know that the hotter a man is on the outside, the less likely it is he's got it going on in the inside." Lola made a choking noise. "Wait. That sounds terrible, but you know what I mean. Nash is a bit of a grump and he's definitely hard to know. Is he still all stern and reserved?"

"Sometimes," Wren heard herself say. "But he's far more open when we're alone."

"And naked?" Lola asked.

"It helps," she said weakly. "But he's amazing when he's not naked, too, okay? This isn't just about the sex. And I know we're not dating for real and that he's never met a relationship he wouldn't run from, but I need to figure this out."

"Naked," Lola said. "Did you at least take pictures?"

"Lola!"

"Tell me all about him."

"He's an amazing guy. He's loyal and stubborn and he's got my back. He lost a whole lot of family early on, so he's fiercely protective of the ones he has in his life now. He loves his brother something fierce and he values his adoptive dad. He's scary smart, super driven, and when he focuses on me, I feel like the only woman in the world even though I know it's temporary."

"Wow. You really went for it. There is a silver lining, however. Now you're not lying to your mom and your sisters about having a serious boyfriend."

"Well, since it's one-sided, I'm going to argue that's not a feature," Wren said.

Lola was silent.

She came to a tide pool and stared down at it. "This is where you tell me I should live in the moment, right?"

"Did he put a timeline on this? Did you tell him this wasn't so fake anymore?"

"Just until I meet Mr. Perfect," she said lightly. "And no."

Lola sighed. "That's great, except you've already met him and his name is Nash."

While flying back to California from Martha's Vineyard, Nash had come to two conclusions. First, adding sex to his friendship with Wren had turned out shockingly well. He had a feeling that things would get complicated when Wren made some misguided attempt to discuss feelings, but until then, it was smooth sailing.

It wasn't weird. At all.

Mostly because he refused to think too closely about it. They liked each other, they had fun in bed and therefore everything would work out even if it was all a tad more real than was safe.

Yesterday, Durant Senior had officially accepted Nash's buyout offer.

Not-so-fake-dating for the win, right?

Because of course the man had called Nash up to explain that he'd just loved meeting Wren at the bachelor's auction. This might have been polite chitchat, the kind of conversation that Nash generally avoided at all costs, but there had also been some very specific hints that the Durants were hoping to be invited to a wedding in the near future. *His* wedding. To Wren. He wasn't surprised she'd made such a positive impression, but he hadn't known what to say, either. He'd settled for admitting that Wren was an amazing woman and he was a lucky man.

When he'd shared his good news with Wren last night, she'd announced that they were perfect partners in crime. But he wasn't so sure about that as he knew that no matter how many signed contracts he had with Durant, he was going to let the man down fundamentally when it came to their unspoken deal because there would be no wedding bells.

Still, they'd done some celebrating, first with a bottle of champagne and then in Wren's bed. She'd convinced him to spend the night at her place, which was a first for them. The next morning he opened his eyes. No Wren, but he could hear voices coming from her living room.

He got up, pulled on the jeans he'd discarded the night before and decided that was enough to avoid going full monty on whomever she was talking to this early in the morning. Following the voices, he padded down a hallway lined with framed photos of Wren's favorite spots. There were a lot of them, but she'd already made room for a picture of the two of them in souvenir T-shirts on Martha's Vineyard. His said "My chemistry is amazing."

"What's he *really* like?"

"And is he a twenty-minute man or can we still expect to see him at the wedding?"

Both questions came from the laptop balanced on Wren's thighs. Despite the ninety-degree weather outside, she was snuggled up on the couch with a fake fur throw blanket around her shoulders. Possibly this was because she was only wearing boy shorts and a little top. He found himself grinning, despite the annoyance of the questions.

He'd clearly nailed the dress code. He loved the way

the soft cotton clung to her thighs, snug to some places he'd enjoyed exploring last night, and particularly the tiny top that skimmed her breasts and seemed one strong breath away from slipping lower. He'd rise to that challenge, thank you very much, and see just how fast he could get her panting.

"Um." Wren stared at her screen. Three sets of eyes stared back at her. Widened as they took in his bedhead.

"Do I get to speak for myself?" he asked. "Because I'm good for at least an hour."

Wren startled. He steadied the laptop with one hand, wrapping his free arm around her. Then for good measure, he rested his chin on her shoulders.

"Do you doubt me?" he asked.

"Nooooo," said a woman who had to be one of Wren's sisters. She looked skeptical so he nuzzled Wren's neck.

She sagged into him for a second before sitting straight up. "Nash, you remember my *mother* and my *sisters*, right?"

The mocking looks directed his way from the sisters said that they knew all too well that he didn't. Not really. "Ladies."

They nodded stiffly at him. Great. He'd interrupted their family time.

"So, Nash," the older woman said. "*Are* you coming to the wedding?"

"Still," muttered one of the sisters.

"I wouldn't kick him out of bed for eating crackers," the other mock-whispered.

"Wouldn't miss it." He looked at Wren. She was chewing on her lower lip. Anxious, and not sure how to handle this. He rubbed his thumb over her lip. "Right, Wren-bird?"

She flushed. He dropped a kiss on her ear and her sisters goggled at him as if he'd just produced proof of life on Mars.

"The seventh of September," Wren's mom said. "Just so we're clear."

"Yes, ma'am."

She nodded. "Call me Calliope. Can I pencil you in for Halloween, Thanksgiving and Black Friday? We'll hold off on Christmas for now, work you up to it."

"Mom," Wren groaned.

Her mother grinned. "What? I'm just getting the dates on his calendar. Licking the cupcake, so to speak. Making sure he knows where to be and when."

"We'll see you in September," Wren said firmly. Then she dramatically pushed the lid shut with her index finger. "Oh my God, they're evil."

"They love you. Me, not so much." He shook his head. Fortunately, the only person he cared about was sitting here on the couch with him. Equally fortunate, he was excellent at both distractions and diversions.

"The jury does seem to still be out," she said.

He slid the laptop out of her hands and set it on the coffee table. "Let me see what I can do to win you over."

Fifteen

The flamingo was pink, sparkly and oversize. Nash took in the carefree way his not-so-fake girlfriend straddled the inflatable pool toy, but decided she wasn't in imminent danger of toppling into the rooftop pool of the very swank LA hotel Wren's cousin May had rented for her bachelorette party.

Wren's increasingly misspelled texts had informed him that it was a "gREaT party." Based on the evidence around him—pink drinks, sunshine and a spectacular California sunset painting the sky oranges and reds— she was right. The guests, including Wren, wore matching pink swimsuits with Friend of the Bride in curly letters on their chests; May wore white and a ridiculous tulle veil stuck to a headband. Wren had expressed a hope that the pictures didn't end up online where her department chair would spot them because, she claimed, none of this would bolster her case for tenure in a few years. He wasn't so sure it would hurt. Who wouldn't want a fun-loving colleague? Plus, she looked gorgeous and she was smiling in that way she had, that lit her up from the inside. He wanted a picture.

Wren's sisters spotted him first. They'd camped out beside the pool, and now they perked up like pointer dogs on a scent. They still didn't like him much. That was a problem to solve later, though, the kind of later that came after he'd retrieved Wren from the pool, brought her home and taken her to bed. Fuck, but he was lucky.

At the far end of the pool, Wren's ex-boyfriend, the very undiscerning Noah, was scooping up his bride-to-be and whispering something that made her giggle. He watched carefully, but Wren didn't seem to mind. It turned out he really wanted her to be happy, but not, perhaps, with Noah.

With him.

Huh. He tucked that thought away for future examination, ignoring the increasingly smaller part of him—the young, left alone, unsure part—that whispered that romance was for other people and not part of his skill set. Wren made him want to learn.

Striding over to the edge of the pool, he knelt down next to his girl.

Her face lit up when she saw him. "Hey."

"Hey," he said right back, ready to give her whatever she wanted. He'd even get in the pool with her, fetch her another pink cocktail thingy and—

"Are you my new cabana boy?"

He smiled. "Aspiration of my life."

That won him a grin. "Are you done with work for today?"

There was always one more experiment, one more meeting, one more patent to win or company to acquire. Why stop at ten miles when you could run eleven? It was all perfectly sensible and how he spent his weekends. He almost never left his lab unless Declan needed him. And now, it seemed, Wren.

"Don't look now, but my sisters are over there," she whisper-shouted.

God, he lo—

No. He was not finishing that thought. Did she know what he was thinking? Should he explain? Lay out the reasons why he—

"Nash?" She blinked up at him.

Right. Not the best place for this discussion. To distract himself, he leaned in and kissed her.

There was some slightly inebriated if good-natured hooting and teasing from the remnants of the bachelorette party. He shot them a look and things got quieter. Hah. He still had it.

"Wow," she said rather dreamily. It had to be at least partly due to the number of grapefruit margaritas she'd consumed (four, if her texts were to be trusted), but still. He thought she was pretty *wow*, too.

"How are you? Are you ready to go?" When she nodded, he scooped her out of the water and stood.

"I'm going to get your shirt all wet."

"Not a problem."

She pointed to a lounger and he carried her over. "I have my own white knight," she giggled.

No. What she had was him. He opened his mouth to

point out that she shouldn't project impossible romantic notions onto him, but one of her sisters—he couldn't remember her name... Ella? Elizabeth? Ember? The E-named one at any rate—gave him a Look.

E-sister had no problem seeing him for who he was.

He set Wren on her feet. "I'll take you home."

She looked pleased and a little smug. "And then what? I know you'll have a plan."

"Whatever you want, Wren-bird."

"He has a pet name for her," E-sister muttered darkly behind him.

"Way to go selling Emily on us," Wren whispered, going up on tiptoe to plant her mouth next to his ear, an ear that was apparently directly connected to a body part that had no business getting hard in front of Wren's sisters.

Still. "I like kissing you," he said.

The kissing felt real. This casual togetherness felt real. Not pretend. Not the two of them against the world like people on a super-weird mission to convince friends and family that he was Wren's honest-to-God boyfriend. Because he was that, he decided. What had happened yesterday, the caring and the closeness and that whole host of unfamiliar but seductively wonderful feelings— that was definitely real. It was a fact, the same kind of knowable, verifiable, scientific fact as knowing that water expanded when it froze or the only solid elements that assumed liquid form at room temperature were mercury and bromine.

Her eyes slid over him, laughing and happy and just Wren. He should share this insight with her. Executive summary: Being with her was, well, everything, and he adjusted his life plan accordingly. The next step in his plan was telling Durant to stay out of Nash's personal life. His life wasn't a performance, and not just because they'd signed the contracts for the company sale. This was private.

"We make a good couple," he said into her ear.

"Yes," she hummed, wriggling away from him to grab her bag, "We do."

Warmth spread through him at her prompt agreement. Good. He wrapped her up in a towel and started sorting through her inexplicably large tote bag for her swimsuit cover-up. Or maybe she'd want to go use the showers and change?

She could do whatever she wanted. He'd wait.

Nash had plucked her out of the pool like Colonel Brandon rescuing Marianne.

It felt romantic and absolutely Jane Austen–worthy, albeit without the creepy age difference. In fact, she thought he might care about her—the way she undoubtedly cared about him. He was reserved and always thinking, sometimes gruff and always present. He saw her, all of her, in ways no one else had before. He was her dearest friend, a friend she loved very much. She was starting to believe deep in her heart that her tiny, small, continent-sized crush-slash-love might be a development he would welcome, too.

Amelia's voice intruded on her happy fantasy. "You're going to owe Wren five bucks," Amelia said.

"As if." Emily snorted. "It's still three days until the wedding."

That was followed by a thoughtful "true" from Amelia.

Nash looked at her questioningly. Oh God.

She stiffened. Her sisters wouldn't bring up that ridiculous bet. They couldn't possibly. It would be rude and… and completely unsisterly. *Or totally sisterly,* pointed out the part of herself that might have pulled a prank or two on them. Her chickens were coming home to roost.

She peeked around Nash, but her mother wasn't there. Oh, thank you, universe. This had all the hallmarks of a Wilson family intervention otherwise.

"Is this for real?" Emily waved a hand between them. "I won't hold you to our bet, Wren. You know I wouldn't.'

"I'm going to go change," she said, chickening out. She didn't want to tell Nash she loved him wearing a ridiculous swimsuit, with her hair wet and standing on end. She wanted the moment to be perfect and she certainly didn't want to do it smelling of chlorine and grapefruit. So she patted Nash's chest, the spot where she'd left an atlas-sized splotch on his no-longer-pristine button-up shirt, and left.

Nash really did (almost) recall having met Wren's sisters once before. At some holiday meal she'd dragged him to. The details eluded him, but they had not been fans.

There was, he thought as he turned around to face them, an obvious family resemblance. They also shot glances at each other, nudged one other, communicating in an unspoken language of little touches. Not only had they grown up together, but they clearly loved each other. It was different from his adoptive family in so many ways, not least because he thought that, maybe, if he put the time and the effort into it, someday he could speak that language, too, and be one of them. They loved Wren the way he loved Declan, so they'd make him work for her. Which was how it should be. Family should never be quick to give away family.

He couldn't help but notice, however, that Wren hadn't answered their question.

Also: What bet?

Amelia—the computer scientist one, he thought— looked at him as if he were a bug in her mission-critical code and she was planning to ruthlessly eradicate him. "You're dating our Wren."

"I am."

"Lovely," she said, in a tone that implied the opposite. "Are you the world's best boyfriend?"

"Am I what?"

Emily waved a hand. "Let me rephrase. Are you really and truly serious about her?"

"Of course." *Serious?* This was not a conversation he should be having with Wren's sisters, certainly not before he explained to Wren herself that somehow, somewhere along the line, he'd changed his mind about fake-dating her and would, instead, prefer to engage in the real deal.

But he also knew that he couldn't walk away from her sisters or even point out how rude their questions were. Because if he wanted to spend a great deal—or any— time with Wren in the future, it would eventually involve these two women. Pissing them off would be counterproductive. It would also be a great deal easier if they liked him. God. He should have hit Declan up for charm lessons, or at least paid more attention to how his brother had won over just about everyone they'd ever met.

"Look," Emily said. "I'm sure you're quite nice—" Nash interpreted *nice* as appallingly awful based on her tone "—but you're not Wren's type. She's never once mentioned you as boyfriend material and yet you've known each other for eight years."

Amelia nodded. "What she means is that Wren has a history of dating the wrong men and then breaking up with them when she realizes that they're not The One."

Nash could hear the capital letters in The One.

"So you think I'm the wrong kind of guy," he said.

"Well, yeah." Emily did not sound apologetic, he noted.

"And you're asking me for a timeline of when Wren will break up with me."

There was an awkward pause, then Emily regrouped. "That's not it. Not entirely. But Wren may have rushed into things with you because she was a teensy bit upset about the whole Noah thing and how she's quite literally always the bridesmaid but never the bride, and then suddenly the two of you are seriously dating the day after she gets the wedding invitation and bets me that she'll still be with her new boyfriend on the day of the wedding."

"She told you we were dating the day after she got the wedding invite?" Nash asked, his voice colder than he'd meant it to be. Because he could do the math here, couldn't he? He and Wren hadn't agreed to fake-date until at least a day after this conversation with her sisters.

"She said she was dating a mystery man, someone she was very serious about."

"Look," Amelia cut in. "We've heard about you, all right? Wren has some great Nash stories, and it seems like you're either impersonating a polar bear in them, or showing absolutely no emotions whatsoever. Wren, on the other hand, is absolutely *made* of feelings. Ergo, you seem like the very last people who would end up with each other."

Of course that was the moment Wren came back, sandals snapping against the deck, cheery smile fading as she caught her sister's words. "Amelia—"

Amelia was on a roll, however, and unstoppable. "And then suddenly she's texting us cute pictures of the two of you, and you're flying across the country to a family wedding, and there's all sorts of highly romantic dates happening and yet she'd always said you were an emotionally stunted work in progress."

Well. At least he was a work in progress—that implied that he could change.

"Amelia!" Wren groaned.

"And then," added Emily, "there are all these pictures on Instagram, where the two of you look downright romantic, and it all seems terribly fast and more than a little impossible."

"So we're just worried about you," Amelia said, looking straight at Wren as if Nash didn't exist, "and we want you to be happy."

Nash's own mental state didn't seem to factor into the sisters' calculations.

"The bet's off, okay?" Emily said. "Come solo to May's wedding. No one will say anything."

Nash straightened. "Bet?"

Wren bit her lip, looking guilty.

"I may," she said carefully, "have made an impulsive

bet with Emily that I would be in a serious relationship when the wedding rolled around. It was silly."

"A serious relationship," Emily added. "And you said that you were already in one."

"And then you came to me about the bachelor auction and offered to go with me, and it all seemed like a good idea."

"You said at the time that it was a terrible idea," he said stiffly.

"Well." She winced. "I changed my mind? I wanted—I *want*—to be in a relationship with you."

"What exactly did you want?" Nash asked. He felt…not hurt. That would be ridiculous. They'd had a friendly deal between friends. Nothing more. She'd held up her end of their bargain, and he had the signed contract with Durant to prove it. And yet he felt somehow off. As if he'd misunderstood or had his methodology all wrong and now his hypothesis had gone sideways. It felt awful and infuriated him.

"Why didn't you tell me about the bet?" he asked. And then he looked at Emily. "What were the terms?"

Emily's gaze bounced between him and Wren, but then she sighed. "Wren bet me that she'd bring her very serious boyfriend to Noah and May's wedding. And I bet her that she'd have broken up with him before then. I might have implied that I didn't think he existed."

"So it was just a game." His stomach tightened unpleasantly. "A made-up story as fake as any Hollywood script."

"Nash," she said, unhappily.

No.

She hadn't ever picked him. He was simply a right-enough guy, in the right place and a very convenient time. She'd never planned on being anything more than his wedding date, and they were fake-dating even if it had felt increasingly real and why in God's name had he thought it was more? This bet shouldn't make him feel surprised or disappointed or a half dozen other really unpleasant feelings. Except. Well he knew exactly how he felt: hurt. Because Nash had thought they were friends and then he'd *believed* they were starting to be something more: a couple. Partners.

"Nash," she tried again. "All right. I did tell them I was bringing my serious boyfriend to the wedding. And I might have implied that he already existed."

"Knew it," Emily muttered.

"And you wanted me to go with you to Martha's Vineyard," Wren continued, "and suggested that we help each other out by pretending to be interested in each other and, well, I agreed."

Nash frowned. "So none of this was ever real."

She stared at him unhappily and he could feel himself icing over, retreating behind his usual shields. Of course she didn't feel anything real for him. This was the woman who looked for romance and a ridiculous white knight of a man who could dash about her life on a white horse or something equally asinine. Why would she care about him? He was hard to get to know and even harder to like.

So, no, he wasn't surprised that she was holding out for Mr. Perfect, someone he wasn't and never could be. Hadn't he learned early on that living up to someone else's expectations was impossible? He couldn't be her perfect man any more than he could be J.J.'s perfect son, or even enough for the birth family that had let him drift out of their lives after his mother had died. Hoping for anything more had been foolish.

"I'll take you home," he said. He'd promised her he would and he kept his promises.

"Should we let her leave with him?" That was someone behind him—Emily, maybe, he didn't care.

"Nash would never hurt me," Wren answered.

Right. He got her into the car, got them both on the road and found he had nothing more to say. He was hurt and it was awful and this was why… Well, this was why he'd learned to shut people out, to make sure that he never, ever wanted more than it was reasonable to expect.

When he pulled up in front of her building an eternity later, Wren turned toward him. "I should have told you about the bet. But it was silly and I felt stupid. And—"

"I don't care about the bet. I—" *I wanted you. I wanted this to be real. To matter. I wanted it to be what you wanted, too. Were you going to break up with me after the wedding? Was it still 100 percent fake?*

Instead of saying any of that, though—because it was too late, it wouldn't help—he got out of the car, walked around it and opened her door for her. She stared up at him.

"Nash," she said. "Nash. It wasn't just… I…"

No. He'd identified the hazard and evaluated the risk. Now all he had to do was put in place the appropriate control measures.

"It sounds to me as if you no longer need a date to the wedding," he said coldly, "as your sister believes you've already lost your bet. We weren't serious."

She slid out of the car then, pressing up against him. He forced himself to take a step back.

"No, Nash. It was serious. Okay? I am serious. I think—I think we're good together. I like us. I don't want to break up. With you. Not at all."

Part of him leaped, stupidly hopeful, but he knew better.

"I love you," she said.

"As a friend."

"I love *you*," she repeated.

"Did you say those words to Noah, too? And to the boyfriend before him? Are you really over him? Or are you just lonely or embarrassed or anything other than in love with me but here I am and therefore why not? Did you think about us before you decided that you loved me and it was serious?"

Her mouth tightened and she blinked. "I'm saying them to you. Right now."

She was gorgeous and funny and so special that she was breaking him apart inside. It was better to end this not-relationship now because it would hurt so much more when she broke up with him in a week or a month, a year or however long he lasted.

"You need everything to be romance and fairy tales," he said. "You bounce from boyfriend to boyfriend. I'm just the next one, and then you'll find someone better after me."

Because of course she would. She would come to him nicely, calmly and completely maturely, and tell him that they would be better off apart and she was ending things with him. That was how almost every relationship in his life ended. With him not being worth holding on.

"It's fine," he told her. "I got what I needed. Durant is pleased. The auction's over. You don't seem to need anything from me anymore. We're just fake-breaking-up ahead of schedule. Apparently, no one will be surprised."

That was the smart thing to say, the safest thing. But as she turned away from him with a quick nod and fled inside her building, the door closed behind her and he was left standing outside alone… He wasn't sure at all that he'd said the best thing.

Sixteen

Nash couldn't remember how he ended up in his lab, just that he eventually did and that nothing felt right. Wren was not an experiment.

Wren also wasn't his. She didn't want to be. The affection and the emotions had just been something she'd made up to sell their story to her family. They'd been friends who had sex, but she hadn't wanted anything more than that. She hadn't wanted to be lovers.

His lover.

That word fit. He'd been happy, thinking they were trying this new thing, their situationship, together. Except it had never been real to her. He'd been happy, unaware that she still thought they were counting down the days until Noah and May's wedding when they'd go back—

To what they'd been before.

Friends.

Yeah. He hadn't been enough, had he? She hadn't loved him enough to want to keep him around. He'd run into that before, as an unwanted kid bounced from his bio family to foster care. He'd vowed never to do that again, never to put himself in the position of wanting someone to care more for him. A fake relationship had seemed safest because the real deal hurt far too much.

Way to go there again.

And yet... Yet. He wanted a do-over. According to his own experiences, that was impossible, but that didn't stop him from thinking about what he could do differently. You know. If he got the chance. He even went so far as to buy a stack of magazines, which included such valuable romantic suggestions as making hearts out of bacon, showing an honest interest in Wren's work, investing in loads of tea lights and hiding notes and tiny presents for her to find. Oh, and he was also supposed to kiss her goodbye and tell her that he loved her every single day. The last one seemed most feasible.

In the meantime, he poured himself into his work. His newest compound had all sorts of implications for the rubber industry. He'd be the king of cheaper, more environmentally friendly tires. His lab team didn't seem to share his enthusiasm, but that was fine. He'd achieve this breakthrough without them, too. He'd always worked best on his own. Work was the best outlet anyhow for all of these ridiculous feelings that had some snuck up on him and moved into his chest, his heart, goddamned everywhere. He wasn't supposed to feel for Wren.

He couldn't do this.

Too late, his head screamed. His stupid heart kept slipping in little observations, like what was she doing? Had she eaten? Was she okay? No. His lab was a Wren-free zone where he did science—logical, practical and lifesaving, moneymaking science. He did not daydream about a woman who had blown into his life and who clearly could just blow right back out again.

At some point, when he looked up, Declan was leaning against a lab bench, arms crossed over his chest, legs outstretched. He looked pissed. "The team called in an SOS."

"Why?" he growled. The last SOS he'd sent had been what got him into this mess.

"What did you do?" Declan countered. "Think about it. It'll come to you."

"Why does this have to be my fault?"

"It doesn't," Declan said easily. "But you're not happy and I'm concerned. So let's fix this thing."

Nash set down his beaker. He didn't need to screw two things up by not paying enough attention. "It's none of your business."

"You've been holed up here in the lab for three days. You look like hell. No one dares come in here. Oh, and apparently your assistant's gone." Declan slapped a sticky note that read "I QUIT" in front of Nash. "So tell me what went wrong with you and Wren."

"Nothing," he ground out. "We broke up. It was never real. I'm not discussing it any further."

"Riiiight," Declan drawled. "You broke up with her. Did she tell you that she also wanted to end things, or did you make a lot of assumptions and rampage around like an angry rhino complaining because you were done fake-dating but hadn't bothered to tell her that meant real dating?"

"She faked being interested in me. It was like a bad rom-com script, one of those Hollywood films you shoot."

Declan looked amused. "You poor bastard. You pushed her away because you're a big chicken."

Had he? Well, yeah. Of course he had. Walk away first and it hurt less. He'd learned that lesson early in life. He and Declan had been shuttled from one foster home to the next, no one willing to take on two small boys permanently. There had been no aunts or uncles, no family, no one close, not until J.J., and even J.J. had wanted them to change, to fit into J.J.'s life. They'd done all the changing and it hadn't been enough. Eventually Wren would have wanted him to change, too. And then when he couldn't or wouldn't, she would have left. So this was fine. Merely an escalation of the timeline.

Loving Wren would be dangerous and risky, something full of variables and completely out of his control. But it was what he wanted. *She* was whom he wanted. So surely he could make this one change for her, to open up, to hope?

I love you, she'd said.

And he'd said—

"I've fucked everything up," he admitted. He'd shut himself off from feeling, walked away from everyone he could because sometimes love did hurt. Sometimes it meant people left, whether they'd wanted to or not. And God, he was the one who'd made the choice to leave, over and over, and then he'd left Wren.

"And?" Declan said.

He didn't deserve her, could never earn a second or a first chance, because those were gifts. Like her feelings, the love and the caring, all the emotions she'd offered to him and he'd labeled friendship—they were gifts. That wasn't a hypothesis or even some really good scientifically based guessing. It was a fact.

"I love her," he said out loud.

Declan crossed his arms over his chest. "Good. Does that mean you're done being an asshole?"

Shit. "What day is it?"

"Saturday."

Noah and May's wedding day. "I need help."

Declan nodded. "You got it."

Seventeen

"There has to be a faster way to get there," Nash growled through his headset.

Declan shot him a look from the pilot's seat. "Don't make me put this helicopter down and make you walk."

The dark blue of the Pacific Ocean stretched out beneath them as they moved northward along the California coast.

"Thank you," Nash gritted out. The distance between him and Wren was still there. It had been days since they'd walked out on each other and almost an hour since they'd lifted off from Declan's current film location. Worse, the physical distance was the least of the challenges facing him.

His original plan had been to get to Wren's condo as fast he could, find her there before she left for the wedding and then list the numerous ways he'd fucked things up and suggest possible fixes. He'd planned on flowers. Groveling. Lots of sincere, heartfelt apologizing because…the thing was… He did have feelings. Heart feelings. He was still a complete and utter novice at this love business, but he was a scientist, he knew how to learn from observation and he was highly motivated.

It had been a great plan, right up until he'd been standing outside Wren's condo, knocking on the door with an enormous bouquet of blue hydrangeas and white roses (they reminded him of their hotel in Martha's Vineyard where things had changed for the better for them), and she hadn't answered the door. Then her next-door neighbor had come out, frowning ferociously, and told him that he should go away because Dr. Wilson was away for the weekend. He'd missed her.

He'd tried texting her, but had gotten no response. Had she blocked his number? Or was she just busy getting on with her life without him? All right. So his first hypothesis was a failure. He wouldn't be knocking on her door, handing her the flowers and then delivering his apology. He'd just have to find the right door, the right place and *then* proceed with his plan. It was, he thought unhappily, not the clearest methodology even if he needed it desperately to work.

"Have you thought about what you're going to say? Or, possibly, letting her know that you're about to crash her family wedding and is she open to hearing you out?" Declan asked.

Nash had a list on his phone. He wasn't leaving this to chance. "Of course I've thought about it. And she's not answering her phone."

"So you're just going to crash the wedding?"

"Technically, she invited me to go with her," he pointed out.

This earned him an eye roll. "And then she canceled you."

True. "Because I wasn't romantic. Or The One."

"And also because you were a total dick," Declan added.

Also true. There was a pause. They left San Francisco and the coastline, swinging inland.

"So now you're romantic?" Declan prodded. "How's that working out for you?"

"I do know how to search the internet, thank you."

He also had hope and his magazine research. It was likely insufficient, but he had to try.

Declan groaned. "So you're going to fake it."

"With heart. Yes."

"And that business about being her one and only perfect man?"

He checked to make sure that Declan wasn't poking fun at him, but he seemed serious enough—and he was the wedding expert.

"I'm working on it," he said because, really, there was no point in airing all of the risk points, was there?

This thing with Wren wasn't just about a second chance. This was everything. Could he imagine a life without Wren Wilson in it? Of course he could. It just wasn't the life that he would choose for himself, and he was a selfish bastard because he wanted her to choose him. Again. And yes, forever was what he was gunning for here, but he'd take whatever she would give him. He wanted all the moments with her, big and small. And he thought that maybe they'd already been each other's perfect match for a long time, but they'd just been calling their relationship by the wrong name. No. Not so much wrong as incomplete. They were friends and he never wanted to stop being friends. It was just that there were other feelings he wanted to add to that equation, feelings like love and trust. Somehow he had to convince her to trust him, although if he couldn't, he'd be her friend the best he could.

He hadn't figured out how to improve his plan—or his chances—when Declan began bringing the helicopter down. He could see a winery spread out beneath them, acres and acres of wine grapes in precise rows in midharvest. The winery sat at the heart of the grapes, a cluster of Spanish-style buildings with a formal garden, a cluster of gazebos and…the wedding. From up here, he couldn't make out Wren, not yet, just the bright white burst of tulle that was the bride. Yelling at Declan to land faster or launching himself out of the helicopter and crash-landing at Wren's feet wouldn't help him win her over, so he kept his mouth shut as Declan brought them down on a landing pad on the far side of a car-filled parking lot. Noah the urologist had managed quite the guest list for a short-notice wedding. Would Wren want a big, fancy wedding, maybe in a castle in Europe? He thought she might. All he wanted was to be invited to that wedding.

As the groom.

Wren beamed determinedly at the guests gathered to celebrate Noah and May. This was a lovely day and she was a perfectly happy wedding guest, thank you very much. Just brimming over with love and affection for the bridal couple. Never mind that it felt like her own heart had been pulled out of her pericardial cavity, possibly with a fishhook through the nose like those Egyptian embalmers used. Or maybe it had been the brain? It didn't matter. She felt like she was missing a critical organ and she suspected that hole wasn't going away anytime soon.

Noah, May and the bridesmaid posse—unable to choose, May had invited ten women to share the bridal honors—started back down the aisle. Wren barely heard the music May had chosen. Her feet were killing her and someone had decided this would be the best moment to land a helicopter practically on top of May's wedding. At least the asshole hadn't buzzed them during the ceremony itself.

Not that May seemed to notice. Nope. She was smiling through happy tears, clutching Noah's arm to her, as the bridal party moved toward the vineyard to take pictures.

"Thank you," she'd whispered earlier to Wren. "You're like the love whisperer."

Wren reminded herself that she was happy for May. She really, really was. It was just that random thoughts of Nash still seemed to keep popping up in her head, sabotaging all those nice, happy thoughts.

What was she going to do about him? She imagined him holed up in his billionaire lair, skulking. Or worse, perhaps he was just getting on with his life like her ex-boyfriends did and finding someone else. Someone who was perfect for him.

Except…wait. If he was looking for that someone else, apparently he was doing it at *May's wedding*? Because there was no mistaking the enormous, dark-eyed, scowling man striding toward her, steel-toed work boots eating up the ground. He looked very determined and impossibly familiar in his usual chinos and a white shirt that was unexpectedly unbuttoned, the sleeves rolled up, the edges flapping. He was wearing a T-shirt. At a *wedding*. For Nash, that counted as undone and naked. Mistake! Her brain yelled. Big mistake! Huge! Do *not* think about him *naked*. Rather than remembering what a delicious beast he was in bed, she needed to plot her strategy. A nice, scientific strategy with those bullets and numbered points that Nash was so fond of.

His face was as inexpressive as ever. So that hadn't changed. She couldn't tell what he was thinking or how he felt about crashing her cousin's wedding. Mostly, though, he just seemed as if he'd quite happily mow down Noah and May's wedding guests if those guests didn't move. Which they did. He had a clear path to her. An errant beat of hope sprang to life in her poor chest. Surely, Nash wouldn't have come all this way just to itemize her girlfriend failings or how he could never, ever harbor so much as a smidge of romantic feeling for her.

Unless.

Crap. He *had* promised to attend the wedding with her and Nash was big on keeping his promises. It was one of his many amazing qualities.

He came to an abrupt halt in front of her.

"Hi?" she said, not sure what to do.

"Hi," he said gravely and then he dropped to his knees. One knee, not two. Her brain froze. This was…

He was…

She should say something. Yes. Ask him how he was or about the weather or didn't he think May made an absolutely beautiful bride? Except this was *Nash*. At her *feet*. Big, inscrutable, private and ever-so-practical Nash was kneeling on the grass in front of her, probably staining the knees of his pants green, and with absolutely everyone staring. Phones were coming out. But what could she say? Or do? She was a mess of feelings from her head on down, although a good many of those feelings were filling up the terrible hole in her chest, swimming around, warm and hopeful and deeply terrifying.

Nash reached out and took her hand. Paused. Then took the other one, too. Her fingers were surrounded by his warmth, the careful pressure of his hands wrapped around hers. She checked, but she still had no idea what to say. So she waited, trying not to hope too badly as Nash frowned. What would he do if she leaned down and kissed his forehead, right where it puckered and wrinkled so adorably? God, the man would have wrinkles by forty. He'd be all delightfully grizzled and silvered and stern at sixty. And at seventy…well…at seventy, she admitted, but only to herself, she'd still love him exactly as he was.

The hole in her chest ached.

"I'm sorry," he said, looking up at her. "I have a list on my phone if you'd like details, but that's really the important part."

"You are?" She swallowed hard. Somehow, the icy spot in her chest melted beneath his watchful eyes, possibly running straight to her tear ducts because she blinked and said, "Me, too."

"No," he said. No? "You have nothing to be sorry about."

She couldn't help but notice that he hadn't gotten up yet. She still had Nash Masterson, all six feet four inches of him, at her feet.

"You offered me a gift," he continued. "And I was too much of a chickenshit to accept it." He frowned. "Although that sounds far less romantic than I would like."

The world spun on its axis.

"Are you—"

"Trying to be romantic? Yeah." He sighed. "It's clearly going to take extensive research and practice."

The crowd of people staring at them made a noise rather like wind rustling through the grape leaves. A sort of sighing sound, she thought, as if maybe she wasn't the only one who thought Nash had understood the assignment and nailed it. She snuck a peek over Nash's shoulder and spotted Emily looking shocked. Her mother was frowning like a semi-enraged mama bear, though.

"Because I love you," he said, squeezing her hands gently where he had captured them. "And I'd like to be someone you could love back. I know I'll never be your perfect man, but—"

She knelt down with him.

"This is probably where I'm supposed to say that perfection is overrated, but the thing is, Nash, you're perfect for me. I don't need you to be different. I just need you to be you. With me. If that's okay?"

Somewhere, far off and yet too close, Amelia said, "Maybe she's not cursed."

Nash frowned, not at her sister (Wren couldn't help

but notice), but at Wren. Life still wasn't completely fair, was it?

"There's no scientific basis for curses," he said.

A beat.

"But," he said slowly, "if we assume for one moment that it's true—" she resisted pinching his side because really—this man "—then I should fall in love with the next woman I meet."

"Date," she corrected. "It's not like my exes turn around and love the next woman they see. That could be anyone—the checker at the grocery store, the cop pulling them over for speeding, the fifty-year-old lady who runs reception at the dentist. Who, for the record, absolutely deserves true love just as much as the under-thirties."

He lifted one broad shoulder. "Will you go out with me tonight?"

Her breath caught. "Are you asking me on a date?"

"Yes." He paused. "I am. But I'm also saying that I already love you. There's nothing you can do or say that would make me love you more."

"So that's a yes on having dinner together tonight?"

"Yes." He smiled. A slow, cautious, completely gorgeous smile that traveled from his mouth to his eyes and back to heart faster than anything should. "But just to be clear, I'm also asking if you'd like to join me in an experiment, a bit of a lifelong one. I never answered your question that night in Martha's Vineyard when you threw yourself at my feet—"

She groaned. "That was a joke, Nash. It wasn't for real."

He pulled her close. "I'm hoping it was. It is. Because, yes, Wren Wilson, yes I'll marry you. If you still want me to. Let's try a true-love experiment."

"I do," she said.

Nash smiled.

Then he was surging to his feet, taking her with him and somehow managing to kiss her at the same time, and she was off her feet, into his arms, and she just had time to whisper *I love you* once when he came up for air.

* * * * *

ONE SUMMER OF LOVE & SNOWBOUND SECOND CHANCE

ONE SUMMER OF LOVE
Valentine Vineyards • by Reese Ryan

Brains *and* beauty? Scientist Delaney Carlisle challenges *all* Nolan Valentine's professional boundaries—and inspires a passion unlike any other. Delaney vows to help turn his business into a success. And seduction is on the agenda...

SNOWBOUND SECOND CHANCE
Valentine Vineyards • by Reese Ryan

Evelisse Jemison wants to escape memories of her ex by returning home to Magnolia Lake. But when a snowstorm strands her with sexy Sebastian Valentine, neither can deny their connection...nor their explosive chemistry.

ALASKAN BLACKOUT & THE WRONG RANCHER

ALASKAN BLACKOUT
Kingsland Ranch • by Joanne Rock

Tech exec Quinton Kingsley won't be denied—but Alaskan bartender McKenna O'Brien refuses to reveal his half brother's whereabouts. She *should* be off-limits. But spending a blackout in her arms leads him to unexpected pleasure...and an unplanned baby!

THE WRONG RANCHER
Heirs of Hardwell Ranch • by J. Margot Critch

Piper Gallagher has to pretend to be someone she's not, for complicated reasons. And then it gets more complicated when she falls for Maverick Kane, her family's rival. Will being with Maverick cost her everything?

THE TROUBLE WITH LITTLE SECRETS & KEEP YOUR ENEMIES CLOSE...

THE TROUBLE WITH LITTLE SECRETS
Dynasties: Calcott Manor • by Joss Wood

Someone is blackmailing Jack Grantham's family and there's hell to pay! But learning Peyton Caron had a child after their one-night stand two years ago complicates everything. He can't trust her—or the attraction that puts them all at risk...

KEEP YOUR ENEMIES CLOSE...
Dynasties: Calcott Manor • by Joss Wood

Entrepreneur Merrick Knowles isn't sure about Aly Garwood. But she won't leave Calcott Manor until they investigate her ominous premonitions—even if the only visions Merrick believes in are fantasies of Aly. But as their attraction grows, so does Aly's mystery...

You can find more information on upcoming Harlequin titles, free excerpts and more at Harlequin.com.

Get 3 FREE REWARDS!

We'll send you 2 FREE Books plus a FREE Mystery Gift.

FREE Value Over **$20**

Both the **Harlequin® Desire** and **Harlequin Presents®** series feature compelling novels filled with passion, sensuality and intriguing scandals.

HARLEQUIN
PLUS

Try the best multimedia subscription service for romance readers like you!

Read, Watch and Play.

Experience the easiest way to get the romance content you crave.

Start your **FREE TRIAL** at
www.harlequinplus.com/freetrial.